LOVE AND OTHER LIES

Also by Ben McPherson

A Line of Blood

LOVE AND OTHER LIES

A NOVEL

BEN McPHERSON

WILLIAM MORROW
An Imprint of HarperCollinsPublishers

HarperCollins books may be purchased for educational, business, or sales promotional use. For information, please email the Special Markets Department at SPsales@harpercollins.com.

FIRST EDITION

Designed by Diahann Sturge

Library of Congress Cataloging-in-Publication Data

Names: McPherson, Ben, author.
Title: Love and other lies : a novel / Ben McPherson.
Description: First edition. | New York, NY : William Morrow, 2021. |
Summary: "A family struggles to stay together and find out the truth after their daughter goes missing during a vicious terrorist attack in this stunning novel of psychological suspense from the acclaimed author of A Line of Blood"— Provided by publisher.
Identifiers: LCCN 2020005482 (print) | LCCN 2020005483 (ebook) |
ISBN 9780062406149 (trade paperback) | ISBN 9780062406163 (ebook)
Subjects: GSAFD: Suspense fiction.
Classification: LCC PR6113.C5855 L68 2021 (print) | LCC PR6113.C5855 (ebook) | DDC 823/.92—dc23
LC record available at https://lccn.loc.gov/2020005482
LC ebook record available at https://lccn.loc.gov/2020005483

ISBN 978-0-06-240614-9

21 22 23 24 25 LSC 10 9 8 7 6 5 4 3 2 1

For Francis

LOVE AND OTHER LIES

IMAGINE A GIRL.

Imagine her sleeping alone on a grassy bank at the side of a glistening fjord.

If you were here beside her you might wonder if the girl is breathing, she's lying so very still. When at last you see the rhythmic rise and fall of her chest you feel foolish for doubting the everyday miracle of breath.

Her kingfisher dress glints like the sun on the water. Seventeen, you might guess, though in truth the girl is fifteen and wishes she were older. A peaceful face, strong-jawed and determined. But something about her makes you want to protect her as she sleeps. All that life ahead of her: all those people not yet met, all those choices not yet made.

And now she's here, on this island, sleeping in the dappled light beneath this tree, because the thought of all those people—of all those possible lives—has left her nervous and exhausted. And so she sleeps away her fears, and in her dreams she is limitless.

In the city at the top of the fjord there is a flash. Then a silence.

Then a roar like a world ending. Glass drops in sheets from the fronts of buildings, becomes sand under the feet of the people as they flee. Songbirds grow silent, then take to the wing. Even crows.

Seconds pass.

In the suburbs people murmur *Thunder*, though the sky is clear and the air pressure low. Dogs do not bark. Cats cower by fences, looking up.

Again, seconds pass.

On her bank by the water the girl hears nothing. For a moment the air tightens. The surface of the water grows opaque. Boats rise, then fall. Hawsers thrum against masts; hulls strain against ropes.

Bare-legged in her sundress of kingfisher-blue, the girl does not stir.

The shock wave from the bomb has passed.

PROLOGUE

Midsummer's Eve
June 23

SHE BLINKED HARD, TWICE.

Some change in the sound of the day had woken her. The pattern of waves against the wooden dock. A boat engine idling.

The engine was thrown into reverse. It whined, then cut.

She sat up, turned to face the water.

A policeman was swinging his foot from boat to shore. A look, she thought, as he glanced down at her. Steely. His uniform was neatly pressed, his belt a little tight. Everything about him was sleek: his flashlight, his nightstick, both shiny and new.

She rearranged herself on the grass, raised herself up on an elbow.

Light danced on the fjord; the mainland hazy now and far away. In the policeman's hand the nylon of the rope shone blistering white. Unused, she thought. Strange. The POLITI decal on the boat was fresh, the aluminum of the hull unscuffed.

The policeman knelt, tied off the boat at the bow. A second officer leaned out from behind the wheel and dropped a figure-eight loop around a pillar. He cut the engine, pinched sweat from his eyes.

Beside her the phone vibrated against the warm earth. She turned it over.

Ropes tightened. Two battered travel bags landed on the dock. The second policeman stepped from the boat, knelt by the first bag, unzipped it, and examined something inside. He stood and handed it to the first policeman.

Cracked leather, water-stained and scuffed. Also wrong, she thought lazily.

The two men were nodding at each other. Small eyes, high cheekbones, prominent teeth. Small mouths too. They could almost be brothers.

"Nothing to worry about," said the first. He had noticed her staring. He had spoken in English.

He flashed her a smile that was anything but a smile.

She smoothed out her sundress. Why would she be worried?

The same non-smile from the second policeman. "Gather your friends." They began to head up the rise.

Her phone began to ring. She rejected the call with a text.

Somewhere out of sight an invisible hand was tapping a microphone. Voices reflected back at her from across the fjord, over-amplified, heavily distorted.

On the rise, the officers were facing each other. They were checking each other's equipment, tapping each other down.

She found herself thinking of her father, though she did not know why. She pushed the thought from her mind.

She looked at the boat straining at the dock. Farther up the coast people were swimming, but here on the island, down by the water, there was no one about. From here you could see only the path that led from the boat dock up toward the camp. She looked up again toward the rise. She could not see the men.

Her phone vibrated. A text from Leela:

You coming?

It had been a mistake to take the ferry on her own. The people on the way over had seemed sophisticated, long and cool in their shades and their sun hats, though many were younger than she was. She had hung back, embarrassed, let them pass up the rise ahead of her, wishing Leela was there with her. It was getting harder and harder to imagine herself among the thronging crowds. More and more tempting to turn and head for home.

She could hear the applause now. Stirring music played.

She texted a reply:

Soon.

The boat key was in the ignition. Strange, she thought. Tempting fate. She looked at the outboard motor. Evinrude 225 E-TEC. Barely used, its white surface completely unscuffed. She looked about her.

No one was watching as she stepped aboard at the bow onto the aluminum tread-plate deck. The boat barely tipped. She sat cautiously at the wheel. She was breaking some law, she was certain of that. But she was fifteen, and she was alone. If anyone stopped her she would speak English. She would be naturally nervous and hesitant, and that would work in her favor. They would let her off with a warning.

Sorry, Officer.

She clicked the key into the first position. Lights on the console. A loud chime. She swung the wheel to the left, felt the gentle tamping as behind her the engine turned in its mount. Everything was expensive. Everything was new. She turned, guiltily—a sudden sense of being watched—looked up toward the rise. No sign of the officers. No sign of anyone.

She slid the key around to position two. The engine thrummed quietly into life.

Where ARE you?

She texted back:

Come down to the dock.

Of course she wasn't going to, but something about the idea of taking the boat appealed to her. It wasn't even tied right. And there was no one here to tell her she couldn't . . .

She stood up, leaving the boat in idle. Everything was showroom-fresh. No oil spills, no salt stains. But the decal on the starboard side was cracked, as if a hand had slipped. Sloppy, she thought, on a police boat. And the hatches . . . why were there no padlocks on the hatches?

On the bench seat at the stern was a blue metal box, rusted at the corners, held shut with a combination lock. She looked at the box. It seemed out of place, like the travel bags.

Her phone vibrated.

Police want to talk to us. You need to get up here.

She texted back:

Sigh . . .

She heard the police boat strain against the jetty, leaned out and looked down. The rubber cladding on the dock was marking the hull. Had they forgotten their fenders? A little random.

The port locker was empty. In the starboard locker there was an anchor, a chain, and a rope. The rope was not tied to the chain, and the chain was not tied to the anchor.

Also random.

What police boat would be so unready? Where was the radio? The life vests? The fenders? She dialed Leela, raised the phone to her ear.

Ringing on the line. Leela's voice. "Finally. Where are you?"

"You know that feeling where you kind of know you're asleep? Which probably means you're only dozing?"

"You were asleep?"

"On the grass, by the water. It was nice."

Leela didn't sigh, but she could feel the edge in her friend's voice. "You need to be up here."

She put the phone on speaker, laid it on the deck before the aft locker.

"I know," she said. "But someone left a brand-new boat down here with the key in the ignition."

"Now," said Leela. "You need to be here."

"We actually could take it out. For, I don't know, twenty minutes or something."

"Or did you somehow not hear what happened in Oslo today?"

"Literally no one would know. Why? What happened?"

"There was this huge explosion. The town hall."

She could feel her mind as it refocused. "Sounds bad."

"It's most probably a bomb," said Leela.

"A bomb," she echoed.

She felt bad. She should call her father, tell him she was okay. But what if her father begged her to come home?

Of course she would never take the boat. She was processing, or something. An explosion in town. Police here to talk to them. She really should call her father.

So far from home.

She picked up the metal box. It was heavy. She shook it, but whatever was inside it was carefully held in place.

"So," said Leela. "So, the police have information they need to give us. And the marshals are taking a roll call. I already told them you were here. Don't make a liar of me."

"Did I ask you to lie?"

Leela sighed theatrically. "Give me a break . . ."

The metal box looked important, but also somehow wrong, like an object kept outside in the rain.

"Okay," she said. "I'll be three minutes."

"Maybe we could go for a ride later?"

"No," she said. "No, this was pretty much our only chance."

What was it that made her take the key from the ignition?

What made her pick up the metal box and stow it in her backpack? Some instinct that she couldn't yet name, some growing feeling. She slid the key and her phone into the side pocket. She jumped ashore. When she looked back she saw a gray half footprint on the deck by the aft locker. She frowned. The earth on the island was dry and brown.

She slung the pack across her shoulder, headed up the hill. She would find the policemen; she would give them the key and the metal box.

She tightened the straps as she walked. The edges of the metal box chafed at her skin through the backpack. She felt sweat gathering where the pack met her dress, felt it pooling in the small of her back. Hard to believe it could be so hot.

At the top of the rise she paused. From here she looked down into a clearing a hundred meters across. There were pinewoods on every side, thick with the heat of the afternoon. Vast faces hung from the trees. Posters. Girls of her own age holding stuff: kayak paddles, stethoscopes, ice axes, phones. All in close-up. All with an eye to the camera, one thumb raised. At the bottom of every poster the letters IFF, white on red, and the thumbs-up logo. Near the middle of the clearing, to the left, was a large red-painted stage. To the left of the stage, banks of seats rose vertiginously towards the pine trees.

Red banners cascaded from the lighting rig:

INTERNATIONAL FUTURE FEMALE: EMPOWERING EVERYONE, STARTING WITH GIRLS

To her right she could see the back of the main house. Here too there was a giant banner: two girls, one light-skinned, one dark, right hands crossed at the wrists, thumbs up, left hands across each other's shoulder. All those eyes, gazing down on you.

Don't be racist!

Take no drugs!

Recycle, recycle, recycle!

"Bring condoms and whisky," Leela had said, laughing. Had she meant it? Hard to be sure. She had brought both, in case Leela wasn't joking, though she wasn't expecting to use either.

At the far end of the clearing were the first of the dormitory cabins. People were trailing from the cabins to the stage; others were already sitting on the banked seats, talking without animation, looking nervously down at the two policemen who stood before them in the middle of the stage.

The policemen were smoking, letting the ash fall from their cigarettes. Behind them at the edge of the clearing was a vast poster of a girl looking down, crushing a cigarette in her left hand, her right thumb up.

She knew she should walk across the clearing to the policemen, hand them the key. But that would draw their attention, and she wasn't sure she wanted their attention. Something about that look they had given her down at the dock, a sense of something out of place.

There were way too many eyes; there would be too much staring. She would wait until the policemen had finished speaking; she would approach them as people were drifting away. There were a *lot* of people here. Overwhelming numbers. There were boys dotted around too, in among the girls, talking earnestly, nodding a lot, demonstrating they were *listening*. Boys got extra points for *listening* to girls.

One of the policemen, she noticed, had his hand on his service weapon. Which was weird, she thought. He hadn't been wearing a pistol as he stepped from the boat. She was certain of that.

She walked forward past the main house and along the rear of the stage until she was standing directly behind the men. Both wore pistols, she could see now, in holsters by their right hips. The shorter of the two was fidgeting the knuckle of his hand against the grip. At his feet were the two cracked leather travel bags.

Random. Something about this was definitely random. She took out her phone, dialed Leela.

"Hey," said Leela.

"Leela, who brings a pistol to speak to a bunch of girls? Like, really, what's the threat?"

"I mean, a bomb went off," said Leela. "Where are you?"

"Yes, but here?" she said. "What's the threat here?"

"I guess sisterhood *is* powerful."

A loud click on the PA system. The taller policeman cleared his throat. "Hello. I would like to ask everyone, whatever their role, to gather in the meeting room of the main house. I have important information to share about the bomb in town. I'm sure you have many questions."

Leela laughed. "Seriously, where are you? I don't see you."

"Leela," she said, "wait."

"Wait, why?"

"We could . . . not go . . ."

The policeman was repeating his words in Norwegian. People began to flow from the seating bank around the sides of the stage and toward the main house.

"How come stealing a boat is not a problem for you, but meeting people is?"

"I mean, it's probably nothing, but I'm getting a vibe . . ."

"You're getting a vibe?"

"It's all a bit too random. Where's the cabin? I want to go find it." The words came out wrong. She sounded as if she were pleading.

"Seriously? No."

"Then tell me what they say. See you later."

She began walking against the stream of people and across the clearing toward the trees.

"Number forty-seven," said Leela. "Past the first bunch of cabins, down the path toward the generator block. I put my towel and my elephant wash bag on your bunk. You utter rando."

She stopped at the first line of cabins. This feeling—it was more than nerves. More than paranoia. She was sure of it. She sat cross-legged on the grass, slid the metal box out of her backpack. Weird that it would be so rusty, so old-looking, when everything else about the policemen was so new. Like it had been stored in a barn or something.

The combination lock had three digits. She tried the easy combinations: all the 1s, all the 2s . . . People were still streaming up the hill and into the clearing. The metal of the box felt cool against her lap; the edges dug into her thighs. On 555 the latch flicked up. The inside was lined on both sides with dense gray foam, custom-cut. In the lid was a row of flattened gray metal boxes. She turned one on its end, saw the bullet readied at the top, the brass casing and the jacketed tip. Pistol magazine, she guessed. In the bottom of the case the magazines were larger, wider, and longer, recently painted green.

Her thoughts stopped her in her tracks. Because the boat, the uniforms, the guns, the travel bags . . . She snapped the box shut, slid it into her backpack, left the pack standing at the side of the path, turned toward the main building. So much here that wasn't right . . . Those were not police uniforms; that was not a police boat: She was sure. She could not believe she had not realized sooner.

She began to walk in the direction of the main house. There were marshals on the path, guiding people toward it. She could see through the bay windows the people thronging the front room.

"Come on," said a boy in a slogan T-shirt. "Come on!"

Important not to panic. Don't arrive out of breath.

"Please," she said, as soberly as she could. "Stop people from going in."

"But the police—"

"They are not police," she said.

"They have come to speak about the explosion—"

"Those men are not policemen," she said. "Stop people. Tell the other marshals. Everyone must leave. Call the real police."

The boy smiled at her blandly.

"But the police are—"

She stifled the urge to scream at him. She was running now, at the side of the path, overtaking the people who were making their way toward the house. She was at the steps. The front door led directly into the main room. She pushed abruptly into the room, found herself standing beside the men in their too-new uniforms.

The shorter one looked directly at her. "Take your place." He motioned toward the people crowding the back of the room. "Don't block the door."

For a moment she felt compelled to obey. It took all her strength to pause, to stand tall, to shout.

"No!"

The policeman heard her. The crowd did not.

"No!" she shouted again, louder now.

"What did you say?" said the man quietly.

She looked toward the faces at the back of the room. "These are not the police!" she shouted.

The room fell silent. All faces, all staring. Where was Leela?

"You are mistaken," said the shorter officer. The tone of his voice was reassuring, friendly almost. For a moment she doubted herself.

"We are here to provide information," said the other officer. "You are mistaken." But she saw his hand tighten on the grip of his pistol and she knew that she was not mistaken.

Her eyes found Leela in the crowd, near the back, her black hair hanging sleekly by her right shoulder, half frowning, half smiling. A moment of stillness.

Leela, she mouthed. *Leela!*

Leela's half smile froze. Her eyes began to dart.

"You need to get out," she shouted, as clearly as her breathing would allow. Her voice sounded hoarse, unreal.

"All of you," she shouted. "Now!"

She turned. She was at the door. She heard the movement of bodies as behind her people pressed forward.

She felt the force of the bullet as it tore through her right shoulder, heard the shouts behind her, then the screams. She brought her left arm up, folded it across her chest and to her left shoulder, pushed out through the door, ran limping along the path.

A marshal tried to stop her. "Are you hurt? What happened?"

"Run," she said. "Please, run."

She could hear gunshots now, in pairs, distant, unreal. But the shouts and the screams were very real indeed.

She turned, saw people piling out through the front door, saw a window thrown wide, saw a distant flash, and another. People began to pour from the window. Beside her the marshal, a girl of her own age, eyes wide, frozen. Still the gunshots came, in pairs.

"You need to run," she said.

The other girl seemed to see her suddenly, to notice the wound in her shoulder.

"You're bleeding."

"I'm shot. You need to run."

"The police are here." The marshal put an arm around her shoulder, pointed toward the house.

"Those are not the police."

"Look," said the marshal.

The gunshots stopped. As she watched, the taller of the men appeared on the veranda, walked slowly down the steps. His pistol was holstered. He had a rifle slung across his back.

"Don't be alarmed!" he shouted. "We are here to prevent further trouble."

"You see?" said the marshal. She took her hand, tried to lead her toward the house.

She slipped her hand from the other girl's. "He is not a policeman."

"I'm going to get you some help," said the marshal. She began to walk toward the house.

"No," she said. "Please." It hurt to talk; she wasn't sure if the girl had heard her.

"Everybody!" yelled the false policeman. "Everybody, come! You're safe! We have the situation under control."

She looked about her. People were arriving from all directions, converging on the house. People who did not know, though they must have heard the shots.

The second man joined the first. They stood, arms folded, waiting.

No, she wanted to scream. *No*.

When the marshal girl was three meters from the men, they drew their pistols. The girl stopped. Around her the others stopped too. The shorter of the men raised his pistol and shot the marshal girl twice. She stayed upright for a moment, swayed, then collapsed to the grass. The second man aimed carefully. Two more shots. A tall boy fell forward. His body struck the girl standing next to him. The girl stood frozen. She did not turn and run. The man shot her twice, and she too collapsed to the ground.

Why aren't they running? she wondered. There must have been two dozen people, standing fanned out around the men in their police uniforms. Not one of them moved. She made to turn, but found that she could not. Two more shots. Another body hit the ground.

You cannot look. You must not look.

The men, she knew, had seen her.

Turn.

They would come for her. She had to move.

Run.

She could not run. She could barely move, but she set off down the path toward the cabins. Still the shots came, always in pairs. *At any moment*, she thought, *two more bullets will come for me.*

Think.

The dormitory cabins. Each was a single room with four bunks, a window at each end, and a door in the middle. There were sixty of them. Would they search every one? Something told her that they would. These men were methodical, efficient. They knew what they were doing.

Once they were inside, you were dead.

Think.

Her backpack, ahead of her, to the side of the path. Her phone; the boat key.

Sharp crack. A bullet tore into a tree to her left.

Don't turn.

A stray.

Don't turn.

She had to believe the bullet was a stray. She had to keep going, toward her backpack. She had to get to the water. Then she would figure out how to get to the boat.

She knew she must not turn, but she turned.

In front of the men were bodies, unmoving on the ground. Six figures stood facing the men, rooted to the spot. As she watched, one seemed to come to life. A girl. She turned, began to sprint toward the nearby trees. The tall man raised his weapon, fired twice. The girl dropped to the ground.

She forced herself to turn away. Five pairs of shots, five more bodies, and then they would come for her.

Two paces and she was at her backpack. She hooked her left hand into the shoulder strap, winced in pain, carried on down the path.

Another pair of shots; then another.

It was obscene to be counting off the shots, counting off the lives of the girls, the boys, who stood, rooted by fear, in front of those men.

Don't look.

Two more shots.

She was at the trees now. From here the path snaked around the edge of the lake, then led down some steep steps cut into the rock to the sea. Off to the right were the dormitory cabins. She wondered if she might be safer there.

She reached into her pack, slid out her telephone and the key to the boat. Then she thought again. She held the pack around the ammunition box, shook her possessions onto the side of the path.

Pain rooted her to the spot. She forced herself to breathe through it. She found the ziplock bag with her toothbrush and soap in it, tipped them out of the bag. She dropped in her telephone and the boat key, sealed the bag, dropped it into her backpack.

It bothered her that she couldn't find a wound on her front. She knew—perhaps she had read—that it was best if the bullet passes right through you. When she reached her hand around to the entry wound it was small. The wound itself didn't hurt a lot, but every time she moved her shoulder nerves shrieked and her jaw clenched shut; it was all she could do not to sit rocking in pain. Still, not having an exit wound on her chest meant she could draw the straps of her backpack tight.

This had to be survivable. There were two hundred young people on the island. Plus a few adults. Those men couldn't kill every last one of them. If she could make it down to the water, perhaps she could swim along the shoreline to the dock.

How many people would the boat carry? Eight, she guessed, easy. Maybe ten or twelve. Maybe more.

"Do not be alarmed."

The voice was chillingly close. She pushed her clothes from the backpack under a bush.

"There has been an incident on the island."

She held her pack in her arms, threw herself into the trees, not thinking about her shoulder. The underbrush was dense here; she could not get more than a few meters in.

"You may have heard shots. We have the situation under control. Be assured that you are safe. Please approach my colleague and me for assistance and further information."

She heard the approach of footsteps. She saw a shadow on the path in front of her, saw it turn this way, then the other. She crouched down, forced herself to slow her breathing.

Hold out, she thought. *You have to hold out.*

A second shadow followed the first. A single muttered word.

The shadows moved off toward the cabins.

A hand reached for hers in the gloom. It took all her strength to keep from crying out. A boy. A tiny little boy.

In truth, she realized, he couldn't be much younger than she was. Her sister's age, maybe. Thirteen, but small. His skin glowed dully. His eyes were wet.

"*De er ikke politi*," he said. *Not the police.*

No, she said. Those men weren't the police.

Were they safe here?

No, she said, she didn't think they were. He should come with her to the boat. He could swim, couldn't he?

Yes, he said, he could swim.

Well then, she said. But she could not persuade him to leave the cover of the woods, no matter what she said.

A pair of shots. A pause. Another pair of shots.

He was clinging to her very tightly. He was hurting her. She was injured, she explained. She couldn't stay here. She needed him to loosen his grip.

"Sorry," he said in English. *So sorry.* He hadn't meant to hurt her.

You didn't, she told him, though the pain was more than she had ever known. She bit the inside of her cheek hard, clutched at her thighs with her nails. The boy was looking at her hands. She could hear his breathing, and her own, ragged and hoarse. She knew she was frightening him. But more than that, she knew she must not cry out.

When the pain subsided she asked him to take her pack, to unzip it and take out the metal box, and to place the box under a long piece of rotting pine bark on the forest floor. The boy did what she asked, wordlessly. His face was streaked with dirt and tears. In the forest gloom the blood from her wound was black on his white T-shirt.

When she told him it was okay, that he would be okay, she saw how hard he tried to smile and it almost broke her. You're being very brave, she told him.

"I don't want to die."

What's your name? she asked him.

"Arno."

"Then we have to go, Arno," she said.

He nodded. She promised him he would not die. But he would not leave, and she knew she could not stay.

She kept to the trees on the left side of the path, by the lake. It was heavy going through the underbrush. She had imagined she would slip past the dormitory cabins in the cover of the trees, but as she drew near, panting—her body twisted in anticipation of the pain that increased with every step—she realized that it would not be simple. The cabins were arranged in four straight rows on the other side of the path. Anyone standing outside could see directly on to the path. Worse, the trees on the lake side had been cut away opposite the cabins to give a view on to the water.

Why hadn't she called someone? Her father? The police? Too late for that now; she would give herself away.

She came to the edge of the woods. Between her and the lake the cabins were small, square, and cheaply built, with miniature terraces and mean little windows.

She began to walk towards the lake. She passed the first row of cabins.

She stopped, crouched down in the shade of a tree, made herself small.

The pattern of the gunshots had changed. Short, jagged bursts. Had they run out of pistol ammunition? She heard another burst of gunfire. She saw, she thought, a muzzle flash; she heard the sound of a heavy object collapsing against wood; she forced herself not to think of bodies. Though it could only be a body.

Ahead of her, in the second row, a face appeared at the rear window of a cabin. The window frame was pushed roughly out, breaking a hinge. A boy of her own age pushed his arms through, braced them against the outer wall of the cabin, pulled hard. He forced one shoulder out, then the other, snaked his body through. He hung, upside down, then landed catlike on the faded grass. He paused, listened, then sprinted up the path toward the clearing. As she watched, another face appeared at the window, a girl this time, looking out.

The unmistakable sound of footsteps on the grass, heavy, relentless. The sound of a door swinging open. She saw—she felt—the panic in the girl's face as she stared toward the door of the cabin. She heard a commanding male voice.

"Please remain calm."

She saw—she felt—the girl's confusion. The girl stood there, her face in profile, framed by the window. How close she was. Three meters, perhaps four.

The girl made to say something.

A sharp burst of gunfire. The girl stood there still, expression draining from her face. Then she fell out of sight. She heard the girl's body as it collapsed onto the wooden floor.

Christ.

She pushed herself in among the trees, stared out at the path. That girl—there and then not there.

Please, Lord Christ, make this stop.

The face of the taller man appeared in the window, looked out. As he did so, his companion rounded the corner, stood on the path between her and the cabin. She hunkered down, made herself smaller still.

Please, Christ. Oh, please. Please, Lord.

She had to control her breathing. She knew she was approaching panic, and that panic would kill her. Weird that she could remember the school drills so well. Macabre. She had to quiet her breathing, her raging pulse. She had to damp down the desire to stand up and scream. Because these men, she knew, would cut her down.

It was dark here in the cover of the trees, and the men were standing in direct sunlight, and perhaps that simple fact would be enough to save her. She began counting as she breathed.

In, two, three, four.

Hold, two, three, four.

Out, two, three, four.

It hurt to breathe deeply, made her wonder where the bullet was lodged, made her hope her lung was okay.

Both men were in front of her, terrifyingly close, though she had not seen the short man move.

"Re-up?"

She saw the smile they exchanged: confident, ready, friendly.

"Yep!"

There was nothing about them that betrayed the horror of what she had witnessed. Their eyes were bright, beady, like dogs on the chase. She could see no aggression in them, no malice. She saw the tall man take what looked like a pill, then wash it down with water from a small metal flask. The short man did the same. She heard the water in his throat as he swallowed, smelled on his breath the chewing tobacco, sickly and sweet.

The taller man took something from a pocket. Three flat metal boxes, which the short man dropped into his own pocket. Pistol magazines, like the ones in the rusted case. Then he bent down, picked up his rifle. She saw him disengage something boxy, which he handed to the short man.

"BRB, buddy." Both men laughed. *Be right back.*

The tall man fitted a new magazine to his rifle, turned, walked toward the third row of cabins. She leaned forward, watched the small man as he too disappeared from sight, then crossed the path. She flattened herself against the first cabin in the third row. She heard his footsteps in the cabin, felt the slow, deliberate cruelty. But he did not fire his weapon. She heard and felt him move toward the door, forced herself forward along the side of the cheap wooden building, made herself watch him leave this cabin and enter the next.

She walked as briskly and as quietly as she could across the gap that divided the third row from the fourth. *At any moment,* she thought, *another bullet will tear into me. A burst of bullets, and they will shatter my lungs and my heart and my liver and all that is me will end, and Christ, please, Christ . . .*

The bullets did not come; the man had not seen her.

She calmed herself.

She wondered. She could save some people. Surely she could. If she tried to enter any of the cabins in the third row she risked being in direct line of sight of the gunman as he moved from building to building. But would he see her if she went to the cabins in the fourth row? How far could she get before he rounded the corner and began to move toward the lake? How many could she save?

She heard a burst of gunfire. Her courage deserted her. She had thought—hoped—that the men would run out of ammunition, that losing the rusted box would cost them, but they had bullets to spare. She was wounded and she was frightened. She needed to get to the water, and to the safety of the boat.

There was no hope for the children in the cabins. How many of them would even move? She must get to the water, save herself and anyone else she could. It was too late for the children in these cabins. It was not too late for her.

She continued down the path to the edge of the island, and down the narrow steps cut into the pink-gray rock, like a tunnel toward the sea below. To her right was a narrow ledge a few meters above the water.

A man on the ledge. An adult. He had cut his leg open dragging himself up the rock face.

"Come up here," he said. She thought again of her father. The man smiled down at her, extending his hand, and for a moment she felt she was saved. But this man was not her father, and she was not yet safe.

The man's hair was wild, his T-shirt torn. She recognized him, she thought. Part of the welcoming committee as she had stepped onto the dock with the other kids. Did something in the office, he had said.

As she frowned up at him she heard an engine approaching, the familiar *ruck-ruck-ruck* of chopper blades. She felt the rush of air, saw the water begin to swirl and dance in the downdraft, and when she looked up she saw the helicopter forty feet above.

Christ, she thought. *Thank you, Christ.*

The man threw himself from the ledge into the water and vanished. She scanned the water. He surfaced, waving wildly.

She looked up again, and saw the camera mounted beneath the fuselage, saw the white-on-red of the TVZ logo. The helicopter hovered, hummingbird-still, and she realized that the camera was lining up on her.

They're filming us.

From the top of the steps a boy and a girl appeared, running as if for their lives. The boy from the woods, she realized, little Arno, with a girl she had not seen before. Another two girls appeared. They pushed past her, stood at the foot of the steps, waving. A burst of gunfire close by. The plexiglass in the near-side door shattered. The helicopter lifted upward, turned, and headed inland.

"Where did they go?" said one of the girls. "Where the fuck did they go?"

The man in the torn T-shirt began pushing past them up the steps, shouting after the helicopter. "Here! I'm here." He reached the top, disappeared, still shouting.

She could see the others looking up the steps after him. One of the girls began to move past her. She put her hand on the girl's arm.

"We should—" said the girl.

"We can't."

"He is the only adult," said Arno very quietly.

"I know," she said. "But we are not going to do that."

She swung the backpack off her shoulder, took off her dress.

All faces, all looking at her in her underwear. The girl at her side reached out toward her, as if seeing for the first time the wound on her shoulder.

"Did you get shot?"

"I'm okay," she said.

Fear on every face.

She pulled on her pack, tightened the straps. "Come on."

The helicopter was fading away. The man was shouting after it, increasingly desperate.

"Guys! Hey, over here! Guys, we're over here."

A shot. Then another.

The man stopped shouting.

No one spoke. The three girls looked at her, terror in their faces. The boy too.

"We're trapped," one of the girls said quietly.

She looked up toward the top of the steps. The other children followed her gaze. She could see them thinking the same thought. The helicopter had given them away.

Every face turned toward her.

I'm the oldest person here, she realized. *I'm the adult.* Funny. Almost.

"We're trapped," said the girl again.

"No." She set her teeth against the pain, tightened the straps on her backpack. She pushed past the girls to the bottom of the steps, crossed her arms over her chest, jumped forward, let herself fall, body tensed and stretched like a dart. For a moment she felt only the air around her. Then the shock of the water, the roar of the sea all about her. She felt herself drop, let her body relax, waited for the water to carry her up toward the light. Her right shoulder ached, but the water cooled it and soothed it, and she found she could swim with her left arm.

Not a sound behind her. She turned to find all faces looking at her. The girls, the boy, rooted in place.

"There's a boat. It's at the dock. I have the key."

One by one they joined her in the water. Only Arno remained. "Arno," she said. "We have to go."

Two gunshots near the top of the steps.

"Arno, please."

Arno crossed his arms over his chest and jumped.

She kicked hard. The straps of her pack cut into her wound and she winced. But if she held her body stiffly she could make progress. Two girls on one side of her, swimming strongly; on the other side Arno and the other girl. The only sound was water; water and breath.

Arno was the weakest of the swimmers. He held his head too high, kicked too hard, tiring fast. The girls swam quietly, efficiently, their bodies low in the water, pacing their breathing to their strokes.

She turned, treading water, waiting for the boy to catch up. Her shoulder was stiff, to be sure, but she was all right. Better now than before. She would survive this. They would all survive.

She looked back at the cleft in the rock. She did not see the men.

"I'm so slow," said Arno as he drew close to her. "Sorry."

"Shh," she said, because as he spoke the smaller of the men appeared on the steps, his pistol in his right hand. If the man turned, if he saw them . . .

She must be calm. The fjord here was shallow, the water dark.

"Listen to me." She put her arms on Arno's shoulders. "Take two deep breaths and dive to the bottom."

"Two?"

His eyes widened. She could feel the panic in him. He wanted to look back.

At the steps in the cliff the man was looking to his right, straining to see up to the ledge. In a moment he would turn to his left and he would see them as they swam for their lives, and everything would be lost.

She felt Arno gasping air. "Swim down, Arno. Grab a rock. Hold on."

She pushed his shoulders beneath the surface; she turned, caught the eye of one of the girls. The girl nodded and slipped below the surface.

She kicked down to the bottom. The water was peaty and dark, but she found the boy quickly, his arms wrapped around a boulder. Bubbles spilled upward from his mouth. She wrapped her own arms around his, brought her face very close, made sure that he could see her.

She smiled, but Arno did not respond. She could feel him trying to free his hands.

She shook her head, tightened her grip on his arms.

Panic in his eyes. *Arno, please*, she thought, *you have to hold on*.

He was grimacing, making a strange kind of *Mmmm* sound.

Please. Just a little longer.

He began to struggle. So tiny, yet so strong.

She let him go. She saw a dark shadow above her as his body reached the surface. He thrashed there for a moment. She watched, certain that he had given himself away, certain that the bullets would strike him, that his body would seize, that blood would leak from him in dark clouds.

Instead his body calmed; she saw him begin to swim again. She released her own grip on the boulder, came up facing the rock staircase, certain that they were discovered, but the man in the police uniform was gone. Ahead of them the three girls surfaced. They swam on, the island to their left, treading water from time to time to wait for the boy.

No one spoke.

As they swam she began to see corpses at the water's edge. You could see people hiding too, boys and girls whom the men had not found, though you could see them clearly from here, cowering in crevices in the cliffs or hiding in the underbrush. Gathering above the children were the news helicopters: three of them now. Filming the children as they hid for their lives. Revealing their presence.

Where were the real police? The army? The camp staff, even?

She began to plan. The boat was held at the dock by two ropes. The engine was in position. They would come on board at the stern; she would be at the console in seconds, the key would turn, the boat would slip its mooring, reverse quietly out into the fjord.

It helped to know what she would do, what she would say. It held at bay the terror that threatened to engulf her.

The men would not hear the engine before she gunned it toward the mainland.

Everyone down.

Stay out of sight.

They were going to make it.

Through her backpack she felt her phone ringing. Still there in its ziplock bag.

Can't speak now, Dad.

Funny.

Almost.

The boat was in sight now. Ahead of her were the girls. Behind her was Arno. She waited until he caught up.

"I'm going to go on board first," she said. Her voice sounded foreign to her, unreal. Out of breath, though she was barely swimming.

The boy nodded. She could see that he was near the end of his strength.

"Need to let the others know. You be okay, Arno?"

"Yeah."

She pressed on toward the girls, swimming swiftly, ignoring the ache in her shoulder. Two minutes. Maybe less. Keep them out of the way.

Everybody stay low.

The water in front of her flicked as if slapped. Twice. She heard the gunshots as they echoed from the far banks of the fjord. She turned to face their attacker, though she knew that she should not; she stopped swimming, though she knew that she must not.

There he was, the short man. He was standing on a rock near the water's edge. His black shirt was open at the neck. There were sweat patches under his arms. His pistol was raised, held in both hands, braced. He was looking at her, she realized. Sighting up. It was casual, matter-of-fact, without malice.

Behind her was Arno. Brave little Arno.

For a moment Arno flailed. Tiny waves radiated out from his body, lapping toward her across the mirror-black surface.

She looked up at the man. *Please*, she thought. *Not Arno.*

How calm the man was. His gaze did not waver. He closed his left eye.

She felt the bullet strike. It crushed her clavicle, tore into the wall of muscle behind, obliterated the lung tissue that lay in its path, lodged itself deep within her.

She gasped. The man paused. The sound echoed back at her.

She saw the man check her position; she saw him check his own position; again she saw him close his left eye.

All was lost now, she thought.

This is the end of me.

The Foreigner

ONE

THE APARTMENT BUILDING STOOD on heavy concrete pillars, held tight to the rock below by deep-driven steel spikes. *Øvre Øvrebøhaugen 4*: an address I could spell but never pronounce. Inside, the dark rooms were low-ceilinged and triple-glazed, built to hold the winter at bay. But today the Nordic summer heat had forced us out onto the terrace at the back.

I felt a low vibration through the concrete of the terrace. The apartment windows trembled in their metal frames.

"Thunder," I said, though the day was bright and the sky was clear.

"Thunder," agreed Elsa, watching me over the top of her glass.

We had loved this place when we first saw it—*so much space, so close to town*—but our daughters never did. There was something about the austerity of the buildings that silenced children, that made them speak to each other in monotones or whispers. Everything was low-slung and hard-lined, the wooden cladding painted black, the concrete gray and weathered. Everywhere there were stern little signs—PLAY NO BALL, RIDE NO BICYCLE, FEED NO BIRDS—and children very quickly got the message that they were tolerated but never welcome: at Øvre Øvrebøhaugen the only voices that carried were old.

Today, though, none of that mattered. Midsummer's Eve was our anniversary. Seventeen years married. Today our elder daughter was at summer camp, our younger daughter at a friend's, our baby son asleep in his crib. And besides, we'd be gone in a week.

On a stone patio table stood two hand-cut martini glasses, emptied now. Elsa was smiling at me as she always used to smile, running her fingertips across my palm. Upright and lean, her dark blond hair scraped and casually tied, her eyes keen and sharp.

Those eyes of Elsa's: the eyes of a wolf, shot through with ice. Her irises are always a shade too blue, a fraction too pale. Nordic eyes, you might be tempted to say, though no one here has eyes like Elsa's. Even now, at times, I feel tracked by an alien intelligence.

She turned my hand over, made a play of looking at my watch. "How about another?"

"We have twenty-five minutes."

"We do."

I picked up the glasses.

On the kitchen wall hung three meter-square prints, all color and photographic grain. Elsa was a photographer. Her work in the years before the children came had been very pure; very expensive; very *art*. All looming shapes, shot without a lens on the camera. *Carmine 12*, *Cinnabar 44*, and *Burnt Umber 11*.

"Why are they so out of focus?" people would ask.

"Keep thinking about that," she would reply. "Because the lack of focus is important."

I could never look directly at Elsa's pictures without a stab of guilt. She would tell me she was done with photography, that she had said all she had to say about color and form, that she loved having time to spend with the girls, but these vast images followed us everywhere, a reminder of a time when my wife was the promising one, and when I had no career to speak of.

A cloud of tiny insects hovered around the fruit bowl. I selected the lemon with the heaviest skin, cut two long strips with a peeler, trimmed the edges straight with a long knife.

From the freezer I took a steel cocktail mixer already filled with ice cubes; two cut-crystal martini glasses, each with a wooden spill onto which I had threaded three olives; and an ice-frosted bottle of gin. I poured a few drops of vermouth on to the ice, then cradled the glasses and the mixer in my hands, jammed the bottle between my right forearm and my chest, and walked carefully back on the other side of the apartment. Here the windowless walls damped down the sounds of the world to a dull hum.

I paused in the box room. In his wooden crib our tiny blond baby curled and uncurled his fingers, wrapped himself tightly into his soft panda, limb against limb. He sucked at the panda's draggled snout with milky lips, as if seeking sanctuary from some unknown force. I stood, watching his chest, listening for the sounds that told me what I already knew.

In. In. Out. Those soft reedy breaths, almost inaudible. An everyday miracle.

Franklin Curtis, his name was, though he did not yet know it.

ELSA WAS LOOKING OUT TOWARD THE HILLS when I returned. I placed the glasses on the table as silently as I could, slipped the gin bottle from under my arm with my left hand. I poured gin into the cocktail mixer. The ice fissured and cracked. Elsa turned.

"That sound. Never fails."

Her transfixing irises; the merest suggestion of a squint.

I stirred gently, poured the liquor into the glasses, held back the ice with a spoon. Elsa watched me all the while. Her eyes flicked to the glass as I set it in front of her, then flicked to me.

"How do you get them so perfect, Cal?"

Always the same words.

"Everything has to be very, very cold," I answered, as I always answered. "Your olives . . ." I stopped.

"What?" she said.

"You haven't actually tasted it."

"Oh, Cal. Don't screw up the ritual."

I smiled, waiting for her to taste. She raised the glass to her lips, took a sip. Winced slightly.

"It's good," she said.

"But not perfect."

"All right." She sighed. "There's a shade too much vermouth, and I feel like you didn't check the strength of the olive brine. What? Stop looking at me like that."

"Like what?"

"You're laughing at me inwardly."

MY WIFE, WHO LIVES BY A CODE of honesty so brutal that it used to terrify me. And still does. Who told me when we met that she preferred men to be taller and a little better-looking, but that she liked my smile and was in the mood for sex. I made a joke about penis size to cover my confusion. She didn't laugh.

"The size of your penis is not relevant. Tonight we shall have non-penetrative sex."

I was crushed, but strangely elated. I could see that Elsa was out of my league, taller than me in her heels and beautiful with it, supple and strong and used to attention.

"Of course," I said, as though non-penetrative sex made perfect sense, given the imbalance between us.

And oh, the many colors in her dark blond hair, and oh, the jut of her thigh and the warmth in her ice-blue eyes. And later, when we were both breathing hard, naked in her vast wooden bed, our lips almost touching, our eyes locked, she said, "Please don't circle your thumb on my clitoris in that way, Cal."

"All right. Just . . ."

"Thank you." Her voice so soft, her eyes smiling at me.

"Just . . . did I misread something?"

She sat up. "Misread how?"

"I thought you were close."

"To coming?" She nodded. "If you keep using your thumb in that way I might come, but it will then make me think of a man who used to make me come in that way. And I do not wish to think of that man. Please find another way."

That night I did not make Elsa come. But in the months that followed I learned how to bring Elsa to orgasm, all fingertips and tongue, in a way that was uniquely mine.

My wife, who cannot tell a lie.

I LOOKED ACROSS THE TOP OF MY glass; Elsa looked back with a level gaze.

"I love you, Elsa."

Even now I can feel the pause, as her eyes dropped away and

lost focus, as the corners of her mouth quivered. It was as if my words had taken her off guard; as if—on this, our wedding anniversary, at this most perfect moment—they were the last thing she was expecting to hear.

"I love you," I said again.

It was almost as if she were considering her response. Her eyes flicked to the horizon, to the trees beyond the garden in the far hills.

"And I love you too, Cal." And oh, the warmth in her voice, and the longing. And oh, how it sounded like love. But when her eyes at last met mine there was an emptiness that did not look like love. And yet . . .

"Seventeen years married," I said.

I took a swig, felt the citrus and the salt as the alcohol warmed me, though the day already was hot.

"Seventeen years." She knocked her glass hard against mine, drained it half down.

She was looking at me matter-of-factly. The emptiness was gone.

"What?" I said.

"He will arrive three minutes early, because he always does. Which means we have eighteen minutes." She must have seen me looking in through the door, toward Franklin, because she said, "Franklin is asleep, yes?"

"Yes."

"Well, then . . ." She reached over, let her hand trail in my lap.

Still that directness about appetites that stops me short.

What is this? I wanted to say. *What are you doing?* But I let her guide me to my feet and into the bedroom.

"Wait here," she said. She crossed to her side of the bed. She turned toward me, raised her arms above her head, let her dress slip to the floor. She looked at me as I looked at her, half-naked, matter-of-fact. And that smile, and the certainty of it, and despite myself I found myself smiling back at her.

"Now you," she said.

I heard you return home, I wanted to say. *The clock said four.*

Instead I undressed and lay down on the bed while she stood in her Calvin Klein underwear, looking down at me.

Where were you, Elsa?

And still I could feel desire gnawing at me. Her smile, her eyes drinking me in. The jut of her lips. The tilt of her thigh. The sheer confidence she had in her body, unlike any other woman I'd known. Her pride in the gentle curve of her belly. She turned. I watched as she walked through the door past Franklin and into the bathroom. I heard the taps run.

From the terrace I heard voices. Neighbors. Elsa wouldn't care that the door was open. I did. I got to my feet, padded naked out onto the terrace, fetched the drinks, and closed the door. I returned to our room, put a glass on each nightstand, lay with my head against the headboard.

When Elsa came in, she was naked too.

I heard you, I wanted to say, *when you came home this morning at four. When I felt you roll in beside me I looked at the clock.* But she had been up at seven with the baby as if nothing were wrong, and I knew that if I asked her she would laugh it away.

It's what we do here, Cal.

And oh, her lips, her breasts, her tilted thigh.

"Venus," I said.

She looked down at me, amused, cupped her left hand across her pubis and her right across her breasts.

"Swollen Venus," she said.

"Venus Venus," I said. "Now and forever."

She sat down on the bed beside me. She looked at me, ran her hand along my jaw. "Why are you so sweet to me, Cal?"

"Take the compliment," I said.

She shook her head. "But thank you. I appreciate the thought." For a moment she looked vulnerable and small. I wondered if I had misread her.

Your confidence, Elsa . . .

Then there it was; her smile returned. She ran her hand down my thigh. "Also," she said, "how can you possibly be so hard?" And when we kissed it felt as if she meant it, for the first time in months. She held me close, pushed her tongue deep into my mouth. I ran my hand down her back, let it rest, flat, at the base of her spine. She bit my lip and I pushed her forward and onto me.

The doorbell. A two-tone chime.

I pulled away. "Fuck," I said.

"Fuck," said Elsa.

The doorbell rang a second time.

TWO

"YOU'RE GOING TO HAVE to answer," I said. "I am going to have to shower."

"Okay," she said, getting up. She turned. "Although, actually, why?"

I got off the bed, threw on my dressing gown, began to walk toward the bathroom. "Because I am not answering the door to your father in this state."

"Okay, that is *not* an image that I want in my mind."

"Or your father's."

"You made your point." She bent down, picked up her dress, pulled it easily over her head and down, smoothed it around her thighs. "Go take your shower, Cal."

I showered my erection away, braced, swearing as icy needles of water bombarded my shoulders, cascaded down my chest, and on to my groin. I took shampoo from the bottle, lathered it into my hair, then stepped forward so that my head was fully under. I counted to thirty through gritted teeth, then reached out and turned off the tap.

IN THE BEDROOM I PULLED ON A T-shirt and a pair of shorts. Elsa and her father were next door in the living room, their voices hushed. Odd. You could barely hear them, but it was enough to put me on edge. Elsa's pitch was wrong, as if her voice had slipped out of tune.

My phone chimed. A text message on the lock screen, from a number unknown.

CELEBRATE

Cheers, I thought. *Whoever you are*. There was an attachment. A video. I turned the phone on the side so it filled the screen, pressed play. A screenful of black.

I deleted it.

I found a pair of black trousers in the drawer of the wardrobe and pulled them on, then went to join my wife in the living room.

"Hey, Cal," said Henrik.

"Henrik, hey."

The television was on, though neither of them was looking at it. On the screen a building, indistinct in the smoke.

Henrik watched me as I crossed the floor to greet him. A strong jaw; his daughter's eyes, like a waiting animal, patient and appraising, all senses firing. He drew me toward him, hugged me solemnly, then looked questioningly at Elsa.

"What is it?" I said.

"There's been an explosion in town," said Elsa.

"A big one," said Henrik.

I looked at Elsa. Elsa nodded.

"Viktoria is all right," said Henrik very quietly. "Frightened, but all right. I spoke to her from the car. Said that Cal, you would collect her. The next train leaves in eleven minutes, so you will leave in five."

I looked at Elsa. Elsa nodded.

"Okay," I said.

"Licia, I could not reach," said Henrik. "Though I did try. Several times. And of course your telephones are switched off." He stepped forward again, held me by the shoulders. "You have no landline, Cal." There was a critical edge to his smile.

I looked at Elsa. She looked back at me. She had her phone in her right hand, my phone in her left. She was turning her phone over and over, her fingers fluid and nimble, though her eyes remained fixed on my face. I smiled. *Are you okay, love?*

Elsa nodded at me. She blamed herself for switching off. I could see it.

I turned to Henrik. "I mean, we decided we didn't necessarily need—"

He cut me off. "Licia's telephone rings, but she does not answer her telephone."

"She's at summer camp," said Elsa. "So she's miles away."

Henrik made to speak.

"What, Dad?" said Elsa.

He turned to me, smiled. "I mean, this explosion . . . probably nothing—right, Cal?"

Elsa switched her phone out of airplane mode and dialed Vee's number.

The explosion didn't look like nothing. On-screen the town hall stood shrouded in smoke. Papers swirled in the breeze, though outside our apartment the air was still.

IN HIS WINDOWLESS ROOM OFF OUR BEDROOM little Franklin, tiny Franklin, slept his own restless sleep. Elsa stood on the threshold, watched the stuttering rise and fall of his chest through the bars of his wooden crib.

"Hey," I said.

"Hey."

We had brought the crib with us from D.C. The first piece of furniture we had bought. Both girls had slept in it. Now it was Franklin's turn.

"Hey." I stood behind Elsa, wrapped my arms across her chest.

She said, "Oh man, the way my dad says *probably nothing*, like it's the end of the fucking world."

"He tried to apologize," I said.

"And I have no idea what conversation he had with Vee, but you can bet he was happy to leave her thinking this was a major terrorist event. Even Franklin looks stressed to me. And I don't think I can blame my father for that."

She was right. Something had left Franklin fearful and tense. His tiny fists clenched and unclenched, his elbows tight at his side.

Elsa leaned gently over Franklin, slipped a hand behind his back and another behind his neck, drew him up and in to her breast as she quietly roused him from sleep.

"Sweet child," she said. "My sweet, sweet baby."

Franklin clung to her gratefully, chuttering and fretting at her, anxious for milk, for comfort, for love.

"Do we need to worry that we can't reach Licia?" I said.

"Licia will be fine," said Elsa. "She's safe on her island."

I TOOK THE PATH TOWARD THE STATION.

At a few minutes after eight that morning Elsa and I had followed Licia down this same path, until Licia turned, and laughed, and asked us please to stop. We had stood there, Elsa and I, smiling at our daughter as she smiled back at us. Her kingfisher dress shimmered brilliant in the sunlight: every imaginable green and blue.

"What?" she said, almost shyly.

World at your feet, I thought.

Elsa held out her hand. "Here."

Licia stepped forward. Around her wrist Elsa placed a heavy silver bangle with a large embossed dragonfly. Licia held up her wrist, turning the bangle before her eyes.

"The first piece of jewelry your dad gave me."

"I know," said Licia, looking from Elsa to me. "Mum, I can't."

"Love," I said, "we want you to have it."

"Thanks, Dad. Thanks, Mum."

Still strange after all these years to hear her say *Mum*—never *Mom*, always *Mum*—the only trace of Britain she and Vee carried with them when they spoke.

"Go and have fun, love."

Something very adult about the look Licia gave me as she tightened the straps on her backpack and turned away. We watched her all the way to the station, holding hands, our hearts full of pride. As she reached the steps down to the platforms I saw her wave to another girl, who approached her and hugged her. I saw Licia hold out her wrist, and I saw how the bracelet glinted and the kingfisher dress shone.

Our daughter, all shrouded in sunlight.

THE TRAIN I TOOK INTO TOWN WAS half-empty. By the doors sat a woman in a headscarf, talking animatedly into a telephone in a language I did not understand. When she ended the call I made a point of smiling at her. The woman smiled cautiously back.

FOOTSTEPS ECHOED AROUND ME AT THE NATIONAL THEATER station. A crowd flowing into town, toward the center of whatever it was that had happened. All heading toward their loved ones. Faces of every kind, all set in the same expression: stoical, impassive, determined.

At the side of the royal park a man stood shouting. His face was bloodied, his clothes torn. At his side a woman stood, a phone by her ear, trying to summon help, listening for an answer on the line that did not come.

THREE

LIGHT BLAZED THROUGH THE stained glass on the stairwell. After the clamor of the streets the stillness of the building felt wrong. There was a grandeur here, a wastefulness both beautiful and intimidating. Painted angels looked down on me from the plasterwork.

I rang the doorbell. From the wooden floors inside the apartment I heard footsteps. A gap between the door and the threshold. I heard my breath too, panting and heaving, though I was only three flights up. My nerves. The windows were out all along the street. There were glass fragments under the soles of my shoes.

The door swung open.

"Hi," I said. Because I couldn't remember her name. Julie's mom.

"Hello," said Julie's mom. Immaculate in three-inch heels and a two-piece suit, her asymmetric bob artfully mussed. In her left hand was Vee's gaming headset.

"Cal," I said.

Julie's mom smiled coolly, offered her right hand.

"Nora. Did we meet already?"

"We did."

Her eyes would not fix on my face; there was something unsteady about her stance.

Behind her stood Vee, lit up with nervy energy, shoes in one hand.

Relief flooded my veins. "My little girl."

"Hey, Dad."

Julie's mom passed the gaming headset to Vee.

Vee hunched her shoulders as she stepped across the threshold onto the tiles outside the apartment, bending away from me. And when I reached down to hold her she slipped from me and headed down the stairs in her socks.

"'Bye," she said without looking back. "Thank you so very much for having me."

"Vee," I said. "Your shoes."

"I'll put them on downstairs."

"Now, please, Vee."

Julie's mom put a hand on my arm.

"Your daughter is a brave girl. A bomb goes off and she does not lose her head."

"If we can be certain it was a bomb."

"Did you not see the glass in the street?" The look she gave me told me she was in no doubt.

"Proud of you, honey," I called after Vee, who ignored me and continued on down.

"Hey," I said. "Wait."

Vee didn't turn around.

"Have a safe day," I said.

"You too," said Nora Gundersen as she closed and locked the door.

Vee heard my footsteps behind her, quickened her pace. When I got to the lobby she was standing there, hunched and shaking, trying to fix the laces on her sneakers.

"Hey, Vee. Vee. It's all right. It's okay." I tried to take her in my arms. "My love," I said. "You're safe. You're safe, okay?"

She shook me off. "Who are they trying to kill, Dad?"

"We don't know that anyone is trying to kill anyone, Vee."

"It was a bomb," she said, her voice soft and matter-of-fact.

"It was certainly an explosion."

"It was a bomb."

"If your plaits weren't screwed down so tight I would ruffle your hair."

"Just don't, Dad."

I could feel the resentment dripping from her. I was speaking to her as to a child.

"Okay," I said. "Sorry."

"You never listen. You . . . you impose your version of what happened."

I could see that she meant it. "I'm listening now. I promise. Okay?"

"Okay."

We sat side by side on the third step, looking out. The building was cool in the summer heat: old and grand, and nothing like ours. The world beyond looked peaceful. You couldn't see the glass fragments that littered the street outside.

"Okay, so, there are two beds in Julie's room. And I was sitting on the spare bed, and Julie was sitting on her bed, and there's just this flash. I mean, it was bright. Julie was just a silhouette. It was so weird. And then the window fell away."

"It fell away?"

"It was like it bent inward first. You'd swear it bent inward. And I kept thinking it was going to shatter, and we'd be stumbling bleeding into the street. It was like I could see that. And then there's this moment where Julie's looking at me, and I'm looking at Julie, and she reaches across and takes my hand. And at the same moment the window was sucked out. The whole pane, and the wood and everything just kind of pivoted on the lower edge and fell away. And there's just this really creepy silence . . ."

"It felt like the birds stopped singing. And then you heard this huge roar. Like the end of the world. And we both turned over on the beds and put our hands over the backs of our heads. We knew what to do. Which is also weird. And then finally you hear the glass shattering in the street. And we just lay there facedown on the beds until Julie's mom came to get us."

I reached out, pulled her gently toward me.

"Mum's going to say I'm dramatizing."

"She won't."

Then Vee wrapped her arms very tightly around me, and I wiped the tears from her face and told her everything was going to be okay, and this time she allowed me to comfort her.

THE STREETS HAD EMPTIED. AT THE SOUND of rotors Vee stopped and looked up. A news helicopter. It made a lazy sweep toward the palace, then tipped and headed toward town.

"Dad," she said, "about Licia . . ."

In my pocket my phone was vibrating against my thigh. Vee made to speak.

"I'm sorry, love. I think this could be important."

"But Dad—"

I raised the phone to my ear.

"This is Lori from WXWD in Washington, D.C." A pleasant American singsong. "Am I speaking with Cal Curtis? Dan said now might a good moment to bring your eyewitness testimony to our listeners."

"Tell Dan I'm collecting my daughter. Could we speak in half an hour?"

"Sure. Speak then."

I hung up.

Vee looked at me, reproachful. "What?"

"Your Uncle Dan wants me to talk about what people are feeling after the explosion."

"What are they feeling, then?"

I laughed. "Maybe it would be better if you did the piece. You have a headset and everything."

For a moment Vee laughed too. Then she stopped, became serious.

"Dad, who's collecting Licia?"

"Licia's safe on her island," I said.

The glass was sand beneath our shoes. We heard sirens, though we saw no police. The few people we did see floated past, empty-eyed, or stood on corners, watching the clouds of smoke and brick dust as they rolled and turned in the Midsummer air.

I STOOD ON THE SUBWAY PLATFORM, VEE'S headset covering my ears, the cable attached to my phone. In front of us was the empty carriage, lights on, doors open. Even down here the air was filled with dust.

"Dad," mouthed Vee.

I lifted the earpad from my right ear. "What, love?"

"Is it true you can breathe in bits of people and not know it?"

From my left ear I could hear the station assistant's voice. "This is Lori. Am I speaking with Cal Curtis again?"

"I'm sorry, Vee. They're patching me through to the studio, love." I replaced the earpad over my ear. The sound of the subway disappeared. All I could hear was my own breath.

"So, Cal," said the voice on the other end. "Dan tells me you are a satirist."

"I am."

Lori laughed as though I had said something funny. "And Cal, we are good for level and we are all set, and the next voice you hear will be Carly's. Patching you through . . . now."

"And from Oslo, Norway, we have Cal Curtis, a Scottish satirist who has lived for many years in Washington, D.C., but is currently on a career break in Norway. Cal, you were an eyewitness to the fearful explosion that rocked the Norwegian capital less than an hour ago. What was your first thought when you heard the bomb that tore through the town hall?"

"Well, my first thought was thunder. My *daughter's* first thought was that this was a bomb."

"Your daughter was a witness to the explosion?"

"My daughter is a very brave young woman." I smiled down at Vee. Vee tried to smile back. "She was in the center of town. The window in the room she was in was sucked out by the blast. She and her friend lay facedown, bracing the backs of their heads, waiting for help to arrive, just as she was taught in school."

"Dad," mouthed Vee urgently. I lifted one earpad. "We need to get on the train."

I replaced the earpad, put a hand on Vee's shoulder. *One second*, I mouthed.

I saw her mouth move. "But Dad . . ."

I turned away, folded my hand over the earpiece. "It's important to stress we don't yet know what has happened. The government has confirmed that there has been an explosion. They have asked us to be vigilant. No word of a bomb. No word on casualties. We are in the center of the city and the streets here are virtually empty."

"Dad." Vee was in front of me, tugging at my elbow.

I held up my hand. *Wait.*

Carly's voice. "Theories must be emerging, Cal."

"Right."

"What are people saying?" I didn't know what people were saying. I thought for a moment. "Yes, at this stage I suppose it's impossible to rule out a terrorist attack. This country has had military presences in many Middle Eastern flashpoints."

Lights flashing. The doors-closing signal.

Vee stepped away from me onto the train. "Dad, come on . . ."

I stepped on board; the doors slid shut.

"Thank you, Cal Curtis in Oslo, Norway. More on that story as it emerges."

A click, and the feed from the studio faded out.

Vee sat facing me, stared me full in the face, arms folded angrily across her chest. I took off the headset.

"What is it, Vee?"

"Why did you say the Muslims blew up Oslo?"

"Vee, you know I would never claim something like that."

"Actually, you pretty much did. And you were speaking in this weird deep voice, like you think that's how radio people speak."

"Please tell me I wasn't," I said. "Was I?"

She nodded at me sternly, then her face broke into a smile.

"Okay," I said. "Well, that isn't good."

VEE STEPPED ACROSS THE THRESHOLD, LEANED IN to her mother, let herself be held, then pulled away and headed toward her bedroom. Elsa watched her go, wondering perhaps if she should call after her.

"How is she?" she said.

"It's all coming out as anger. She was very close to the bomb."

"If it even was a bomb."

"From what she says, it was."

"Maybe." She said it on the in-breath. A strange little sighing sound.

I followed Elsa through to the kitchen, stood looking up at her unreadable pictures on the white wall above the table. The pictures were of crime scenes in Washington, photographed with the cooperation of the police. Elsa would work methodically, using whatever light was available, shooting on large-format film cameras, always without a lens.

Carmine 12 was taken at the scene of a stabbing; *Cinnabar 44* a shooting; *Burnt Umber 11* a hammer attack.

"Why murder?" people would ask.

Elsa never explained.

The serious newspapers loved my wife's work; critics made comparisons with Munch. "A Postmodern Scream for the New Post-Enlightenment" was my favorite headline; the article was as hard to decipher as Elsa's pictures.

"Elsa," I said, "there's something I need your help to understand."

She looked levelly back. "What's that?"

That video file, I wanted to say. *Time-stamped three a.m. When you came home at four. On the morning of our anniversary.*

No hint of guilt in Elsa's gaze. Instead there was something complex and loving and warm.

"You guys about ready?" Henrik's voice from the hall.

Elsa smiled. "Dad's going to drive us to the marina."

"You sure, Henrik?" I called out.

Henrik stepped into the hall from the kitchen. "Important not to be dramatic. I shall drive you."

"I mean, Henrik, that's great, but it doesn't feel—"

Henrik cut me off. "If it is terrorism, we do not want such people to win. And if it is not terrorism, what is the risk? Your marriage is a precious thing to you, no?"

"Wait," I said. "Henrik, no disrespect, but Vee is in pieces, and we haven't spoken to Licia."

"Viktoria is playing a computer game, which involves shooting people and then dancing. I do not think she is *in pieces*."

Elsa smiled. "I texted with Licia. She was fine."

"I don't know," I said. "Something about this doesn't feel right."

"Cal, you must go," said Henrik. "Simple."

"Henrik," I said, "again, with respect, it isn't simple."

"What Viktoria needs is calm and normality. A good walk, out in nature. Pine trees and forest animals. Maybe we will see an elusive moose."

"Or I could come with you, Dad." Vee's voice. She had slipped into the room, unseen. "Please, Dad?"

FOUR

ELSA SWUNG THE WHEEL, slipped the motor into gear. The engine note rose, and our little rented speedboat continued its arc out of the bay and into the fjord beyond. Vee lay on the sun seats by the motor, staring up at the sky. Beside her, her laptop bag and her gaming headset.

I sat beside Elsa, the passenger seat angled toward her, my bare feet on the edge of her seat, watching her. A woman perfectly in command of a boat, in a strapless black dress and fitted life preserver. An everyday sight in Norway, perhaps; still exotic to me.

"What?" said Elsa.

I grinned. "You, at the helm of a small speedboat."

"Eyes on the water in front, Mum," shouted Vee from behind us. "And Dad, shut up."

"Okay, love." Elsa grinned, and turned to face forward.

The boat was an indulgence. We couldn't afford it, but everyone we knew in Oslo had one. And besides, Elsa was comfortable on the water. She stood behind the windshield, sunglasses pushed high on her head, turning from time to time to check for other boats coming in from the side, watching the marina disappear behind us, poised and in control. The engine pitch rose to a soft whine; the bow of the boat kicked up.

Elsa looked at me and nodded. I rose and we took a step forward, used our weight to bring the nose of the boat down, stepped back into place. I sat down. In seconds we were skimming fast across the fjord, cutting a perfect wake across the glassy water.

Vee's eyes were closed now.

Elsa leaned in to me, whispered. "You smell of really good food."

"I smell of sweat and sexual frustration."

"Trust me, you don't."

Behind and to the left, the scattered bays, the painted houses by the water. The land was green, the rocks pink, the water a deep northern blue.

On islets near the shore you could see wood stacked neatly in vast piles, ready for the evening's bonfires. Farther out, birds divebombed shoals of herring fry, and ahead, though it was partly hidden by the headland, you could see the sweep of the Oslo waterline, the cruise ships and the grain towers and the monstrous industrial cranes.

"We could buy a little boat back home," said Elsa. "Be good for the girls."

"Yes," I said. "Maybe we could."

The smoke. We saw it as we rounded the headland. It rose in a vertical plume from the middle of the C-shaped bay. Elsa eased off the throttle; the boat dropped down onto the surface of the fjord. Vee sat up, instantly awake.

The bay was divided in two between light and dark. In the center of town the buildings lay shrouded in a gray pall. The twin towers of the town hall vanished into the smoke. News helicopters dipped in and out, rotors shifting the edges of the swirling gray column above, ruffling the water below.

Elsa's eyes scanned the shoreline.

"We can turn around," I said.

"It's not as bad as it looks," said Elsa. "The ferries are running."

To our right were the islands. The smoke from the mainland had not reached them. They stood there, jewel-green in the sunlight.

"Still," I said. "We really don't have to go."

"No, Dad," said Vee firmly. "That way the bad guys win."

THE ENGINE TICKED QUIETLY. ELSA EASED US past the boatyard and into the shallow channel in front of the restaurant. A single-story building, its wooden cladding painted green, with a fleet of small boats moored to the pontoons outside. Ahead, on the outermost pontoon, our friend Jo stood waiting, a bottle of beer in each hand, looking blond and fresh. On his T-shirt an inverted swoosh, and the words MATE, JUST DON'T.

As we drew level with him, he passed a bottle to Elsa, took from her the rope she carried in her left hand, pulled the boat gently toward the pontoon, and tied it off at the front.

"Hey, Cal!"

"Hey, Jo."

He handed me the other beer. I leaned across, put an arm around him, felt the scrape of his stubble on mine.

Jo turned toward Elsa. "Hey, nice dress, darling," he said, in his practiced London English. "Seriously *frodig*, darling."

Elsa took Jo's hand, stepped easily onto the pontoon. She embraced him, cheek against cheek. Jo turned toward me. "Don't you think?"

"What's *frodig*?" I said.

"Yeah, Jo, don't be dirty!" said Vee.

"Sorry, Vee. Didn't see you there."

Vee smiled. "You so did. Stop laughing, Mum. And Jo, don't say that stuff."

Jo put his hands up. Guilty as charged. "You've got it, *darling*. Where's your sister?"

"Feminist summer camp."

"Ooh. Fun."

"Not if I know my sister. Where's the new boyfriend?"

At this Jo became serious. "Edvard sends his love. He's trying to put a helicopter in the air."

Vee said, "There are lots of helicopters."

"Not a single one from the police," said Jo.

We stared toward the town. Jo stood between us, an arm over Elsa's shoulder.

"Edvard says no one died," he said. "Can you believe that? Literally not one person. Come on, you." He took Elsa's hand in his and led her into the restaurant.

I hung back with Vee. "Well, that's a result," I said. "You okay?"

"Can I tell Julie?"

I looked at the ash cloud that hung above the town. It must be half a mile across.

"Don't want to cause trouble for Edvard and Jo."

Vee nodded. "All right. Got it."

On the wooden steps outside the restaurant was Hedda, smoking a cigarette, a beer in her left hand. Tiny compared to Elsa, barely taller than Vee, in stacked heels and black knee-length dress, her dark hair hanging in ringlets around her face, watching the town.

"Love," I said, "why don't you go in, get Mum to get you set up with a table? I want a word with Hedda."

"You don't even like her."

I laughed. "I do like Hedda."

"*I do like Hedda,*" she mimicked through clenched teeth. "You always say that in exactly the same way. And anyway, I asked Mum if you liked Hedda—"

"See you inside, Vee."

"Don't you want to know what Mum said?"

"See you inside."

Vee began to walk toward the bar. I put my phone in my pocket, walked toward Hedda, whose eyes remained fixed on the horizon.

"How was your night out?" I said.

She looked up at me, eyes twinkling. "Which night out?"

"With Elsa? Last night?"

"Oh, that night out." She got to her feet, stood swaying slightly, examined her cigarette as if trying to remember something, then smiled again. "Nice, thank you. Why aren't you asking Elsa?"

She hugged me demonstratively, as if making a point, then planted a kiss on my cheek.

"Elsa came home at four," I said.

"Sounds about right. All those married men at Lorry, quietly slipping their wedding bands into their pockets, sending over trays of drinks, sliding in at our table, bumping hard against our thighs . . ."

I pulled away slightly, trying to read her expression.

A smile twitched across her face. "Obviously I'm joking."

"Obviously." I put my arm around her, patted her twice, then tried to step out of the embrace, but she held on to me, pulled me toward the restaurant, then pushed me gently through the door and into our anniversary party.

"*Skål* for Cal and for Elsa, everyone!"

"*Skål!*"

A toast. To us.

A hand exchanged my beer for champagne. I raised my glass, met the eyes of each person around the table in turn, ending with Elsa.

Seventeen years, mouthed Elsa.

I know, I mouthed.

Elsa stood up, raised her glass to me. We drank to each other, standing at the head of the table, as around us our friends got to their feet. Knives chinked on glasses. People at the other tables were watching us. I rested my hand in the small of her back. "Well, this isn't in any way embarrassing."

A half smile from Elsa, knowing and complex. She leaned in very close. She smelled of sunlight on clean skin. The white-blue iris of her left eye; the amused curl of her lip; and below her the faces of our friends, smiling up.

"Speech, Cal," someone shouted.

"Yes, speech!"

"Elsa," I said. "Did you say I would speak?"

"I did."

"I don't understand you," I said. Elsa looked at me, serious now. I stood at the head of the table, looking around. Faces were turning toward me, our friends becoming an audience. "Seventeen years married," I said to them, "and still that question: Who is this woman I share my life with?"

People from other tables were watching too.

"I don't know where the rest of you are in modeling the psyche of your wife, your husband, your—forgive me for saying this, Jo—your *life partner*, but I'm stuck in the black-box model of marriage."

No one laughed.

"Tough crowd. Okay, let me give you an example. The sexist version of this joke is this: I know, through observation, that a dropped pair of underpants on the bathroom floor—that's stimulus A—results in icy atmosphere at dinner—that's response B. But the route from A to B cannot be mapped, because it's taking place inside a black box."

Sporadic laughter.

"For anyone who hasn't figured it out, the black box in this joke—the sexist version of this joke—is the inside of my wife's head. Because *women are a mystery to men*."

A couple of good-natured boos.

"Okay, good. We agree that no one looks good in that version of the joke. Right?"

People nodded.

"Right. But you guys are way beyond the black-box model, right? You formed a *hypothesis* about why underpants on floor equal icy atmosphere at dinner.

I selected Hedda.

"Hedda, you hypothesize that Elsa is mad because I left my underpants on the bathroom floor, and she feels—reasonably, I should stress—that as an adult . . ."

Hedda smiled. ". . . you should pick up after yourself."

"Now my wife is no longer the butt of the joke, and I come across as an imbecile who is incapable of change. But . . ."

Elsa's eyes locked on to mine.

"Twenty years ago I slipped a note onto the desk of a girl sitting on her own in the New York Public Library. Six months ago the third of our beautiful children was born. And I know there's got to be a connection there somewhere . . ."

I looked around the table. The laughter was indulgent. Eyes were shining.

"Here's the point in the routine where I say something that demonstrates that I'm not a complete imbecile. That's my shtick, right? Idiot savant says something profound. And I've been searching blindly for what that thing is, and truthfully, I don't know. I have a wife who is more intelligent than me, and who demands from me a level of honesty which no man can reasonably be expected to achieve; I struggle to see connections that are obvious to her, and most likely to all of you. Though, Elsa, I genuinely do try to meet the standard you set."

Elsa was looking at me levelly. She nodded, half smiled.

"Also, full disclosure about a little lie of omission: I've started shaving the outside of my ears and hoping you won't notice." Elsa pretended shock. I turned away from her. "But here I am with the most beautiful woman I know, with our beautiful family, in the happiest country on earth. I don't know how I got so lucky."

"So why won't you stay?" said Hedda loudly.

"We should, Hedda. We should. These past eight months have been amazing. But you guys knocked me off my game. Everyone's so fucking incorruptible and so fucking nice. And I can't make satire about good people doing good things. I need sleaze, American-style. Quickly, before the newspaper closes my column."

People were laughing again. At the far end of the room I could see Vee looking up from her screen at me, anxious. There was the real reason we had to return home. In the most perfect place on earth, Vee was unhappy. We had not understood how hard she would take moving to this strange and beautiful land; what it would cost her to leave behind her friends and her social status, to find herself at the bottom of the heap.

I smiled at Vee. Vee smiled back, uncertain, then returned to her game. Elsa, who had followed my gaze, turned toward me, nodded.

I said, "I thought I was used to being a foreigner. I thought it came easily to me. And in Washington, D.C., it pretty much does. But here I really am a foreigner. You all very kindly speak my language to me, but here I can see there is this part of Elsa that I can't fully know, and it's available to all of you, and not to me. And if I'm honest I'm a touch jealous of you all for having that part of her, when I don't." Our friends clapped and smiled.

"And Elsa told me it was an easy language, but you know and I know that's simply not true. Which leads to the horrible question: Have I—finally—caught my wife in a lie?"

Elsa smiled, meeting my eye, and I was sorry I had doubted her.

I looked around at her friends. Such warmth. Such kindness. "Thank you for listening, you beautiful people. I'm Cal Curtis, and I used to be a lot funnier."

Elsa was on her feet beside me, eyes sparkling. We toasted the brightness of the summer day, and the resilience of the Norwegian people. All the while I watched Elsa, thinking how happy she looked.

I love you, I mouthed.

"No, Cal, I love you," she said, loud enough for people to hear. "You strange, sentimental fuck."

I had a bad feeling about taking her home to America, a sense that it would do her some quiet violence, that at some level Hedda was right, that we should stay. But for the sake of our children . . .

VEE SAT IN A QUIET CORNER OF the bar, laptop plugged in, headset on, lounging in her chair. On her screen an avatar, a slim white girl in a tight T-shirt, short black hair covered in a blue beanie hat, staring out. Lasser8. Another avatar appeared beside the first, dark-skinned and muscular. Marldathug.

"A week from Tuesday," she was saying. "So maybe, I don't know, like a pizza or something? Good to go here, by the way . . ."

"You all right, Vee?"

"Wait a second . . ." She smiled, lifted the earpad from her right ear.

"I was asking if you were okay."

"Dad, can I go out for pizza Tuesday when we get back?"

"Who with?"

"Marlon. A couple of Marlon's friends."

"Sure, love. Sounds like a good idea."

"Thanks." She replaced her headset over her right ear and picked up her control. "Good for Tuesday. And we are . . . go . . ."

On-screen her avatar was skydiving toward an island. "Marlon, low building top right." Below, other avatars were landing, picking up weapons, disappearing from sight.

I stood watching her face, looking for some sign of trauma.

She noticed me staring. "I'm really okay. You should go be with Mum."

Her avatar landed on a roof, picked up a rifle, ran to the edge of the roof, and began to shoot.

FOR A WHILE THE EUPHORIA CARRIED US along. We drank white wine and ate crab from steel platters, half dazzled by the sun on the fjord.

Only Jo kept checking his phone.

I leaned forward. "Everything okay with Edvard?"

"Am I being that obvious?"

"Come and talk."

The bar was fuggy with the heat of the afternoon. Fruit flies flew lazy loops above the beer taps. In the corner, Vee seemed lost in the world of her screen. She was talking easily to Marlon. Excited about going home.

The barman and a few customers stood watching a large TV screen showing pictures of the waterfront. Through the windows you could see the same cityscape, the buildings gray-brown in the smoke. I chose a table near the door, away from the television, facing Vee.

Jo sat opposite me. "Please tell me I didn't just see my god-daughter pickaxing a guy to death."

"It's a game. Tell me about Edvard . . ."

"Yeah, Edvard," said Jo, serious again. "Edvard is having a really shitty day. He spent the afternoon trying to scramble the police helicopter. They have three pilots, and guess what? One pilot's with his family in the Arctic, one can't be contacted by phone, one is with her family on Tenerife."

"Wow," I said.

"I realize you think this country is some kind of *safe space* where nothing ever goes wrong, but Edvard can't track down a helicopter pilot because it's Midsummer, and *everyone deserves to be with their family* on Midsummer. I mean, why aren't you satirizing that?"

Through the doorway I could see Elsa, sitting talking intimately to Hedda. She must have felt my eyes on her; she looked up, then away. There was something furtive about her glance now, something very different from the way she had looked at me earlier, as if talking to Hedda made my wife love me less.

"Cal, mate?" Jo was staring at me.

"Sorry. Yes." Elsa had turned in her chair. She was facing away from me. I looked at Jo. "I think maybe Edvard should speak to a journalist."

"You have news connections. Edvard likes you, Cal. He'd prefer to speak to you."

Cheers from all around. They were announcing it now: no one had been killed in the bomb.

I STOOD AT THE FAR END OF the pontoon, earpiece in. "Patching you through to Carly in the studio." A click, and I could hear the studio feed. Carly's voice was clear and strong.

"Back to that explosion in Oslo, Norway, and to eyewitness Cal Curtis, whose family experienced these traumatic events at close hand. Cal, everyone here is delighted that your family is safe."

"Thank you. And yes, you can almost feel the country breathing a collective sigh of relief. Sources close to the police tell us that not a single person lost their life in what looked, at one point, to be a major terrorist incident. The town hall bomb appears to have been something of a damp squib, an act of spectacle terrorism on a building where no one was working, though it does raise important questions as to the level of preparedness of this proud little Scandinavian nation."

"Thank you, Cal Curtis in Oslo."

I took off the headset, looked out across the bay. The entire city was shrouded in smoke and dust. Terrifying, but strangely beautiful, cut by heavy shafts of sunlight.

A voice shouted. "Cal!"

I turned. Hedda, framed in the light of the bar.

The plume of smoke on the mainland. The concern in Hedda's face. The urgency in her voice. "Cal, you have to see this."

Fear beginning to take hold.

I was on my feet, running. Hedda turned, moved out of my way, touched my hand as I passed, followed me in. There was Vee, fighting her way through the people, and next to Vee was Elsa.

"My daughter," I said to the couple beside me. They moved to let me pass. I reached out. Vee grasped my hand. I pulled her toward me.

New images on the screen.

A girl sheltering by the water's edge, a man waving desperately from the water. In the downdraft from the helicopter the fjord frothed and turned.

We crowded around the bar, every face staring up at the screen.

"*Lyden*," said Elsa. *Sound*.

The barman nodded and turned up the volume.

Pictures from TVZ. A sundress of kingfisher-blue. A shooting on an island near Oslo.

I saw the terror in Vee's eyes.

"Licia," she said.

I STOOD OUTSIDE THE RESTAURANT, EYES FIXED on the water, phone in hand. I could not look at Elsa or Vee, though I could feel their eyes on me, willing Licia to pick up.

A click. Licia's voice.

Can't speak now.

Funny.

Almost.

Punch line to a horrific cosmic joke.

FIVE

THAT DREAD SILENCE.

Farther along the coast bonfires lit up the fjord. Here the pyres remained unlit. The sun was down now, the air cold.

We stood on the mainland opposite Garden Island, watching as the boats came in.

A hundred of us, maybe more, looking out across the fjord, waiting for our children to return, barely daring to speak. From time to time a hand sought out a hand, a body leaned toward another. Whispered words, furtive almost. But mostly I remember the silence.

In my hand I held the form that we had filled out:

NAME: Alicia Curtis
HEIGHT: 5´ 6˝
AGE: 15
SKIN COLOR: white (pale)
HAIR: blond

CLOTHES: blue dress (kingfisher, sequined). Silver dragonfly bangle. Converse sneakers?
IDENTIFYING MARKS: none

Elsa had crossed out the height, had rewritten it in centimeters:

HEIGHT: 167.5 cm

As if that might make the difference.

I leaned toward Elsa.

"Focus on New Year in Whistler," I whispered. "Focus on Licia coming back."

HEAVY WINDS HAD BEEN FORECAST IN WHISTLER that New Year's morning, but it was lunchtime and the storm had not come.

I tried to hand Licia her phone.

"No need, Dad." She smiled, dropped her skis to the snow, stepped into them, began fish-boning up the slope. Vee was waiting by the lift, arms crossing and uncrossing, tiny and impatient in her helmet and her stormproof one-piece. They were skiing without us for the first time, drunk on the excitement of it. Licia was the better skier, fearless, skillful, and fast.

"Licia!" I shouted after her. "Phone!"

She stopped and turned, waved, called out, "Enjoy your meal!" Then she turned to face her sister, who cuffed her playfully across the temple.

And so Elsa and I sat drinking Riesling, toasting the New Year in, eating Swiss fondue from long skewers as we held hands under the table. We did not see the blackening sky. We were happy in each other's company, easy in the warmth of the wine, and of the food, and of the fires in the grates.

That first gust. A metallic shriek, not easily forgotten.

We were on our feet, outside before we knew it, looking up.

Heavy sheets of rain beat down across the slopes, freezing as they hit the snow. Clouds curdled across the mountainside. Chairs swung in the lifts.

I ran up the slope, skis in hand, tried to make my way through the barrier.

"Lift's closed," said the man in the booth.

"It's still turning."

"For people heading down. You can't go up."

"My daughters," I said.

"Give a description to Mountain Rescue."

An hour Elsa and I stood in the doorway to the restaurant, wet through, waiting for our daughters, each hiding our fear from the other. I pleaded with a god I did not believe in to return them to us, safe and unharmed. Vee was so small and Licia so naive. How stupid we had been to allow them to go.

And then they were there in front of us, laughing, high on the electric excitement of danger, wrapping themselves into us as we held them close.

"It's her fault," Vee was saying. "She made me not take my skis off. I must have fallen like fifty times."

"Dad, she snuck onto the lift again."

"Liar! You frickin' dared me!"

I said, "I thought all the upper lifts were closed."

Vee gave her sister a conspiratorial look. "Not if you know what you're doing. And you didn't have to come with me the second time, Licia. Or the third."

Licia turned to me. "Dad, you might want to think about having my sister baptized. For her own safety. Before something bad happens."

Whistler had become part of the lore of our family. A disaster averted. A narrative of sisterly heroism.

"CAL, THIS IS NOTHING LIKE WHISTLER," ELSA was saying, quiet as breath.

I tried to take her hand. She tried to take mine.

We could not do it; we could not touch. And when I looked around us I saw that the other parents stood as we stood, holding papers with their children's details on them, undone by nerves, separate and alone, eyes fixed on the island across the water where something had happened, some dread thing for which we did not yet have a name.

A larger boat this time, bullet-nosed, striped green and orange at the bow. It seemed to lift itself above the fjord as it rounded the headland. Every face in the crowd watched. The boat turned a lazy arc, came to rest by the slipway. From the bow, two armed policemen surveyed the crowd, submachine guns readied. In the stern were two female officers, rifles half-shouldered as they scanned the shoreline.

Two more uniformed officers emerged from the wheelhouse, one tall, one small. Both men were blond, both were unarmed. Something strange in the way they carried themselves; some unnatural swagger. They stood on the deck, looked out at the crowd, expressionless. Narrow white bands cuffed their wrists. Two further female officers appeared close behind them, pistols drawn and pointed at the men.

I turned to Elsa, wanting to know if she felt my confusion, but she simply stood staring. I looked from face to face in the crowd. In every face I saw that same blank incomprehension that I saw in my wife.

Police officers.

I had not thought the perpetrators would be police officers. I thought they would be darker-skinned, that they would be . . . had expected to see the words *jihadisme* or *islamisme* in the news feeds, to hear those words whispered knowingly among the other parents, spoken carefully into microphones by the reporters on their live links. *Our values. Their values. Allahu akbar.*

To be plain: I had not expected these men to be white.

In the bow an officer lowered his submachine gun, dropped a gangplank into place. Metal slid on concrete. The officer beside him stepped ashore, his weapon at the ready. Grit crunched beneath his shoes. Both officers were onshore now, surveying the crowd, weapons readied. They glanced at each other, nodded. One of them turned, nodded toward the escort.

The unarmed men—could they really be police?—began to move toward the gangplank and on to the shore, each followed closely by a pistol-carrying officer who tracked their every move.

The crowd split into two, made room. These men—these suspects—were not just white, they were archetypically, almost comically white. Their hair was bleached, their noses narrow, their eyes blue, their foreheads high. So close they were now. You could almost reach out . . . I caught the eye of the first, the taller of them. The man nodded. I felt myself beginning to nod back.

I checked myself. Because this man . . . because surely no policeman would have done . . . what? What had these men done?

Please, where is my daughter?

None of us spoke. We parted quietly, made room for the police escort and for the two unarmed men who could not—*surely* they could not?—be policemen themselves. Their collars were undone. Their boots were scuffed and muddied. Badges hung from their shoulders, as if torn by briars.

The shorter man spat something onto the slipway. A gobbet of chewing tobacco, gray-black and shiny.

I caught the eye of another father, a man of my own age, saw in him my own confusion and rage. *These men walk easily by us, arms cuffed, uniforms torn. When our children . . .*

What have they done with our children?

Elsa was muttering something. I could feel her stiff staccato words, could hear the *s* sounds, and the *k*'s and the *t*'s. I did not look at her—could not look at her—must not let her see my fear.

The pistol-carrying officers led the men up the rise to two waiting police cars. The policewomen in the stern tracked the path of the men with their rifles, while the officers on the slipway scanned the crowd. I looked around. Still that dread silence. Still the faces, empty of emotion, though every parent there was thinking the same thought: *Please. Our children. What have you done with our children?*

The machine-gun-carrying officers moved away to join their colleagues at the cars. Doors opened. The officers separated the suspects, one into each car. The men sat calmly in the backseats, facing forward; they offered no resistance. An armed officer got in beside each man, and another into the passenger seat.

Doors closed, headlights lit, engines started. The cars stayed where they were.

In my pocket my phone vibrated. I held it in front of me like some alien thing.

Dan.

I stepped carefully up the slipway and away from the crowd. I brought the phone to my ear.

"Hey," said my brother's voice, "just wondering . . ."

"Nothing yet." My own voice sounded jarring, even at a hoarse whisper, as if I might cry.

A thin man in a black suit was quietly collecting the forms. Something familiar about him.

"Sorry, Dan. I just . . ." I turned away from the man.

"Listen, Cal, whatever you need, you tell me, okay?" I could hear the catch in my brother's voice, though he did what he could to disguise it. The knowledge that things were bad, that Licia most probably wasn't . . .

I couldn't allow myself the thought, so I said, "We're good. We're really looking forward to this whole thing being over."

"Everyone here is sending love, Cal. Daisy wanted you to know she's thinking of you. Oh, but Lyndon's at soccer practice, so he doesn't yet know."

"Love back," I said, and ended the call.

The thin man in the suit approached me, hair mussed, shoes covered in dust. I looked down at the sheet of paper in my hand. I held it out to him, began to turn toward Elsa.

"Cal." I felt his hand on my shoulder, saw the concern in his eye.

"Oh my God, Edvard. Thought you were at police headquarters. Jo said . . ."

"We're all doing everything we can," said Edvard. "But it's a mess. I'm really sorry."

"What do you mean?"

He nodded at the men in the police cars. "You don't bring them ashore somewhere crowded. Things could have got out of hand. No one's following protocol."

"So those men . . . ?" Again I couldn't finish the thought.

"Yeah," he said quietly. "This is bad, Cal."

I swallowed down my fear.

I nodded. "Wait . . ." I reached into my pocket, pulled from my wallet a strip of passport photos that Licia had taken and never used, folded at the middle. I had rescued them from the trash, carried them with me without her knowing. I held out the strip of pictures to Edvard.

"These will help," he said. He took a paper clip and attached them to our form, added the form to the top of the pile in his hand.

"You'll tell me?" I said. "When you know something?"

His look told me not to expect too much.

ANOTHER BOAT, CLOSING FAST.

Behind, around, voices murmured, then fell silent. Paramedics opened ambulance doors, unloaded equipment onto the slipway, waited. The boat was closer. I searched for Licia's face, but Licia was not there.

Elsa knew it too.

Licia is not here.

Parents stepped forward, reached out, held to them their boys, their girls as they stumbled forward from the boat. Some drew their children gently from the scene and away. Others knelt beside gurneys, ruffled hair, kissed foreheads and backs of hands. Beside them, nimble fingers found veins, attached cannulas, fitted monitors. These sons, these daughters: among us again now, but changed.

Water lapped. Wood strained against wood. Gurneys slid into ambulances, doors slammed, motors started. Around us, among us, newspeople spoke hushed words into shielded microphones. Ambulances began drifting up the rise, silent, blue lights flashing. We forced ourselves to turn to face the island. Too early for despair, too late for hope.

Down by the slipway children were standing in small groups, confused, waiting for parents who had not yet arrived.

A hand pressed gently against my back, another placed a coffee cup into my hand. I could not see Elsa.

"Here." An arm in a gray sleeve, steadying me, so that I might not spill the coffee.

"Thank you," I murmured. That small unbearable kindness: I looked only at the hand that offered it, afraid that I would give myself away if my eye met the eye of this stranger.

"Be assured that all will be well." Words spoken softly, in accented English, the man's mouth by my ear.

I glanced upward, saw a shock of black hair, a gray vestment.

You can't know that all will be well, I thought. But there was kindness in the man's eyes. I nodded and thanked him for the coffee.

Farther down the slipway I saw Elsa, staring out across the fjord. A new boat was crossing the mirror-flat water. A fresh wave of ambulances was approaching from the rise. All else was silence.

When I looked around again the priest was gone.

I was about to return to Elsa when I felt the phone in my pocket vibrate.

CELEBRATE

That same word. Another film clip that was not a film clip. This was either a mistake or a cruel joke. I deleted the clip and blocked the number from my phone.

THERE WAS ONE CHILD ON THIS LAST boat. A boy, shockingly young, statue-like in the bow, arm in a blood-blackened sling. The officer at the wheel took the key from the ignition; his colleagues moored the boat to concrete posts on the jetty.

"Oh please, God, no."

Every face turned toward Elsa. The boy stared at her, eyes wide. She had spoken the words loudly and clearly. I took my wife by the shoulder, drew her away from the group toward a rocky spit that pointed out toward the sea.

She looked across at the jetty. I followed her eye, saw the boy carried up into the air, held tightly in his mother's arms. The arc lights picked out the wetness of their faces, the relief, the love.

"I mean," Elsa said, her voice level, "we don't know, of course, because no one has told us. But actually we do know, and every other parent here knows."

She looked over her shoulder at the other parents. The group had scattered. Some stood looking out across the ink-black fjord. Others sat huddled in groups, blankets around their knees, clustered around the arc lights and the heaters. Elsa sat down, stretched her legs out along the rock.

"How many of us are there left?" she said.

"Sixty?" I said. "Seventy?"

"So that's, what? Forty missing kids? Fifty?"

"These are just the parents who live near Oslo," I said. "I'm guessing."

"So it's more?"

"I don't know."

"So strange," she said. "Right now I feel calm."

"Because we aren't out of hope."

"Yes," she said. "Yes, actually we are."

The boy looked smaller than ever. He sat bolt upright, saying nothing, still in his orange life preserver, as his mother talked to the medical crew.

"Cal," said Elsa, "you need to understand this: that boy is the last of the children."

AS THE NEXT BOAT DREW NEAR WE saw the shrouded bodies on the deck and turned away.

A new wave of adults began to arrive. The parents of the missing, contacted by the police, setting out across the country, desperate for news.

Farther up the rise were four rows of white tents. Officers were leading people inside, singly or in pairs. Lights on metal stands threw vast shadows. You could see the stark outlines of the parents on the white nylon walls, as they stood and identified their children. We saw hands raised to faces, saw shoulders bend and heads shake in disbelief.

When our turn came, a police officer led us to the nearest tent on the first row. On the canvas wall silhouetted figures slid a gurney into place.

"I can wait with you, if you like," said the officer.

I shook my head. Elsa shook hers.

"Thank you," I said. "No."

"Someone will be with you shortly."

It was only then that we cried, wordless, by the white canvas wall that separated us from the body of our murdered child. We cried to prepare ourselves for what was to come: the fragmenting of bone, the tearing and obliteration of muscle and lung. We cried silently because we could not surrender to the pain, could not let it consume us, could not scream and rail and shout when we were surrounded by other parents who knew—but had not yet seen the proof—that their sons and their daughters would not be coming home.

"Cal Curtis and Elsa Steen?"

I looked at Elsa. Elsa looked at me. She nodded.

"Yes," I said, my voice as steady as I could keep it.

"Yes," said Elsa.

"This way."

Dry earth. Stale air. Disinfectant.

The body had been covered with a hospital sheet, ruched at the thigh. Pearl-white underwear on milk-white skin in the blinding light of the arc lamp.

"Is this how she was found?" I asked.

The officer nodded.

Half-naked, and so very vulnerable. She must have jettisoned the kingfisher dress.

I LOVED HER FOR WEARING THAT DRESS. Those iridescent blues, constantly changing. So exuberant; so very unlike Licia.

"Promise me you will have fun," I had said in the hall.

"Why would you think this time would be any different?" Vee had said. "You know she never does."

"I promise I will." Licia smiled a serious smile as she leaned in to kiss me, as if having fun would require preparation.

"Love you, Licia."

"Love you so much, Dad."

My little girl.

HOW UNLIKE HERSELF SHE WAS NOW. HOW strange her hand looked, palm up, fingertips bleached in the glare of the arc light, like an object I knew but could not recognize.

I turned to the police officer who stood between us and our daughter. She looked exhausted, worn out by other people's grief.

The officer stepped out of the way. Elsa knelt down, began to draw the sheet down Licia's torso.

"Please," said the officer. "You mustn't touch."

The child-white skin. The pair of bullet wounds in her shoulder, a finger-length apart, just above the left clavicle. The bruising that radiated outward.

Seawater had emptied the wounds of blood.

Elsa's hand up by her mouth. "Oh my . . ."

Something odd. Wrong.

I stepped forward, crouched down. A beautiful face. A girl's face, tiny pink spots the only disturbance on her otherwise perfect skin.

Elsa put three fingers on the strap of the girl's bra, ran them up and down.

"You mustn't touch," said the officer again.

"Elsa," I said. "Step back."

"This is not . . ."

"I know . . ."

"But . . ."

The girl's lips were a fraction tighter than Licia's. Her forehead a fraction broader; her hairline a fraction higher.

"Fuck," said Elsa. "Oh fuck." She gave a confused laugh.

I turned to the officer. "I'm sorry," I said.

"Laughter is not uncommon," she said levelly. "People often swear."

"She doesn't understand," said Elsa.

"There is no correct response," said the officer reflexively. "You are both very much in shock. I am here"—she gave a professional half smile designed to reassure—"to help."

"This is not my daughter." Elsa's eyes were blazing.

"Also a common reaction. Would you like me to call someone?"

"It isn't her," I said.

"Would you like to be alone?"

"You don't understand," I said, keeping my voice as steady as I could. "This girl is not Alicia Curtis. This is someone else's daughter."

AT FOUR THE SUN CAME UP. AT six someone brought us waffles and hot chocolate. At eight we agreed with the police that we would go home. All the while that other girl lay there on her steel gurney in her plain white tent, still and alone, waiting for parents who did not come.

After the last ambulance left we stood on the shoreline, eyes fixed on the fjord, as if something might change, as if some new and better reality might dislodge this one. And as the lights in the tents were extinguished one by one I felt a guilty, vertiginous hope take hold of me.

What if our daughter were not among the dead?

The Skeptic

SIX

WE THANKED THE POLICEMAN who had driven us home, walked the last fifty meters up the tarmac path, turned left at the barrier.

Another police car was parked on the path outside the apartment. Its doors were thrown open, blocking the way. Next to it was a gray van.

At the front of the van Elsa's father stood talking to a detective in a dirty suit.

"Henrik," I said.

Henrik turned, began to walk toward us. "Oh, Cal," he said. "Elsa."

The detective moved with him, tracking him. He was fifty, I guessed, face ugly with lack of sleep, his cuffs stained with late-night food.

Henrik and Elsa held each other, all sinews and silent suffering. I knew Elsa. She and her father would not cry, either of them. Not here in front of strangers.

Henrik embraced me. I heard him whisper, "Courage, Cal."

I stepped away. We looked at each other, nodded. After all, we still didn't know.

The door of the apartment building swung open. Two pony-tailed female officers. The first carried Licia's iMac in a large plastic crate, along with Vee's gaming laptop. The other woman carried a smaller crate that contained two iPads, two old mobile phones, and my own laptop. She smiled at me as if we were friends. I saw the green drinking glass from the bathroom, spattered with toothpaste, and in the glass our toothbrushes. I did not return her smile.

Some tiny movement at the edge of my vision.

Vee was standing in her sister's window. She looked bleached out, drained of blood.

You okay? I mouthed. Vee blinked hard and looked away. When she lifted her head to face me again, she nodded.

"Mr. Curtis?"

I turned. The detective in the dirty suit. His smile was friendly, though there was something behind the eyes that was not. He held out his hand. "May I have your cell phone?"

LICIA'S BED WAS MADE. THE BLIND WAS closed, the air stale and lifeless.

I walked to the window and wound the handle. Outside, metal slats jerked open. Light flooded in. Everything was neat, with none of the easy disorder of Vee's bedroom. The plain blue carpet and the clean white walls and the cheap IKEA bedframe, none of which we owned. Licia had never made the room her own.

I sat down on her bed. My little girl, I would say, and she would sigh, and roll her eyes, and make her voice deep. "Don't tell me I'm little. Who wants to be little?" Still, she would lean in to me briefly, before thinking better of it, pushing me laughingly away. The closest she ever got to rebellion.

I lay my head on the pillow, smelled the washing powder and the soap and the patchouli scent that made up Licia's smell.

My little girl, I thought. *Fifteen and gone.* But my other daughter's voice pulled me back.

"Dad!"

"Coming, Vee!"

There was Vee in the living room, balled into the rented blue sofa, a bag of cheap yellow candies on the table in front of her, flicking through the channels on the rented TV. On every channel a new opinion over the same images, over and over and over. The bomb, the obliterated town hall, the ash raining down through the burnt air. Hard to know what you were looking at; everything gray and indistinct.

Above the sofa a two-meter square of deep red-brown. Another of Elsa's photographs, *Carmine 34*. The only object in the room that we actually owned.

From the kitchen I could hear Elsa's bare feet scuffing about.

"Vee," I said. "Let's eat."

"Not hungry. Thanks, though." Looking at me all the while.

"What you got in that bag?"

"Scum bananas. They're actually pretty good." Still staring at me. "Are you really not going to get that?"

"Get what?"

The doorbell chimed.

Vee turned toward the hall. "You didn't hear it the first time?"

"Did it ring before?"

Vee nodded.

I walked through the dark interior of the apartment to the hall, looked at the screen on the intercom. Edvard, staring awkwardly down at the camera.

I pressed the button, heard the door to the building swing open. I opened the front door, watched as he appeared around the corner. He was carrying a scuffed plastic bag, wearing yesterday's shirt. He looked flat and ragged, as if he had been up all night. He reached out, hugged me awkwardly, patted my back as he stepped away.

"Jo sends his love."

"Thanks, Edvard," I said. "Appreciate it."

He gave a little half smile. "I did think you might need these." He looked down at the plastic bag in his hand. "Normally they'd just download your phone and hand it back, but they're up to their eyes right now."

He opened the bag, handed me three simple gray mobile phones.

From his shirt pocket he took three folded envelopes. "SIM cards."

"They didn't take mine." Vee was beside me, blinking up at Edvard.

Edvard smiled. "They will. Once they realize they haven't."

"Okay." She reached into her jeans pocket, held out her phone.

Edvard shook his head. "I'm not on the clock." He stood there for a moment, staring at Vee. "I can't imagine what this is like for you, Viktoria." He smiled awkwardly, turned, and walked briskly along the passageway.

Vee watched him go, listened as his footsteps faded down the passageway. The main door swung open; it swung shut. She turned to me. "Jo's so great, and Edvard's so weird."

She headed into the living room. I heard her sit heavily down on the sofa, followed her in.

The images had switched to aerial shots from the news helicopters. Clothing lay scattered. Bodies lined the water's edge, some in bags.

"Love," I said, "I don't think watching this is a such a great idea."

"But yesterday, that clip they showed. Same dress. Same hair. So we know she was alive. And they never showed that bit again. Which is weird, right? We agree on that? And we agree that the bomb was a diversion? And the children on the island were the real target?"

"We don't know that for certain."

"Actually, yes, we do." She picked up her phone, unlocked it, handed it to me.

PRESS RELEASE
All media
From the desk of Commander John Andersen
12 p.m., 23 June

"What is this, Vee?"
"Read it."

At first you will call us child-murderers.

The actions we will take today are horrible, unthinkable to any civilized person. Yet the "children" we eliminate on this peaceful island would soon enough have on their hands the blood of our white brothers and sisters. And so we are compelled to act.

We must learn the lesson our enemies learned long ago: that

the child is never simply the child. Children are soldiers. They are transmitters of ideology. We underestimate them at our peril.

Their parents and their parents' parents have opened our borders and left us at the mercy of an ideology that would enslave our women and emasculate our men. And thus we target this new generation of traitors. Thus shall we dismantle tomorrow's treacherous elite, for they are lost to the ways of God and of our people.

I felt bile rising in my throat.

Our civilization must survive. The unthinkable must be thought. Children are both our greatest threat, and our most underused resource. Great men must step forward to prevent indoctrination, and when it is too late, when the child is too far gone, great men must eliminate that child as we crush the tiny flies that infest the fruit in our kitchens.

My brother and I face a stark choice—Killer or victim: which is it to be? The question is horrific to us in its cruelty, yet we ask it with love in our hearts and an easy spirit, for the answer is clear. And so it is that today we fire the first shots in a war for the emancipation of our people.

This is our gift to the nation, and to the entire European race.

Commanders John and Paul Andersen
Tactical Brigades of the Knights Templar

I looked up. Vee was watching me intently.

"Brilliant, right?" she said.

"Brilliant?"

"Everybody here trusts the police. These guys are first on the scene. I mean, you see the cleverness, don't you, Dad? It's using people's naïveté against them. And literally no one is discussing that."

"How did you find this?"

"Not BBC or CNN or NRK, that's for sure."

"Cal. A word?" Elsa's voice from the doorway, flat and affectless. How long had she been standing, arms around Franklin, watching us?

"Sure." I got up. Vee looked at me. "Dad, they killed ninety people. And not one of the mainstream channels is telling us why. It's like someone deleted Licia."

I stood, staring at my daughter. Did she really believe there was some sort of cover-up?

"Now would be good, Cal." Elsa's voice again.

"Coming," I said.

I turned toward Vee.

The intensity of her stare. "So go," she said.

Elsa waited in the middle of the kitchen floor, arms still folded around our son, who began kicking excitedly as I approached.

"The police window for finding Licia alive is closing," said Elsa, "and you're trading conspiracy theories with Vee?"

"That's not—"

"They should be camped out here, asking us everything we know. And you should be as worried as I am." Every line in Elsa's face was etched a little deeper today.

"I want to be sure Vee's okay," I said.

"All right, then, sorry." She stepped forward and we embraced. Franklin kicked enthusiastically in Elsa's arms. "I keep calling the police," she said quietly. "Because the first twenty-four hours are meant to be . . . I mean, they say that if you don't . . . Fuck, Cal, it's been, what? Sixteen hours? How exact is the twenty-four-hour thing?"

I really had no idea.

FRANKLIN WAS LYING ON HIS CUSHION IN front of the TV, staring up at his fingers, entranced. Vee was on the sofa.

Ninety-one were now confirmed dead, the majority of them children.

"A tragedy." A man's voice, warm and deep, yet full of melody. "And an outrage that they should attach our name to their racialist agenda."

Vee put down the remote.

The man wore a gray shirt with a neat gray collar. He was forty, I guessed. His hair was wild and black and had not been combed. The gold bands on the shoulder of his shirt looked almost military; the vertical creases were ironed straight.

A voice from off-screen. "Do you distance yourself from the actions of these men?"

"We try to further God's work. What these men have done is very far from that, no?"

I heard Elsa swear under her breath.

A caption on-screen:

Father Bror
Patriotic Order of the Temple Knight

A concerned smile was playing at the corners of Father Bror's mouth. There was something familiar about the kindness that radiated from him. I remembered the coffee he had passed into my hands as we waited for news of Licia.

"That man," I said. "He was on the shore by the slipway . . ."

"No, Cal," said Elsa. "No, that isn't possible."

"Elsa, I swear. He handed me a coffee. Told me all would be well."

"Father Bror . . ."

"It's Bror," he was saying. "No need for the Father."

"Mr. Bror, your organization describes itself as 'furthering the chivalric aims of the crusader knight.' As do the Andersen brothers."

The man Bror smiled a patient smile. "The Patriotic Order of the Temple Knight practices the chivalric virtues," he said. "The so-called Tactical Brigades of the Knights Templar copy-and-paste our texts. We farm vegetables. They murder children. We seek enlightenment. They spread dark lies. You see the difference, perhaps?"

"But Mr. Bror—"

"*Bror* means brother," he said. "So it really is just Bror."

"In their press release the Andersen brothers link prominently to this film."

A blocky Internet video filled the screen. Bror as a younger man, in jeans and a fisherman's jumper. "These little flies," he was saying. "On our fruit. Began to enter Norway in the 1970s. And at first the cold winters killed them. Now, though, they have learned to adapt and they are everywhere."

In the studio Bror gathered himself. "As I have explained on countless occasions, I am talking, in that clip, purely about fruit flies. This is not a veiled reference to something else, no matter how others may wish to exploit it."

"Yet you have described yourself as skeptical toward immigration . . ."

"And I think perhaps you are confusing skepticism, which is

part of our religious *praxis*, with acts of violence, which do not form any part of our praxis. The peaceful Muslim is our brother, our sister, our friend. No? And this video is not a racist dog whistle, no matter what you in the media might wish."

Elsa's fingers played across her lower lip. Her wolf eyes glowed.

"So you are not," the announcer was saying, "an anti-Islamic organization? And you condemn the actions of the Andersens?"

"Would you hold me responsible for the misuse others make of our good name?"

The interviewer was not letting go. "But you, like they, are immigration skeptics."

"And now you too are twisting our words. We teach skepticism in all things; it is the bedrock of our praxis. We insist that our recruits question every orthodoxy. Especially political orthodoxies. We demand that they speak with radical honesty about their innermost feelings. We are no more against immigration than we are against life itself. About which our recruits also have many skeptical questions."

Elsa was staring at the screen as if entranced. Vee was watching her mother intently.

"Mum," said Vee. "Mum, how do you know that guy?"

Elsa's hand curled around Vee's. "Wow, Vee. You are *good*."

"You got this secretive smile."

They looked at each other, Elsa's eyes shining. "He was a friend once."

No, I thought. *No, he's more to you than that.* Because the way my wife was looking at the man on-screen, you would swear she knew him well.

"He seems okay," said Vee.

"Yes," Elsa said. "He is okay."

Vee made to say something more. Elsa's phone rang. She got up off the sofa.

"But Mum," said Vee.

Elsa picked up her phone. "Just a minute." She answered the call, listened, nodded. "Finally." She turned to me. "Police. Can we meet them in an hour?"

SEVEN

WE SHOULD NOT HAVE let the police divide us up. It created the sense that we were not in this together. It was the beginning of a fracture between Elsa and me, though it was tiny at first and I did not see where it would lead.

A policewoman showed me to a brightly lit room. The windows were obscured by heavy black drapes. In front was a low table. There were two blue pens, and two red pens. There was a stack of paper. There were two empty coffee cups, and a carton of chewing tobacco.

The policewoman motioned for me to sit.

Three low armchairs faced each other across the table. The chairs were mid-blue, the carpet mid-blue, the walls cream. On the wall opposite, a pair of red checked curtains.

"What are the checked curtains?"

"The curtains are not relevant."

I walked to the wall, drew back the curtain on the left.

A plate-glass window, so dark that it was almost black.

I looked about me. The room was entirely bare, save for the chairs and the table.

"What kind of room is this?"

"Please sit down."

She walked out through the door and shut it.

I chose a chair and sat down.

Two gobbets of chewing tobacco on the carpet by the table, still slick.

Those men.

Here.

In this room.

I could hear computer keys clacking in the office beyond. The door must have opened. I looked up to find eyes appraising me. A bald man, dark-skinned and powerfully built, in a pressed white shirt. He crossed the floor at a brisk pace, stood facing me, a shade too close.

The door hissed shut.

"Ephraim Tvist. Chief of police." He grasped my hand.

"Cal Curtis."

"And you are a . . ."—he looked down into the corner as if trying to remember a complex detail, snapped his fingers—"a satirist?"

"I try to be."

Ephraim Tvist smiled. "The world needs laughter. No?"

"Laughter is a by-product of satire," I said. "It isn't really the point of it."

"So if the point is not laughter . . ."—he let go of my hand—"then what?"

"It holds people in authority to account."

"Ah."

He turned away, sat in one of the chairs, waited for me to join him. I sat down. He turned on a recording device, satisfied himself that it was working. His lively dark eyes came to rest on mine.

"A man who uses humor as a way of dealing with the most horrific aspects of human existence. Our greatest fears. My own greatest fear is an armed man walking into my daughter's kindergarten. I have some idea of what you must be feeling."

I laughed.

"I wonder, Mr. Curtis, is that a satirical laughter? Or is it an angry laughter? Perhaps a satirical laughter is an angry laughter?"

"This is an interrogation room."

A shrewd look from Tvist. "An explanation for your anger." He looked very deliberately at my hands, then at my face, as if making an assessment. "Yes. This is an interrogation room." He got up, opened a window blind. He turned to me and smiled. His voice was quieter now, more intimate. "The idea is that the architecture is open, and that instead of facing each other across a desk, we sit as if we are having a nice coffee, and our suspects— and I really want to stress that you are not a suspect, and that you are not being 'interrogated'—our suspects know all this, because we explain the internal geography of the room to them. It's all so very open and Scandinavian."

"You provide them with chewing tobacco?"

"Worthy of satire, I'm sure. And yet they feel inclined to share their guilt."

"So what have the Andersens told you?"

He made a noncommittal gesture. "These are early days. We are analyzing the attack cycle. They are not being cooperative."

I laughed.

Tvist smiled. "I appreciate the irony. These people work in loose networks that have no organizational structure. But I am hopeful."

"Why would the chief of police be interesting himself in our case?"

"You're right to be skeptical, of course. Normally my role would be purely strategic, but this is a very extreme case and I want to know we are doing it right. Now . . ." He arranged himself, relaxed his shoulders, made his posture open and receptive. "There's a troubling fact that has come to light. One with which I need your help. Because we have discovered your daughter's telephone." He reached into a drawer in the desk, produced an evidence bag with a white iPhone in it, and another with Elsa's bangle. He handed the bags to me.

"You're asking me if these are hers?"

"That is not the question. We know that this is Licia Curtis's phone. Your wife confirmed that this was her bangle. *To Elsa, all my love, Cal.*"

He was smiling: a studied, sympathetic smile. "The phone was found on Garden Island near the boat dock, without a SIM card. The bangle was found in some underbrush near a box full of ammunition. The question is, can you explain these facts?"

A horrible thought was growing, a sense that I was being walked into a trap. Behind Ephraim Tvist's smile there was a keen intelligence, and something that felt increasingly like an accusation.

"What are you actually doing to find Licia?" I said. "We are seventeen hours into the twenty-four-hour window."

"I'm sorry if you feel let down. But twenty-four hours is for cases of kidnap, and we have no reason to think Alicia Curtis has been kidnapped. Unless you know something that would affect our assessment?"

He was looking at me levelly. Nothing about his demeanor said he was sorry. "And there's another question that arises from this, because although this phone was found on the island, simultaneously your daughter's SIM card was being used to send encrypted text messages to phones that we cannot trace. From the mainland."

"Maybe if you took the time to ask us about Licia . . ."

"Teenage girls lead complicated lives. They shout and slam doors, and you have to remind yourself that they're crying out for your love, because that's the very last thing they will express to you. Sometimes they lead many parallel lives. Perhaps Alicia Curtis lost her bracelet and somebody else picked it up?" He smiled, as if daring me to say it; as if we both knew the idea was absurd. "Perhaps your daughter has more than one phone? Or more than one SIM card? Did she confirm to you that she was on the island?"

"To my wife."

"Is there a reason she didn't speak to you?"

"No. We're very close."

"All right." He brought his hands together, tapped his forefingers on his upper lip, waiting for me to fill the silence.

"They spoke at around ten," I said.

"Which is two hours before the boat to the island began to run." He sniffed, rubbed his nose with the side of his thumbnail. Any trace of a smile was gone.

"Look," I said. "I can see, on what you've got, that you might think we were connected to this."

"Have I said anything of the sort?"

"It's always the parents. Right?"

"I'm surprised that you would satirize what you perceive to be my attitude, in a case where the stakes are so high. Perhaps you feel I need to be 'held to account'?"

I saw the warning in his look. *Tread carefully.*

The door opened. The detective in the crumpled suit, eyes red and painful-looking from lack of sleep.

"Detective Mikkel Hansen," said Tvist. "You already met, yes?"

Mikkel Hansen ignored me. He slouched across the floor, leaned close to Tvist, said something in Norwegian that I did not catch. Tvist passed him the evidence bag with the bracelet. Detective Hansen slouched out.

"What questions is that man asking my wife?" I said.

A shrewd look from Tvist. "Complementary questions." He was watching me, studying my reaction.

"I'd like to go home," I said.

"And soon you will. I do still need to know something from you, though. As I'm sure you're aware, much of the white extremist movement is gathering around the idea of crusader knights." The same smile, the same careful, watchful look.

"I didn't know that."

"Going on crusade? Crushing the dark-skinned man? These ideas are their stock-in-trade." Again that keen, appraising gaze. "Please understand that this is not an accusation."

"So . . . ?"

"Someone in your apartment has accessed these extremist Knights Templar websites."

"Okay," I said. "Not good."

"No, really not good."

"I'm mortified. Vee's fourteen, though, and she has a lively mind, and I guess after what just happened—"

He cut me off. "And if someone were researching these people in the wake of these horrible attacks, that would not be noteworthy." He sat down across from me again. "But here we have some serious red flags against your family. For months, there have been regular contacts between a computer on your network and these frankly repulsive websites. Most evenings."

"You're spying on us?"

"This is not spying. This is information we requested from your service provider this morning. Though contact ended a week ago. All three of the computers from your apartment have been scrubbed by someone who knows enough to write new data over the old. There is nothing on any of your telephones. So I wondered if you might have an explanation for any of this? Because cleaning up is good Internet practice, yes, but it's unusual for a family to be so thorough."

Those unblinking eyes of his, so endlessly dark that the pupil and the iris seemed to merge.

"I have no explanation," I said. "We are not extremists."

"But you have a political alignment, surely?"

I shook my head. "We teach our daughters to think for themselves."

He considered this. Something about my answer did not satisfy him. His mouth twisted one way, then the other. Then he smiled.

"I have one final question, after which you may go. You received a link by SMS at three a.m. yesterday morning. You downloaded a file. You received a second such file while you were waiting on the shore for news of your daughter. You deleted both files. My colleague Mikkel Hansen was wondering—"

"Unknown number," I said. "Blank files. I assumed they were spam."

"All right. Okay. Though the files were not in fact completely blank. Mikkel Hansen undeleted them. Here is the first of them."

He turned his screen so it faced me, then clicked an icon on the desktop. The screen turned black.

He pressed play. The merest hint of something else, tiny patches of gray against the black. Tvist stopped the clip. He adjusted first the brightness, then the contrast, his eyes flicking to me all the while. "You really didn't try this?"

"No."

He pressed play on his keyboard. The picture was clearer now. The profile of a woman, her face in close-up. She was lying on her back, eyes closed. That familiar nose, long and straight with a curved tip; those full lips and those planar cheeks.

I felt his eyes boring into me as I watched.

"What's your question?" I said.

Tvist reached out, pressed stop, watching me all the while. He smiled a sympathetic smile. He reached into a drawer in his desk, took out a headset, plugged its lead into the computer. He handed the headset to me. I put it on. Tvist pressed play.

There was no mistaking the familiar sound of her breathing.

In.

In.

Out.

"A colleague will be in with your phone." He watched me for a moment. "I'm very sorry to add to your burden." And with that he was on his feet. "But you are a strong man. I am sure this will not break you."

Oh, Elsa, I thought. *What have you done?*

IN THE PARK BELOW THE POLICE STATION the grass was greener than in our suburb. Men lay, shirts off, or kicked soccer balls up the incline, laughing and shouting. A clamor of children's voices; birdsong; traffic. If you wanted Scandinavian multiculturalism, here it was. Blond girls in bikinis sunbathed next to dark-haired women in headscarves. Young men grilled meat on portable barbecues, drank beer from cans. For a moment it was possible to believe that yesterday had not happened, that the country had not been attacked.

Was Tvist trying to knock me off my axis? Showing me that video had been a cheap move. And all the while he had smiled, and all the while he had expressed concern. It was misdirection, I thought, pure and simple: *Trust me. Doubt your wife.*

I found a bench in the shade of a tree. I would wait here for Elsa, and she would have an explanation. As Elsa always did. We would not allow this man to divide us. There was a strength in Elsa and in me that Tvist could not hope to understand.

I half turned, sat watching the smokers at the entrance of the police station as they laughed and flirted in the sunlight. I could almost taste their smoke in my mouth, could almost feel their nicotine coursing through my veins. Perhaps Elsa would have cigarettes. Perhaps we would sit here together, smoking, as we planned our next move.

EIGHT

FIDELITY WAS ELSA'S RELIGION. She insisted that it become mine.

We must each focus on the other's left eye; we must put all desire from our minds. We must make love. We must not fuck.

And so in the early days of our relationship we tried not to fuck. In numberless positions. Time and again. We would manage for a while to fill our minds with thoughts of respect and of peace, to listen to our partner's breaths and to hear our own breaths reflected. But desire took over every time, and we would laugh, and kiss each other deeply, and I would feel the orgasm begin to build within me and Elsa's spine would arch and she would push back hard, and we would forget tantric breathing and ignore inner peace, and one of us would begin to thrust, and we would agree—breathless now—that we should slow down, and neither of us would, and oh, her breasts and her lips, and oh, and the strength in her supple thighs.

And in the stupid way that young men do, I asked Elsa the most stupid of questions:

"Do you ever think about other people?"

"Do I ever think about other people?"

We were lying naked on Elsa's bed, legs entwined, exhausted by an afternoon of whisky and failed tantric sex.

"I mean, sexually."

"I understood that, Cal." She reached across me for a cigarette, which she lit.

"And?"

"If you don't withdraw the question, I will be forced to answer it."

We locked eyes.

"You seriously want me to withdraw the question?"

"You seriously want me to answer?"

"Yes," I said, because I was twenty and stupid. "I seriously want you to answer. Do you think about other people?"

"Okay, Cal. I do think about other people. Sometimes I long to be touched by other men. Sometimes. But this is a fantasy, and you are a jealous man, and I do not want my fantasies to hurt you. Please do not ask me more such questions."

"Good-looking men?"

"Who fantasizes about ugly men? Of course, good-looking men. Please stop."

"Because you cannot tell a lie?"

"Because you do not need to know my every thought. Jesus."

"Okay," I said, trying to force down the jealous anger that was rising in me. "That's fair. That's a reasonable point."

After all, Elsa had a right to her own thoughts. I breathed out heavily, tried to refocus my mind.

Although . . .

"Matter of interest," I said, as casually as I could. "What is your type?"

"What is my type?"

"Or who?"

"Please, Cal."

"Anybody I know?"

"Don't do this."

"You want me to withdraw the question?"

"I want you to withdraw the question."

"I won't."

She reached across me, rolled the tip of her cigarette around the ashtray, then she sat up.

"Then before I answer your question, please understand that, although I do think about other men, I do not plan to be unfaithful to you."

I laughed. "That's reassuring."

"You should be reassured. Assuming you care what I do. Instead you are sarcastic. Which makes me think that you do not care." She was staring very hard at the tip of her cigarette. For the first time it occurred to me that I had hurt her.

I ran my hand down her arm, eased the cigarette from her fingers into mine. Still she would not look at me. I took a draw, then offered her the cigarette.

Her eyes flicked to mine, then flicked away. "You're a fucking idiot if you can't see I have feelings for you." She looked at me, checking that I understood the weight behind the words.

"Maybe I am a fucking idiot." A moment of pure elation. "I really didn't know."

She was watching me keenly now, and a thought was forming in my mind. A terrifying thought that I almost didn't dare speak.

"What?" she said.

I shook my head.

"No, Cal, I'd really like to know your reaction to what I just said."

"You don't need to know my every thought."

"Don't laugh at me. I really want to know what you're thinking."

"Okay. All right." I took a long, tantric breath. "This is what I was thinking: I was wondering if you love me, Elsa."

She laughed in mock outrage. "Not fair."

"That was—in all *honesty*—what I was thinking . . ."

"You're going to force me to tell you if I love you?" She was smiling at me, almost daring me . . .

"Am I going to like the answer?" I said. "Because in that case, yes, I am going to force you to answer."

"Slightly fuck off," she said, as if she were considering the thought. "But also, okay. Here goes." She paused. Looked at me. Laughed. "Fuck."

"What?"

"Ask me the question again."

"Elsa," I said. "Do you love me?"

She sat up, composed herself formally, legs crossed, arms at her side. "Yes, Cal. I love you."

"Wow," I said.

"Wow, what?" I could see the beginnings of uncertainty, of disappointment.

"Elsa?" I reached out, brushed the hair from her face. "You are completely out of my league. You do know that, don't you?"

She smiled. "Kind of, I guess. But also no. You're funny, and you're gentle, and I'm pretty sure you love me. I feel we are on the way to something very intimate. But you didn't ask me quite the right question yet."

"What question is that, Elsa?"

"Ask me if I love you more than any man I've ever known."

AND NOW, THE IMAGE OF HER, ON that screen, at night, in somebody else's room.

NINE

SOME CHANGE IN THE balance of the day, as if a cool wind were blowing.

The smokers parted, turning as he passed among them. He paused, stood for a moment, watching over the park as a king might watch over his people, magnificent in his vestment of gray. Father Bror, whose hands had steadied me as he passed me a cup of coffee, while we stood watching the island from the shore, waiting for the news that never came. It had been a simple gesture, filled with humanity and kindness, and for a moment it had made me feel that after all there might be hope for Licia.

Bror. *Just Bror.*

He was walking slowly down the path toward me, looking neither right nor left. Behind him the smokers drew on their cigarettes, watching him all the while. I should thank the man, I thought, for the comfort he had brought me at that moment. Such quiet power he had; such peace; such charisma. Did he see me sitting under my dark tree? He passed so close I could have touched the hem of his vestment, yet I did not move.

I let him pass. I got up, walked to the center of the path, stood shading my eyes against the light, watching him go. By the road at the bottom of the slope he stopped, arms folded, as if waiting for a gap in the traffic.

I should speak to the man. It was that simple. I looked around. There was no sign of Elsa. But as I resolved to approach Bror a silver Land Cruiser drew up. He got in and the car sped off.

WHEN I GOT HOME I STOOD AT the threshold of Vee's room, watching my daughter playing her game. She was frowning at the screen, her bottom lip curled against her teeth, hands gripping the game pad, eyes wide. On the screen her avatar was attacking the roof of a house with a pair of hand axes.

I began to turn away.

"Hey, Dad."

I turned back. "I didn't know you'd heard me, Vee."

She smiled, but did not turn from her screen. "The key, the door, your footsteps . . . you know . . ." Her avatar picked up a large sniper rifle from behind a bookcase.

"All right, Miss Supersense. Mum not home yet?"

"I thought she was with you."

"So you put Franklin to bed by yourself?"

"Yay expressed breast milk. Yay carrot smoothie. Yay soiled diaper."

"Vee, I'm sorry—"

She turned, smiled, cut me short. "Don't sweat it."

I had waited on my bench for an hour. Elsa had not appeared. Her phone was off.

I walked through the living room to our bedroom. Franklin lay in his cot, clutching and unclutching his fists, sucking on the nose of his bear. I slipped my hand into his, and he gripped it. "Beautiful child," I whispered, and he stirred, turned on to his back, opened his eyes, shook his fists excitedly.

"Dddd," he said.

"Shhh, love. Shhh." I shielded his eyes with my hand, sang the only Norwegian lullaby I knew:

> *Sleep in peace*
> *Little man*
> *Dream of mint and clover*

"Mmm," said Franklin. "Mmm."

"Sleep, little man."

> *Dream so sweet*
> *And travel, fleet*
> *Sleep, my sweet wild rover*

When I lifted my hand away, Franklin's eyes were closed.

I stood in the hall, watching Vee in the light of her screen. Behind her the door to her sister's room was open, but Licia's window blind was closed.

Vee's avatar crouched at the top of a high tower, aiming with a hunting rifle at a girl in a blue beret far below. Vee fired twice. The girl crumpled to the ground. Her possessions scattered on the grass.

Eliminated WhoKTDid

No sound beyond my daughter's breathing. Her avatar jumped down from the tower to where the girl with the blue beret had stood.

"Vee, have you had any weird friend requests recently?"

"Dad, we had this talk literally a hundred times." She turned so that I could see the exaggerated roll of her eyes. "I don't friend with randoms." She turned back to her screen. Her avatar climbed up the tower, began scanning the horizon for movement.

"Okay. But how about people calling themselves knights?"

"Ew. People with knight gamer tags are the worst. They're all, like, I don't know, *Sir Fragalot*, or *Damselpleezer*. Easy to kill, though. Watch."

Her avatar switched weapons.

"Is that a rocket launcher, Vee?"

An amused smile. "Yepp."

On the screen Vee's avatar fired two rockets at a distant tower. The tower came crashing down. A tiny figure began running from the scene. Vee's avatar took her hunting rifle, aimed, and shot the figure dead.

Eliminated Kruse8or

"Kruse8or," said Vee. "See what I mean?"

"And how big a thing is racism in this game?"

"I really wouldn't know." She turned toward me again, irritated now. "It's a game, Dad. It helps me not to think." She turned to the screen again. "You can watch, but I need to concentrate."

That question of Tvist's: it could wait until she was more receptive.

I walked across the floor, through the door into her sister's room. I opened the blind. I lifted the latch, tilted the window open. Beyond the hedge I could see dogs running lazy arcs across the open parkland, crazed in the heat of the sun.

Around me, everything as Licia had left it. No pictures. No mess. Everything simple and unadorned, tidy and orderly, though the mirror was coated in dust, as if appearance did not much matter to Licia; as if the way she looked were merely a detail. So strange for a teenage girl to be unaffected by the usual social pressures. It had gotten so that we almost wished Licia would share the normal teen neuroses, we would joke, that she would put herself out there on Instagram, make a few very public mistakes. At the very least she could go out and have some proper fun.

The dress Licia had worn to the island had been so uncharacteristic. How lovely to see her looking so young and so poised.

World at your feet, Licia.

On the desk was a recent edition of the Bible, and beside the Bible a small pile of math books. By Licia's mirror was a poem written on plain card:

> *Be simple*
> *Be pure*
> *Be true to the faith*
> *Be mindful*
> *Be kind*
> *Be true*

The card was torn at the end, cut vertically after the word *true*, as if the lines were part of a longer poem. I took the card, turned it over. On the reverse was a handwritten note:

You are exceptional, Licia.
You will achieve the exceptional.

Until that day keep putting one foot in front of the other. Remember to breathe!

She had written the note to herself. My sweet Licia, so dogged and so determined to succeed. She had signed and dated the note. Six months ago.

I felt a sob threatening to engulf me. But I would not let myself cry; not now, while Vee was being so strangely adult. I walked back into Vee's room, sat on the table beside her screen, facing her. Her eyes flicked to me, then to the screen. Her gunsight hovered over a distant figure.

"You know your mum was a good shot, Vee . . ."

She shook her head. "Was she?"

"She never told you? She could down twelve single foot-square metal plates at one hundred meters. Eight seconds. With a .22 pistol."

She sighed. "I get where this is going. You think I'm a weirdo sicko freak for playing this."

"We don't. As I was saying, your mum—"

She turned to me. "Mum stopped shooting, right? That's the end point of this story? *We're not gun people.*"

"Your mum realized each of those targets could have been a human being."

Vee took off her headset. "Fine."

"Vee, honey . . . it's not that we don't understand your need for escapism."

"You don't, Dad."

"Sure I do."

She turned for a moment. "I'm pissy and I'm mean and I don't deserve a sister."

I ruffled her hair. "Only sometimes."

"Yeah. Well, this time I called her Alicia Don't-Call-Me-Stupid Curtis."

"Okay, that's not great, Vee."

"I know." She bit down hard on her lower lip.

"Want to tell me what provoked it?"

"She called me unhygienic. Like I smelled because I didn't shower before school. I don't smell. And Licia showers way too much. Like three times a day. Anyway, I feel terrible for saying it."

I took her in my arms and held her for a while.

"Do I smell unhygienic to you?" she said at last.

I laughed. "You smell of soap and candy."

The sound of footsteps on the computer speakers. Vee pulled away, swung in her seat, picked up her controller. On-screen her avatar picked up a shotgun, crept into the shelter of a bush. Another figure appeared on-screen. Vee's avatar sprang from the bush and fired twice, killing her opponent.

A key in the lock.

I heard the front door swing open. A bag dropped to the floor. Vee's eyes flicked toward the hall. "You should be asking Mum about that priest guy." I heard Elsa take off her shoes, heard her pad through to the living room. The television came on.

Vee was looking up at me, making sure I had understood her meaning. I nodded.

We had both seen how her mother reacted to Bror.

TEN

IN THE LIVING ROOM Elsa sat slumped in the sofa.

"I went to Hedda's for coffee," she said. "I walked home."

"I waited for you. Which left Vee looking after Franklin."

"Sorry." She avoided my eye, flicked the channel on the TV. "The police and their fucking questions, you know?"

"Franklin is asleep, so it's all good."

Something stopped me from asking her about Bror. Some need to digest what I'd seen before sharing it with her. That strange sense of godliness, as the smokers parted around him.

She took my hand, though she did not look at me. She seemed worn out. Done in.

I sat down beside her. On CNN a woman in a red two-piece was looking down at a large notebook. "Mounting criticism of your response during this rapidly unfolding crisis. Particularly on the issue of locking down the islands after the explosion in town."

"The Internet stuff bothered me," I said.

Elsa turned. "What Internet stuff?"

Had the police really not asked her about the websites?

Her eyes flicked back to the television. On-screen a dark-skinned man turned toward the camera, shaven head glistening under the lights.

A caption:

Ephraim Tvist, Chief of Police, Oslo District

"Mr. Tvist," said the woman on television, "Mr. Tvist, you are Oslo's first black police chief. You have been in the job three weeks."

"Jesus," I said. "Today is like one long psychotic break. That's the man who interviewed me."

"Yes," said Tvist cautiously. "I'm not sure what either of those facts—"

The journalist cut him off. "Why was Garden Island not on lockdown after the explosion in town?"

"We had four islands in the Oslo Fjord on lockdown."

"Again: Why not Garden Island?"

"Garden Island was rated as a medium-risk target. The four islands on lockdown were considered high-risk targets."

This was not the Tvist I had met. The camera reduced him; he looked shifty and out of breath.

"On those other four islands," the journalist was saying, "there were career politicians present. Garden Island was a youth camp with only youth politicians. Is this the reason for the medium-risk designation?"

"The designation was signed off by my predecessor, six months ago."

"My God," said Elsa quietly. "Did he really just blame the last guy?"

The journalist on-screen was studying her notebook. "Mr. Tvist, how many helicopters did you mobilize?"

"I'm not certain that a helicopter is the correct response to an event of this type."

"So, no police response helicopter was available? Seems barely credible."

Tvist looked away, tapped the tips of his fingers together.

The journalist looked severe. "May we take that as a no?"

Tvist made himself tall. He was looking directly at the camera.

"Elsa," I said, "he thinks someone in this apartment was accessing crusader knight websites."

Tvist was speaking slowly, as if appealing to the nation. "We did not consider a helicopter to be the best use of police resources."

"This is absurd," said Elsa. "Obscene."

"Elsa, did you hear what I said? Those are basically the people who carried out the attack. Someone in our apartment was downloading their material."

"And Mr. Tvist . . ." The reporter on-screen was consulting her notebook. "Mr. Tvist, the first shot was fired on the island at six-oh-three p.m."

"That doesn't in any way worry you, Elsa?"

Elsa did not respond.

"At six-oh-three p.m., Mr. Tvist," the journalist was saying. "Can you confirm?"

"That sounds correct."

"Who's that man?" said Vee from the doorway.

An uncomfortable pause. Elsa and I exchanged a look.

"Dad, who is that?"

I studied Vee's face. She gave no sign of having heard us arguing.

"It's the police chief, love."

"He interviewed Dad." Elsa smiled, a little too brightly. "So we have his attention. That can only be good, right?"

"I suppose," said Vee.

"Mr. Tvist, at six thirty-one p.m. two police officers arrived at the slipway on the mainland, but did not make the crossing to the island. In fact, they returned to their vehicle, citing safety concerns."

"My briefings did not include mention of these officers," said Tvist.

"But you can confirm that at seven fifty-one p.m. your tactical weapons unit brought the two perpetrators into custody?"

"Fuck," said Vee, eyes wide.

"That's to say: between six-oh-three and seven fifty-one these two men, armed with assault rifles and nine-millimeter automatic pistols, were free to roam across the island, executing children at will, and they did exactly this until seven thirty-three p.m., when they ran out of ammunition. At which point they sat and waited patiently to be arrested . . ."

"That's like a kill a minute," said Vee. There was something almost admiring in the way she said it.

". . . and all this despite the fact that you had officers at the scene, at the slipway on the mainland. Mr. Tvist, did those first officers at the scene have firearms in their vehicle?"

"Cal." Elsa's voice, very quiet. "Maybe it's time we switched this off."

I nodded.

Tvist was speaking again. "This was a complex and rapidly evolving situation, with many variables and many dangers."

"Particularly for the children," said the journalist, "who waited in vain for rescue. The only officers in the vicinity waited in their car on the mainland, concerned solely for their own safety, while on the island these children were cut down by men impersonating your officers. These men claimed they were there to put the island on lockdown. You appreciate the irony, I'm sure . . ."

I almost felt sorry for Tvist. The air had been knocked out of him.

"Mr. Tvist," the reporter was saying, "your country has a population of, what? Five million?"

"Five-point-three."

"And in an average year you have twenty-five murders, and in a bad year you have, what? Thirty? Perhaps?"

You could see it in Tvist's eyes: the realization that he was being walked into a trap. He made to speak, but the journalist cut him off.

"So how would you describe ninety-one dead in a single afternoon, Mr. Tvist, the majority of them children?"

While Tvist sat there considering his response, Elsa walked to the television and switched it off.

I WAS BATHING FRANKLIN IN THE KITCHEN sink when Vee walked in. Franklin made fists of his tiny hands, shook them excitedly at his sister. Vee held out her pinkie, and he grasped it.

"Okay, so look," she said, "if I watched things I shouldn't have . . . I mean, I'm not saying I did. But if I had, how bad would that be?"

"What things?"

She looked down. I had not seen the phone in her hand. She unlocked it and held it out to me. "This is the only one left up."

I took the phone.

On the screen was a video. A tomb in a medieval church, and

on the tomb a carved stone knight in full battle armor, arms folded across his breast. Across the bottom of the screen was the text *Tactical Brigades of the Knights Templar.*

"You need to press play, Dad."

The shot held on the knight's tomb, then began slowly to zoom in to the hands crossed on the knight's chest. The music swirled, grand and romantic in intent; through the phone it sounded tinny and bombastic. The music dipped. A voice began: "Today we honor our forefathers. Today the fightback begins."

"Vee, why would you be looking at this?"

An evasive little flick of the eyes.

The camera was tilting down the knight's sword. The shot dissolved to two men in combat gear, bearing Ruger short-barreled rifles. I felt my throat beginning to tighten. These were the men Elsa and I had seen being led off the boat and into the waiting police cars.

I pressed stop. "You understand these people are fascists?"

"Fascist is what you call people who don't agree with your articles."

"Listen to me, Vee, I'm not joking now. These men believe in racial hierarchies; they want to concentrate power in the hands of a small number of people; they believe violence justifies their end."

She was looking blankly at me.

I said, "That's about as good a working definition of fascism as you can get. How much have you been visiting these sites?"

"A bit. I guess. A lot, maybe."

"Oh, Vee."

"They had answers to some difficult questions."

"Like what?"

"Like who's actually in control."

"Let me guess: the Jews and the Marxists?"

"Plus Muslims. Plus bankers."

"The Marxists and the bankers and the Jews and the Muslims? All on the same side?"

"Okay, it sounds extra-stupid when you use your satire voice."

I sighed. "Really not using my satire voice, Vee . . . But can you not see where this kind of conspiratorial thinking leads?"

"I'm not saying I think they're right. But what do we do that's so great, Dad? Mum takes pictures that no one understands and that no one wants to buy anymore. You write articles telling people to get angry about the government. Every week. I mean, how are these things even jobs? And I don't know if it's the Jews or the Muslims or the Marxists, or if it's the government and the bankers, but the world's kind of going to hell right now and what are we doing about it? I mean, when did you last grow your own food, or rescue people from hunger? This is pretty much the richest country in the world, Dad, and one family in ten is below the poverty line. Why aren't we helping them?"

"So these people are attractive because they offer meaning in a meaningless world?"

"No. Maybe. I don't know."

"Vee, I want to understand. Because this stuff normally appeals to people whose lives are spiraling downward. And I don't think that's you."

Vee sighed heavily. "I mean, yeah, shoot me for looking for a little meaning in my life. Dad, I didn't know those men would actually do what they did. I promise you. And anyway, we're supposed to be going home next week . . ."

She paused. She must have seen the look on my face. "Except we can't now, can we?"

"Vee," I said, "was it you who deleted all the browsing histories?"

Vee nodded.

"So you knew at some level that engaging with this stuff was wrong?"

"I guess . . ." Her eyes flicked away. When she looked at me again I could see they were misting with tears. "Dad," she said, "am I responsible for what happened to Licia?"

"No, Vee, no. You couldn't have known."

ELEVEN

I GOT UP AT six, all hope of sleep gone.

I stood for a while in Franklin's room, listening to the snuffled in-in-and-out of his breathing. The children all breathed in the same pattern, inherited from Elsa. They would pause in the middle of the in-breath, inhale a second time, pause again for the tiniest moment, then exhale fully.

In, in, and out: always most noticeable in sleep. In the early days it had terrified me, the thought that Vee or Licia might simply stop breathing and never begin again. I would keep watch over them for hours, though Elsa always told me there was no need. With the passing of the years I relaxed a little.

These days, my children's breathing was a detail, like eye color: at least it was for Franklin and for Vee. Licia had not been so lucky. On top of her mother's breathing, she inherited the asthma that shortened her grandmother's life. *Not a problem*, the doctors had said. *Entirely controllable*. And it was, with her Ventolin inhaler.

Licia was not among the dead. Not yet. But if she was alive, what then? Was she lying alone somewhere, hurt and afraid and gasping for breath?

I felt tears pricking at the backs of my eyes. *Tell me at least that she has her inhaler.*

I wiped the tears away with the pads of my hands. I opened the door to Vee's room, thinking to sit awhile on the wooden floor, to watch her as she slept.

Vee's bed was empty.

I walked into the living room, opened the door onto the balcony at the back.

Vee was not there.

I walked into the bedroom I shared with Elsa.

Elsa must have felt my presence. She sat up in bed. "Everything okay?"

I said, "Did Vee mention anything to you about having plans?"

"No."

"She went out."

Elsa swung her feet across the bed. She picked up her phone, squinted for a moment, checking the time, then dialed Vee's number.

We watched each other, anxious.

"Straight to voice mail," said Elsa.

IN THE MIDDLE OF THE PARKLAND WAS a play area. A sign warned children from the neighboring areas to keep away.

"Vee!" I shouted uselessly. "Vee!"

I walked on. I stood on the high metal bridge above the station, but there was no one on the platforms and I could see no one on the tracks. On a balcony in an apartment building very much like ours an old woman turned to watch me. From another balcony, farther away, a man with binoculars tracked me as I walked.

"Vee!" I shouted again. "Vee!"

I walked the path that skirted the perimeter, eyes searching the ground forty meters below. I found a smaller, narrower footway that led me down on to a dry mud track, and followed that until I could follow it no more.

Elsa would have called Julie's mother, and after Julie's mother her own father, then a couple of friends back home in D.C., in case Vee had called.

I took the footbridge down to the main road, walked along the high grass bank, heading past the mall. Nothing would be open there, not at this time, but it was the only place I could think of going. Outside were the cleaning staff, sharing cigarettes, waiting to be let in, speaking in languages I didn't recognize. Every one of them was a foreigner, I guessed.

The vehicle fumes smelled of burnt licorice and ammonia.

Elsa called.

"Hey," I said.

"The boat key's gone."

AT THE MARINA I TOOK MY KEY fob from my pocket, held it up against the reader. The gate clicked open. I could see that our rented boat was not on its mooring, but I ran out along the pontoon, needing to be sure.

Four tensioned ropes, two on each side. Vee had set them neatly in place on the spits; she had folded the tarpaulin canopy of the boat into four and left it on the pontoon, along with the steel hawser and the padlock.

I called Elsa. "Boat's not here."

Elsa's breathing, the sound cutting in and out on the line.

"You there?" I said. "Jo and Hedda brought it back for us, right? Elsa?"

"Vee took Licia's life jacket off the peg. I'm assuming she took the boat."

"So, what, she has some kind of a plan to find Licia?"

"I'm going to call my dad. Ask him to drive up and fetch Franklin."

THE HIGHWAY CUT THROUGH COMMUTER TOWNS, LOW-BUILT and ugly. Elsa drove without speaking, eyes flicking from mirror to mirror, rarely settling on the road.

"What are you thinking?" I asked her after a time.

She glanced at me. "Same as you, Cal. Exactly the same as you."

She reached across with her free hand, and I clasped it tightly, threaded my fingers through hers.

We drove on in silence, hands entangled, until we came to the exit for Garden Island.

WE STOOD ON THE SLIPWAY. THE BODY bags were gone from the shoreline. Farther up the coast children were swimming. Hard to believe, after what happened here. But out across the water there was nothing to suggest the violence done so close by. The fjord was mirror-still. From here the island looked inviting.

I could see the diver units farther out: the marker buoys on the surface, the boats tracking the divers under the water. Elsa watched a diver as he handed something to the man at the helm of the boat.

"Cal," she said, "don't bodies float in seawater?"

"I guess."

"Then Licia is not down there." She took my hand. "Come." She led me along the shore to a small sandy cove. Just above the waterline lay a white fiberglass boat with a small outboard engine.

"Pull from the bow," she said.

"You serious?"

"We'll bring it back."

I looked toward the phalanx of police cars on the slipway.

"We're day-trippers," she said. "Far as they know."

No one was watching. "All right," I said.

I bent down, took off my shoes, threw them onboard. Elsa stepped easily over the side as the boat slipped into the water, while I stood knee-deep, steadying the hull. She leaned forward, pulled out a pin, lowered the outboard into the water. She braced against the side of the boat, drew evenly on the start cord. I felt through the hull the tug and thrum of the engine. I jumped in, took my place in the bow, facing my wife. We pulled out into the bay, Elsa scanning the horizon, leaning forward, steering by instinct.

Halfway across she slowed the engine. "There." She stood, hands shielding her eyes. I turned, saw ahead of us the silhouette of our wooden speedboat on the brilliant fjord, and at the helm a resolute little stick figure.

Vee turned to face us, then turned away.

I began to get to my feet.

"Cal," said Elsa. "Down."

I was tipping us. I didn't have her instinct for the sea.

I hunched down, watching the little red speedboat. Vee was heading behind the dock on Garden Island.

"Did she see us?"

"Who knows?"

We continued on our course until we were past the island, then turned in. Soon we drew level with the dock, emptied now of boats. Signs in Norwegian and English warned us not to moor.

Vee had not stopped here. Elsa nodded toward a spit of red-pink rock that ran out into the sea, hiding the coastline beyond. She turned. Her eyes flicked to mine.

There?

I nodded. Out of sight, I knew, were the cliffs, and the staircase cut into them. Licia had been alive on those steps; we had seen her reaching up toward the helicopter.

We rounded the spit. There was the cliff wall. There was our wooden speedboat, moored at the foot of the steps.

Elsa was frowning. Where was Vee?

As we drew level with the speedboat Elsa hooked an arm across the side of it, passed a rope through a metal ring and back. She stood up, looked down into the boat. Her hand brushed my shoulder.

I stood up, cautious. There was Vee, crouching low in the boat, hands across her face, rocking backward and forward.

"Vee," I said.

I felt Elsa slide past me, saw that she was securing the boats at the bow. I swung a leg across, stood, finding my balance as the speedboat gently rocked.

"Vee."

When I crouched beside her I could hear the rapid in-in-and-out of her breaths. I put a hand across her shoulder. She leaned in toward me, and I held her very tightly. A tiny, sighing sound, then another, as she gulped air.

I heard a splash, heard chain links on the fiberglass hull of the little white boat, looked up to see Elsa letting the anchor rope run through her fingers.

Vee took her hands from her face. Her eyelashes were matted and wet. I kissed the hair on top of her head, held my palms against her cheeks.

"Dad," Vee whispered. "I'm sorry."

"My poor tired horse."

She looked guiltily at me. Her eyes were shot with blood.

"I wanted to see."

I nodded. Last known whereabouts.

"I get it," I whispered. "We both get it."

"Dad, I want to go on land."

WE FOLLOWED A SHORT DISTANCE BEHIND VEE. I walked along the cliff edge toward the sheer wall of the staircase, looked down to where the girl matching Licia's description had hidden from the gunmen. The churning fjord was still now, mirror flat.

Elsa trailed her fingertips across the palm of my hand.

"Hey."

"Hey."

You would never know, I thought. When you looked about you, the island was perfect. The neat lines of the cabins by the lake, the straight-sided path: the placing of man-made objects in nature, everything simple and rational. Ahead, Vee was walking the path toward the cabins.

"So it was Vee," I said. "The Knights Templar websites. Looking for answers, she said. Been going there for months."

Elsa watched Vee for a time. Then she turned to me. "And if we freak out about that we make things worse."

"Yeah. I resisted making a point-by-point breakdown of why everything those people believe was wrong. Figured it would make it more attractive. We should catch up with her, though."

She put a hand on my shoulder. "Let her do this, Cal. Let her understand for herself the implications of what those men believe."

"All right."

I stood looking down through the cut rock at the slash of fjord water. That intense Nordic summer blue. If you dived in, the water would be warm on your body. But keep diving down from the surface and you would soon feel the cold peaty dark of the fjord. Winter was always there, ten feet down, patiently waiting for summer's end.

"Elsa," I said, "why did you never tell me about Bror?"

"How could I guess he would become relevant?" That evasive little eye flick. So unlike Elsa. She seemed to notice it herself. She turned, made a point of meeting my eye. "I mean, here's the thing, Cal . . . Oslo's a small place. If you were going to parties at the Blitz squat, you knew Bror. He hung with the young Marxists. He was all *Durkheim this* and *Lacan that*, which was hilarious because he was a trance DJ. But he could make you feel that what he was saying made perfect sense, even when it didn't."

"So you guys used to fuck?"

"Okay." She glanced at me, then glanced away. "I mean, he's kind of an ex."

"Kind of?"

When we locked eyes there was something apologetic in her gaze.

"We went out. Half a life ago. I didn't want to talk about it in front of Vee."

"And?"

"I was sixteen," she said. "He was nineteen. I liked that he took me seriously. He had a sense of his own ridiculousness, which is a quality I like in men."

"So that's a yes?"

"The sex was vanilla. Take a breath, Cal, and remember what sixteen means."

She was right. I was being ridiculous.

"Look," she said, "I mean, I doubt if we'd get on these days, but he was kind to me. You know, first my mother died, and then Dad went completely off the rails. And in the middle of all that I had this unplanned pregnancy, and Dad insisted I terminate it but he wouldn't come to the hospital, so in the end I went on my own. And I was sitting in the hospital canteen afterward not knowing if I felt good or bad about what I'd done, but dreading going home to Dad, and I guess Bror was there and he could see I was suffering, because he came over and offered me coffee and a cigarette."

I knew about the termination. She had never told me about Bror, though.

"He was patient with me, you know. Didn't pressure me into anything. I'd gotten really thin, and all my friends were telling me I needed to eat, or worse, that I needed to see a doctor or a shrink. Bror didn't care about any of that. He was the only person who just seemed to get that I was in pain, and he listened to me—every evening for weeks, it seemed like—and then at the end of the summer he gave me a pile of books he hoped would help bring me clarity, and he never minded that I didn't read them. The sex was the least memorable thing about that time."

We stood, watching the divers as they reentered the water, closer to the shore this time. Here and there, I realized, you could see patches of dark red on the rocks, on the grassy banks. Vee was crouched by the side of one of the cabins, examining the wood near the door.

I turned toward Elsa. "Would you be okay with me going to see him?"

"Bror? Sure. You might like him." She turned my hand over in hers. "Just don't punish me for decisions I made when I was a kid."

"I know," I said. "That was stupid of me. I'm glad you had someone who listened."

Ridiculous to be jealous over something so far away.

TWELVE

THE THREE POLICE OFFICERS who stopped us were kind and showed us nothing but respect. They understood, they said, our need to see for ourselves. But Vee could not be here on the island. None of us could. They escorted us back to the boat and shook our hands. "We feel for you," they each said in turn.

Vee and I sat in our wooden speedboat, holding it in against the slipway, while Elsa stood on the pebbled beach, thigh-deep, holding the transom of the little white boat. Vee was carrying something delicate and soft, folded into her hands, held artfully against the side of her belly. I didn't think Elsa saw it.

"What's that, Vee?"

"We don't need the police to feel for us. We need them to do their jobs."

The object in her hands glimmered softly.

"Vee, what is that?"

Vee looked at me, guilty, then at her mother.

"Please," she said gently. "She . . . she wouldn't understand."

"Vee," I said, "I am not a softer touch than your mum."

"She will freak."

Elsa shouted. "Cal!"

"Vee," I said quietly, "do not play us off against each other."

"Dad, you know she will."

"No, she won't."

"Cal! Now would be good."

Vee's eyes flicked toward her mother. "Shouldn't you go and help her?"

Elsa was standing in the water, arms folded, the boat braced against her thighs.

"Hold the boat to the quay," I said to Vee. I jumped up on to the jetty, walked a few paces toward the shore, jumped down onto the beach. At the water's edge I took off my shoes.

The water felt colder. The wind was getting up.

We slid the little white boat up the beach. When we returned to our own boat Vee's hands were empty.

WE SAT ON THE SOFA, ELSA AND I, drinking our martinis as we watched the news on NRK, desperate for anything that could help our case. The announcer introduced a dark-haired woman, who began to hold forth about immigrants in heavily accented English.

"Tasteful," I said.

Elsa sighed heavily. "So there's this stupid thought I have about Licia, and I can't shake it."

"Tell me your stupid thought."

Our eyes met for a moment. We were on edge, worn out, could barely look at each other. She reached for my hand instead.

She said, "Did I ever tell you about driving her to that house church in the eastern suburbs? I mean, God knows why she asked me and not you, because it was four days before Franklin was born and I could barely walk. But anyway . . . I have this image of Licia standing there in the parking lot in her oversized woolen coat, folding and unfolding her hands, staring up at the open walkways that led to the apartments. And I had the window open and the snow was gusting into the car. I asked if she had her inhaler, and she nodded and smiled the most beautiful smile and said, "All I need is to remember to breathe."

"She was so painfully nervous, so I went up with her. The elevator barely had room for two people and smelled strongly of sweat, and we took it all the way to the twelfth floor, and when we got up there the walkway was slick with ice and the guardrails were low, and Licia got worried that I was going to fall, and she very sweetly held my hand, and we walked slowly up to this plain unmarked door. And from the inside there was just this music. The most beautiful melody, Cal: twenty voices—thirty, maybe—all singing in unison. And she turned to me and thanked me for not being *weird* about her coming here and asked me if I'd be okay getting back to the car. I called her my sweet child. And then the door opened, and there was this girl with white-blond hair wearing these ugly clumpy shoes, and she smiled the most beautiful smile and asked if she was Alicia Curtis. And Licia nodded, and let go of my hand, and began to walk across the threshold, and the girl asked if I wanted to join them. And I looked at Licia, and I could see what she was thinking. You know, *No, Mum, please don't,* so I went downstairs to wait."

The woman on-screen was ranting now. Her Norwegian accent got stronger by the second: "We need to look away for a moment from the obvious crimes committed by the Andersens because these crimes are a distraction from their actual message. And that message is that people in Europe are tired of their homelands being a dumping ground for the cultural detritus of Africa and the Middle East."

"God," I said, "this is chilling. What are they doing, interviewing her? What can she usefully tell us about Garden Island?"

"She's from a free speech think tank."

"Free speech?"

"She makes a living winding up people like you, Cal. She's a provocateur, and she'll be finished soon. Can you please focus on what I'm trying to tell you? Because I was sitting there with the engine on and the heater on high, and the snow was falling all around, and the apartment building was beautiful in the snow. And when Licia returned to the car we drove quietly along the highway, and she was singing to herself under her breath, but she was shot through with excitement. So I asked her how it went and she said, "I wish you could know the happiness that true faith can bring, Mum." And it was like the most perfect moment. Except . . ." Elsa was shaking her head, biting back tears.

"Except what?"

"What if the island was her opportunity to get away from us? What if Licia actually wanted out?"

I reached out a hand, drew Elsa to me. "She was happy with her life."

"Was she?"

"Wasn't she?"

"I guess I always thought so."

The woman on-screen seemed calmer. She was speaking slowly, but her words were no less chilling. "Our culture is being held down by the ankles and raped, and it is being mongrelized. These are the real crimes being committed daily against the Norwegian people through this mass immigration, and that is what the Andersen brothers are trying—imperfectly and clumsily, I concede—to communicate."

The presenter on-screen was trying to hold her to account. "But what these men did is not communication. What they did is murder."

The woman turned contemptuously to the camera. "You see? Instead of reporting the message, you and your media colleagues brand them criminals and murderers and side with the people who would see our heritage disappear."

I could feel the anger rising in me. "Seriously, though," I said, "you can't separate those men's 'message' from the killings. The killings *are* the message. Can we please watch something else?"

"With pleasure." Elsa picked up the remote and flicked the channel.

On-screen a ginger-haired man was speaking English, slowly, to a very tall black man. "You are perfectly nice," he was saying. "And entirely welcome here. But Norwegian research proves your reaction time is likely to be slower than mine. And your IQ significantly lower."

I said, "I guess I was hoping we could watch something a whole lot less racist."

"Our TV *is* racist," said Elsa. "How did you never notice this?"

"Just weird." I picked up the remote. "When everything else is so right on." I flicked through the channels till I found a quiz show. The room filled with the sound of audience laughter.

Elsa watched distractedly for a moment.

"What, love?" I said.

"We need to visit that house church."

SHE DROVE PURPOSEFULLY, HANDS CLAMPED ON THE wheel. Franklin sat in his car seat, alert and excited, very far from sleep.

The eastern suburbs looked very much like our western suburb. The same no-nonsense architecture, though the buildings were placed closer and there were fewer trees. There were basketball courts here and a soccer field on green-painted tarmac that was floodlit, though there was light in the sky. There were more dark faces among the players here than in Øvre Øvrebøhaugen. Fewer cars.

As Elsa turned left up a narrow road that wound to the left, the players stopped to watch. The road surface was dusty, the grass at the side spattered with dried mud. We reached the top of the rise. Elsa parked the car, got out. I got out too. In front of us a hole, three stories deep, and behind it a towering wall of rock. Around the edges of the pit stood vast industrial machines: earth movers; cranes; pile drivers.

"And this is definitely the address you came to?" I said.

Angry tears were forming in Elsa's eyes. "I should have taken a telephone number from someone, or gotten an email or a name . . . I just didn't think . . ."

I took her in my arms. "This is a blow, love," I said. "But we'll tell Tvist about the house church, and maybe he'll turn something up."

THIRTEEN

MY BROTHER DAN CAME for the memorial service. I was late to the airport. He was standing there, alone in a black suit, hair cropped close, a tan leather bag slung across his shoulder, coffee in hand.

"The traffic," I said. "Sorry."

"Christ, man, don't be daft. I would have met you at the kirk. C'mere." He dropped his bag to the ground, bear-hugged me. Always the older brother, though there was only a year between us.

There was whisky on his breath. I stepped back. A tracery of red veins in the whites of his eyes.

"You didn't sleep on the flight," I said. "Did you?"

"Wrong way around, pal." He laughed, shook his head. "You don't get to worry about me." His eyes were searching my face, all brotherly concern.

"We're getting by," I said.

"Right. Yeah." He exhaled heavily. There was something more than concern in his eyes. Something more like grief. He ran the palm of his right hand across his right eye, blinked hard.

"The station are being understanding," he said. "So's Daisy. She wanted us all to be here, but we didn't feel we could take Lyndon out of school."

"Dan, the official line is that Licia's coming back. Great if Vee could hear that from you as well as us."

"Aye. Sure." He nodded, swallowed. "What's your instinct, Cal?"

"My instinct is she's coming back."

He was searching my eyes. Perhaps he heard the catch in my voice.

BRAKE LIGHTS IN FRONT FLASHED TWICE. I cut and swerved to the inside lane, swore under my breath. I felt my seat belt jam. We came to a stop.

"Hate it when that happens. You okay?"

"Are you?" said Dan.

My phone began to ring. I checked the mirror. Gridlock in front. Gridlock behind. I unclipped and unjammed my seat belt, let it flow back into the reel, reattached it. Dan did the same.

I answered the phone hands-free.

That rich voice filled the car. "Cal Curtis? It's Ephraim Tvist."

I felt my brother's eyes on me.

"Hello," I said.

I heard Tvist say, "A girl matching your daughter's description . . ." I felt my muscles tense against the news I was sure was to come. Licia's body, borne by the currents . . . I avoided my brother's eye.

"A girl matching Licia's description?"

"Saved the life of a young boy. Got him out of the woods and into the water. While she was in the woods she appears to have jettisoned an ammunition box along with the silver bracelet.

I thought you'd want to know. Cal, the men ran out of bullets. When my tactical unit arrived they offered no resistance. It seems your daughter may have shortened the massacre."

"Oh my God."

The relief was overwhelming. I felt Dan's hand gripping my arm. I could almost see the smile on Tvist's face. "I wanted you to hear it from me and not from the press, Cal. You will have many questions, I'm sure, but a piece of the puzzle has fallen into place. We shall speak more." And he was gone.

"Wow," I said, "Fuck."

"That's my Licia," said Dan. "You can be proud."

"So fucking proud."

"We both know Licia's a survivor, Cal."

I took the roundabout at the top of the slip road, turned left across the bridge that crossed the highway.

"Just the one wee note of caution," said Dan "You do understand that man has already released this story to the press?"

"Do you think so?"

"I'd say that's pretty much what he was telling you."

ELSA WAS FRESH FROM THE SHOWER, HAIR wet, a towel knotted over her breasts.

Dan stepped into her waiting arms. "Good to see you, darling. Wish the circumstances . . ."

"Circumstances just improved a little," said Elsa. "I think."

"Dan, tell Mum we have five minutes. She literally needs to get dressed now." Vee was standing, impatient for her mother to end the embrace, in a blue sequined dress exactly like her sister's, a thin black cardigan across her shoulders.

"A journalist called," said Elsa, eyes shining, "to tell me Licia saved a little boy. Called her the hero of Garden Island. Said she ended the massacre."

"Yeah. Tvist called me," I said.

"So this can only be good," said Elsa. "Right?"

Dan stepped away from Elsa. "I'd maybe switch your phones off for the next couple of days. Give some thought to how you manage this."

Confusion in Elsa's eyes. "Manage this?"

"Mum," said Vee, "you really need to get ready."

Elsa looked at Vee, seemed to see for the first time the king-fisher dress. Vee crossed her arms self-consciously across her body, drew the cardigan tight.

"Where's the dress from, Vee?" I said.

"Julie," said Vee, suddenly defensive.

"Because it looks awfully like—"

"Are those your sister's shoes?" said Elsa, her voice full of sim-mering fury.

Vee, defiant, all jutting angles. Her mother staring daggers. Was that what she had found on the island? Her sister's dress?

I saw the tremble in Vee's jaw, saw the clenching of her right fist, saw the nail of her right forefinger digging into the quick of the thumb. "They're Licia's shoes. Julie lent me the dress."

"And if I check with Julie's mum?" said Elsa.

Dan walked toward Vee, took her in his arms, looked at Elsa, then at me. "This is a tribute," he said. "Right, Vee?"

Vee nodded. Her eyes were filling with tears.

"Might be an idea to change, love," I said, as gently as I could.

"You're thinking of your sister." Dan turned to Elsa. "Thinking of her sister sends exactly the right message."

"I agree with Dad, Vee," said Elsa, her voice tight with control. "It might be a good idea if you changed."

Dan put a protective arm across Vee's shoulder. "Family line is you're looking forward to welcoming Licia home. Hence the dress."

I stood very close to Elsa. "Dan's good on this stuff," I said, as quietly as I could. "And Vee clearly needs this. Let's deal with the rest when we get home."

"All right," said Elsa, quiet as breath. "We mustn't fracture. I see that."

"I THANK EVERYBODY WHO WAS ON GARDEN ISLAND for the courage they showed on that terrible day." The prime minister was looking out across the cathedral at the survivors, at the families of the dead, with his buzz-cut hair and his Boateng suit. "Whether you faced down these two very disturbed men, as our tactical weapons unit did, or whether you simply survived to tell your story, as so many of you that I see before me, you have proven once again that courage is the defining Norwegian virtue."

I felt eyes on me. I turned to the left. On the pew beside me was a small boy in a perfectly fitted black suit. I tried to smile, but the boy would only stare. So much stress in his sinewy, bony frame.

A hand reached out for the boy's. His mother, an older woman, elegant in gray silk. I recognized her too now. She ruffled her son's hair, then leaned across him to whisper to me. "I wanted to say thank you. On Arno's behalf."

"That means a lot," I whispered.

Arno. Of course. The last of the children. Rescued from the water after Licia helped him escape. In the days since Garden

Island his face had changed. His features were drawn, the flesh below his eyes puffy.

"Courage," the prime minister was saying. "Courage is the . . . great . . . Norwegian . . . virtue."

Arno's mother squeezed my hand. "We are all very much hoping you will have news of your daughter soon. Without her . . ." So she knew, then.

Arno turned his blank stare on me again. "How are you, Arno?" I said.

"He hasn't spoken," said his mother. "Not once."

"Give him time."

She nodded, and I nodded, then we turned to face the front.

The prime minister was not done discoursing on courage. "Courage defined our forefathers when they faced down the Nazi threat during the war. Courage defines the young people who faced unspeakable dangers on Garden Island. Courage is the virtue shared by every man, woman, and child in this great Norwegian cathedral of ours."

Beside me, Elsa said something to Vee that I did not catch. I turned toward Vee, who leaned across her mother. "That boy knows things, Dad." She stared across at Arno. "Bet you anything you want." Arno returned Vee's stare, suspicious.

"This isn't the time, Vee," I said.

"He should tell us what he knows, Dad."

Arno's mother, sensing something, reached out and drew her son close.

"As the man in charge," the prime minister was saying, "I accept responsibility for what went wrong on that most terrible day."

Murmurings behind us. Ahead people were nodding, visibly moved.

"But I also accept . . ." He paused dramatically, leaned forward on the lectern. "I also accept responsibility for the things that went well."

"What?" whispered Dan. "What were the things that went well?"

"Nothing," said Vee. "Not a single thing."

The prime minister stopped. Had he heard? His eyes flicked across to our pew. A look of displeasure crossed his features. "We are," he said, "the most courageous of nations."

I turned around, expecting to see my family's disbelief reflected in other faces, but if there was anger it did not show. People sat in rapt attention, tears pouring down their cheeks, as if listening to a different speech. Arno's mother seemed profoundly moved.

The prime minister looked down at his notes. He pulled at the ends of his cuffs, cleared his throat, drank water from a crystal glass, made himself tall. "You will forgive me, dear friends of Norway, if I continue my speech in the language of our forefathers. *Kjære alle sammen . . .*"

And so we sat there at the memorial service, surrounded by the families of the dead, as the prime minister promised the television cameras that his country would not change, that he would meet this atrocity with *more democracy, more openness*. Dan sat beside Vee, holding her hands very tightly. Vee did not cry. None of us did until the final hymn. "To Those in Peril on the Sea," sung in Norwegian by a choir of two hundred. The deep bass of the organ took hold in our bones, wrenching the emotion from us, while the descants in the choir soared high above, ethereal and timeless.

We cried then, huddled together, my wife, my brother, my daughter, and I, as Franklin gurgled happily on my lap. We cried for Licia, who was yet to come home, and we cried for the lives lost or ruined that day, for those who would not be coming home, and for those who had come home changed. And all the while little Arno sat staring rigidly ahead, saying nothing.

When the service was over we slipped from our pew past the journalists and the camera crews.

"Viktoria! Viktoria Curtis!" one shouted.

Vee turned. A man in a suit was stepping toward her, microphone extended. "Your sister, the hero of Garden Island . . ."

Vee made to speak.

"No, Vee," I said.

I could see Vee's confusion.

"Viktoria Curtis," the man was saying, "do you have a message for your missing sister?"

I handed Franklin to Elsa, stepped between the reporter and my daughter, guided her away.

"They shouldn't be trying to speak to you, Vee."

The reporter moved to intercept us.

"Do the right thing, pal," Dan said to the reporter as gently as he could. "Step away."

I began drawing Vee to the side.

"But Dad." She turned back toward the reporter. "She needs to know we're looking for her."

"This is not the time, Vee."

"Your dad's right, Vee," said Dan. He stepped in front of the reporter. "Page one of the ethics book, pal. No mics in kids' faces."

The reporter was not giving up. "When you feel the time is right to give your side of the story, Viktoria—"

"She doesn't," Dan said.

"She won't," I said.

I could feel Vee trying to pull away. "Who said you could speak for me, Dad?"

I took her hand. "Excuse us," I said. "Please. Vee, we need to go." I bundled her past the reporter and out onto the steps of the cathedral. From both sides of the path people watched us.

When we reached the gate on to the street, Vee stopped. "I want to wait for the others."

There were camera teams everywhere. "They'll catch up with us," I said.

Back on the cathedral steps I could see Bror, speaking to Arno and his mother. Arno's mother said something to Bror, and he turned toward us. His eyes seemed to meet mine, even at this distance. A hint of a smile, the merest of nods. Then he turned back toward Arno and his mother.

"Dad," said Vee.

Almost as if Bror knew us. Had he seen us together with Elsa?

"Dad," said Vee again. She motioned toward a camera team farther up the street. They were lining up on us.

I took her hand and we turned and began to walk away down the street.

"Can you promise me something?" she said.

"What, Vee?"

"Just promise me you don't all think she's dead, and I just don't know yet."

"Oh, love. No. We don't. Of course she's not dead. She's a hero, Vee, and we're going to find her. But Dan's right about keeping to the family line."

She laughed. "What's Dan scared we're going to say?"

"It's more subtle than that." I stopped, turned to her. "Love, if you felt lied to or patronized, I'm sorry."

She swallowed hard. "Patronized, maybe."

"That was never our intention. Listen, your Uncle Dan thinks we need to manage our relations with the press. So the story they are reporting is ours, and not someone else's."

"Oh." Her manic energy seemed to drop away. She stood thinking for a moment. "Yeah, that actually makes sense."

VEE'S DOOR WAS AJAR. I STEPPED TOWARD it, heard movement, stopped. There was Vee in her windowless bedroom, facing away from me, taking off her dress. Behind her, the connecting door into her sister's room was open. Light was streaming through the window at the far end. The sequins at the edges of the dress flashed in the low evening sun. Like fish scales.

Vee laid the dress out carefully on the bed. She reached to the top bunk, took an old Bauhaus T-shirt of mine, pulled it on.

I smiled, about to turn away.

I saw Vee kneel, reach out to the rear panel of the dress, run her fingers along it. She lifted it away from the front panel at the strap, held it in the flat of her hand. She crossed the floor to the door into her sister's room. She walked toward the window, stood, silhouetted, dress in hand. Tiny specks of light on every wall.

I stepped forward, stood in the doorway of Vee's room, watching. The area Vee was holding seemed duller than the rest, and when its sequins did glint it was not blue but orange-red.

"Vee! Cal!" Elsa's voice from the kitchen.

I slipped out into the hall, stood watching through the hinge jamb as Vee returned to her own room. She folded the dress at the middle and slipped it down between her mattress and the wall.

"THAT DRESS TODAY," I SAID TO ELSA, as we stood washing dishes at the sink.

"I know," she said. "Something really not right there."

"I saw her hide it down the side of her bed. I mean, it feels wrong to breach her privacy . . ."

"We need to know," she said. "Absolutely we do."

"So what do we do?"

"Vee!" she shouted. "Honey! Can you go fetch the ice cream from the freezer?"

Vee sauntered in. "Dan's smoking cigarettes on the patio. What do you want to do about that?"

"Nothing."

Vee rolled her eyes. "Hmm." She opened the fridge, made a play of opening the icebox.

"The freezer downstairs," said Elsa. "In the storage room."

"Why can't Dad?"

"Your father and I are talking."

Vee rolled her eyes again. But she took the key Elsa handed her and headed out of the door.

I FOUND THE DRESS AT ONCE, BETWEEN Vee's bed and the wall.

Elsa was waiting in the kitchen. I held the dress by the straps, let it unroll. The sequins sent tiny shards of light onto every surface. Elsa took the dress from me, turned it around. A brown stain in the rear panel below the right shoulder.

I said, "She brought something home with her from the island."

"And you didn't tell me."

"I wish I had now."

I heard the door of the apartment swing open, heard Vee kick off her shoes in the hall, heard the door slam shut.

"We agree it's a bloodstain?" said Elsa.

I nodded. Elsa blinked hard, handed me the dress. From the front it looked perfect. You wouldn't know. But when I turned it over there was no mistaking the small tear in the darker blue fabric underneath, and the stain that radiated out from it. Like Elsa's pictures. Carmine 12 shading to cinnabar 14.

FOURTEEN

WE ASKED DAN TO take Vee out.

"Vee," said Dan as she entered the room. "Vee, what say you and I go for a walk?"

"I'm fourteen, Dan."

"Which means what? You don't do walks?"

"Which means there's nowhere to walk to. Literally, like, nothing." She looked at Elsa, suspicious, then at me. "What are they planning?"

"What about that Viking grave?" I said.

"It's barbed wire and dead grass," said Vee. "Maybe some skater goths drinking beer and smoking weed."

"Sounds edgy," said Dan. "Let's go."

"Thanks, Dan," I said.

"It's not edgy. It's lame." Vee looked at me, then at Elsa. "Fine," she said. She walked from the room, angry.

"Thirty minutes?" said Dan.

"An hour would be good," said Elsa.

WE DREW THE BED AWAY FROM THE wall, but Vee had hidden nothing there beyond the dress. I pulled the sheet from the mattress, pulled the cover from the duvet. Elsa rifled through Vee's diary. I searched Vee's schoolbag. We searched every drawer, opened every jeweled box.

Nothing.

Elsa stood on a chair and ran her hand across the tops of the wardrobes. Nothing more than dust.

We put everything back exactly as we'd found it. We agreed that I would speak to her, but when Vee returned something went wrong. I heard shouting from the kitchen, and when I walked in Vee was in tears and Elsa's eyes were white with fury.

"Fucking hypocrite," Vee spat at her mother. She turned on her heel and strode out.

"I'll take this," I said.

"I think that might be best," said Elsa.

Vee was sitting on the bed. I sat down on the floor, facing her.

"Unbelievable," she said. "Can you believe she would do that?"

"Do what, love?"

But Vee was looking around at the bed, at the bookcases, at the wardrobe. She could tell.

"She searched my room, Dad."

"*We* searched your room, love."

"Oh." She sat for a time examining her foot, rubbing her thumb across the side of the arch. Her voice, when she spoke, was very small. "What did you find?"

"Vee, you know what we found."

She nodded as if to herself.

"I know I have to take the dress to the police," she said, her voice small.

Then she got up and sat down beside me on the floor. I put my arm around her and we sat for the longest time, saying nothing.

AT ELEVEN, WHEN DAN AND I SAT drinking whisky in the living room, and the sun was still up, and the sky was red and the clouds feathered to gray, when we heard Elsa's footsteps in the hall, heard the front door sliding open, my brother looked at me as he shouted, "Elsa?" And Elsa walked into the apartment, and through the dark space that we called the library. And she stood there at the edge of the room in the pool of light from a spotlight in the ceiling and said very simply, "Maybe you can manage to get Vee off her computer. I'm meeting Hedda."

Dan looked at me, and I could tell he expected me to say something, so I said, "Sure," because I didn't know what else to say.

"Want to go with her, Cal?" said Dan. "I can hold the fort."

I looked at Elsa.

"Better not," she said.

As we watched, Elsa stepped out of the light and I saw her shadow move through the library and into the hall, and Dan was looking at me all the while.

"You okay with that?" he said, as the door swung shut.

And a part of me was running after Elsa, asking her not to go, but I said, "Price of a good marriage. Bit of give-and-take."

"So your marriage is good?"

"Sure."

"So you're okay with bars and late nights? Wow."

I said nothing.

He reached across, began to pour himself another whisky. "I don't buy it, Cal."

"Drop the concern. It's what we do."

"Elsa goes to bars while you sit at home, seething."

"Do you see me seething?"

"And, I mean, these pictures of hers." He gestured up at the print above the sofa. "All those huge swaths of Rothko red. All those purples. I've never known what they mean. I'm not even sure that I like them. But they express something, for fuck's sake . . . Some kind of inner landscape . . ."

I looked up at *Carmine 34*. So young she had been when she had taken it. So full of confidence. So certain that this would be the picture that would make her name. And it did. For a time.

"They're American crime scenes," I said.

Dan laughed. "Aye, right."

"No, they actually are," I said. "Elsa had this agreement with the PD. She would travel out with the detectives, hang back until the crime scene technicians were done."

My brother stopped laughing. "Okay."

"Once the body was gone she would photograph what was left without a lens, using their lights."

"Blood," said Dan.

"And the other stuff. You know, transforming the viscera and the ooze and just the unbearable fucking cruelty of murder into something better, I guess."

"She actually said that?"

"No, she said if she knew what her pictures were about, she wouldn't have needed to make them."

"Wow. That is some hinterland your wife has there. When did she last take a picture?"

"It's been years, mate."

"So Elsa has this whole churning inner world," said Dan. "And it's no longer finding expression. And now with Licia gone . . ."

"Missing. Important distinction."

"Missing," he said. "Aye. But, Cal, are you surprised that your wife goes to bars without you?"

AT FIVE I WOKE TO ELSA'S ARM, trailed carelessly across my chest, her hand grazing my right nipple. I lay for a while, watching her face, listened to the gentle wheezing of her breath.

In. In. Out.

Smiling now, eyes closed. Beautiful in sleep.

"Elsa," I said.

"Mmm."

"Elsa, I love you."

"Mmm," she said.

I lifted her arm carefully from my chest. I sat for a while looking out from the terrace toward the trees, watched as a cat chased butterflies on the lawn.

I searched through my phone, found the video files that Tvist's people had undeleted. That female figure in darkness, breathing in-in-and-out, beautiful and indistinct. But if the figure was Elsa, and surely it was, what did the files actually show? The first was time-stamped 03:01 on the twenty-third, an hour before Elsa returned home. Perhaps then she had betrayed me with another man. Perhaps that man had filmed her as she slept. But the time stamp on the second file was 02:57 on the twenty-fourth, while Elsa and I stood waiting on the slipway for news of Licia.

I unblocked the number and called it. No longer in use.

I sat for the longest time, watching the files and watching my wife, wondering what this was. Was it evidence of betrayal, or of something else?

What am I not seeing, Elsa?

Stupid, really, because all I had to do was ask. But some instinct warned me that catching my wife in a lie would be the end of us.

FIFTEEN

CHIEF OF POLICE EPHRAIM Tvist sat, hands clasped, watching my daughter, his thumbs resting on his chin. He looked down at the plastic bag on the desk in front of him. He leaned forward, turned it so the opening faced him. He examined the dress, then let go of the bag.

"It's already contaminated," said Vee.

Tvist tilted his head away. Hands still clasped, he traced a line from temple to crown with his right index finger. "It's contaminated, you say . . ."

"I wore it. To the memorial service. My dad didn't know. And I do realize that this compromises its value as evidence. It was impulsive and immature of me. I truly am very sorry."

"Viktoria, it sounds as though your parents have already had with you the discussion I was planning to have."

Vee nodded, sniffed hard, blinked twice. "They have."

Tvist looked at me. "Then perhaps we don't need to have that discussion a second time."

"She gets it," I said.

"I've learned my lesson. I swear. Is it true you don't send children to jail?"

Tvist looked at Vee, amused. "I would expect your parents to know this."

Vee pulled her chair forward. "So you can murder someone here and your family stays together?"

"Vee," I said. "Don't go getting any ideas."

"No, it's cool."

Tvist smiled very broadly.

"All right," she said, sitting up. "First, I need to declare that I was the one looking at the Tactical Brigades' stuff on the Internet."

Tvist's smile did not leave his face. If anything it broadened, becoming kinder and more open. "May I ask why?"

"They had some answers I sort of agreed with. Not the violence, though."

Tvist turned to me, still smiling. But there was a question in the look he sent me.

I said, "We work hard to transmit our values to our daughters."

Vee said, "Being politically incorrect isn't a crime, Dad. And I didn't agree with everything they said about black people and Muslims." She turned to Tvist. "Back in D.C. my best friend is black. He's really not trying to pollute the white race. I'm pretty sure he's actually a virgin."

Tvist was looking at me with his dark, dark eyes, an eyebrow half-raised.

Vee said, "If you're thinking I'm a fascist, Mr. Tvist, I'm not."

"Why would I think that?"

"Because if I was, would I be helping you?"

The look on Tvist's face: somewhere between disbelief and amusement.

"She's fourteen," I said. "Figuring stuff out."

"Dad," said Vee, "don't apologize for me. I really do not view violence as a solution to complex social problems, Mr. Tvist."

"Good," said Tvist.

"Some of what they're saying isn't so extreme, though. A lot of people are against immigration."

Tvist pressed the tips of his fingers together. "Are you against immigration, Viktoria?"

"In America we have whole cities that are run by black people, for the benefit of black people."

"Really?"

"No offense."

"None taken," said Tvist, his expression unreadable.

"I mean, look at Gothenburg in Sweden. Look at the East End of Oslo. They're practically no-go areas. Ordinary white people are scared to cross the Aker River. The police won't go there."

"Won't we? That's news to me, Viktoria. Perhaps you should spend a little time down there, take a look."

"Vee," I said, "you don't think maybe you're letting the prejudices of people in our neighborhood inform your judgment?"

"You're the one who wants us to live in a white neighborhood, Dad."

"That is not why we chose the apartment." I turned to Tvist. "It's set in parkland. We thought it was for six months."

Was that disappointment in Tvist's smile? Very hard to tell. "Viktoria," he said, "what makes people like the Tactical Brigades difficult to investigate is that there actually is no physical brigade.

Most of them never meet in real life. They exchange ideas on discussion forums and recruit people who seem receptive to those ideas. We call it radicalization, but it's a slow and painstaking process, and it takes months. Beginning with ideas that don't seem so very far from the mainstream. They're watching for shares and for likes. Then they invite you to private discussions. They're especially interested in people of your age."

Vee looked down at her feet, weighing her thoughts, wide-eyed. "I never shared anything. I swear. I may have liked some stuff."

"Oh, Vee," I said. "Love."

"It gets exhausting, always having to say the right-on thing all the time, you know, Dad. But I swear on my life I didn't think I was putting anyone in danger."

"All right," said Tvist. "Lesson learned. Why don't you tell me about the dress, Viktoria?"

Vee brightened. "I took photos of where I found it. Here." She reached across the desk, handed him the phone that Edvard had given her. "I'd like my actual phone back, by the way."

"And you may have it when you leave." Tvist began scrolling through the photos. "You tell me you think this is Alicia Curtis's dress?"

"It is her dress."

Tvist sent me a questioning look.

"Yes," I said. "I think it is."

His eyes returned to Vee.

"But you can see there's one bullet hole." Vee turned, tapped herself on the back just below her right shoulder blade. "About here. Surrounded by blood."

"Possible bullet hole," said Tvist. "Possible blood."

"I know you have to say that. But a bullet wound like that would be survivable. Wouldn't it?"

"Hard for me to know."

"It would," said Vee, as if the fact were nonnegotiable. "So you know she was alive, on the island, probably after the massacre."

Tvist had his elbows on the desk, was sucking at the joint of his right thumb.

"Vee," I said, "that's not really something you or I can judge."

"But this moves the case forward, doesn't it? Because it's not a fatal wound. And your people didn't find the dress, Mr. Tvist."

"Viktoria, I don't think we can exclude the possibility that she took off her dress before she got in the water."

Vee's face fell. She seemed to shrink in on herself. "Yes," she said. "Yes, I see what you're saying. God, I can be stupid. But it does show she was there, on the island, at least."

"VEE! CAN YOU GO FETCH THE ICE cream?"

Vee sloped into the kitchen. "If you and Dad want to talk, tell me. You don't need to lie."

"Vee," I said, "don't call your mother a liar."

"If it's about me being a fascist, Mum, I'm really not."

"No one believes for a moment that you're a fascist."

"Dad does. I'm going to play *Battle Royale*."

Elsa watched as Vee sloped from the room. She turned to me. "Well, at least we know it wasn't Licia."

For a moment I thought I'd misheard, that Elsa could not possibly mean what she had said. But her eyes told me I had not misheard.

"You seriously thought it could be Licia on those sites?" I said.

"I'm relieved it wasn't. Vee's so smart and so cynical. She'll figure out the problems with what those men believe. With Licia I would be truly concerned. She is too easily overwhelmed by other people's arguments. She's so out of place in the modern world."

"Licia's not one of life's losers, Elsa."

"Really? I'm not sure that's how she feels about herself, Cal. The modern world is cruel to the unexceptional and the unbeautiful."

"She's both beautiful and exceptional."

Elsa was looking at me candidly. She raised an eyebrow.

"Fine," I said. "She's a doer, not a thinker."

"She has twenty-three followers on Instagram. That tells you how the world sees her, Cal."

WE HAD TRIED TO PUSH LICIA TOWARD rebellion, but she had remained dutiful and devoted. She helped about the house; she carried out the trash and washed the dishes and did her homework, always diligent, always slow. She completed not only her own chores but Vee's too, singing all the while, though Vee would not let Licia near her schoolwork.

When Licia first began to attend a house church, in the northern D.C. suburbs, we wondered if she was growing away from us. But if anything it made her more devoted. She would come into my study while I was working, empty my wastepaper from the basket, then ask if there was anything she could do to make my life easier, if her attitude was all it could be.

"At her age, I was lying to my parents and hanging with the bands at the Rockefeller," Elsa said.

"And we should be glad she isn't living your life."

Licia only ever fought with Vee, and every time it was Vee who provoked her. Little Vee, to whom everything came so easily, who at fourteen knew so much more about the world than her older sister. "C-minus," she would whisper into Licia's ear. "D-plus." And Licia's eyes would fill with furious tears, and she would fly at her sister, and tear at her, and Vee would give as good as she got.

Ten minutes later they would be the best of friends again.

SIXTEEN

THE NEXT DAY WE sat on the stiff white chairs of a studio behind a white table covered in a gray linen cloth. We wore clothes that were formal but not excessively so. On Elsa's lap Franklin gurgled happily, gnawing at her thumb. We would answer the same three questions for the BBC, NRK, WSJ, NBC, FOX, CNN, TVZ, and a Christian rock station from Richmond, Virginia. Four minutes each, plus three minutes for turnaround. Elsa had balked at Christian rock, but Dan had insisted it was a *key demographic*. And so we answered eight sets of identical questions, exactly as he had briefed us:

—**Tell us about the moment you first realized Licia was missing, Elsa.**
—Well, as a mother my first thought was . . .

—**Cal, what kind of person is your daughter, Alicia Curtis?**

—Licia is the kindest, funniest, and sweetest child a father
could wish for . . .

—Viktoria, do you have a message for your sister?

Vee paused when the Christian rock journalist asked her that
final question. She sent me a look that said, *Do I really have to?*
"Go on, Vee," I said.

Vee looked at Elsa. She looked at me. She looked at the camera. "I know I'm not the best sister you could have, Licia. I know
I should be more like you. I know I could be kinder, and sweeter,
and funnier, and when you come back I promise that I will be all
of those things. But this is all just so . . ." She looked at the camera, at the lights, at the vase on the table with its single white lily.

The journalist smiled encouragingly from beneath a black
beanie hat. She was dressed in a black singlet and a long black
jersey skirt. Nothing about her said Christian rock, except for the
steel crucifix that hung on a looped leather thong from her left
wrist.

Vee's gaze shifted from the journalist to the camera. "We're no
good at this, Licia. I mean, look at us. You can see we're close to
falling apart." Angry tears were forming at the corners of her eyes.
She smudged them away with the flat of her hand.

I looked at Dan, who was standing close by. Surely he would
step forward, crouch down, and whisper to the journalist, suggest
a break and a sip of water and a second take? But Dan simply nodded at me, then nodded toward Vee.

"Oh my God," said Vee under her breath. She turned to me. "I
promised myself I wasn't going to cry."

I reached out, put my hand on hers. Elsa did the same.

"Almost done, honey," whispered Elsa.

And then my little daughter sniffed heavily, and looked straight down the barrel of the lens. "Please, Licia, it's time to come home." And her eyes were raw, and tears were cascading down her cheeks.

I leaned forward and took her in my arms.

After the longest of pauses the journalist said, "Viktoria, that was amazing. I've cut." She stood up, turned off the camera, slid out the memory card, and placed it in a small metal holder.

Dan crossed the floor to the table and crouched in front of us, eyes shining. "That, people, was the one."

The journalist was at Dan's side, crouching down.

"Viktoria, that was very moving. People will share what you said." She turned to me. "Mr. Curtis, may I ask you a question off the record?"

"Sure." I got to my feet.

"Okay. Would you wish Alicia had her gun with her during the events on the island?"

Elsa raised an eyebrow. Vee looked as if the someone had slapped her across the thigh.

I looked at the journalist. She was serious. I laughed. "What a strangely American thing to ask."

"This in no way affects the way we will present your case," said the journalist. "It's just a question that's been troubling me these last few days. I can't quite pray it away." She smiled a self-deprecating smile, then produced a photo, which she handed to me. "Someone at the station found this. It's being widely shared."

The picture showed Licia, wearing ear protectors and clear plastic glasses, her stance upright and confident, her shoulders locked. Her right forefinger curled around the trigger of a heavy black pistol, the fingers of her left hand bracing her trigger hand, her right eye half-closed. Vee looked furtively at the image, then away, as if she didn't want me to read her reaction.

"This has to be a fake," I said. "Right?"

Elsa nodded. Vee avoided my gaze.

"Okay," said the journalist. "Sure." I could see there was more she wanted to say about the picture. Instead she said, "The interview will be up on the website by seven. I hope it will make a difference. And—again, personally—please know that your family, and most especially your adorable blond children, will be in my prayers over the coming days."

"You're praying for us?" said Vee. "Wow."

"I have been. I will continue."

Vee smiled, a little uncertain.

"Thank you," I said. "I'm strangely comforted by the thought of your praying for us."

She smiled and embraced me very warmly. "And that is the wonderful thing about the power of prayer, Mr. Curtis."

"THAT PICTURE, VEE," I SAID, AS THE journalist was packing away her things.

"Yeah, honey," said Elsa. "What was that?"

Vee swallowed hard. "So, the picture's not a fake."

I took out the photo again. "It isn't?"

How confident Licia looked in the picture. Lithe and alert.

Vee said, "You know when you and Mum were at the modern art museum, and we said we would go to the aquarium?"

"Virginia Beach," I said.

"Yeah. Licia got ID and we went to the range."

"Damn," said Elsa, almost admiringly.

"Yeah," said Vee. "I mean, we did go to the aquarium, but we were there like half an hour."

"Vee," I said, "did you get ID too?"

"No, because Licia was my 'designated guardian.'"

"You fired a weapon?"

"Only a two-two. Licia fired a Glock."

"Wow," said Elsa.

"Licia was actually pretty good," said Vee. "We both were."

"You guys about ready to go?" I looked up. Dan was standing with the journalist by the door of the studio.

"We're going to need five minutes," I said.

"Sure, bro." He opened the door for the journalist and stepped through it after her.

The door swung slowly shut. Elsa's expression was unreadable. I looked at Vee.

"What?" said Vee. "Are you going to tell me, *We're not gun people*? Or all about how Mum stopped shooting?"

"Please don't anticipate my reaction, Vee . . ."

"You can stop judging me. I promise I will never again do such an irresponsible thing."

"I'm not judging you. If anything I'm judging your sister. What was she thinking?"

THE NEXT MORNING I DROVE DAN TO the airport. He sat in silence all the way to the terminal. "No need to come in," he said as I drew up.

"Wish you weren't going to be so far away," I called after him.

He stopped, turned, looked at me for a moment. "Me too, brother," he said, and headed inside.

I WAS BACK BY SEVEN, MAKING BREAKFAST. The smell of coffee in the grinder, of oranges in the squeezer: these things made me feel Licia's absence so keenly.

At home in D.C. she and I were always first up. Licia would sit at the breakfast bar, finishing her homework from the night before. Sometimes she would look across as I was fitting the filter into the coffee maker, or pressing oranges through the squeezer, and we would stop what we were doing and smile and say nothing. Then she would go back to her math, and I would return to making breakfast. I would cut bread and boil eggs and fill lunch boxes, and when I looked up she would be frowning quietly at her exercise book.

"I would like to be exceptional, Dad, of course I would," she would say if I noticed she was struggling. "And maybe one day I will achieve something exceptional."

"Licia," I would say, "you are utterly exceptional to me."

"I'm more a doer than a thinker, I guess. And you don't need to over-praise me."

She didn't want my help. I would watch, a little heartbroken, as she forced her way through the problem, quietly speaking the numbers to herself. Mostly, though, this was a happy time. Just the two of us, without her sister there to remind Licia of what she was not.

ON THE COUNTERTOP MY PHONE CHIRRUPED. ALREADY people were attaching hashtags to the video of our appeal: #blondgrrl and #islandheroine, as well as #Licia and #fightback. Dan had good instincts. In the video we looked united in our grief.

Dan had been right about Tvist too: the police had briefed the press about Licia. Thanks to them, people knew that a girl matching the description of my daughter shouted out a warning in the main house; that she comforted a boy she met in the woods; that she shielded that same boy from harm in the water despite the wound in her shoulder. Licia had cut short the massacre, it seemed, by throwing away the metal case so that the men had eventually run out of ammunition. She was a hero. An actual, all-American hero. Amid all the uncertainty, that one thought brought me comfort.

I didn't like the picture of my daughter holding the pistol. I didn't like the way the image began to mutate, to combine with images of the Andersens and calls to action. I hated the hashtags #blondgrrl and #fightback. But people were angry about the attacks on Garden Island and wanted revenge. They needed a hero too, and in my daughter they found someone they could believe in.

None of us had predicted that future for Licia.

SEVENTEEN

THE ROAD WAS UNSURFACED; neat hedges lined both sides. I drove across one cattle guard, then another, then a third. A hand-carved wooden sign stood to the left of the path:

PATRIOTIC ORDER OF THE TEMPLE KNIGHT

Ahead of me a woman stepped into the road, smiling. I wound down the window, leaned out, smiled in return.

"*Hei.*"

"Hello," I said.

Her white-blond hair spiraled into a stern bun. She was twenty, I guessed, but dressed like a woman of sixty in a gray smock and black lace-up shoes. A simple leather bag lay slung across her shoulder.

"I'm looking for the Order of the Temple Knight."

She smiled. "Isn't everyone?"

Beyond us ash trees stood protectively around a white farmhouse. The gabled roof sloped steeply to keep snow from gathering in winter.

She said, "You are in the wrong place, friend. Bror is seeing no one."

I opened my door, got out. "You make it sound as if I am in the right place."

This time the edges of her mouth twitched downward. "He is not expecting you. Ahead you will find the gate is locked."

"Maybe I'll climb the gate."

From her bag she produced a phone. She held it up, took a picture of the car. She dialed a number, spoke in English, making sure I understood the threat.

"Bring dogs to gate number two."

"My daughter is missing," I said as calmly as I could.

She hesitated. "You're not a journalist?"

"No."

Her stance softened. I saw curiosity in her eyes. Sympathy, perhaps. "You seek Bror's counsel?"

"He showed me kindness. He might remember me."

From the farmhouse the sound of barking. She glanced toward the house.

"Please," I said.

She studied my face for a moment. She reached out, put a hand on my elbow. "Are you the father of Alicia Curtis?"

"You know who she is?"

"Bror would not forgive me if I sent you away. Come."

"And the dogs?"

She smiled. "No one is bringing the dogs."

The kindness in her smile almost broke me.

I slid Franklin's car seat out of its mount, slammed the car door shut. The sound cut harsh and sharp across the drowsy heat of the day. In the hedgerow the crickets fell silent, though Franklin did not wake.

"This way," she said.

By the house was a large meadow. Above the meadow a sparrow hawk hung noiselessly, watching for the rustle of mice in the long grass below. I heard a cuckoo and, farther off, crows. We came to an iron gate. It slid open on silent hinges. The hawk hung in the air, wingtips shimmering. As we passed, it tilted and slid toward the far edge of the meadow, hung there watching silently down.

Our footsteps echoed off the white stone building ahead. In an upstairs window I caught movement. I looked up to see another female figure, also in gray. There, then gone. Like breath.

Above the open door hung another carved wooden sign:

YOU ARE ENTERING A PLACE OF CONTEMPLATION

"After you," said the woman.

The air in the hallway was cool. I called out, "Hello?"

The timbers of the house flexed and creaked. I heard a large dog barking close by, then another. When I turned to look behind me the woman had disappeared.

"Hello?" I called out, louder this time.

"Ah."

Bror stepped into view from a doorway halfway down. He pulled the door to, then turned, stood there in his gray vestment, arms open in welcome.

"Cal Curtis," he said, as if I were his long-lost friend.

"Yes." How did he know?

"And what a luminously beautiful child."

"His name is Franklin."

"You are welcome. Franklin is welcome. Perhaps your son would like to continue his nap on some lovely soft cushions?"

"He'll be okay in his car seat. Thank you." I set the seat on the flagstones.

"Handsome little fellow," said Bror. "He will be fine there by the door. Now, we're just finishing off . . ." With that same open-armed gesture, he turned away from me and into the room behind him.

I heard voices. A woman appeared. Heels and a pressed linen suit. She saw me and hesitated, a look of surprise on her face.

I stepped forward. "I'm Cal."

Arno's mother narrowed her eyes.

I said, "I'm Licia Curtis's father."

"I know who you are. I just . . ." She smiled, took my left hand. "Anyway, hello again. I'm Mari."

"Hello, Mari. I didn't expect to see you here either."

She looked toward the side room. Bror emerged, his arm around Arno's shoulder. The boy saw me and stopped. With empty eyes he looked at Bror. Bror bent down, whispered something. Arno nodded, walked slowly past me toward the front door.

"Nice to see you, Cal," said Mari as she passed. "This is an extraordinary place. The man has something . . ." She took her son's hand, and together they stood for a moment on the front step. Then they were gone.

I turned toward Bror. "That was unexpected," I said.

"Sadly the boy is yet to speak. I do what I can to provide counsel." That same reassuring gentleness. That same disarming smile. I tried to imagine Bror twenty years earlier, in the days before he became a priest, smoking cigarillos and talking earnestly about politics. I could not.

"Now," he said. "Follow." He waited until I drew level, then turned down the hallway. "I understand Police Chief Tvist is taking an interest in your case? Did he cite 'exceptional operational circumstances'?"

I laughed. "Why?"

Bror was not smiling as he turned to me. "You must be careful of this man. He may not be the ally he appears to be. Coffee?"

"Coffee would be good," I said.

The kitchen was a huge vaulted room, wood-beamed and white-painted, with glass doors that gave on to a vegetable garden. On the facing wall a single oil painting showed a young girl kneeling in a dark stone vault, gazing upon the tomb of a knight.

I stood listening. You could almost feel the house breathe, feel the timbers as they expanded and contracted.

From a cupboard above his head Bror took a stiff-sided paper bag. A single fruit fly zigzagged up into the air. It hovered above him like a mote of dust trapped in the sunlight. He caught my gaze, looked up, smiled. "Ineradicable little buggers. They come in on the coriander plants. Then they make the kitchen their own." A twinkle in his eye, as if he were challenging me to challenge him.

My phone rang.

"Your wife, perhaps?"

I looked down at the screen. "Excuse me a moment."

"Of course."

I walked out into the hall.

"Cal. You disappeared. With Franklin. I got a little worried."

"Franklin's here, with me, sleeping peacefully." I walked to the front door, stood on the porch, watching the doves in their pear tree. "I was about to call you. I'm having lunch."

"Kind of a late lunch."

"Coffee, really."

"You're in town? The car's gone."

I could feel the next lie coming. *Yes, Elsa, I'm in town.*

I stopped. I looked about me, at the gravel drive and the courtyard and the birds circling a tractor in the field below.

"I'm not in town. I'm at Bror's farmhouse."

"With Franklin." The longest of pauses.

"You told me I could meet him."

"I did."

"Can I be honest with you?"

"Honesty's always good . . ." she said cautiously.

"He's actually kind of an amazing guy. I can see how you would have hit that . . . I mean, spiritually, at least . . ."

She laughed. "You're not actually jealous?"

"He radiates something I don't have. I wish I had his charisma."

She gave a theatrical sigh. "You beautiful jealous lying fuck of a man."

"Forgive me?"

"Sure. Just don't go getting converted."

I ended the call and returned to the kitchen. In the middle of the kitchen floor the young woman in the gray shift dress was standing with her head inclined toward Bror. She turned as I entered, stood facing me, hands folded formally at her waist. Her feet were bare now.

"Hello," I said.

She glanced at Bror. Bror nodded.

"I was abrupt when you arrived." She looked at me, then looked down at her feet. "I am contrite. You are the father of a heroine. You are always welcome here." Far too young, I thought, to be speaking so formally.

"I believe Milla wishes to apologize," said Bror, his hand on her arm.

She smiled, her gaze still averted. "I do. I wish to apologize." She glanced up at me, eyes dancing, smiled the most charming of smiles.

"No need," I said.

"I believe there is," she said. Again she averted her gaze.

Bror said, "I'm sure Cal understands that your instinct is to protect, Milla, and that you were dutifully protecting me." He looked at me. I nodded. "And perhaps you will serve him with coffee? As a token of your contrition?"

"Gladly." She turned toward the counter.

Strange to see this woman so submissive, when before—

"How is your extraordinary wife?" asked Bror, breaking my thought.

"She's well," I said. "All things considered. She sends her very best."

My mind flashed to an image of Elsa, fresh from the shower, throwing her arms around this strange otherworldly man.

Bror stepped toward me, studied my face. He smiled a wry smile. "You have my respect. To take on a woman so committed to her cause requires moral strength."

I laughed, but he was serious.

"Elsa set a standard that I could not meet. Her radical honesty defeated me in the end. Though she inspired me perhaps to seek out my own calling." He smiled, placed a hand on my forearm. "But total honesty is not easy when you are dealing with a missing child. People blame each other, and say things that are better left unsaid. Are you being kind to one another?"

"We are."

"Good."

He turned toward the woman Milla, who handed him two cups of coffee. He nodded, and she returned to the counter, where she stood watching us, her hands folded at her waist. Bror turned, offered me a cup. Milla hovered by the sink. I smiled. She half smiled, then looked away.

"Will you not join us in a cup?" I said.

Her eyes flicked to me, then away. Bror sent her a look that I could not read. Now she was slipping from the room. Sound of bare feet on dry stone, the gentle swish of her shift dress.

"That was kind of you," said Bror. "But unnecessary. Tell me, why are you standing here before me?"

"I want to know who you are."

"Ah." He considered this. "How very direct. Do you mean the Patriotic Order of the Temple Knight? Or do you mean the student who once knew your wife?"

"Is there a difference?"

"Locking horns with the priest." He smiled a wry smile. "This is the job of the satirist, no? You are wondering if we are in some way connected to those men and their brutal acts? After all, we—and they—carry the name of the Knights Templar."

"I have asked myself that question."

"The Patriotic Order of the Temple Knight is a chivalric order, committed to honor and valor. With our young followers we meditate on the figure of the crusader knight, whom we consider the most complete embodiment of courage and honor. We seek inspiration from his deeds. But he is a metaphor. Which should be obvious. We are not literal knights and nor is he. We do not wish to rampage through the Middle East, spilling the blood of our Muslim brothers. Though we do have some very fine horses in our paddock."

"And those other Knights Templar?"

"The—quote-unquote—Tactical Brigades?"

I nodded.

He shook his head. "These boys have a narrow understanding of metaphor: the gun is the lance; the boat is the horse; the refugee is the Saracen. They lack the intelligence to understand that this is a ridiculous proposition. But they outwitted our police. And their talk about employing children as actual soldiers? If that's where we are headed in the West, then we know from other countries it's a terrifyingly effective tactic, no? What decent man would dare to return fire, knowing his target was thirteen?"

"These men admire you. They quote you very widely."

"We've taken down our websites. All materials. You can't even google us now. I will not have these acts on my conscience." A sorrowful look passed across his features. "I sincerely hope better people admire us too. What I teach—the praxis our true followers observe—is more akin to Buddhism or Sufism. Balance duty with pleasure. Take time out to breathe."

"I still don't really understand what you believe."

"Cherish and protect those you love. Beyond that I don't really care what my followers believe. It's the *praxis* that counts. Live the good life. Know the consoling qualities of a good cup of coffee . . ."

"You brought me coffee on the day of the massacre."

A sober look. "You really mustn't thank me."

"Still, it did console me a little. To know we were not completely alone."

He studied me for a moment. "You're father to a heroine. To two heroines, most likely. These things run in the family, you know."

I laughed. "I'm not a hero, Bror."

He laughed gently. "And yet you married the most exceptional woman. Let us take with us our coffee as we walk."

WE STOOD AT THE TOP OF A rise that looked down over the outbuildings. A single vast shed, two stories high, painted red; and beside the shed a lower building, long and narrow and painted black, where the horses were stabled in winter and the dogs were housed all year around. In a field beyond the outbuildings three young women in shift dresses were crouched, turning the earth with trowels and hoes, each working her way along a neatly plowed row of potato plants. One paused for a moment, rubbed the dry earth off her hands. She glanced up the hill toward Bror, who nodded in her direction. The girl nodded back and picked up her trowel. How happy they looked in their work; how comfortable Bror seemed in his role of protector and guide.

"Okay," I said. "Where do I sign?"

"I would welcome you as a member today." He turned to me. His eyes searched mine. "If I thought for a moment you were sincere."

"Almost makes me want to get down on my knees and pray."

He laughed. "Then let us pray together."

"I said almost."

"I welcome the fallen. Bring them back to the fold."

That strange charisma of his. Where was it from?

He seemed to catch the question in my gaze. "What?" he said.

"You're unusually *alpha* for a priest."

"Says the alpha-satirist."

I looked at the girls in the field, at the gray of their shift dresses blending with the parched farmland.

"Were those girls *fallen* when they came to you?"

"No more than you are, Cal," he said. He smiled a warm, enveloping smile.

"I don't consider myself fallen."

"What fallen man knows that he is?"

I pointed at myself. "Not fallen."

His eyes were dancing now. "We are sparring a little. This is fun, no? The alpha-satirist and the alpha-priest. But in answer to your question, you would have to ask the girls themselves. We really are very nonjudgmental."

"Okay," I said, "I can see there's something to what you do here."

He became serious. "Then I have a question I wish you to consider. In the midst of all you are going through it is easy to feel cast adrift, to lose sight of what you are fighting for. There were very few heroes on the day of the massacre. We all want to believe that we would have the presence of mind to do what your daughter did, but in reality most people simply freeze when confronted with mortal danger. And because of this Alicia Curtis will be turned into public property, and in ways that you cannot control. People will claim her for their side."

"Already happening," I said. "We're trying to ignore it."

"So I wonder this: Is there an image of your daughter that you wish to preserve?"

"An image that I wish to preserve?"

I took a swig of coffee. I could feel his eyes on me. The coffee was strong and black, its bitter edge tempered with a gentle sweetness.

Beyond the shed was a large field. A small herd of horses stood by the trees at the far end, feeding from a hay bale.

"Are those your horses?" I said.

"They are."

"They hardly look big enough to wage war."

Bror smiled. "No need to answer my question. But do think about what I'm asking you."

He put a hand on my arm. I blinked, and in that instant I saw Licia in a sea of light.

I opened my eyes. Bror was staring off toward the horses.

I said, "She was in a blue sequined dress that day. People saw her sleeping under a tree by the water, wearing that dress. I imagine the sun on her hair, and the sun on the fjord, and the light dancing on the dress, and I imagine that she was happy as she slept."

"That is a beautiful image."

"Licia is so quiet and so modest. Her bedroom mirror is covered in dust. Literally." I could hear my voice cracking. "That dress was such a gesture of confidence. And I realize this is a grandiose thought, but in that small moment before the killings I imagine she had the world at her feet. And I hope she was happy and excited. Because she deserves to be."

Bror was silent for a long time. He looked out over his farmstead, as if seeking answers in the landscape. At last he turned to me. "What if we could help anchor for you that image of your daughter?" he said. "Would that be useful?"

"Through meditation?"

He laughed, sought my eyes with his. "You find us a little ridiculous. And that's okay. But hear me out." He put an arm on mine, turned me so that I was facing him. "What if your family were to plant a tree by a grassy bank?"

"We don't want a memorial."

"I agree. And certainly not on Garden Island, in that most godforsaken of places. But might not planting a tree turn that moment of yours into something more permanent? Might it anchor the thought of who Alicia Curtis is, until the day she returns?"

I considered this. Most likely Elsa would like the idea. Vee too.

"It might," I said. "It would certainly be in Licia's spirit."

"Then there is another island a little farther down the fjord that I would like you to see."

EIGHTEEN

WE TOOK OUR BOAT, traveled an hour down the fjord to the island Bror had told me about. *Håøya*. Unpronounceable but beautiful, all abandoned factory buildings and wild-roaming goats. German troops had been stationed in this place during the war. The officers' quarters had been converted to weekend cabins; a small workshop made goat cheese and served coffee.

We moored in a natural harbor on the western side of the island, followed the path up past a simple tarred-wood cabin.

"Strange," said Elsa.

"What is?" said Vee.

"I'm pretty certain that's Quisling's cabin."

Nordic carvings decorated the heavy front door, roughly cut. Smoke curled from the chimney. Plants hung in baskets from the heavy roof beams. Through the windows I saw plates and pans lined up in the white-painted kitchen; the table was set for a meal of crayfish and crab.

"Who's Quisling?" said Vee. But Elsa was disappearing fast up the rise, pushing Franklin's stroller ahead of her, as if sweeping a path.

"Wartime leader," I said. "Under the Germans."

"What, like a *Nazi*?"

"An actual Norwegian Nazi. Sent a lot of Jewish people to their deaths."

"Why are people using his cabin?"

"I don't know."

ELSA HAD STOPPED IN A CLEARING WHERE the redbrick mess hall stood. Through high metal-framed windows you could see the stage where German troops had cheered and entertained each other with music and song on chill Norwegian nights. The guts of a piano were spilled across the floor. Someone had taken an ax to it in cruel revenge for the songs it had once played.

"Why are we doing this here?" said Vee. "If this really is a Nazi island?"

"It belongs to people like us now," said Elsa. "Not to people like that."

We sat for a while at a picnic table outside the mess hall, listening to the wind in the trees, and, farther off, the bells that hung around the necks of the goats. Sunlight dappled prettily on the brickwork. There was an eerie stillness to the buildings that appealed to Elsa, I guessed; something unresolved and unfinished. She knew this place from her childhood. She had said yes to Bror's suggestion at once.

"Who's that?" said Vee, staring toward the far end of the clearing. But when I looked up there was no one there.

HENRIK MET US ON THE EASTERN SIDE, at the water's edge. He had taken the ferry over from the mainland. He nodded at each of us in turn, embraced Vee. Then he took Franklin's stroller wordlessly, walked ahead of us up a gentle rise to a piece of flat land that overlooked the harbor. And here by the spreading canopy of an old willow tree we planted a small willow for Licia.

Elsa hung a copper band on the tree onto which Vee had stamped the words:

TIME TO COME HOME, LICIA

We stood in a ring, closed our eyes, held hands around the sapling. From the fjord you could hear boat engines, and far away the sound of blasting.

"Licia," said Vee, "what I miss most—" Her hand clasped tightly around mine.

"What you're looking forward to," said Elsa's voice, gently correcting her.

"I mean, what I'm *looking forward to* is you and me going back to Whistler. Or anywhere with shitty weather, really. And skiing till Mum and Dad freak the frick out."

I could hear Elsa laughing gently. I squeezed Vee's hand. She squeezed mine back.

"I'm looking forward to breakfast and homework," I said. "Our time, in the mornings, before the chaos of the day."

A long pause. I could feel Elsa's weight shifting, as if she were searching for the words. I leaned toward her. "Are you okay, love?"

I felt her nod. She tightened her grip on mine. She said, "Licia, I'm looking forward to listening more. I don't think I've done enough of that and I plan to make a change. I'm looking forward to learning."

We left the longest of pauses for Henrik, but Henrik said nothing.

"So here we all are, Licia," said Vee. "We're talking to you through a tree. That's how much we want you back. Hope you can hear us. Because otherwise this would all be kind of lame."

Henrik's breathing sounded labored. When I opened my eyes he was there in front of me, stiffly holding Elsa's hand, and Vee's. His eyes were misting with tears. He took a half step backward. Vee stepped with him, taking her hand from mine. She stood there for a time, holding her grandfather's hands in hers, saying nothing, then she let go and turned toward the sapling.

"Oh. Hey there."

A goat and her kid had wandered up, were nibbling at the base of the slender trunk. Vee stepped toward Franklin's stroller and lifted him out. She crouched down, held him close to the kid. Franklin reached out gingerly. The kid sniffed at his fingers, licked carefully at his palm. Franklin burbled and kicked. Henrik caught my eye and smiled.

We had with us bamboo canes and green garden wire. Henrik made a little enclosure to keep the goats off the sapling. Then he walked with us back to the little harbor and we drove him across the sound to Drøbak, where we moored the boat in the guest marina.

The sun was out. It was almost warm. We walked down narrow streets of delicate clapboard houses toward the market square, bought pizza and sour-cream dressing from a restaurant in an ugly gray villa. We sat on the plastic benches outside, eating meditatively, saying very little.

"This was nice," said Henrik. "Thank you for the food." He patted me on the back, got stiffly to his feet.

"Where are you going?" said Vee.

"Home."

Vee stood. Henrik hugged her tightly, nodded to Elsa and to me, then headed off.

"Why's he being weird?" said Vee.

"Because he's your grandfather," Elsa said. "And because the police interviewed him and asked him a whole lot of questions about how close he was to Licia."

"But he would never . . ."

"I know."

We sat for a while, finishing the pizza. "Seriously," said Vee, "why is that woman staring at us?" I looked up. Elsa and I exchanged a look. Because there was no woman.

"Let's go get you an ice cream, Vee," I said.

"Sure," she said brightly. But I saw how she shivered as she got to her feet.

We found a place that sold five flavors of ice cream, with a soft-scoop machine at the back. Elsa and I bought dispenser coffees. Vee bought a white soft-scoop, obscenely large and obscenely soft.

The air was warmer. The breeze had fallen away. We scuffed along through the narrow streets, with their picket fences and their orchards heavy with fruit. Crickets chirped. Apples and pears rotted in the dry grass. Our shoes made little *ruck-ruck* sounds on the softening tarmac.

No one was following us. Just Vee's mind turning paranoid circles. Except . . .

It was then that I saw the woman, at the far end of the park. She was turned away, waiting on the bench outside the baker's, nondescript in her gray shift dress and her flat black shoes, quietly blending in.

"Vee," I said, taking her by the shoulders, turning her in the other direction, "help your mum get Franklin back to the boat."

"Why, Dad?"

Elsa sent me a questioning glance.

"I'd like to take a couple of minutes for myself," I said. "To think about your sister."

"You all right, Dad?"

"Please. Just to . . ."

You okay? Elsa mouthed.

I nodded. "I will be," I said softly.

I watched them disappear down the narrow street with its white-painted fishermen's cottages. I felt a stab of guilt. Wrong to use emotional pain as an excuse. But Vee would be full of questions if I told her the truth. Elsa too.

Milla shielded her face until my wife and daughter were out of sight. I sat down beside her on the bench, looked out across the park.

She said, "Did you like the island?"

I turned to her. "Tell Bror the island was perfect."

She smiled. "I'd prefer him not to know I'm here."

She opened her leather bag, took from it a folded sheet of paper, which she passed to me. "I am sure you will do the right thing with this."

I unfolded the paper. A color photocopy of a Post-it note. The note itself was pink, the handwriting blue, backward-sloping:

16:12
til Ephraim Tvist

"What is this?" I said.

But she was shaking her head. "Thank you for offering me coffee. That was kind." She stood up, nodded a goodbye, began to walk from the square.

I looked at the note. I understood most of the words. The center of town. Two black-clad men. The registration number of a car. I would need Elsa's help to be certain of what I was looking at. But already I had a fairly clear idea. The note was addressed to Ephraim Tvist. Five minutes before the town hall bomb went off.

THAT EVENING I SANG MY LITTLE SON to sleep, my back resting against his crib, my hand trailing through the bars. Franklin held my index finger in his tiny fist as I sang to him the lullaby of mint and clover. When I felt his grip relax I slid my finger out of his. I counted to a hundred, then got quietly to my feet.

From her doorway I watched Vee as she liquidated opponents with rifles and shotguns. She was catlike and alert, talking easily with her American friends over her headset.

In the kitchen I took an orange from the fruit bowl and a peeler from the drawer. I shaved off two strips of peel, which I laid on the chopping board, one above the other. I cut the edges straight with the sharpest of our knives.

The gin bottle was frosted white from the freezer, the shaker so cold that my fingertips stuck to its steel surface.

Over the ice in the shaker I poured a capful of vermouth, then three teaspoonfuls of brine from the olives. The ice cracked. Now the gin, viscous and heavy. I stirred, counting to twenty, poured the liquid carefully down the sides of the crystal glasses. The ritual slowed my thoughts, calmed my nerves. Tiny suspended ice shards refracted the light.

Elsa was sitting on the terrace, staring out at the purple hills. She heard me as I approached and turned. "So there's a new meme," she said. She held out her phone. That picture of Licia, her hands locked around the pistol. Someone had added, "This is what a #feminist #fightback looks like."

"Was she even a feminist?"

"Good question." She gave the tiniest shake of her head, put the phone down on the table. "She'd find the whole thing very strange, I guess, the uses to which a picture can be put. But it keeps her alive in people's minds. I'd kind of prefer it without the gun, though."

"Me too. Maybe a gun is what it takes."

"Maybe."

I sat down. I set a glass in front of Elsa. She lifted it to her eyes, turning the stem.

"How do you get them so perfect, Cal?" she said, her voice full of warmth.

We drank, holding each other's gaze. The ice shards were almost gone now.

I put down my glass. "Elsa, do we ask Bror to speak to Vee?"

"Interesting." She rearranged herself in her chair. "Why?"

"I guess I am starting to worry a little about her gaming . . ."

"Thank you. Finally. That fucking game."

"Yeah. That fucking game. So if Bror could start a conversation with her?"

"Which would be what? I don't really get what he stands for these days."

"Believe what you like, and try to be good. More a discipline than a religion."

"Sounds like a match. Except the bit about being good."

I laughed. We drank to each other again, holding each other's gaze.

I put down my glass. "There's something else." I slid the scanned Post-It note across the table to her. She read it, tracing the words with her thumbnail.

"Okay," she said. "It's a message to Ephraim Tvist from Switchboard:

" 'Four twelve: Man called with description of two individuals behaving in a suspicious manner in the vicinity of the town hall. Both were men, both appeared to have dyed their hair blond, both were wearing black coveralls, and walking at a swift march to a white Volkswagen Polo with the registration plate XR310701.' "

"Bastard," I said. "He's such a master of deflection."

Her blue-gray eyes, quietly appraising me. "I think he might be playing you, Cal."

"You know what's so hard in this place?" I said. "Everyone's so nice, so understanding, so welcoming that you never really believe someone could be taking you for a fool."

"And we are sure this is genuine? Where did you get it?"

"One of Bror's people. Milla. Waiting for me in the town square while you went back to the boat. Why would it not be genuine?"

The tiniest of frowns. "So from Bror . . . ?"

"I don't think Bror knows."

"All right," she said. "This note is significant."

"Significant? Elsa, Tvist could have prevented the whole fucking thing. And all the while he smiles and tells us he understands how we must be feeling. And all the time he's deflecting our attention away."

"You can't confront him. That isn't how we do things here."

"Yeah, I'm starting to realize that."

"I'm serious. If you confront him he will keep on smiling and he will freeze you out, and he will do it so slowly and so imperceptibly that you won't notice he's done it."

"Bastard, though."

"Cal," she said, "this is the knife in the table between you and Tvist. Cool your head. Show yourself willing. Cooperate. Then choose with great precision the moment when you reach for the knife. Because when you go for him you need to go hard."

NINETEEN

I PULLED INTO A street that ran parallel to the fjord. Fancy area, expensive, though the September air was full of diesel and smoke. On the other side of a high fence a train yard blocked off the water. Elsa got out of the car and slammed the door. I opened the passenger window.

"Thank you," she said.

"I wish you were coming to this thing at the kindergarten," I said.

"Believe me, so do I. But they want fathers to bond with other fathers, so you know . . ."

"I already have my support group for that."

"You know they're not the same thing. This is for the kids."

"Or you could shoot me now."

She laughed. "I didn't bring my gun. Go bond with some fathers."

She watched me, smiling, as I drove off. In the rearview mirror I saw her turn toward her therapist's office.

I drove around the corner, parked the car in the next street, switched off the engine.

Why was I lying, and about something as trivial as my support group?

For a while in August I had gone along to the meetings, but I was unable to follow because the Norwegian they spoke was nothing like the Norwegian I was learning. I would sit for whole hours absorbing the feeling of other people's grief, trying to guess what they were saying. I never dared speak myself. I was a foreigner here. It felt crass to ask people to translate their suffering into my language. I quickly found reasons not to go.

Awake in his car seat, Franklin kicked his legs, energetic, smiling. I leaned toward him through the gap in the seats, brought my face very close to his.

"D," said Franklin. "D."

"Yeah," I said. "D. Daaaad. Dad."

"D."

"Oh, Franklin, buddy. My beautiful boy . . ."

"Mm . . ." said Franklin, pointing.

And there, suddenly, was Elsa, walking briskly along the other side of the road, away from her therapist's, her trench coat buttoned tight across her chest. I watched her, ready to open the door, but she did not see the car. She passed by on the other side, stood outside a bar, looked about her, then ducked her head and entered through the low door.

"M," said Franklin. "M-mmm." He had seen Elsa as she passed.

I started the engine. I drove the car slowly up, stopped outside the huge plate-glass window. There was Elsa on a high stool, alone at the bar. I watched for a while, saw her order a drink.

"M-mmm," said Franklin again.

I could walk in. I could ask her what she was doing. But Franklin was in the backseat, and we had an appointment at the kindergarten. Besides, I didn't want to make a scene, carrying my baby into a bar to confront Elsa.

I wanted to believe I could trust my wife.

THE KINDERGARTEN WAS A LOW-SLUNG BUILDING, UGLY and functional, with a playground around the edges. To the right a sea of baby strollers, to the left crates of toys stacked neatly at the side of the path. At the double gates parents were greeting their children, scooping them up, all laughter and soft loving words, lifting them high. In my arms Franklin kicked happily as he scanned the faces of the children, eyes wide, making happy little *ah-ah* sounds.

"Okay, love," I said. "Here we go."

"EEh," said Franklin. "Oh."

Other new fathers sat in the sunshine in overalls and heavy shoes, talking easily among themselves, already forming bonds. I headed nervously past them and in through the door, beneath a finger-painted Norwegian flag, all red, white, and blue.

"Franklin?"

A ponytailed woman with an efficient smile, reaching out with two hands.

"Yes," I said. "This is Franklin."

I passed him over. A look of surprise in Franklin's eyes, and for a painful moment I thought he might cry. The woman turned him toward her, smiled into his face, said, "Hi, Franklin, I'm Leni."

Franklin smiled back, delighted. "Lll," he said. "Ni."

"Hi, Leni. I'm Cal." I reached out.

She offered me her elbow, then laughed. "Perhaps we do not

need to be formal. Hello, Cal. Hello, Franklin. Welcome to father-child evening. Franklin and I will get to know each other while you work with the other fathers, Cal. We will discuss my assessment next week."

"Wait. You're assessing him?"

"Mmm-hmm." She nodded, as if this were obvious. "We assess the child's needs. First through discussion with the child, then with the parents. Your family is multicultural, yes?"

I looked about me, at parents with dark skin, at light-skinned parents with dark-skinned children, all speaking to kindergarten workers.

"I don't know," I said, suddenly aware of our whiteness. "I mean, I guess . . ."

"You're English?" she said.

"Scottish."

"Your wife is Norwegian?"

"But that's not—"

"For us, this is two cultures. Let me go talk to Franklin and assess his needs. And then we can see if you agree. Say bye-bye to *Papa*, Franklin."

She turned, began to walk away, ponytail swishing halfway down her back.

"He speaks Norwegian too," I said. She turned to smile and I felt foolish. Then she headed from the room.

"Could this place be any more politically correct?" A voice I recognized. I turned. A bald man, dark-skinned and powerfully built, in T-shirt and carpenter's trousers, carrying a large green toolbox in each hand. The immaculately shaved skin of his head, the unmistakable set of his jaw, his eyes so dark that I could not see where the iris ended and the pupil began.

"Jesus," I said.

Tvist laughed. "It is good to see you too, Cal Curtis."

"You have a kid here?"

"My little Josi. That's why we're all here, isn't it? Fathers together. For the good of the children. Enforced bonding. This . . ." He looked about himself, laughing. "This is how we build our perfect little social-democratic world." He handed me a toolbox. "Here is your electric drill."

"Isn't *this* about three conflicts of interest already?" I said.

He punched my arm gently. "I must not forget that you are a satirist. Now, to the diaper room."

I stood there in the diaper room, with my drill and my bits, and Tvist stood there with his boxes of screws and nails and Rawl-plugs and pencils. Around us men painted cupboards in primary colors. In the garden outside, other men swept leaves into green plastic sacks.

"So I'm wrong to think this would be a problem?" I said.

He smiled. "There is no conflict of interest. Precisely because this is for the children."

There was an openness that I did not remember from the police station. In other circumstances, I thought, we could almost be friends. And yet . . .

And yet that Post-it note. How long had it sat on his desk? While on the island those men murdered four adults and eighty-seven teenagers?

"Nothing can be a problem," he said, "when it is for the children."

"All right."

And so we worked quietly and efficiently, and I swallowed my feelings and concentrated on building shelves for my baby son's diaper room. Tvist passed me screws and drill bits and Rawlplugs, made neat little marks on the painted walls with his 2B pencil; and for a time the awkwardness between us did disappear. Men at work. *For the children.*

Afterward we sat on the large wooden planters outside, drinking instant coffee and eating pink wafer biscuits. The older children stood in line for sausages in potato pancakes. Tvist offered me a cigarette, which I accepted.

"Can you imagine this place with an armed guard at the gate?" he said.

"No," I said. "No, I really can't."

"I used to read stories about men walking into kindergartens with automatic weapons, and I would think, that's America, or that's Chechnya: that will never happen here. And now I fear that our safe little world is changing, and such a thing can and will happen here, and I shall be forced to put armed guards at the gate of Josi's kindergarten." He turned to me. "I can only imagine what it's like to have a child not come home. We failed you on that day. We are doing what we can to put that right."

His smile—the sadness in it—looked absolutely sincere. And yet . . .

"Can I ask you a question, Ephraim?"

Tvist looked about him. "We are in an informal situation, no?" He waved his hand demonstratively. "Ask away."

I said, "What if you had information that could have prevented a massacre?"

"Then I would act on that information and prevent the massacre." Another sincere smile. "What kind of information?"

A Post-it note with a car registration on it, I thought. But this was not the place to show my hand.

WHEN I GOT HOME VEE WAS PLAYING *Battle Royale*. Her avatar was watching from a high tower, scanning the horizon through the sights of a rifle. Far below, another avatar was jumping. Vee sighted up and pulled the trigger. The avatar below her disappeared mid-jump.

"And . . . head shot," she said, under her breath.

"Vee, where's Mum?"

She laughed. "Who ever knows the true answer to that question?"

"So, not home yet?"

She shook her head. "But guess who I found today?"

"Who did you find?"

She put her headset onto her desk, became very serious. "Arno."

"You . . . what do you mean, you found him?"

She smiled. Her excitement was electric. No sense that she had overstepped a boundary.

"Vee," I said, "you do know you mustn't speak to that boy, don't you?"

"Dad, he knows something, I swear."

She had gone to Arno's school; she had followed him home; she had asked him about Licia. Arno had run away. She had followed him for miles.

"Vee," I said, "I need you to understand that you're dealing with someone in a fragile emotional state. I had no idea he was even back at school."

"He was."

"You cannot approach him. Do you understand me?"

"Sure. But I didn't."

"You just told me you did."

"Fine. I won't do it again. Sorry I spoke . . ." She looked toward the hall. "There's the answer to your other question."

I looked at her. What did she mean?

She said, "You didn't hear her?"

I listened. I heard Elsa's shoes drop. I heard her pad toward the kitchen. I found her by the cooker, reading from her phone screen.

"Hey," I said.

"Hey."

She looked up, turned her phone over, placed it on the worktop, smiled.

I slid my hand into the small of her back, drew her to me. She rubbed her cheek against mine, then half stepped away. I caught the scent of mint on her breath. Alcohol too, though she had done what she could to disguise it. She stepped backward, half sat on the table.

"How was your session today?" I asked.

"Actually weirdly great." She nodded, as if remembering some detail. "Yes. Today was definitely a breakthrough day."

I looked at my wife, trying to find the lie.

Elsa looked levelly at me, smiling. "Why don't you fix us a drink?"

"To celebrate your breakthrough?"

"Sure . . ."

If I hadn't known better, I would have sworn she was telling me the truth.

I went to the freezer, set the gin and the shaker on the worktop. A thought stopped me. I turned to Elsa.

"Would you fetch me some ice?" I said.

"We out?"

"So it seems."

She padded out into the hall. I heard the front door open, heard it swing shut behind her. I turned her phone over. A message from a man named Sverre. Billing her for missing today's session.

A strange, vertiginous moment, catching Elsa in a lie like that. The end of something, I thought. When the foundation of our relationship was truth . . .

I bit back my anger, tried to push all thought from my mind. I replaced Elsa's phone on the worktop, facedown. I began cutting peel and decanting olive brine. When Elsa returned with a large bag of ice, I had two martinis standing on the counter, ready to drink.

She frowned. "I thought we were out of ice."

"I checked again. We weren't. What was your breakthrough, by the way?"

"It's not supposed to leave the therapy room."

"Huh."

I handed Elsa her drink. *My wife, who cannot tell a lie.*

"What?" she said.

I said, "Okay, look. I understand that you may have emotional needs I can't meet. And we are in the middle of something truly terrible. So if there's something I need to know, then please tell me."

"What do you mean?" she said lightly.

"I mean, in times of stress people turn to other people. People who make them feel understood. People more like them. Often someone from their own culture."

"Is this your way of asking, would I be happier with a Norwegian man?"

"Would you?"

"Mostly no." She smiled. "It would make some things easier, of course. Fewer misunderstandings, for sure."

We were standing very close now. Her pupils were large. The flecks in her gray-blue eyes danced silver and gold. No trace of guilt.

"Where are you going with this, Cal?"

"I mean, marriages survive affairs. If the foundation of the marriage is strong enough."

She laughed.

She smiled.

She shook her head.

"You're a sweet, generous man. And an idiot. I am not having an affair." How easily she laughed as she crossed to the sink to pour herself a tumbler of water. She turned, leaned against the worktop, made sure she looked me in the eye once more.

"We don't have affairs," she said. "You don't. I don't. Affairs are not who we are."

How comfortably she held my gaze. How lightly she said the words, though she set down the glass so hard that I thought it might break.

Still, anybody watching would swear she was telling the truth.

TWENTY

MIDWINTER WAS UNSEASONABLY WARM. By evening the pavements were slick with meltwater. I was already cursing myself for agreeing to meet Jo at the Muscular Arms. But Elsa had insisted: "We both need time away, once in a while." She was right. We were together for days on end, and the ground between us was fissuring and eroding.

THE SOUNDS OF THE CITY WERE DISTANT, damped down. Snow on water, water on ice, ice on frozen ground. I fell twice on the short walk from the station.

The Muscular Arms was half-empty. The upholstered booths were threadbare, the wooden tables chipped and pitted. Jo bearhugged me as I crossed the threshold, his stubble scraping mine, and at once I felt like his long-lost friend. Soon we were drinking hard, talking and laughing about soccer and darts.

Three beers down, Jo set down a new glass in front of me. I raised it to my lips, took a long swig. Oslo porter, dark and sharp and strong.

"Not a bad half liter," I said.

Jo shook his head. "It's a pint, mate. Why do you think we're sitting here? Proper working pub. London-style." He gestured around him. Settlement cracks ran the length of the ceiling. The walls were painted yellow, the floor tiles crazed and split.

"And just so it's out of the way," he said, "the police interviewed me about my relationship with Licia."

"I'm sorry," I said. "I know they ask some pretty intrusive questions."

"It's got to happen, mate. They're being thorough for once. *Skål.*"

We toasted each other the Norwegian way, holding eye contact as we drank.

"How are you guys bearing up?" he said as he set his glass down.

"Did Elsa ask you to invite me out?"

He laughed, shook his head. "I . . . thought you might like a drink."

"You're a mensch," I said.

"Plus Edvard's not a big beer drinker. Doesn't really get this place."

He took another long, appreciative swig.

"How are things with Edvard?" I said.

A pained look crossed his face. "God," he said, "where to start?" "*Hei.*"

We looked up. Two women, both in their early thirties, each carrying a pint.

"*Hei,*" said Jo, turning back to me. "I did a stupid thing, Cal."

"English? Mind if we join?" The women were smiling. The taller one was dark, her hair worn high on her head, elaborately pinned. Her friend was blonde, with smile lines around her eyes.

"Other seats are available," said Jo. "And neither of us is English."

"But we could sit here, with you. And you could tell us about yourselves. And that would be nice." The tall woman. She said it so disarmingly that I began to move out of the way. An open face, intelligent and kind. No edge. She pushed in beside me, and I was aware of the shortness of her skirt, could feel the strength in her exposed thighs. Her friend slid in beside Jo, an expectant look on her face. I pushed up along the booth so as not to sit too close to those thighs.

"It's just . . ." I said. I caught Jo's amused smile. "We're both spoken for."

"And what?" said the blonde woman. "Married men can't talk to us?" Pretty, I thought. Interested in Jo.

"To be clear . . ." said Jo, "neither of us fucks."

The women exchanged a look.

"My friend Jo prefers the company of men," I said. "Sorry."

Jo sighed. "My friend Cal is prone to making irrational choices. A fuck with a woman he just met in a bar will not make him more rational. You ladies will find better pickings at one of the tables over there."

"Okay, Jo," said the blonde woman, making a point of shaking his hand. "Nice to meet you. Thank you for being clear. I'm Solveig. I do not wish to fuck you. Either of you. And this is Nina. I think also Nina does not wish to fuck you."

They got up to leave.

"Sorry for the interruption," said Nina.

"I'm sorry too," I said, and meant it.

We watched them go. They stood at the corner of the bar, ruffled.

Jo said, "And now your foreigner's mind is thinking I had no right to speak to those women like that."

"Yes," I said. "Something like that."

"And maybe you want to flirt with a girl in a bar, buy her a few drinks, and go home to Elsa. In which case, my bad. And I will walk over there and tell Nina that, and maybe she will come back and you can buy her some drinks. But Cal, man, you have *needs an actual fuck* cut into the lines in your face."

"What are you saying?"

"Oh come on," he said. "I saw the way you leapt away from her when her leg brushed yours. You yelped."

"I did not yelp."

"You yelped. What's that, if not a guilty conscience?"

"Tell Elsa, from me, that I don't fuck other women."

He laughed, shook his head.

"What's funny?"

"Just . . . Elsa's pretty much erased me from her life."

"I didn't know that. I'm sorry."

His eyes searched mine. He looked away. "Maybe you can understand that I worry about you guys."

"Do you think she's faithful to me?"

He took a long slug of his pint. He put the glass carefully down on the table. "Cal, mate, no one comes easily through losing a child."

"So that's a no?"

He ignored me and carried on. "People become strangers in their own home and they fuck other, easier strangers in bars." He took another long swig. "But I really don't think that's Elsa. She's completely devoted to you."

"I always thought that."

"So what's changed? Have you and Elsa stopped having sex?"

"Well, I can't speak for my wife . . ."

Jo was looking out at the snow, orange in the light of the streetlamp. "I'm not an audience. Don't turn this into a joke."

"I don't seek an audience."

He was right, though. He was my closest friend here; he had known Elsa since they were children. I wanted to tell him that our marriage was eroding, that I had lost a daughter and now I was losing my wife. But Jo was Elsa's friend before he was mine, so instead I said, "You were about to tell me about Edvard."

"Okay. Let's do me instead." He made a bridge of his hands, fingertips pressed together. "I am coming to the conclusion that the man I love actually hates me."

I laughed.

Jo stared at me for a moment. The look in his eyes told me he was serious. "Since Garden Island, Edvard works stupid hours, and last Friday he called me and asked if I could bring his uniform and his shaving kit to him on my way to work, because he'd been up all night and had to be at a press conference. And I was running late, but I said sure. And then my train was delayed, and I didn't think . . ." He was looking down at his feet, shaking his head. "And you're going to find this ridiculous, Cal, because it is utterly ridiculous, but I left the uniform in his rucksack behind the counter at the café opposite the station, because I've done it a million times. But that was before Garden Island. Everything's changed now, hasn't it?"

I thought of the Andersen brothers in their police uniforms, the badges torn by briars. "Yes," I said. "I guess it has."

"And when Edvard got there it was gone. On the CCTV there's

this little wiry kid hanging about, but you don't see him take it, and the staff remembered nothing. And it's probably not terrorists and it's probably just a kid being a kid. But it doesn't matter how many times I try to speak to Edvard's boss, because she really doesn't care that it's my fault and not Edvard's. Edvard is responsible for his own uniform. And Edvard hates me. I mean, he tries not to, I know, but he does. I humiliated him. I put him under suspicion."

"Did you get it back?"

"No. And you can't talk about this."

"I can see that."

"He's the best thing that ever happened to me." He laughed bitterly. "Was. Now he turns away when I kiss him."

I said, "I'm sorry, mate."

"I am so fucking stupid. Because I know the uses a police uniform can be put to . . ."

TWENTY-ONE

AT HALF PAST EIGHT the streetlights in Oslo would go out, all at once. Sunrise was officially at nine, though we rarely saw the actual sun. The filtered daylight felt like a mistake, an unintended interruption to the unending dark.

Elsa and I settled into our new reality as parents of a missing child. We grew used to television cameras and microphones, to stares in the street and to journalists who could not quite meet our gaze. We dressed like concerned parents in respectful, conservative clothes. I took to wearing dark suits; Elsa to high-buttoned blouses and long-flowing skirts.

We read prepared statements to the press, which we agreed in advance with Tvist:

If you have any information, anything at all . . .
We miss you, Licia.
Please come home . . .

We were kind to each other inside the home, made a point of holding hands and kissing in front of the children. To look at us you would think we were getting by. But Jo was right to be concerned. It was February. The truth was that in eight months Elsa and I had not fucked once. And the lie she had told about her therapist: I could not let go of that.

LATER THAT MONTH I LOST MY COLUMN in the *Beltway Times*.

"Your writing's gotten serious, Cal," my editor said. "This is a satirical column."

"Satire's purpose is serious, Gina."

"And your writing always had a point behind the laughs. But white supremacist murderers? Every week? Do you want to be on these guys' radar?"

"Isn't that my risk to take?"

"Plus our readers need some actual laughter . . ."

The argument was lost. I could come back, she said, when I was ready. But I knew that—in the kindest, nicest way—she was firing me.

Now I was adrift in this country and it frightened me. I knew I should tell Elsa about my column, that by not sharing the truth I was failing her, but I was ashamed at my own lack of resilience. I was afraid that the winter would finish us as a family. I knew that it must not.

I learned everything about the murders on Garden Island. I memorized the coroner's report, learned the Norwegian terms for *hollow point* and *jacketed*, for *bone fracture* and *lung collapse*. I forced myself word for word through the articles that detailed the time and the manner of every death. Hard to explain, but knowledge kept at bay the fear that threatened to enfold and engulf me. It kept Licia alive in my mind.

We had to survive the next few months. The trial date was set for June.

We hunkered down. We coped, though how Elsa managed I was not sure. She floated around the apartment like a heroine in an Ibsen play, all buttoned-up blouses and long flowing skirts.

At night I would hear Elsa in the bathroom. She would turn on all the taps, stand naked under the shower screaming her fury and her frustration at the cruelties fate had dealt us. When I met neighbors on the stairs I would see in their faces that they heard her too. Perhaps she thought the water disguised her screams.

I TOOK TO GOING FOR WALKS. OCCASIONALLY I would catch sight of Elsa in a grocery store, talking easily with the staff, or see her laughing happily with people I did not know as she waited for the train into town. I would marvel then at how easily she fit into this place, while I stood on the periphery, watching. How easily a person might think my wife was happy, when I knew for certain she was not.

ONE AFTERNOON I FOUND MYSELF AT THE coffee bar in the mall. I stood by the thick plate glass, scanned the interior. Baskets of bread hung from a heavy wire, slowly making their way down from the bakery to the walnut-topped counter. There were candles; there were tablecloths; there was raw blackberry jam. All very clean, very *hygge*.

Bored-looking women in slack suits drank fruit drinks through steel drinking straws, their lips plumped with collagen. One of those moments when you could imagine everybody who lived in this country was tall and white and blond. Every tooth was straightened, every blemish removed, every strand of hair professionally lightened. And there was Elsa, alone at a table, listlessly reading *Posten*.

Elsa reached for her coffee, took a slug, winced at the taste. A strange erotic thrill, watching my wife, unseen. So beautiful, as she sat there, radiating *don't-come-near*. So unlike these other women, with their puffed lips and their smoothed cheeks, their foreheads stiff with botulinum.

Where was Franklin? I looked about me, at the strollers lined up outside the door, their wheels resting in loose slush. In a stroller very like ours, a child swaddled very like ours reached out a fist and beat at the air. I leaned toward him, ready to lift him and carry him into the café's warm air, but it was not Franklin. I turned. Elsa was looking down now, speaking softly. She had Franklin at her side, I guessed, just out of sight.

I began to lean my weight against the door. I paused.

That man at the next table, staring at Elsa. His entire being was directed at my wife. I took a step into the shadows, amused. How could he be so obvious? For a time, Elsa did not seem to notice him. Then she looked up, met his gaze, dismissed him with a half smile.

I smiled too. *Not a chance, friend.*

Elsa turned the page of the newspaper. But something had caught her off balance. She took a sip of her coffee, and this time—I could see it—she forced herself not to wince at the flavor. Every time she looked up, there was the man, all eyes. His hair was disheveled, his movements staccato, but his clothes were clean and his trousers pressed.

The man leaned across, rapped twice on Elsa's table. I noticed his shoes now, leather-soled, highly polished, not a salt mark to be seen. He spoke a word that looked like *Hello.*

Elsa looked up. This time she did not smile. The man spoke again. His fingers hovered by the pocket of his jeans, then by his breast pocket. Elsa's brow knotted in annoyance. From beside her she picked up Franklin, asleep in his car seat, put him gently down on the table.

You see? I thought. *My* wife. *My* son.

Now the man was on his feet. As I watched, he walked to the end of the counter, where he stood by the coffee machine. He exchanged words with the girl behind the machine. The girl smiled.

Around me the babies slept peacefully in their strollers. Foot-steps crunched heavily on gritted paths. Car wheels spun on ice. The man laughed gently with the girl behind the machine. In a concrete gym across the parking lot blonde women in leotards danced to a beat I could not hear. Soon they too would be making their way to the café, to detoxify their bodies with wheatgrass and ginger.

The man was walking toward Elsa carrying two cups of coffee. He slid one carefully to Elsa's side of the table. Surely now she would ask him to let her be?

But no. She nodded politely. The man sat down at her table, his back to me.

I could end this. All I had to do was enter the café, approach Elsa, introduce myself to this man, and ask him his business. But I stayed in the shadows, watching as Elsa took Franklin's seat from the table, placed it carefully at her feet.

THE MAN WAS THE FIRST TO LEAVE. I hung back as he walked toward his car, shoulders hunched against the wind. A gray Volvo, rust-stained around the wheel arches. He got in, slammed the door shut. A line of wet snow fell from the roof on to the tarmac.

I took out my phone and wrote the plate number into it.

DINNER THAT EVENING WAS DOMINATED BY FRANKLIN: he pushed food from his plate; he burbled; he dropped his spoon experimentally onto the floor and watched, fascinated, as Elsa picked it up. Every time. His eyes fizzed with delight.

Elsa was on her hands and knees, reaching under the table.

"Actions have consequences," I said. "Maybe leave it there, love."

Elsa got to her feet, passed the spoon to Franklin. "Don't use the word *love* like that, Cal. Like it's a control mechanism."

"He's right, though, Mum," said Vee. "Why are you being Franklin's bitch?"

"Vee," I said, "don't."

"Or what? Mum will get worse? How could she actually be worse than she is right now?" She folded her arms, angry with us both.

Elsa sat in her place. "I guess we're all a little on edge." She reached out across the table, took my left hand. "Sorry, Cal."

"Sorry, love." I smiled a careful smile. "How was coffee at the mall today?"

"Good," she said levelly. "Coffee at the mall was good." But I could feel the racing of her mind. Had she told me she was having coffee? Had she told me she was going to the mall?

"Franklin sleep all the way through?"

Perhaps Elsa could hear the edge in my voice. She smiled as if puzzled.

"Yeah," she said. "Franklin slept."

"Good," I said. "Sorry if I was sharp."

We both turned to look at our daughter.

"What is this?" said Vee. "How come suddenly it's the two of you united against me?"

"This isn't about sides," said Elsa. "But in the future please don't use the word *bitch* in front of your brother."

"Fine. Just—"

She was on her feet, heading from the room.

"Vee, would you please—"

"No."

"—pick up your plate—"

The door swung shut behind her.

I sat staring at Elsa, waiting for her to speak, but she simply sat staring back.

"I wasn't completely straight with you," she said at last. "I've been feeling weird about that." She smiled; her wolf eyes fixed on mine, gauging my reaction.

"I wasn't straight with you either," I said.

Franklin pushed his dish across the platform of the high chair, over the edge, and onto the floor, where it landed face-down. He sat staring down at it, transfixed. Elsa looked at him, then at me.

"Here's the thing," I said. "I know you met someone at the mall."

She laughed. "You followed me?"

"Kind of by mistake."

She turned, looked me very deliberately in the eye. "See, I'm pretty sure I saw you, lurking in the shadows outside."

"Did you?"

"Yes." She said it on the inhale.

I said, "Who was the man?"

She sat for a while, as if weighing her options. She gave a tiny grimace.

"Elsa?"

Then she looked me very directly in the eye with her blue-white wolf eyes. "Hedda thinks our policy of honesty doesn't work in my favor."

"What's that even supposed to mean?"

But she simply sat there staring at me, refusing to answer my question.

I WENT OUT, ANGRY AND CONFUSED.

I walked into town along the freeway, hands freezing, shoes and trousers stained with salt.

What would Elsa have seen if she had been watching me? That I fell twice on the icy street. That I entered the bar self-conscious and covered in snow. That I sat, talking to a woman on a high stool.

"Where are you from?" the woman said.

"Here," I said.

She looked at the stain where the snow had soaked into my jacket, amused. "No," she said. "I really don't think you are."

A tall woman with elaborately pinned hair and a short skirt. She remembered me, she said, and I remembered her.

"Okay," I said. "What was your name again?"

Nina. Her name was Nina. With her open face and her strong thighs.

We retreated to a booth in a dark corner. When I told Nina that I had no friends in this town she reached across and mussed my hair, and although that was a friendly gesture, I suppose it was open to misinterpretation. If my wife had been watching through the plate-glass window she would not have liked it.

Outside the bar, electric cars cut silent paths through the snow.

From the street perhaps it looked as if we were caressing each other's hands, though, for all my longing, it was innocent and chaste. I did not once look at Nina's thighs, despite the shortness of her skirt.

The truth is I wanted to talk to someone who didn't have an opinion about me, who hadn't seen me on television, and who didn't know that I was the father of the missing girl. I wanted to flirt and laugh for an hour or two, and for it all to mean nothing. And Nina was kind and funny, and I told her at the start that I was married and loved my wife. And she admired my wedding ring and told me it was beautifully designed, and I in turn admired hers.

I wanted to tell Nina that the foundation of my marriage was honesty, and that something had begun to erode that. But even the thought felt like a betrayal.

AT ONE I WENT HOME TO MY wife. My troubling wife, who met men I did not know in coffee shops in malls.

I lay down beside her. "Elsa," I said. "I want to know the truth about that man."

She muttered something I did not hear, turned on her side.

I lay staring at her back, angry at myself for wanting to hurt her.

When I was certain she was asleep I got up from the bed. I sat at the computer, typed the license plate into the register:

Pavel Lisowski
Thor's Gate 41

Pavel, mate. What's your interest in my wife?
What's my wife's interest in you?

TWENTY-TWO

THE CAFETERIA AT THE hospital was almost empty of people. The walls were white-painted, the furniture ash. I hung by the door as Pavel Lisowski ordered coffee. He was wearing a gray-black coverall, carrying a leather satchel in his left hand and a tray in his right.

When he sat down I bought a machine cappuccino for myself, then approached his table.

I put my coffee on the table opposite him.

He studied my face. "Please sit."

He was not surprised to see me, then.

I said, "Why did you contact my wife?"

"Your beautiful Elsa. Please. You have nothing to fear." His smile was weary; there was a wounded sadness to it. I sat down.

He was staring at me again. "Elsa told you that she has met me?"

"She did not tell me that."

"So perhaps you follow your wife around? Like a policeman, only jealous?" He laughed a mirthless laugh. "I apologize for joking. This is your job, no?"

"Joke away," I said. "If that's what it takes."

He sniffed hard. "And now you google me and you follow me to my place of work. And here am I, working hard flying my air ambulance—I'm joking again, of course, because I am grounded pending psychological assessment. Which is routine, but also sounds serious, no? The helicopter pilot who must not fly?"

I said nothing.

"Hm. So I came to see your Elsa because your daughter came to see me. This I thought was not good, because I knew who she was. Everybody googles everybody now, yes? And she knew who I was, and that I also fly for television stations, and she knew I was flying for TVZ on the day of the killings."

He looked to check that I had caught his point.

"I imagine you saw some very bad things," I said.

"All those children, you know?" He brought his hand toward his face. "These are scenes you never forget. My colleague Mikal was filming that day, watching everything, very close. He did not cope with this so well. He assembled his family shotgun. His daughter found him at the kitchen table . . ." Pavel's voice trailed off. He pressed his thumb and forefinger against his brow, then forced his hand down on to his lap. "He was a friend, you know."

He smiled and nodded. I found myself smiling too. The strange kinship of people who have known bereavement. "I'm sorry for your loss," I said, because I understood Pavel Lisowski's sadness.

He nodded and looked away. He said, "Viktoria remembered a girl down by the water, filmed from our news chopper. She thought that it might have been her sister. Alicia, yes? She asked me if our helicopter made it more likely that her sister was killed."

I said nothing. I could think only of the kingfisher-blue sundress, of Licia lying alone and undiscovered, of Vee setting out to find her in our little red speedboat.

"I told Viktoria . . ." I saw Pavel swallow hard. He faced me, looked me straight in the eye. "I told Viktoria that I was not sure; that we might have made the situation worse; that I knew we attracted the attention of these men. Because many of those children were murdered shortly after we filmed their . . . predicament . . . I understand what this means now, that by being at Garden Island we made a bad situation worse. In the heat of the moment I did not understand this. I thought we were bringing people the truth."

"Okay, Pavel," I said. "I appreciate your honesty."

I could hear the bitterness in my words, could feel tears forming at the edges of my eyes, could see my vision begin to cloud.

"Please understand that I did not know the consequences of our presence . . . Once we realized, we stopped filming . . . I told your wife this too." His mouth was open; his shoulders were shaking. I was afraid that this man would cry, afraid that I would not know how to comfort him. I could think of nothing to do; I took a slug of coffee.

He leaned forward. "It is not my intention to exploit your empathy. I hope you and your wife do not think I am asking for your forgiveness."

"Forget forgiveness," I said. "Do you have the footage your colleague Mikal shot?"

He was looking at me appraisingly. "Yes."

"And does it show a girl in a kingfisher-blue dress?"

"Yes."

"Then I would like to see it."

"It shows things no father should see."

"Nevertheless . . ."

"Cal, this will not bring you peace."

I felt anger spike in me all over again. "Who are you to judge what will bring me peace, Pavel? You come to us to unburden yourself, to tell Elsa that you contributed to our daughter's death."

"Please," he was saying.

"Maybe you're worried that we could sue you, so you're trying to head that off? Is that what you were doing with my wife yesterday? Establishing your good-guy credentials with the woman? Because you need to know that Elsa is attuned to lying. She can spot it where other people can't."

A stricken look on his face. "It is not my intention to add to your burden."

"Then tell me this. Do you have proof that my daughter is dead?"

"No."

A moment of terrifying hope. "Do you have evidence that she's alive?"

"I have evidence of a timeline."

"Which you won't show us." The hope began to leach away.

"My colleague Mikal: I cannot risk that this might happen with other people."

"So you came to Elsa offering exactly what?" I knew I was being harsh, but I could not escape the feeling that he was trying to play me.

"I need you to know: We tried to land the helicopter. Two times. Each time these men shot at us. When we tried to land to pick up your daughter there were bullets striking the fuselage. We had to take off quickly." There was a pleading note in his voice.

"So to summarize, Pavel: You tried to do the right thing on the day of the attacks. It didn't work out. Your presence made things worse. Lots of children died." I could see the hurt in his eyes, but I couldn't stop myself. "We need to know the truth. Show us what happened. You know you have a moral responsibility to us now."

"It is not in my gift."

"Not in your gift?" I laughed. "I can see you're kind of trying to do the right thing, Pavel. You gave the footage to the police, right? But you have to follow through. You have to show it to us." I was on my feet now, heading for the door.

He was in front of me—I wasn't sure how—blocking my path.

"The police," he said. "They specifically asked me not to share this material with you."

"Specifically with me?"

"You. Your wife."

"They mentioned us by name?"

"They're clever, and it's all implication, but it was clear they were talking about you."

"Because—let me guess—your footage doesn't show the police in the greatest of lights?"

"I will try to help you in other ways. This is a complicated situation."

"No, Pavel, this is simple. If the police had done their jobs, my daughter would still be here. If you cared about the truth, you would be showing me what you have."

"It was never—"

"—your intention. I know. Find someone else to absolve you of your sins."

THAT NIGHT I CALLED MY BROTHER.

"People aren't telling me the truth, Dan."

I was a little drunk. He could hear it down the line.

"Who isn't telling you the truth, Cal?" That slight undertone of concern.

"The police. Elsa. Everyone."

"Elsa lied to you? Wow . . ."

"It wasn't an actual lie. Anyway, I want a press pass. For the trial."

"A press pass isn't going to fix your marriage, Cal. Could do the very opposite." He said it very gently, a smile in his voice. *Always the older brother . . .*

"You know what? Forget what I said about Elsa. Delete it from your brain. But, Dan, you liked what I did on the day of the attacks. And we need to keep Licia's name alive."

"I know," he said softly.

"Plus I have a source. Two, maybe."

He laughed. "Are you pitching for a job?"

"Would that be completely ridiculous?"

"You realize that people won't start telling you the truth just because you're a journalist? I have a world of people lying to me too. Who's your source?"

"One was flying a helicopter on the day of the attacks. He has footage. The other's in the police. Dan, there's a story here that isn't being told. The authorities are holding something back."

"You're saying there's a conspiracy?"

"I realize that sounds extreme. Maybe, though."

I could hear my brother sucking the air in across his teeth.

"I should go," I said. "Sorry."

"Wait." He exhaled heavily. "Cal, did you ever sit in on a murder trial?"

"No."

"Point one: Murder trials are shitty. They do not provide closure—"

"And I get that—"

"—and point two: These guys had plenty of time to take their own lives. When they ran out of bullets they sat and waited for the tactical unit to arrive. That means the plan was not to die. This isn't a school shooting. It's not a suicide bombing."

"I do realize the difference."

"I don't think you do. Cal, for men like this the trial is a key part of the exploitation phase. It's a way of getting their message out. *Amplifying the signal.* And that will open wounds you didn't know you had . . . Are you ready to sit and watch as they talk about Licia as collateral damage in the war of the races? Cal, for the sake of your mental health, for the sake of your marriage, for the sake of your relationship with your kids—"

I knew he was right, but I could feel the anger rising in me. "My mental health is okay, Dan. So's the other stuff. But thank you for your time."

"—and if you let me finish, you will hear that I'm not telling you no."

"You aren't?"

"I look at the news value of this and—what do you know?—kind of a tantalizing offer."

For a moment I thought I might cry. To be listened to . . . for Licia's story to be heard . . .

"Dan," I said. "Thank you. Thank you. From the bottom of my fucking heart—"

He cut me off. "I mean, let's forget for a moment your conspiracy theory—"

"This is more than a theory. The police knew who these men were, and they did nothing. They could have prevented the attack. They had the license plate. And they have footage that proves something, which we're forbidden to see—"

"So let's say you do have a source—"

"Let's say I have two sources—"

"And if you can show your conspiracy, great. But you're not an investigative reporter, so I want you to do what I know you do well. Which is the family stuff. You cover the trial and you tell us what it feels like. You have instincts, and your instincts are good. Tell us the story of your family, and people will listen."

"That's not the story I want to tell."

"Cal," he said. "Take the offer on the table."

TWENTY-THREE

THE LATE SNOW CAUGHT us off guard. Huge flakes were falling fast through the still air, obscuring the island. They settled on the oil-black surface of the fjord, held there for a moment, and were gone. Below our feet the engine thrummed. Chain links clanked in across the bow. A heavy rope was thrown from shore onto the deck and the ferry rocked forward into gear. People stumbled, reached out with their hands, but kept their footing.

It was the first Monday of May. An official court day, though the trial would not begin for six weeks. The judges were here to examine each of the ninety-one murders, following the timeline minute by minute. The survivors and the families of the bereaved were here to watch the reconstruction. The whole thing would be broadcast on television and live-streamed on the Internet. Here, perhaps, was what the prime minister meant by *more democracy, more openness.*

Around us were the families of the dead. Eighty people, I guessed, and not a one speaking. They huddled into their jackets, pulled their hats low across their faces. Strange what ten months of loss can do to a face: the bagging of the flesh below the eyes, the lining of the forehead and the cheeks, the graying of the skin. Dark faces. Light faces. All clouded with the same pain, etched in hard lines around their mouths. You could see in their eyes the awful resignation. Their son, their daughter, their brother, their sister: never coming back.

Toward the aft I saw Arno and his mother. Mari noticed me looking and smiled. Arno looked away. In his hand he was carrying something heavy. A book, bound in leather.

As the ferry began to near the other side, I saw a cameraman on the dock lining up on Vee. I jumped ashore, put myself between him and my daughter, pushed him gently away as I helped Vee and Elsa ashore.

At the top of the rise volunteers were handing out blankets and warm soup. There were a hundred and eighty of us, all told. Maybe two hundred. They lined us up on red plastic chairs arranged in rows behind heavy ropes that kept us from the main house.

Elsa leaned close to me. "They won't let us into the buildings," she said. "We have to follow things from out here."

"You serious?"

"Yeah," said Vee. "Which you have to admit is fucked up."

"Hush."

Vee turned toward the man who had spoken. "Don't hush me."

Near us sat a couple with the saddest eyes you can imagine. I tried to make some kind of contact first with the woman, then with the man, but before I could nod they turned to each other, speaking quiet words into each other's ears, glancing toward us as they spoke. Then they both turned full on to us; they stared at Vee with an expression very much like reproach.

She's fifteen, I wanted to say. *Please understand . . .*

"I'll stay here with Vee," said Elsa. "Go use your press card."

"Yeah, Mum," said Vee, looking toward the couple. "Chaperone the frick out of me. Because apparently I shouldn't say what everyone else is thinking."

"Vee," I said very quietly. "Shh."

I put my press card on a lanyard around my neck, walked slowly over toward the house. When I looked back, the man with the reproachful eyes was staring at me.

THE WOOD ON THIS SIDE OF THE house was rotting beneath the yellow paint. The window glass had not been replaced. It was hard to make out the figures moving through the gloom inside.

There were two male stand-ins, placed where the brothers must have been as they addressed the children. Actors dressed casually in T-shirts and jeans with white sneakers, allowing their bodies to be moved, their limbs to be repositioned.

There was Tvist too, his face glowing red in the light of a space heater, his long woolen coat turned up at the collar. He caught me looking, nodded a greeting. I nodded back.

Nearer the window, lit by the low sun, was a young woman, blond-haired with a pretty, open face. She turned into the room, listening to an instruction read by a court official from a large ring-bound file. She was playing Licia, then.

Funny.

Almost.

The actress turned away. I realized with another lurch that Paul Andersen was speaking to her. The actual Paul Andersen, the murderer of children, correcting some minor detail of Licia's position. There he stood, with his brother, at the far end of the room. A court official crossed the floor, moved the girl a couple of paces closer to the door. The actress turned, looked questioningly toward the Andersen brothers. Paul Andersen nodded.

The actress walked out of the light and toward the center of the room, where she joined the huddle of lawyers.

"Cal."

I turned. Elsa was walking across the snow toward me.

A guard stepped toward her. Elsa said, "I left my press card in my bag."

The guard nodded. "No pictures."

"I have no camera," she replied.

The guard waved her through.

"Should it be that easy to lie your way in?" I said.

Elsa laughed. "I know." She stepped toward me, brought her head close to the window, looked in.

"The actress is the stand-in for Licia," I said. "Those guys are standing in for the Andersen brothers."

"Huh," she said.

Inside the room, something seemed to be decided. A tiny, bird-like woman stepped forward. The chief judge. She nodded, spoke words that we could not hear. The actors took their positions, the young woman very close to us. A court official approached, tapped the actress very gently with his fingertips. On the back of her right shoulder, where the first bullet had struck Licia.

I looked at Elsa, saw the pain and the shock in her eyes. I reached out, took her hand.

The actress stood with her back to the door. The court official approached a second actor, tapped him twice on the forehead. The chief judge said something. The actor turned toward the judge, nodded, then joined the girl near the door. The court official approached a girl who was kneeling near the window. He tapped her once on the stomach. The girl looked up, looked at the chief judge, listened to an instruction, then lay lengthways on the floor. The court official knelt at the girl's side, tapped her once in the back of the head.

For a moment I could see the scene. The hundred children gathered in that room, the panic as they spilled outward and away from the Andersen brothers from the doors at each side; through the plate-glass window, forcing it from the frame as they hurled themselves against it. And Licia, who had shouted the warning, who was the first out of the door, clenching her teeth against the shock of the bullet wound, running scared.

I forced my thoughts back to the people in front of me, to the actors and the court officials, and the gentle taps where the bullets had entered. The Andersens had killed four in that room. They had not yet found their rhythm, I thought grimly. Their kill rate improved as they went.

The men were led outside. They stood on the veranda, just above us, arms free, relaxed in their blue winter jackets and heavy black trousers, speaking easily with each other, and with the defense team who joined them. There was something so nondescript about them, something quiet and unexceptional. Pimples and shaving rash. If you had met them in the street, or in a bar, you would never have guessed what they were planning.

People behind the rope were beginning to notice, nudging each other, turning to watch.

Paul Andersen turned, as if relishing the audience. He spat a yellow-black gobbet of chewing tobacco onto the snow, took from his pocket a small box, which he opened. From it he formed a piece of tobacco into a small cube, fit it to the gap between his upper lip and his gum, then put the box in his pocket.

"You'd think at least they would cuff them," said Elsa.

"I know," I said. "You'd think."

A new stand-in, a man, stood on the lawn in front of the house. There were marks on the ground, silver crosses made with duct tape, numbered from 5 through 16.

"Where's Vee?" I said.

Elsa looked anxiously toward the empty chairs where she and Vee had been sitting. "She was there just now."

Paul Andersen said something to his brother. John Andersen raised his arm, pretended to fire a shot. The men laughed.

The birdlike judge walked toward the men's defense team. She spoke to the huddle of lawyers, though she kept eyeing the men. There was a long pause.

Elsa was gripping my arm tightly. "Is it bad that I want those men dead?"

"I know what you mean," I said.

"What was I expecting, right?"

The simplicity of the scene made the whole thing so much worse. The standing figures; the taps to the shoulder, to the leg, to the temple, to the right lung. And throughout it all the Andersen brothers, eyes bright and chests puffed, all fighting-cock bravado and private jokes, as they made small corrections to the positions of the shooters, of the victims.

Elsa let go of my arm. "Oh." She jumped across the rope, began running toward the chairs. I looked up, confused. There was Vee, and there was Bror, with his wild hair and his gray robes.

A voice, very close. "Hello, Cal Curtis."

I looked around. It was Tvist, smiling, carrying three cups of coffee in a triangle he had made of his hands. "Like one? You'd be doing me a favor."

I reached forward, took the cup nearest Tvist's fingertips.

"Stupid way to carry hot drinks." He bent his knees, put down the two remaining cups, shook spilled coffee from his right hand onto the pristine snow.

Paul Andersen's voice, saying no, not like that, like this.

Seven paces. Not eight.

Tvist was standing now, sipping experimentally from his cup.

"Why aren't those men handcuffed?" I said.

"We don't deal in gestures. No one here is in any danger."

We stood watching the men. I saw that Paul Andersen remembered every step, every shot, every face that passed before his gunsights. I felt how he savored the memories, how he breathed in the disgust in the faces of the survivors, of the bereaved. I knew that there was in him an enjoyment of the precision of the killing. In his brother too.

"And meanwhile . . ." said Tvist, gesturing beyond the huddle to where Bror stood talking to Vee. I looked at Bror, saw how his hand rested on Vee's back. I felt Tvist's eyes on mine. "For a man who dislikes white supremacism, you're surprisingly relaxed about its advocates. Old friends?"

"That man is emphatically not a white supremacist."

"He's clever. He hitches it to progressive causes. But he is widely quoted and shared. By white supremacists."

I looked him square in the face. "Found any trace of a network?"

"No . . . But has he mentioned female emancipation to you yet? Sustainability? A general suspicion of the police?"

Bror had noticed us, could see that we were speaking about him. He smiled, raised a hand in greeting.

I said, "He has shown us great kindness. He listens. It's nice to feel someone is on our side."

Tvist made a little scoffing sound. "That comment about fruit flies. That's the real Bror."

"He never linked it to immigration."

"Perhaps because he knew other people would?"

Elsa was picking her way across the snow toward Bror. He caught sight of her, took his hand from Vee's back, smiled very broadly, stepped toward Elsa. They hugged. He was turning away, was saying something to Vee. Vee began to speak. Elsa put her hand on Vee's shoulder, shook her head, smiled.

I turned back to Tvist. "There's this thing you do," I said. "You sow doubt. About good people."

"I sow doubt?"

"I mean, yes, Bror is odd," I said, "and yes, his sexual politics are a little off. But so what, if he's spreading hope?"

Tvist considered this. He gave an exaggerated frown. "And what if he's using you?"

Elsa was crouching down now, speaking directly to Vee, while Bror looked down upon them, smiling his benevolent smile. He gestured to one side, and there were Arno and his mother, approaching across the snow. Vee stood, held out a hand to Arno, who eyed her suspiciously. Bror said something to the boy. Arno stepped forward, still holding his large, leather-bound book. A Bible. Bror put his left hand on Arno's shoulder, his right hand on Vee's.

"Man's doing what he can to help," I said. "Seems unfair to write him off as a racist."

"Oh?" Tvist turned to me. "How easy would Norwegian racism be for you to discern?"

"Given that I'm not black?"

"People speak more freely in their own language." Tvist smiled sadly, as if my question disappointed him. "Perhaps that is hard for an outsider to understand?"

For a moment I wanted to apologize. I valued this man. Those moments we shared in the morning as we handed over our children at the kindergarten felt like something close to friendship. But he was a master at placing blame elsewhere.

Vee was pulling her coat tight around herself, walking toward me across the snow. I waved. Vee waved back. Tvist watched her, that same sad smile playing across his lips.

"So is it true," I said, "that you had the Andersens' license plate, and that you took no action?"

"That was an abrupt and rather journalistic turn."

"And you don't much like journalists?"

He considered this. "You feel let down. When you experience a loss of this magnitude, you look around you for someone to blame."

"There you go," I said. "Deflecting a question . . ."

He shrugged, smiled, took a slug of coffee, smiled again.

Always that same smile.

I took from my pocket the color copy of the Post-it note.

Tvist glanced at it, handed it back. "How useful it must be," he said, "to have a friend in the police." There was no hint of warmth in his smile now.

"That is not how I came by it," I said.

"And yet there is no other possible source." He crouched down, picked up the last of the coffee cups. When he stood up, his dark,

dark eyes were so close to mine that I could not bring them into focus. He smelled of lip balm and expensive cologne.

"Nothing personal, Cal, but perhaps you should not be so seduced by other people's agendas." And with that he was walking away.

I looked across at the Andersen brothers. The two men were staring at Bror and at Elsa. John Andersen was whispering in his brother's ear. I could see in Elsa's face that she sensed them looking. I could feel her unease.

"Dad."

Vee crossed elegantly beneath the rope in a single fluid move.

I stepped toward her. "Hey, Vee." I reached out, drew her to me.

Vee turned in my arms, looked toward her mother. Bror was smiling at Elsa, all charm, arms thrown wide, shielding her from the gazes of the Andersen brothers.

"So, that guy Bror . . ." I said to Vee.

"Yeah, why is Mum pushing me toward him?"

"Is she?"

Vee's eyes narrowed. "What did you arrange?"

"Why would you think we arranged something?"

"You raised me cynical. Suddenly I'm supposed to be, *Ooh, breathing techniques*?"

"Look how he's helping Arno. You see that, right?"

"I guess . . ."

"Would it hurt to be a little happier?"

Vee rolled her eyes. "Can I please go for a walk? There's literally nothing to do here."

I looked at the chairs, at the ropes, at the court officials, at the armed police. What harm could it do?

"Sure, love. Go for your walk."

Paul and John Andersen stood where they were, watching my daughter go. They turned to each other and laughed. Then John Andersen made a gun of his fingers and sighted up on Vee.

In the depths of my soul I wanted him dead too. But I put the thought from my mind. Because we are not that kind of family and I am not that kind of man.

The Spectator

TWENTY-FOUR

THE SPRING MONTHS WERE the making of Franklin. Once a serious baby—old-mannish, heavy-jowled—with the coming of the spring he had lightened and lengthened, grown supple and strong. This June morning he had escaped the confines of his diaper, thrown it from his crib to the wooden floor beyond. He had climbed the bars that held him, lowered himself gently down, run naked through the apartment, all limbs and untamed hair.

"Wheee!"

Vee shouted back at him, "Wheee!"

Franklin skidded to a stop on the kitchen floor, arms high. He swayed, became serious, fixed his gaze upon his sister.

"Wheee?"

"Yeah, Franklin," said Vee. "Wheee. Right, Dad?"

"Yeah, honey," I said. "Wheee!"

"Wheee!" said Franklin.

We were a family again, no longer simply individuals adrift in our own grief.

These precious moments when Vee would allow herself to be

young. Lately she had put aside childish things, had become so very adult.

"Wheee!" shouted Franklin.

"Yeah, guys. Wheee." Elsa was standing in her nightgown, hair across her face, knife beside her, pressing oranges through the squeezer.

My eyes found hers. We had made it through the year. We had given each other space. Moving forward, I thought, separate, but together.

Faithful as ever.

"What?" she said.

We stared at each other, each surprised to find the other smiling. There was a lightness today, even in this god-awful place, an ease between us that could not be denied.

A bark.

A dog loped up, stood at the garden door looking in. An Irish setter, daft-faced, russet-coated, out of breath.

Franklin waved, shouted, "Do'!"

Another setter joined the first. The two dogs stared in, drool spilling from their pink-black gums, panting heavily, amazed to find four pairs of eyes staring back. They dipped down, inviting Franklin to join the chase.

"Vov!" shouted Franklin. "Vov!"

The dogs barked in reply, then sprang from the garden and out to the path. Franklin stood in the doorway, watching them go. In seconds you could see them in the parkland far beyond, leaping and tumbling over each other, dizzy in the gathering heat.

Licia was on the front page of *Posten* today, along with the ninety-one who had fallen on Garden Island. A tiny square image in a grid of faces. A memorial, on the first day of the trial. Her image was ringed in red; a note explained that she was missing, presumed drowned.

"Let me see that," said Elsa.

I handed her the paper.

"They used the one from her Instagram," I said.

"I always liked that picture."

Five counts of attempted murder. Ninety-one counts of murder. One disputed charge of murder, which the defense moved to have struck. Because we did not have Licia's body. And for that reason, I thought, we had hope.

Elsa handed the paper back to me. Her hand brushed mine. Something passed between us: some understanding beyond the words.

The winter had not unmade us. We had grown strong, it seemed, each in our own way. No one dared use the word *closure*, but at breakfast that morning there was an expectant energy. My wife; my daughter; even tiny Franklin, as he pushed his Tripp Trapp chair to the head of the table, climbed into place, took a banana in his right hand, and squeezed till the sides split.

"Here, little friend," I said. "Let me get that for you."

I reached across, peeled the banana, handed it to my son.

"Bann," said Franklin. "Banan."

Anyone looking in through that window, I thought, would say we had it pretty good.

WE STOOD OUTSIDE THE APARTMENT BUILDING, THE four of us.

Elsa laced her fingers into mine. She searched my eyes, smiling.

"What?" I said.

She drew away, looked at me again, smiled.

Vee stood on the tips of her toes, threw her arms around her mother's neck.

Elsa put her bag down on the tarmac path, lifted Vee off her feet.

"Hey," said Vee.

"Still my little girl," said Elsa, laughing.

"Put me down."

The bag on the path. Stiff-sided, gray, the strap a simple wide loop.

"New bag?" I said.

"Mum," said Vee. "Mum, I mean it, put me down."

Elsa lowered Vee to the path. She turned to face me. "New bag. Yes."

The eye contact: So deliberate. Calculated, almost.

"Hope that's okay," said Elsa. Money was tight, she meant, though she wouldn't say it in front of Vee.

I looked down, caught Vee looking at us. I looked at Elsa.

Elsa's smile: It was good, but it wasn't quite right. Her eyes flicked to a tree farther down the path, then flicked back to mine.

I said, "What would you call that color?"

"Battleship gray."

"I like your new bag." *Unusual choice*, I wanted to add. *A Mom bag. Not really your style.*

ELSA AND VEE WAITED OUTSIDE WHILE I dropped Franklin at kindergarten. I handed him his lunch box and his water bottle, which he dropped into a large plastic crate.

"*Hei*, Franklin!"

Franklin stood on the threshold of the Red Room, looking in, unsteady. Then he ran to Leni, let himself be swept into the air, wriggled around in her arms so he was facing me, and smiled.

"Hey, Leni," I said.

"Just wanted to say good luck," she said.

I nodded. "Thanks. Good to know Franklin's in safe hands."

"Sure." Her ponytail swished reassuringly as she carried him from the room.

On the way out I saw Tvist coming toward me, carrying Josi.

"Hello, Cal Curtis," he said evenly.

Josi turned to look at me. I looked at her, smiled. Her face lit up. "He'o, Ca' Cu'is."

"Good luck today," said Tvist.

"See you there," I said, watching after him.

SCANNERS AT THE COURTHOUSE. SHOES OFF. KEYS and belt in a plastic tray. Standard precautions—the familiar routines of the modern world.

We walked across the slate floor toward the wooden staircase. Vee hung back.

"Want us to save you a seat, honey?"

"I'm good."

On the floor outside the courtroom a chaos of tape marks and cables and tripods. Men and women in sober suits standing in pools of light, speaking test-words into microphones, joking quietly with the crews behind the cameras.

Elsa held my face in her hands. Around us people flowed toward the court.

"Handsome fuck," she said.

My phone vibrated. I took a step away, pulled the phone from my pocket.

Dan.

I held my phone up to Elsa.

"I'll find you a seat with translation," she said, serious suddenly. "Say hi."

We looked at each other. "Courage," she said, very quietly. I nodded. *Courage, love.*

I raised the phone to my ear. "Sorry, Dan."

"Three things. One: I'm calling to wish you guys luck."

"Thank you."

"Two: I want to let you know I have options."

"Options?"

"If you need to back out."

"I do not need to back out."

"I want you to promise—"

"What's the third thing?"

"The third thing is a piece of advice. Do not engage with these people."

"Sure, Dan, whatever you say."

"I'm serious, Cal. These are not people you want anywhere near the inside of your head. Do not look them in the eye."

A WALL HAD BEEN BUILT FOR THE trial, a three-sided glass box ten feet high. They stood there behind their wall, these men who had murdered so many people's children, so many people's brothers and sisters, in their nondescript black suits, their hair unbleached now. Mousy.

I saw Tvist take his place in the front row.

You do all this for these men, Tvist: your airport scanners, your glass walls, your special officers with their submachine guns. Yet you couldn't protect our children.

Tvist turned, as if he sensed my eyes on him. He caught my gaze and smiled. I turned away, surprised at my own anger.

In the back row of the courtroom Vee sat with some girls I didn't know, holding hands. All adult dresses, minimal makeup. I tried to meet Vee's eye, to ask her if she was okay, but she was lost in conversation.

Elsa curled her fingers into mine.

The men stared out at us from behind their bulletproof glass. Two officers approached them.

The Andersen brothers held out their hands. The officers removed the cuffs.

There they stood, massaging their wrists, surveying the room. They turned to each other. *Why were they not separated?*

A look passed between them. Each man folded his right arm across his heart. They turned again to face us, stared out again at the faces in the courtroom. Slowly, in unison, each unfolded his right arm, clenched his fist, fixed his gaze on the press at the back of the courtroom.

A frenzy of cameras.

A salute. A white power salute. The men exchanged a look, smiled, adjusted their pose. Their fists clenched a little tighter, their right arms extended a little farther. *Amplifying the signal.*

Elsa was gripping my wrist. The sinews in her arms and face were tight.

"I know," I said. *Courage, love.*

I heard a laugh in the row behind. An actual laugh, ringing bell-clear across the court. I turned to see a girl of Licia's age, dark-skinned and pretty, sitting among friends. The girl covered her mouth as she met my eye, appalled at her own reaction. The men turned toward her, anger in their gaze. They had not expected laughter. The tiny female judge spoke, asking for silence. The girl nodded an apology.

Beside me I felt Elsa turn too. She and the girl exchanged a look. Elsa put a hand over the girl's and smiled; the girl smiled back, glad of the support.

More cameras were turning. The girl couldn't be more than sixteen.

I looked toward the men, foolish and ashamed in their black shirts and their bully boots. The girl had punctured their moment, destroyed the drama of their performance, left them standing half-cocked and pathetic.

Laughable.

I put on my headset. I heard the translator's words in my ears. "Defendant Andersen, J., will stand." The judge began to address the first defendant. I could hear her voice through the foam padding of the headphones.

The tall man nodded at his brother, then stood facing the judge.

The translator continued. "Defendant Andersen, J., do you understand the charges made against you?"

The man nodded.

"Respond."

The man nodded again; he spoke, a single syllable.

The translator's voice, flattening out the dialogue, rendering both sides. "Yes." A pause. "How do you plead?"

There was another, longer pause. The man looked about him. *Checking he has the attention of the court*, I thought.

Bastard.

The man began to speak. After a moment the translator picked up his words, without inflection.

"As a . . . Knight of the Temple of Solomon . . . I decline to recognize the authority of this court. I refuse to plead."

I looked around at the girl behind us. She was not laughing.

I lifted the headphone off my right ear. Absolute silence in the courtroom. Beside me, Elsa was quietly shaking her head. The chief judge sat stock-still, staring at the man. The defendant looked around to his brother, nodded, then turned toward the back of the courtroom, stared defiantly out at the survivors, at the families of the dead. No one spoke. There were no camera shutters. I turned to look at my daughter, but Vee would not meet my eye. She was staring back at John Andersen.

The judge leaned across and consulted with a colleague, her hand across her microphone. She turned, sat watching the man for a few seconds. She took her hand from her microphone.

"Defendant Andersen, J., a refusal to enter a plea will be recorded as a plea of not guilty."

"I understand."

"Then your plea will be entered as not guilty."

"I do not recognize the authority of this court."

He looked across at his brother, who nodded, then leaned forward and spat a gobbet of chewing tobacco into his water glass.

The judge remained composed, but you could feel her anger. She spoke two words.

"Noted," came the voice in the headphones. "Sit."

Elsa leaned toward me. I raised an earphone.

"Look at them with their little uniforms, their little salutes, their little speeches." She gave a bitter laugh. "Look at the fact that they rehearsed the whole thing. Like, *We are the Knights of the Round Table*. That's funny, isn't it? It's like fucking Monty Python."

From the bench the chief judge was staring at Elsa.

"Elsa," I said. I nodded toward the judge.

"Yeah," she said quietly. "Okay."

Now the prosecutor stood looking out across the faces of the public. An accomplished woman, blond-haired, eyes of granite. Elsa and I sat up and faced the front.

The prosecutor spoke slowly, left long pauses between sentences, gave the translator time to catch up. She turned to address the judges. In the headphones the translator was affectless and calm, her words seconds behind the prosecutor's. "In the time between the parking of the van and the explosion, a witness called the police to say she had seen two men in navy overalls as they walked toward a small white car. Something in the men's demeanor caught in her mind: their behavior was hurried, feverish even.

"The eyewitness gave the police an accurate physical description of the men you see before you: the high foreheads, the wide-set eyes, the West Oslo accents. Both men were blond, she reported, though the eyewitness wondered if the shorter of the men you see before you, Paul Andersen, had dyed his hair; there was something about the eyebrows that did not match. The eyewitness had the presence of mind to note the license number: XR310701. This was indeed the license number of the car that the men drove to Garden Island."

Ahead, Tvist turned to a colleague. None of this was new to him.

I felt a movement beside me. Elsa's face was clouding with anger. Around us people were exchanging looks, shaking heads. I turned around. Vee's eyes met mine from the back of the courtroom, full of fury.

The translator's voice in my ear. "In other words, the police had the information needed in order to apprehend the suspects with no loss of life."

You could hear the translator sipping water while the prosecutor continued to speak. I caught Tvist's eye and he smiled; a careful smile, studiedly neutral.

"In fact," the translator began again, "at one point a police cruiser was directly behind the suspects' car. We know this from camera footage taken from the police cruiser."

The anger in the courtroom was intensifying. Elsa was gripping my arm tightly. I could sense the mounting outrage, could feel it rising in me too.

The Post-it note.

The white car.

The police cruiser.

Licia missing, presumed drowned.

The prosecutor finished speaking; she stood looking out across the court; she walked to her desk; she sat down. The translator's voice continued, catching up with the prosecutor's words.

"No one at police headquarters thought to pick up and read the note until seven fifty-seven, by which time both suspects had been in police custody for six minutes. And on the island ninety-one people, eighty-seven of them teenagers between the ages of thirteen and seventeen, lay dead. The police, of course, are not on trial here, but . . ."

I saw the look on Elsa's face. *They should be.*

I took off my headphones. Elsa leaned in. "I'm okay," she said.

"Tvist lied to me," I said. "About the Post-it note. Or it wasn't exactly a lie . . ."

At the back of the courtroom something clattered to the floor. I looked around. Vee was on her feet; she pushed past her friends and out into the aisle. Her eyes met mine. Her face was streaked and blotched.

"Let's go," I said to Elsa, my voice a low whisper.

"You stay, Cal," said Elsa. She got to her feet.

Vee was at the door of the courtroom.

"You sure?" I said.

Elsa leaned in, spoke very quietly. "One of us needs to witness this."

In the rows nearby people were staring at us. A woman, a court official in a dark skirt, was making her way toward Vee. Elsa reached the aisle, headed toward the rear exit, exchanged words with the official. The official opened the door and held it. Elsa put her hand on Vee's back, guided her through it.

The accused men watched as my wife and daughter walked away down the corridor. John Andersen said something to Paul. Paul smirked.

They had noticed our daughter's distress. They liked it.

TWENTY-FIVE

TVIST CAUGHT UP WITH me on the way out of the courtroom. "Cal."

I could think of nothing to say to him, so I half smiled and turned away. I carried on down the stairs and out through the lobby, eyes fixed ahead of me. I could feel him at my side, matching me step for step, could hear the heavy leather of his soles as we crossed the polished marble floor.

We stood on the steps of the court, blinking in the harsh summer light. Before us the temporary studios, each a twelve-foot cube, raised from the road on stilts, walled by translucent white tarpaulin. The sides of the studios were rolled up. Journalists on high office chairs were joking with colleagues on other continents, checking their hair in the screens of their phones.

Tvist gestured toward the studios. "This is nice."

I half turned toward him. "Is it?"

He smiled a neutral smile. "Practical and elegant and egalitarian . . ."

Another voice cut across Tvist's: "The very best of our Scandinavian values." I turned to see Bror, his arms thrown wide as if I were his long-lost brother. I hesitated for a moment, uneasy at the intimacy, then stepped forward and felt the warmth of his embrace.

"Cal Curtis," he said. "I feel you are close to a breakthrough." He turned toward Tvist, his arm still on the small of my back. "And Mr. Police Chief. What a trying morning this has been for you. You have my sympathy."

"Bror," said Tvist. "Cal." He nodded to me, then walked down the steps and away.

"Well, now," said Bror, watching him go. "This man Tvist is highly intelligent." He turned to me, the most radiant smile on his face. "Is he not?"

I found myself smiling too, relieved to be in his presence. "I mean . . ."

"He must protect his carefully constructed lies. You must not underestimate the lengths to which he will go." He took a half step backward, his hands loosely holding my forearms. Healing hands, I thought, radiating warmth. Kind eyes, searching mine. "You tried to break the story about the police delay, no?"

So Bror had known about the Post-it.

I looked about me. "I guess I should file my piece."

He reached out, took my hands in his. "Expect another of Milla's little gifts."

Then he was walking away.

"That was you?" I said.

"I don't know." He turned, gave a self-conscious shrug. "Was it?"

"Who is the source?"

He smiled, shook his head. "A priest has a duty of silence to his flock."

"I can respect that."

"With that in mind, if ever there were any particularly difficult thought you couldn't share with Elsa . . ."

"We're getting by," I said, because I trusted this man, but only so far.

He smiled. "Keep building your case." And he was gone.

AT JUST BEFORE ONE I ROLLED DOWN the sides of a studio at the far end. One hundred and fifteen seconds on the clock.

"Cal, we're seeing outrage at the behavior of the defendants in the Garden Island trial in Oslo, Norway."

"Some. When defendants John and Paul Andersen were brought into court, their first move, once the handcuffs were removed, was to make what I can only describe as a white power salute, right arms out, fists clenched. A gesture intended to shock, but which was met with derision. Far more serious were details that emerged about the Oslo police, who failed to act on an eyewitness description of the suspects, along with the license plate of the vehicle they drove to Garden Island. That number was on a handwritten note that sat on the desk of Police Chief Tvist himself. Yet no one thought to look at the note. Not until after the massacre was over and the men were in custody.

"Meanwhile, we await clarification on two major points: The police are stating that the organization to which the men claim to belong, the Tactical Brigades of the Knights Templar, is simply a dog whistle to other white extremists, and does not exist beyond the imaginations of John and Paul Andersen. Given the demonstrable incompetence of the police, how far can we trust such a claim? And point two: These men tested and perfected a powerful fertilizer bomb. So where is the laboratory where the men produced that bomb? No mention of this rather significant hole in the investigation. You have to ask: Are the police even looking?"

I looked up, saw the clock tick down to zero.

"Thank you, Cal." A click on the line and Carly's voice became distant. "A brave man bearing witness at the trial of the presumed murderers of his daughter."

I stepped out from the white tarpaulin walls of the studio. I joined the line for the scanners; I put my press accreditation around my neck, took off my belt and my shoes, put my laptop and phone in a gray plastic tray.

TVIST TURNED IN HIS SEAT AS I entered the courtroom. I smiled and nodded. Tvist smiled carefully in response, but I saw the scowl he tried to suppress. He had heard my radio piece, I guessed.

Elsa's seat was empty. On it was a small envelope, with *Cal Curtis* written in fine cursive script. I looked about me. Tvist had turned away, but I felt eyes on me.

I looked up. The judges were entering.

I looked down at the envelope in my hands.

I looked up. Paul Andersen now, fitting a lump of chewing to-bacco between his upper lip and his gum, all the while trying to lock his eyes onto mine.

I turned to the woman on my left. "Excuse me," I said as I got up to leave.

THE IMAGE IN THE ENVELOPE WAS A simple one. A red rubber dinghy, photographed from above. There were figures in the boat, heavily foreshortened, wearing some kind of uniform. Two had rifles slung across their chests. The rubber of the boat bulged around the figures of each of the men, as if it could not contain them.

A still from a video. I turned the picture over. In the same cursive script a hand had written, *The real story*.

TWENTY-SIX

I SAT ON THE terrace drinking whisky. There was a psychotic intensity to the evening light. The fjord glowed gold and green; there were purples and indigos in the trunks of the trees: a parallel spectrum, some great supernatural darklight.

Did I imagine hearing the front door slide shut? It was quiet, but there was a distinctive click.

I went through to the bathroom. There was Elsa in the shower. She turned off the water, opened the cabinet, her body slick.

"Strange," I said. "I thought . . ."

"You thought?"

". . . that you'd slipped out."

"And yet, here I am." Water beading on her breasts, on her belly, making gentle tracks down her thighs. A smile that was more than a smile. "Perhaps you want to join me in the shower?"

An invitation that was not an invitation. A challenge, almost, her wolf eyes searching mine.

Water drops marking tracks on her thighs, on her breasts.

"I love you. It's just . . ."

I saw the desire in her eyes, saw it curdling with disappointment. She nodded sadly. "It's just you don't want me anymore."

"Vee went out."

"Which should give us the perfect opportunity. But I get it."

"I'm going to go after her," I said.

"Of course."

As she turned away, water ran in rivulets down her back.

IN TREES TO THE SIDE OF THE path crows had gathered. They watched silently, eyes flicking white as they caught the lights from the apartment buildings.

Ahead, small and determined, Vee was striding toward the station. Lights on short poles at the side of the path threw her shadow crazily onto trees.

As she passed by the Viking ruin, I slowed. This place disturbed the rational geometry of the parkland, of its neat green lawns and its blue-black tarmac paths. The site was overgrown by gorse, guarded by barbed wire. Vee huddled into herself, though the evening was warm. She hurried on. Here too the crows gathered, blinking silently down. Something older lurked behind the wire, wilder than any of us. Burials, people said. Dismemberments and blood rituals.

Vee came to a stop on the platform, stood blinking under the lights, while I watched her from the bridge above. My little girl in a black dress she must have taken from Elsa's wardrobe, starkly lit, alone on the heavy gray platform. I watched as she bought a ticket from the machine. I bought a ticket on my phone.

I stepped on at the rear of the train, watching my daughter as she chose a seat near the front. I pulled out my phone, sent her a text message.

Where are you?

Ahead of me, at the far end of the carriageless train, in a dress a size too large, Vee bent forward. A pause, then my phone vibrated in my hand.

Julie's.

I watched Vee for a while. Had it come easily, to lie to me?

WHEN THE TRAIN PULLED INTO MAJORSTUEN, I waited until I was certain Vee was off before stepping onto the platform and heading for the main road.

People from the bars were spilling onto the street. Vee was walking swiftly now. I followed from the other side of the road. People hung about on the sidewalks in twos and threes, called out to each other across the traffic. A man leaned on the hood of an idling car, stood swaying, then bent over and vomited into the gutter. Vee clasped her hands tightly around herself as she passed him.

A bus crossed between us, then another, and when they cleared I thought I had lost her, that she had slipped down a side street, but she was there, her face lit up by the windows of the Broker winebar. Men in suits watched her as she walked, swiftly, arms folded across her chest. There was something in the air, something heavy and salacious and adult in the way they looked at her, then looked at each other.

She's fifteen, you fucks.

From a doorway someone spoke to her. Vee hovered, uncertain. I should intervene, but I wanted to know where she was going, why she had lied. I stood, sinews tensed, planning my route through the traffic, but Vee walked on, and the man did not follow.

Twice more Vee turned to look about her. I hung back, let her pass out of sight. The sidewalks down here were emptier; she would see me if I followed too close. I took out my phone. There she was, a white dot passing down the right-hand sidewalk, gliding into Magnussons vei, coming to rest outside number four. I enlarged the map, clicked on the wineglass icon next to Vee's. A bar. Mikrokosmos. And as I watched, Vee's white dot seemed to enter the bar.

THE AIR SMELLED OF SPILLED BEER. PINE-SOL soap too, and the tang of old men's kidneys.

"What can I get you?" asked a barwoman, smiling.

I picked up the beer card, pretended to look at it. The barwoman moved away.

The bar had three sides, with lines of beer taps all the way along. It was late. Men swayed in their seats in front of rows of empty glasses, or stared furtively at women, who stared candidly back. From the far corner came the *thock-thock-thock* of darts.

There was Vee, in a dark booth directly opposite me. And there, opposite Vee, was the helicopter pilot Pavel Lisowski. I texted her:

Still up?

She said something to Pavel, busied herself with her phone. My phone vibrated.

Julie's mum says hi.

What was she doing?

Pavel looked disheveled and unwashed in his pressed black shirt. There was a fresh glass of beer in front of each of them, and beside each beer a shot glass. Pavel was leaning forward; he seemed to be spitting words at my daughter. Vee was looking evenly at this man, head close to his, perfectly unafraid. Even as the anger spiked in me I felt a strange stab of pride.

My little girl. Holding her own.

As I turned left along the second side of the bar a woman barged into me. Beer spilled down my shirt and onto my leg. The woman did not stop.

People milled in both directions. I turned to look at my daughter, and as I did, Vee picked up her shot glass, drank it down, watching Pavel all the while. I saw how she winced, though she hid it well. I looked about. No one but Pavel was paying Vee any mind. Except for me, of course, and she had not yet seen me.

Vee set the glass down on the table, said something to Pavel.

"Excuse me," I said. A group of women smiled amiably at me, though they carried on blocking my way.

"I need to get past," I said.

The women smiled. They stayed where they were.

I began moving women out of the way, guiding them by their shoulders, anxious not to be seen as rough or inappropriate, but still the women smiled. The last of the group, a dark-haired woman in a laced fitted top, stood in front of me, right arm on the pillar at the corner of the bar, made a play of refusing to let me pass.

"Please," I said.

"So polite," she said. "Would you like to drink beer with me, Mr. Englishman?"

I looked across at Pavel. He was speaking animatedly. He had not yet seen me.

"Scottish," I said, "and in other circumstances this would be fun."

"What is it about this that isn't funny?" said the woman, a look of mock-disappointment on her face.

I pointed. "That's my daughter. She's fifteen. That man has bought her alcohol."

"Oh." The playfulness dissipated. She stepped out of the way, put a hand on my shoulder. "Do you want me to call the police?" she whispered as I passed.

"I've got this. But thanks."

I rounded the bar, walked straight up to the booth, stood staring down at Vee. "Because they got it excluded," she was saying, "or ruled inadmissible, or something. You know this."

Pavel leaned closer in. Had they really not seen me?

"Find someone who DVRed it," he was saying. "This is not my responsibility, Viktoria."

"Pavel," I said.

"What do you want?" He said it calmly, but his eyes darted toward the exit. In Vee's eyes I saw horror. She was calculating fast, looking for the words that would defuse the situation.

"Vee," I said. "Go and wait outside."

She wanted to say something. She stopped herself. She stood up. I stepped out of her way. From the corner of the bar the woman watched. Vee began to pass me. She made to say something. I shook my head.

"Stand outside," I said. "Do not speak to anyone."

I slid into the booth opposite Pavel.

"I'm going to go," he said, as if it were the most natural thing in the world. He began to get up.

I put a hand on his shoulder. "There's a camera, Pavel."

Pavel looked up at the security camera in the corner. "And?"

"And I told that woman not to call the police." Pavel looked over toward the bar. The dark-haired woman was watching our exchange, concerned. "But we both know what she and the camera saw."

He looked at the drinks in front of him. He looked at the camera. He slumped down into his seat.

I watched as Vee made her way through the bar, saw her tapping gently on people's shoulders, making herself as small as possible, slipping through gaps between bodies. The dark-haired woman moved out of the way, put a hand on Vee's shoulder, guided her past her friends at the bar.

I said, "What did Vee want?"

"Proof that her sister is alive. Which you know I don't have."

"And you arranged to meet her here?"

"And then you come, and you threaten me that I will lose my pilot's license. That's what you're implying, isn't it?"

"Pavel, she is fifteen. You knew that."

He stared sullenly at me. He had the look of a man who had been drinking steadily for hours. Matte shadows were forming around the armpits and the neck of his neatly pressed shirt.

"No," he said, "I do not think I can allow you to threaten me like this."

"No one is threatening you." I took out my phone, opened the video still of the boat. He sat forward, instantly alert.

"Where did you get this?"

"Anonymous source."

"You mean police." A statement, not a question.

"What happened to that boat?"

He exhaled heavily. "I can't help you."

"You can," I said. "You won't."

"Cal," he said. "You do not wish to put your children's lives in danger. Do not pursue this material."

VEE WAS STANDING ON THE FAR SIDE of the street, tiny and humiliated, fingers worrying at the hem of her dress. I crossed the street. As I approached her she held up her phone with the texts I had sent. "Who were you even going to show these to? The police? Mum? *Oh, look, honey, our daughter's a liar.*" Her makeup was smeared. She had been crying.

"I'm not building a case against you, Vee. We'll both delete the texts from our phones and we'll call that the end of it."

She looked at me, surprise in her eyes. "You're not going to show her?"

"Look, I've been fifteen, and your mum's been fifteen, and I guess we all had a traumatic day. But promise me you'll stop trying to investigate this, and that you'll stay away from that man. He's damaged, and he's unstable."

"The police are doing nothing."

"I swear to you that I will hold the police to account for Licia's disappearance. But you have to stop pursuing Pavel."

"Because you think he could hurt us?"

I said nothing. Some instinct told me that what Pavel had told me was right, that to investigate too closely would be to put us in danger.

WHEN WE GOT IN, ELSA'S NEW GRAY bag was standing in the middle of the hallway. Such an odd statement for her to make: so rigid; so colorless; so determinedly practical. Vee noticed me looking, gave a little mock-frown.

"Do you think if you open it all her secrets will fly out?"

"Bed, Vee."

"I'm pushing my luck now, aren't I?"

"Bed, love."

She threw her arms around my neck and hugged me very tight, then walked quietly away, as if embarrassed by the show of emotion.

TWENTY-SEVEN

THE NEXT MORNING THE bag was still standing there.

I could hear Elsa in the kitchen making breakfast, cooing to Franklin. I could hear Franklin cooing in reply.

I crouched down, slipped the clasp. Inside was a black leather wallet. In the wallet were a credit card and a pistol license dated 1998. No cash.

Some slight shift in the balance of the light. I looked up. Vee was standing in the doorway of her room. Our eyes met. Three hours' sleep and a quick shower, but she looked better; held together by nervous energy. There was something adult and appraising in her gaze. "Where is she?" she said.

"Making breakfast."

I slipped the license into the wallet, and the wallet into the bag.

Vee's eyes flashed toward the kitchen, then to me. "Dad, no one is that tidy."

"Have you been going through your mother's things?"

She gave a little scoffing sound, made a backing-off gesture with her hands. "You're the one with your hands in your wife's bag. But sure, make me the bad guy."

I considered this. I stood up. "I'm sorry."

"You know I won't tell her," she said.

"You can tell her if you like," I said.

"But I won't."

A moment of complicity, strange after all that had happened. We were smiling at each other, sharing in this small betrayal.

"Just so you know," said Vee, "I'm an empiricist, not a fascist."

I frowned. "What?"

"I base my beliefs on the facts in front of me."

I smiled, but Vee was serious.

"Racial hierarchies are based on emotion. I thought about this a lot. They're not rational."

"Tell your mother. She'll be delighted. Come on let's eat."

Elsa was standing by the table, reading from the court schedule. There was something too perfect, too staged in the arrangement of her limbs, and I wondered for a moment if she had heard us in the hall.

"I'm going to sit today out," she said.

Vee stared. "Why, Mum?"

Elsa picked up the sheet of paper from the table. "'Today the court will examine the beliefs of the accused, in connection with the psychiatric report compiled by Doctor Blah, blah blah blah professor emeritus of the University of Meh.' I'm translating. You get the gist."

"Meh," said Franklin from his highchair. "Mmmmeh."

Vee took the piece of paper from Elsa's hand, scanned it, put it down. I simply stared at my wife.

"Don't look at me with concern, Cal. What happens inside

those men's heads is irrelevant to me. It's what they did that counts."

"And it's not that I disagree with you."

"Then don't."

Only Franklin seemed truly happy this morning, though the day was just as bright and the birds sang just as loudly.

"DO YOU HAVE TO BE CRAZY TO plan the murder of children? This is the question that the Garden Island courtroom will consider today. Paul Andersen and his brother John admit that they set out to do exactly that last year on Midsummer's Eve, when they murdered ninety-one people in cold blood, eighty-seven of them minors. In front of the court are two competing psychiatric reports, which draw two chillingly different conclusions."

I paused. Through the window of my office I could see our upstairs neighbor, standing on the path, peering in. I looked at the telephone on the desk in front of me, at the headphone lead connecting me to the phone. I picked up the phone, stood up, walked toward the window.

Carly's voice in my ears, comforting and professional. "Cal, talk us quickly through those conclusions."

"The first report states the brothers were in the grip of a psychotic break, suffering paranoid delusions about a Muslim invasion, after a year spent in near-isolation in a rented worker's cottage, in which the police found two gaming consoles, countless cigarette butts, mounds of used chewing tobacco, and not a lot else. That's both men. Suffering the same delusions. Your listeners won't be surprised to learn that the judges asked for a second opinion."

The neighbor was waving and smiling. I smiled up at her, then twisted the handle on the blind. The neighbor's expression changed to one of surprise as the dark bands obliterated her shape.

"Now walk us through that second opinion, would you, Cal?"

I turned, sat on the edge of my desk. "The second report concludes that the Garden Island murders were the result of meticulous planning. It points out that the isolation was self-imposed, and that the men spent that year alone together educating themselves in bomb-making, studying and rehearsing firearms techniques, only coming into the city sporadically, to pick up girls and visit their mother. In other words, these men were not delusional. They were bad and not mad."

"Now, Cal, as many of our listeners know, you lost a daughter in these savage attacks."

"That is correct." I could hear the catch in my own voice, wondered if Carly could hear it too.

"And your interpretation of the evidence?"

"I'm not a psychiatrist."

"But I'm asking you as the father of Licia Curtis, who disappeared that fateful day on Garden Island. You spent yesterday observing the Andersen brothers in court."

I thought about the men, about how they had watched my younger daughter, enjoying her distress. When I spoke I had to choke back my anger.

"Those men . . . they planned the murder of our children. They killed with ruthless efficiency. Now they are exploiting the trial to spread their poison to a wider audience. These men are not insane. *Evil* would be a better word."

I CHANGED MY SON'S DIAPER, DRESSED HIM for kindergarten, placed him in his rocker chair. Elsa was still packing his lunch.

And when she sent me to the bedroom to fetch her phone I realized she had left it unlocked. I stood looking at the phone where it lay on the bed. I picked it up. The thought of what I was about to do worried at the edges of my conscience. My finger hovered over the lock button. But before I locked the phone and returned it to Elsa in the kitchen I enabled location sharing.

"All good?" I said as I passed it to her.

"Brown goat's cheese sandwich." She handed me the lunch box. "Cucumber chunk, tomato chunk, banana chunk, chocolate chunk, satsuma."

"Modern Norway in a lunch box." I bent down to the rocker chair, picked Franklin up with my spare arm. Elsa sent me a neutral half smile.

We were brisk and efficient. We did not hug. Second day of the trial, and already we were coming apart.

AT THE KINDERGARTEN I MET TVIST. HE had delivered Josi, was placing her lunch box into the plastic crate by the door to the kitchen. I lifted Franklin, my hands in his armpits, lowered him into his Crocs. "One foot," I said. "And the other foot."

"Foo," said Franklin excitedly. "Foo!"

"I enjoyed your piece today."

I looked up, wary.

No edge to Tvist's smile. "You are right," he said. "Of course those men are sane."

I bent down. "Franklin," I said, "go and play." Franklin, suspicious in his dungarees and his Crocs, threw his arms tightly around my thigh.

"Separation anxiety," said Tvist.

I lifted Franklin up, stood facing Tvist. "Is that all?"

"I'm not sure I understand." He knew what I was saying—of course he knew—but he kept his gaze level and his smile polite.

"*Hei*, Franklin!"

In my arms I felt Franklin kicking, stretching away from me. I turned to see Leni walking toward us. Franklin was making little *oh oh* sounds, kicking happily. I kissed him on the forehead and passed him over.

"Hey, Leni," I said.

Leni smiled. "Hi, Cal. *Hei*, Ephraim." She knelt, picked up Josi in her free arm, and carried the children into the Red Room, knocking the door shut with her thigh.

"Perhaps I will see you in court today," said Tvist. He turned. He was ending the conversation.

I caught the door as it swung shut behind him, followed him out along the path. As he reached the gate I touched his shoulder and he turned.

"You lied to me. About the Post-it note. And I know there's more."

"Is there?"

"Maybe your problem isn't police incompetence? Maybe it's active corruption?"

"How would one even prove such a thing?" For a moment he looked almost amused, though I could feel the underlying anger. "Why are you pursuing a narrative that is harmful to the police, and harmful to our country?"

"Are you telling me not to make an enemy of you?"

"That's one interpretation, isn't it?"

There was an analytical coldness to him now, a hardness in his quick black irises. Then he was smiling. "If only ethics did not prevent us from taking a beer together."

"A beer?"

"I am certain this could be cleared up over a beer."

He walked toward a gray Tesla SUV, lifted the gull-wing door on the driver's side, sat down. The door closed. The car moved silently off.

IN THE COURTROOM I CHOSE SEATS TOWARD the right-hand wall, placed myself on Vee's left. If the men made eye contact with her I would lean in to block it. But today they sat slouched in their chairs, paying us no mind. Every now and then one turned to the other and made some kind of joke. They would smirk, then turn to face the glass wall, glaring out at the public.

I took out my phone, unlocked it, opened Find My Family. I looked about me.

Vee was staring at the screen of her own phone. She caught me looking and held it out to me. I placed my phone facedown on my thigh and took Vee's.

REMEMBER: THIS IS WHAT THE #ANTIFASCIST #FIGHTBACK LOOKS LIKE

That same image of Licia, the gun braced in her hands.

"Pretty cool," said Vee, taking her phone. "Don't you think?" She flicked into Instagram and began to write.

I turned my own phone over. There was Elsa on the street outside our apartment block. A flashing orange dot.

Vee leaned toward me. I shielded the phone with my hand.

"Which one would you drop, Dad?" she whispered. "If you had a Glock?"

"Vee, you can't talk like that here."

Vee rolled her eyes, turned to face the men.

I looked at my phone screen. Elsa was on the move.

Vee leaned in again. I shielded the screen.

"Just because we're 'pacifists' doesn't mean you can't answer the question. Say you have one gun and one bullet, which one would you drop?"

I looked about me. No one had heard her. But still. "That's not why we're here. We're here to learn."

Vee rolled her eyes, faced forward, made a play of listening.

I watched my screen for a while, tilting it so Vee could not see. I assumed at first that Elsa was heading for the mall, but she took a road that led into town, walking swiftly.

"Dad," said Vee. "Put that away."

"Sorry." I turned my phone facedown. I sat forward, tried to listen. The absent father; the abusive, neglectful mother; the social work reports recommending removal of the boys: there was nothing here that we did not already know; all those markers that so many killers share, but which do not in themselves make a killer.

The men looked unaffected when the psychiatrists read out the injuries they had sustained at the hands of their mother: the broken arms and the scalded legs, the kettle-cable marks, and, once, the imprint of an iron on the skin of Paul Andersen's lower back. Time and again the social workers had recorded their concern. Time and again the boys' mother moved them to a new district, and the social work evaluations began again from scratch.

"The answer is you shoot the little one," whispered Vee after a time.

"Vee, no."

"What? This is a game. You shoot Paul Andersen. John Andersen shrivels up and dies. Two men, one bullet."

"Vee."

"It's okay. I'm done."

I turned my phone over in my hand. There was Elsa at Stein Erik Lundgrens plass, an address I didn't recognize.

"Put it away, Dad."

"All right."

I dropped the phone into my pocket, tried to concentrate on the trial.

After a while I began to see small differences between the men. It was the smaller brother, Paul, who made most of the jokes. The taller brother, John, did most of the laughing.

Vee was right. John Andersen was completely dependent on Paul.

ELSA SPENT AN HOUR AND A HALF at Stein Erik Lundgren's plass number 2. When she left, it was at a slow walk. As if something had calmed her.

In the café during morning break, while Vee fetched drinks and cinnamon buns, I dropped the address into Google. A low-rise industrial building, painted white.

Skarpsno Pistolklubb.

A pistol club in Skarpsno. Was this Elsa's idea of *therapy*?

I felt Vee hovering at the edge of my vision. I looked up.

"It's their sanity," she said. I put my phone on the table, face-down.

"What is?"

She passed me a black coffee in a paper cup. "That's what those men find funny." She put down her soda. "Every time someone says the Andersen brothers are insane, that's when they laugh. They find it hilarious that anyone could think that. Like they gamed the system."

And she was right. For the rest of the morning I watched the Andersens closely and the pattern was the same. Details from the reports were read out. Same facts, different conclusions. At every finding of insanity, the men sniggered. At every mention of planning, they looked bored.

AT TWELVE ELSA COLLECTED FRANKLIN FROM KINDERGARTEN. There was her flashing orange dot. At quarter to one she put Franklin down for his nap. She was on the terrace at the back of the apartment for seven minutes. Nothing grows on our terrace, so she could only be drinking coffee or smoking a cigarette.

The tracking on Elsa's phone is very precise.

I RECORDED MY PIECE. I CLIMBED THE steps to Security. There was one person in front of me. Edvard, taller and thinner than ever, in an ill-fitting gray suit, dropping his belongings into a gray plastic tray.

Perhaps he felt my eyes on him. He turned, made himself smile. "Hello, Cal."

"Hello, Edvard."

We embraced. "How's Jo?" I said.

He turned to face the scanner.

"Oh, Jo's okay," said Edvard. "I'm sure he sends his love."

"Send mine back."

"I'll be certain to do that."

The woman nodded at him. He stepped briskly through the scanner. Some strange edge to his behavior; something untruthful.

The scanner woman smiled. I passed her my telephone.

Edvard turned to me. "I thought perhaps I'd sit with you in the courtroom?"

"That would be . . . that would be nice, Edvard . . ."

The woman was inspecting my phone. I put my keys and belt onto the conveyor, and stepped through the scanner.

Edvard was watching me, expectant.

"I'm going to see you in there, Edvard. I have a couple of calls to make."

"See you in there."

I watched him go, then called Jo.

"Hey, Cal," said Jo. "Good piece. Moving."

"I worry I come across as angry. So anyway—"

"Righteous anger."

I was in the foyer now. I sat on a low wooden bench. "So anyway, Edvard's here at the courthouse, and he wanted to sit together, and I guess I was wondering how things were between you, because he was being a little odd."

A long pause. "*Odd* is a pretty fair description of how things are between Edvard and me."

"I'm sorry."

"And you really don't want to hear about our problems."

"Actually, I kind of do."

"Really?"

"Really."

"Cal, he moved into the spare room. Says he wants us to *experi-*

ment with celibacy. Like it's something I should be getting excited about."

"Wow."

"And then he asks me if I think Mila Kunis is hot."

"Okay . . ."

"It's like he's practicing not being gay," said Jo. "Or being married. I mean, is Mila Kunis hot to married men? And who in the world decides it's a good idea to *experiment with celibacy*?" He was making light, but I could hear the pain behind the words. "It's like when his parents came to stay and I pretended to be his roommate. Only no one's coming to stay. The flat is like a morgue."

"Wait a second," I said to Jo, because there was Vee, coming down the stairs, computer bag in hand.

I moved to stand up, but Vee did not see me. She began walking toward the exit. I watched as she passed, then stood up. At the top of the courthouse steps she looked about herself, then headed quickly away.

"No offense about being married, by the way," Jo was saying.

"None taken. I'm so fucking sorry, Jo. Listen, I should go . . ."

"I know," he said. "I'm being an energy sink. Sorry. You don't need it."

"No, mate. I want to hear."

"Not what you signed up for."

"Beer soon," I said. "Gotta go."

I reached the top of the courthouse steps, thinking I'd lost Vee, but she was striding back toward me from the edge of the square.

"Mum's right," she said as she reached the top of the steps. "Today's pointless."

Still, though: She was avoiding my gaze. She turned and looked out across the square as if checking some detail.

"What's happening, Vee? Where were you going?"

She turned and looked me in the eye. "Nothing, Dad, and nowhere. Don't spy on me."

So convinced she was of her own position. I felt a strange protective surge of pride. *Our stubborn little girl.* "You can tell me later," I said. "When you're ready."

"Tell you what?" she said, her own eyes flashing. "What are you looking at me like that for?"

Because, Vee, I thought, *you are every inch your mother's daughter.*

TWENTY-EIGHT

ELSA AND I WERE on the sofa, drinking martinis in front of the evening news.

I said, "I want to know your reaction to something Vee said."

Elsa reached across, took my hand in hers. "How do you get them so perfect, Cal?"

"I'm serious," I said.

"I am too."

On the news was an interview with the immigration minister, in Norwegian. Arrest photographs of dark-skinned people. Cameras roaming through dusty African towns. Handcuffed figures being led up airplane steps. The minister in a studio, all bottle-blond hair, her lips and cheeks rouged, like a child's drawing of a white woman.

"So," said Elsa. "Vee . . ."

"Yeah, Vee asked me, if I had one gun and one bullet—"

"—which one of the Andersens you'd kill?" That smile, as if the idea amused her. "I can see where she's going with that . . ." She took a long swig of her drink, rolling the glass appreciatively in her hand as she swallowed. "My reaction is that it's normal to play around with ideas."

The immigration minister used the word *ghetto*. I turned to face the TV. The minister seemed to be making a point about Sweden.

Elsa put her glass on the table. She turned to me. "That really is a great martini. Why don't you tell me about the olives you used?"

The immigration minister's job appeared to be sending refugee children back to Afghanistan and Central Africa. A Facebook page full of love-heart emojis celebrated successful repatriations.

"The olives, Cal?"

I answered sharply, "You just . . . you buy the right fucking olives, Elsa. Is that really more important to you than Vee's state of mind?"

The interviewer was asking the minister if she was as *skeptical about immigration* as the Andersen brothers were.

Elsa reached forward to take my hand again. "This is our ritual. Cal, why are you getting hung up on a child's game? And will you please look at me, and not the TV?"

On-screen the interviewer was asking the minister precisely how her views differed from the Andersens'. The minister replied that her views were nothing like the Andersens'. The interviewer quoted the prime minister's words from the memorial service: "*More democracy. More openness.*" His tone was sarcastic. An argument broke out in the television studio.

Elsa picked up the remote control, began flicking through the channels.

"Okay," I said. "So what's your answer to Vee's dilemma?"

"It's hardly a dilemma, Cal. You shoot the strong one. Paul Andersen. Without him the weak one crumples. Everybody wins."

How strange to hear my wife speak so casually about murder, even if it was a game. She turned to look at me, seemed to read my thought.

"You do understand I'm joking?" she said. "Cal? Or do we not make jokes anymore?"

I looked at her as she sat, rolling the stem of her glass between forefinger and thumb. Something about her had changed. There was a purposefulness to Elsa these days—though surely it had come gradually and imperceptibly—something decisive and hard, and sharp as new-forged steel.

I SHOULD HAVE ASKED HER. THE QUESTION was a simple one.

What did you do today, Elsa?

Instead I went out, angry and confused. I went to a bar with a stage where Mark Steiner & His Problems were playing. The songs were slow and melodic, the guitars full of discord and Nordic pain: "Insomnia'; "Fortitude'; "Sea of Disappointment'; "Don't Explain." *With your voice of gravel and honey*, I thought, *you could be singing for me*.

Beside me a woman leaned in. "Guy can really move." The warmth of her breath on my ear. Her dancing eyes.

I nodded. She must have caught the look in my eye.

"Hey," she said. "Why so sad?"

I had no answer to that, though we sat and we talked for hours on the steps outside. If Elsa had been watching, I know she would not have liked it. And when we parted, I felt her fingertips lingering on mine and wondered if this was an invitation to something more.

But I love my wife, so I headed for home.

VEE FOUND ME ON THE TERRACE. SHE looked at the cigarette butts that littered the soil of the planter, at the bottle of gin on the table in front of me.

"I can't get back to sleep. You woke me up when you came in."

"Sorry." I put an arm across her shoulder, and we sat, father and daughter, looking out from our strange oppressive apartment into the black trees and the purple hills beyond. The night was at its darkest, though there was color in the sky. A cat roamed the long grass behind the apartment building, blue-gray and shadowless in the grasses below the trees.

That expectant look on Vee's face, all fired up.

"What?" I said.

"Dad, can I show you a thing?"

But she was already on her feet and out of the room.

She returned, carrying a bundle neatly wrapped in a dishcloth. She placed it on the table in front of me, sat down opposite me, watching for my reaction.

The corners of the cloth were folded into the middle.

"Did you go searching among your mother's things? Because that's an abuse of trust, Vee."

"So wake her up and tell her . . ."

I lifted a corner, felt fabric drag across the object inside. Something heavy and dark and metallic. I unfolded the cloth, corner by corner.

The handgrip was textured, the trigger guard square. I leaned in. Engraved into the gunmetal were the words *Glock 17 Gen4 AUSTRIA*.

Vee's face was flushed, her eyes electric with excitement. "Aren't you even going to pick it up?"

I shook my head. "Vee, I'm sorry."

I could feel her disappointment. This was not the response she wanted.

"Why?"

"We are not providing the stability you need."

"Did you know she had this, though?"

"It's not a complete surprise."

I began to fold the corners of the cloth back over the body of the pistol.

"Dad, is Mum having some kind of breakdown?"

I laughed. "Your mother is the sanest person I know."

She looked at me, unconvinced. She made to say something. She stopped.

"What is it, Vee?"

"There's another thing. Only now I don't know if you'll be interested."

"Is this other thing also about Mum?" I said.

"No."

"All right, then. What sort of a thing is it?"

"A story. One nobody else has."

She left the room and returned with an iPad.

"Vee," I said, "where is this from?"

"I promised not to say."

"Vee—"

"You can take it to the police if you like, Dad. But please watch what's on it first."

TWENTY-NINE

IT BEGAN LIKE A feature film, though there was no sound. The camera skimmed the glassy fjord, raised up as it came to the island, followed the path from the boat dock up to the clearing. It hung suspended, looking down at the main house, at the bodies that lay strewn on the sun-scorched grass beyond.

Children. Other people's children. You could almost imagine they were sleeping.

I reached across, pressed pause, turned the iPad on its front.

"Okay," I said. "Vee, I want you to go to bed."

Vee met my eye. "I already watched it, Dad. Twice. It's not like I'm going to sleep *better* if I go to bed now. But if that's what you want . . ."

I pushed the tips of my fingers together, tapped both index fingers against the tip of my nose, breathed out heavily. I turned the iPad over. Vee pressed play.

Even in close-up, the camera held steady. Now it followed a dark-haired boy as he ran along a path, panning and tilting with him. So close. You could see his eyes, read the fear in them, see patches of sweat around the collar of his T-shirt. The camera watched as he left the path, made his way into a wooden cabin.

The cabin was one of many. The helicopter stayed in position for what must have been about a minute. The shot held wide, staring down. In that time you saw another boy, then two girls, each running to a different cabin. The camera tilted up, zoomed in to a path, found a man in police uniform.

The tall brother. John Andersen. Carrying a pistol. The merest hint of a smile.

John Andersen holstered his pistol. A rifle raised into position. He checked something on the side of the weapon, then looked through the gunsight at the helicopter, taking aim. The helicopter jerked upward, John Andersen dropped out of shot, and the screen was a blur of faded greens and browns.

Fleeing.

I looked at Vee. There was something very adult about the set of her chin, about the determination in her eyes. She looked older than her sister ever had, and I wanted to tell her that I was sorry, that I could see sometimes how Licia's disappearance had robbed her of her childhood.

"Dad," said Vee, looking up, "you're not watching."

"Of course I'm watching."

On-screen the water was an indistinct gray-black mass.

The camera steadied. The world fell into focus. There was the slipway on the mainland. At the waterline a red rubber boat, and on the boat four men. Figures around the boat busied themselves with levers and ropes. The boat seemed to be floating free. I had seen that boat before, in the video still that Bror had left for me on Elsa's seat in the courtroom.

"You see that, Dad? No one's even holding it."

Two more men jumped aboard. The rubber of the boat seemed to swell around them.

"Fucking amateurs," said Vee.

"Vee, please," I said.

"Okay, but do they look to you like they know what they're doing? It's way too low in the water."

Another two men approached and jumped in. The boat pulled slowly from the slipway. Water plumed out behind the motor.

"This is what they didn't want us to see."

"Maybe," I said.

"No, Dad, it is. That's the police tactical weapons unit."

The helicopter was returning across the sound toward the island.

"You're right," I said. "That is a little odd."

"That's not the end of that story, Dad . . . But you have to keep watching . . ."

Now the helicopter was back above the island, hovering over a block of flat-roofed buildings at the side of the clearing.

The shower block.

At one end of the block a door opened. Two girls appeared on the steps. They waved frantically up at the helicopter. The shot began to close with the ground. Yellow-green grass filled the frame, then the screen turned dark gray. Pavel was landing, I realized, in the clearing by the shower block.

He had tried to help. He had been telling the truth about that.

"Vee," I said, "was it Pavel who gave you this?"

"I know you told me to keep away from him. But if you're going to shout at me, can you at least wait till you've seen it all?"

I took her hand. "I'm not going to shout at you. I promise."

She appraised me for a moment, puzzled.

The shot jerked yellow-green. Vee's eyes flicked back to the screen. The camera was in the air again, looking down. There were the two girls looking up at the helicopter, desperate now. And there, at the edge of the frame, a man in police uniform. Paul Andersen looked up, locked eyes with the camera. The helicopter continued to climb.

The girls disappeared inside the shower block. The door closed.

The short man unslung his rifle, walked toward the door of the building. From the other side of the screen his brother appeared, walking toward the door at the other end, his rifle held casually in his right hand.

For a sickening moment nothing happened. There was the red-roofed shower block, there was the yellowed grass, and there, at each end, stood the two men. Avatars, foreshortened, black-clothed, blond-haired, each with rifle in hand.

Were they hesitating? Were they gathering themselves? *Don't do this*, I wanted to say. *There is hope*. But of course there was no hope, because that story was already written. And so the men entered the shower block at precisely the same time, and in that building out of sight of the camera they would kill nineteen children.

For two minutes the camera held where it was. It stared dis-passionately down at the yellowed grass and the red-rusted roof, observed the length of the shower block and the broken concrete steps at each side. If you saw this shot on its own, you would never know. It was peaceful—boring, almost—while under that cheap rusted roof nineteen young people were executed at close range. *Enemy combatants*, the men had called them in their psy-chiatric interviews, *tomorrow's treacherous elite*, and for that those children paid with their lives. The oldest of the children in the shower block was fifteen; the youngest thirteen.

"It's weird what your brain does," said Vee. "A part of me expects the tactical unit to arrive and save them. But we both read the report. We both know that doesn't happen."

The men emerged from the steps at the left of the shot. They turned and looked up at the camera. The helicopter rose rapidly and turned, headed out across the fjord, still looking down.

Halfway across the fjord it stopped. There, in the middle of the frame, facing right to left, was the red rubber boat, with its black-clad special forces team. Spray was pluming from the engine; the boat was barely moving.

I looked at Vee. "They've turned . . ."

"Yeah," she said. "They're heading back to the mainland."

"Fuck," I said.

"Yeah," she said. "Fuck."

As we watched, the two men at the front took oars and began to paddle.

"It's sinking," said Vee.

"Let's put this on pause, Vee."

Vee touched the screen, freezing the image of the red rubber boat, of the tactical unit pathetically paddling for the mainland. So this was what Bror had wanted me to know.

"They kept this out of evidence," I said after a time.

"I know," she said. "Do you think it's a story?"

I didn't have to answer. We both knew it was . . .

We watched the rest of the footage without speaking. The camera hovered above the island once more, quietly bearing witness, as the men entered buildings, as they left. If the helicopter approached too closely, the men would raise their weapons; the camera would move to a safer distance, then continue to watch the calm exteriors of the buildings while inside the children were cut down: seven dead here, five here, twelve here. Two shots every time, as we knew from the coroner's report, while somewhere out of sight the tactical unit foundered in their too-small rubber boat.

The only sound now was Vee's breathing. In, in and out. *An everyday miracle, in the midst of all this death.*

Suddenly she was there: the girl in the kingfisher dress. Above her a man on a ledge in a torn T-shirt. Both looked up at the same time. Hearing the helicopter, I guessed.

As I watched, the man threw himself from the ledge into the water and turned toward the shore. He was waving to the camera. You could see him shouting.

"*Thank God,*" said Vee very quietly. "That's what he's saying, right? *Thank God.* He thinks they're going to drop a rope or something."

The girl on-screen raised her hands to shade her eyes. She was smiling. You could feel the relief in her, even at this distance.

Vee leaned across and pressed pause. She picked up the iPad, stared at it very closely. Then she passed it to me.

"She thinks she's being rescued."

I looked up, nodded. Vee nodded back.

"Can you make this bigger, Vee?"

"You could. It won't really help, though. There's no extra detail."

I handed the iPad to her. Vee pressed play.

Four more children on the steps now, waving upward. The girl who must be Licia at their head, in her kingfisher dress. The shot began to pull away as the helicopter moved upward. Why was it abandoning them?

Something in the girl changed. Every muscle in her seemed to slacken. She grasped the handrail at the edge of the steps. Strange how you could read the emotion, even at this distance: the realization that no one was coming to save her.

The world failed you, Licia, I thought.

NEITHER VEE NOR I SLEPT. I SAT in the kitchen, making phone calls and drinking coffee; Vee sat with me, listening to every word.

Dan wanted TV pictures.

"Why?" I said. "You're a radio station."

"We're that, and we're whatever else we need to be."

Elsa came through from the bedroom at six and I explained to her what I was going to do. I expected her to ask if I was crazy, but she listened, then asked if I needed help.

"No," I said. "But thanks."

The conversation about the Glock would have to wait.

The Assassin

THIRTY

AT EIGHT I STOOD on the courtroom steps. The cameraman looked up from the viewfinder, nodded, and looked down. The record light glowed red.

Ready.

I heard Carly's breath in my ear.

"Over to Cal Curtis in Oslo, Norway. Cal—"

I didn't wait for the question. "There's something I've never understood about this little country: How could two armed men roam freely across an island near the nation's capital for the best part of two hours, murdering young people at will, and not be stopped? If this were America or France, an armed unit would have been there in minutes. But last night a video came into my possession. And that video gives an answer, of sorts."

Carly's voice in my ear. "Cal, describe the footage that you have exclusively received."

"It's news video from a Polish helicopter pilot, from the day of the Garden Island massacre, and most of what it shows was never broadcast. This video is an important historical document, and records police failings that delayed the arrests of Paul and John Andersen."

"Cal, how many of the ninety-one murder victims does this new information affect?"

"Roughly half. Plus my own daughter, who is not included in that figure of ninety-one dead. We already know that Police Chief Ephraim Tvist failed to act on information that identified the men responsible. We already know that a police cruiser was directly behind their car as they drove out to Garden Island, but did not have the information needed, because nobody had passed it on. What this video shows is that Mr. Tvist's most highly trained men are badly equipped and underprepared. Because at 6:48 p.m., forty-five minutes after the first bullet was fired, at a time when we know that fifty-two of the victims were still alive, the police tactical weapons unit arrives at the slipway on the mainland. Yet it takes those same men sixty-three minutes to make the trip across the water to the island. And if you look at the footage—"

"Which is up on our website so that viewers can judge for themselves."

"—you can clearly see that the rubber boat in which the tactical unit set off is inadequate for the job at hand. The boat is sinking under the weight of the men and their gear. The engine can barely move it. Halfway across the fjord they realize they're not going to make it over, and the unit turns around and begins limping back toward the slipway on the mainland. It's utterly pathetic."

"And at this point, Cal, roughly fifty of the victims were still alive, including, of course, your own daughter."

Licia.

"I used to wonder if it was a conspiracy that cost me my daughter. But now I see that it's simple incompetence."

A pause.

A moment of dead air.

"I . . . I mean, she was just . . ."

The cameraman looking up from the viewfinder.

The fear that grief might overwhelm me.

I swallowed the pain and stepped closer, stared straight down the lens. "I don't know which is worse: the cowardice of the first two officers, who were unwilling to lay down their lives—for children, Carly, for our children—or the incompetence of the tactical unit, whose rubber boat nearly sank on the way to rescue those same children's lives."

Anger was coursing through my veins. I heard Carly's breath in my ear. I felt the cameraman's eyes on me as he tightened the shot. I turned away. I blinked the image of Licia's face from my mind.

I turned to face the camera. The cameraman sent me a questioning look. I nodded. The cameraman nodded back. He put his eye to his viewfinder.

Ready.

"It's the anniversary—a year to the day since the massacre on Garden Island. The police failed our children on that day, and a year later those same police are still failing our children. That this film was kept out of evidence is a national disgrace. They knew the truth. Tvist must be brought to account."

DAN CALLED ME IMMEDIATELY. "WHY WERE YOU ever a satirist? You were honestly never that good at it. This is clearly what you were born to do."

"Thanks," I said. "I think."

"This was great work, brother. Sincere and relatable. You threw a bomb at the man, Cal. You threw a fucking bomb at him.

"A bomb?"

"Of course, you have to assume he's going to throw a bomb right back. But that's the job. Get ahead of these people, or they will screw you."

I heard the call-waiting tone.

"Dan, I think Elsa's calling."

"Love you, brother. You're a newsman, Cal. A fucking news-man."

I selected Elsa's call.

"Hey."

"Hey."

"So, I'm kind of dumbfounded." The warmth and the love in Elsa's voice. "And on the anniversary too. That was . . . yeah . . ."

I realized with a jolt that Elsa was crying. And God, at that moment, how I longed for the world as it once was.

"Cal? Would you please say something?"

Tears were smudging my vision. I wanted so badly to believe in my wife, and in her innocence.

"Sorry," I said. "Yes."

"Anyway, I called a few people. Because Midsummer's Eve is *our* anniversary, and I won't let it belong to those men. I'm going to buy gin and lemons and olives. And we can toast each other, and we can think about Licia. And then we will go out and meet our friends."

I blinked the tears away. "Put the gin in the freezer, Elsa. Along with the shaker and a long spoon."

PEOPLE WERE SHARING MY REPORT. AS I entered the courtroom I could see on their phone screens the red roof and the yellowed grass of the shower block from the helicopter footage, even as the court discussed those same murders.

And there was Tvist smiling up at me, from the seat beside mine. I smiled as neutrally as I could. I sat down.

The short brother was speaking. Paul Andersen.

"Hun sa nei. Holdt armen foran ansiktet."

She said no. She held her arm up in front of her face.

Tvist leaned across to me. "Did you notice?" he said. "The short one remembers each gunshot with absolute clarity. And the tall one simply watches his brother, and then he watches the family's reaction. These are men who enjoy the details of suffering."

The Andersen brothers were looking directly at the father of a murdered girl, checking his response. The man sat rigid in the front row, listening to the brothers' account.

I turned to look at Tvist. I could see the cleverness of the man. The way in which he used the truth—because he was right about the Andersens—to throw me off the scent. And Tvist smiled his smile, and gave nothing away.

I nodded and turned toward the Andersen brothers.

Paul Andersen continued speaking. I heard the word for *angle*, and the word for *bullet*.

Tvist leaned forward. "Is he really saying that? That his greatest worry was that the girl's arm might deflect the round from its trajectory?"

"I guess he is."

"This is an outrage, no?" Tvist leaned very close to me. "Even as they are watching this poor soul you can feel them seeking out the next family with their eyes. Because our laws say these men must have access to the media. And so they familiarize themselves with photographs from the newspapers."

The father of the girl had turned his face from the men. Such quiet dignity in the face of their unrepentance.

"How does he do it?" whispered Tvist. "How does that poor man keep from screaming his hatred and his contempt for these men and what they have done to his family?"

I looked at Tvist. He was staring levelly at me, waiting for a reply. I stared levelly back.

"Right?" he said again.

"Right," I said quietly.

"These brothers, though. They're very caught up in the detail of what they have done. They are not planners. Wouldn't you agree?"

"Maybe."

"Then you do wonder what kind of logistical help they must have needed."

"Isn't it your job to answer that question?"

He laughed quietly to himself, folded his fingers together in front of his face as if thinking. He said, "Who is your source?"

I leaned in very close, whispered into his ear, "I'm not going to tell you."

Tvist's turn to whisper: "This is an issue of national security."

I half laughed. "I genuinely don't know the identity of my source."

"But you have your suspicions? No?"

I looked about me. People were reacting to our whispered conversation. I turned to Tvist. "The internal meanderings of my brain are not the business of the police."

"Very satirical." He got up, brushed himself down, sniffed.

"Have you thought about how you will bear it when the time comes for these men to talk about Alicia?"

He had spoken the words loudly and deliberately.

"No," I said just as loudly. "I haven't thought about that."

People were turning toward us.

"Perhaps you should," he said.

Some nagging voice told me that taking on Tvist was a mistake, that perhaps he was neither corrupt nor incompetent, that he was simply playing the long game. But a year had gone by and we were no closer to finding our daughter. I watched him go, doing nothing to disguise my anger.

When I turned toward the court I found Paul Andersen trying to lock his gaze onto mine.

That smile. As if the two of us shared some horrible secret.

THIRTY-ONE

AFTER TWENTY MINUTES I could bear no more of the men's cruelty. I took the train home.

I stood outside the apartment building, looking in. No sign of movement. No trace of Elsa's phone on my screen. Why had she switched it off? Was she out buying gin and olives at the mall? Perhaps the simplest explanation was the best.

On a terrace two floors up a woman was polishing shoes, stopping from time to time to examine the sheen. She noticed me watching, raised a hand in greeting. I waved back. Then I went down to the garage and drove out to Garden Island.

I HAD COME TO REMEMBER. I HAD half expected to be alone, but the road was filled with cars parked all the way down. I had to walk the last mile on foot.

One year.

People filed along the grass at the side of the road. Most were in their twenties. Many were younger. Some cried as they walked. Some spoke to each other in hushed words, as our shoes scuffed the path and our breathing filled the air around us. Some of us smiled private smiles, as if lost in thoughts of our loved ones. Many of us carried flowers. Had they, like me, simply felt the call?

At the slipway people were scattering their flowers onto the surface of the fjord: tulips and roses, chrysanthemums and lilies. The current today was strong. The flowers fanned out in a swath that reached halfway across the sound. I sat, my legs overhanging the water, watching as others paid their respects. Five hundred of us, maybe more.

Grief welled up in me. The tears seemed to come from nowhere, huge racking sobs from a place deep within.

My Licia.

My little girl.

I thought of the time on the mountain at Whistler, and of the moment when Licia returned, laughing, full of joy at surviving the snowstorm. I thought of the mirror in her bedroom, of her empty bed, of the dust that had settled over the fingerprint powder in the year since she had gone. . . .

I don't know how long I sat there, at the edge of the slipway, hands pressed hard against my eyes. When I could cry no more I took off my clothes and folded them beside me.

I filled my lungs with air. I stepped toward the water's edge. *How long since I last felt the sun on my skin?*

I stopped. I was naked. I looked about me, self-conscious, foolish and out of place. But no one was paying me any mind. I took another breath.

I jumped, piked in the air, straightened first my arms, then my legs. I felt the shock hit my torso as I dropped below the surface. I pulled myself downward—one stroke, then the next—into the chill peaty dark, tasting salt on my lips. After a time I sensed a darker shade of black. I slowed. My fingers found the branch of a tree. I gripped it gently.

I turned on my back, looked up. I could not see the surface, though I could sense light far above. I exhaled, watched as my breath gathered in a bubble that rose slowly away from me, contours disappearing into the gloom.

My calf muscles brushed against rock. My back came to rest in the soft silt. I was calm now, calmer than I'd been in months.

I emptied my lungs, saw my breath plume and join into a single vast bubble, watched as it rose directly above me, softening and disappearing as it went. If I did nothing, if I did not push myself toward the surface, then I would stay here. I would merge with the water, become one with the fjord.

Calm.

I could feel the beginning of the ache in my stomach, and in my throat, could feel my body preparing to inhale.

Perhaps Licia was down here? Perhaps Licia too had merged with the water? Perhaps she was waiting for me, just out of sight. Perhaps she wanted me to stay.

I was very, very calm, though I could feel my body fighting me, trying to force me to open my lungs and breathe.

Calm.

If I stayed, perhaps I could merge with Licia?

For a moment I thought I saw the surface of the water, saw above it the faces of Elsa, and of Vee, and of Franklin, seeking me out. All was light and color and laughter.

I looked about me. All was dark.

"I'm sorry, Licia," I said with the very last of my breath.

A tiny bubble rose swiftly through the dark.

Gone.

Nothing now but the sound of blood pumping in my ears, of my heartbeat slow and strong.

But Elsa. But Franklin. But Vee.

I can't stay, Licia.

I curled my knees into my stomach, crouched for a moment, feet planted on the fjord's rocky bottom. I raised my arms above my head. I pushed hard, upward, toward the world of the living, swimming for my life, fighting to keep the water from spilling down my throat.

Three strokes, and the water began to lighten. I saw shadows above me. Two more strokes, and the shadows resolved into shapes. Arms. Legs. Bodies in motion.

I was at the surface, breathing gratefully, surrounding by light and by people, laughing now. United by something more than grief, as we swam together in a sea of flowers that reached almost to the island.

MILLA WAS WAITING AT THE GATE, AS if she had known I would come.

"He's at the barn," she said as I got out of the car.

I walked past fruit trees where turtledoves billed and cooed. There he was at the side of the red-painted wooden building in his gray shirt and his gray robe, kneeling beside Arno. On the ground before them four rabbits were laid out, each bleeding delicately from a tiny wound in the shoulder. Two small-bore rifles stood nearby, barrels pointing toward the sky.

Arno saw me first. He smiled. He tapped Bror lightly on the shoulder, staring at me all the while. The dark rings around his eyes were gone.

Bror followed Arno's gaze. He jumped lightly to his feet. "The hero returns." He stepped forward. We embraced.

"You . . . are less troubled, Cal Curtis."

"Doesn't sound like me."

He held my forearms, scanned my eyes. "No, something in you has changed."

"You saw the broadcast?"

"Very good it was. And yet . . ." His eyes were searching mine. "I feel it is more than this."

"Maybe . . ."

He looked back at Arno. "The boy's mother will be coming for him soon. You don't mind if we continue?"

"Of course not."

Bror returned to the rabbits. He knelt. From a pocket he took a roll of canvas, which he unfurled on the grass. A set of cook's knives, black-hilted, eight in all. Arno looked down at the knives.

"Choose," said Bror.

The boy's hand floated toward an eight-inch blade.

"You need a four-inch knife."

Arno looked at Bror. Bror took Arno's hand, guided it toward the shorter knives at one end of the roll. "This," he said. "Or even this."

Arno looked at him again, then reached for a blade with a slight curve.

"Good choice," said Bror. "Very good."

Arno smiled, briefly, and Bror returned the smile: an enveloping smile full of warmth and kindness. "Here's how you hold it." Guiding the boy's movements, gently and with confidence. "And here's how you make the first cut."

He must have seen me turn away.

"Not a fan of blood, Cal?"

"In my world meat comes from the supermarket."

He laughed. "You disapprove?"

"Not judging. Just not my thing."

"I like your honesty," he said. "Take a short walk."

I glanced at Arno. He had made a neat cut on the abdomen of one of the rabbits.

Bror caught me looking. "Or stay." He smiled. "It's really not so bad."

Arno nodded at me and smiled too. Unthinkable a year ago. Even a few months ago his eyes had been lifeless and empty. I smiled at the boy, and he nodded at me and picked up the next rabbit.

"I will go for a walk," I said.

"Introduce yourself to my dogs."

I began to walk toward the low black-painted farm building.

A dog gave voice. Then another.

"Hush!" said Bror from behind me. That same reassuring gentleness. The dogs fell silent. I saw a yellow eye in a gap between the black-painted slats. A second eye appeared. Watchful and poised behind thin wood. No sound now beyond a low, hoarse panting.

I crouched down, held out the back of my hand. A snout appeared, black and very close. I saw an open jaw lined with heavy teeth, felt the dog draw my scent in through its mouth. "Hey there," I said. "Hello." I pushed my hand closer to the slats, and a pink tongue appeared, lapping at my wrist.

"The door is around the side," said Bror. "They really are very friendly."

I opened the door to the barn, heard the rasping of breath and the clanking of chain on concrete, saw their dark lurking shapes in the gloom. Three dogs, all haunch and shoulder and pointed snout. Muscular, like sprung steel.

At this end of the barn light fell through the slats and from the open door. I could make out a wall at the far end, and in that wall a door. I hunkered down, held out a hand, but the dogs kept their distance, pacing just out of reach. I took a half step toward them, heard the smallest of them growl in warning.

"Hey," I said. "I'm one of the good guys." But none of them would greet me now that I was inside.

WHEN I RETURNED, THE RABBITS WERE LAID out in a row, their entrails stacked in a neat pile by the fence. Arno was gone.

Bror smiled a disarming smile. "There's a definite spring in your step today."

I looked at him. "You want to guess Tvist's reaction to my piece?"

"Misdirection?"

"He asked me who might have provided the Andersens with logistical support."

Bror gave a cynical little laugh. "And whom did you suppose him to mean?"

"You."

"Well, I'm an easy target, am I not? We've established that." He gestured at the rabbits. "Shall we carry two each, my friend?"

I looked at him. He was not exactly my friend, I thought. But he listened. A part of me almost wanted to confide in him.

I bent down beside him. The rabbits were still soft, their fur silky, their bodies warm.

I said, "I've come to understand that the police and I are not on the same side."

"Yes. That's what I see, I think." He smiled, as if he found an answer in my eyes. "You, Cal Curtis, are . . . a man reborn."

"Is that a blessing?"

He raised his right arm, his forefinger and middle finger held almost straight, ring finger and pinkie curled. "Would you like it to be?"

I stood up, a rabbit in each hand. "Actually, I had an almost religious experience. In the waters of Garden Island."

He picked up the two remaining rabbits in his left hand. He stood up beside me. He laughed gently, walked to where the rifles stood, knelt and picked them up in his right hand. "And did you see the face of the Godhead?"

"I saw the faces of my family."

"Good. Very good indeed." He was nodding, as if to himself, serious now. We began to walk toward the farmhouse. "There is something heroic at your core. You did not believe me when I hinted at it before. But you are beginning to discover what I meant."

"Am I?" I laughed. He turned and looked at me almost gravely. I stopped laughing.

"Follow." He marched into the house, along the stone-flagged hall and on into the kitchen, where he laid the rabbits on the workbench by the sink.

I said, "Arno seems . . ."

". . . better? Much, though he hasn't uttered a word since he arrived. And the girls terrify him. We quarter as many as eight a time. All of them exceptional. So hard to be a teenage boy these days. Even without Arno's additional challenges. And yet still I say to Arno, you may open any door, enter any room, but you must not climb the stairs to the girls' dormitory! Because even in the land of equality, men are still men."

"You're schooling him in the chivalric virtues?"

"All very chaste. Though I imagine that's not easy for a pubescent boy either, and I can see that a part of you wishes to satirize me for it. But a young man must know how to behave in the presence of women. You're a father to two daughters. I know that at heart we agree." He looked at me, smiled a wise smile. "What we teach is really not so old-fashioned. Me-too, and all that. Think of our girls as a new template for womanhood, and Arno as a new template for manhood. The modern world wants to use women and cast them aside. We do not, and Arno will not."

"So Arno is your little knight . . ."

At this he became very serious. He put a hand on my arm, looked me in the eye. "Cal, friend, even a good man knows how a bad man thinks. Surely it's better that he respect women?"

"All right," I said. "Yes. And I do see the change in him."

"Now . . ." He gestured to the rabbits in my hands, which I passed to him. "Let us talk instead about this change in you, Cal . . . I'm tempted to say it's an acceptance of calling."

"I have no calling."

"Oh, but you do. You spoke truth to power, and with such angry clarity. This is what the fightback looks like, my friend. And you know now for whom you are fighting."

"Do I?"

"Your tribe, of course. You must not deprecate yourself. This is a huge achievement. And now that you have identified your enemy—with startling clarity, may I say—you are declaring war upon him with the truth as your shield and the pen as your sword."

"Thank you," I said. "For helping us get this far."

"Oh, but you mustn't thank me. Not yet. You must go home to your wife and your children and prepare for something utterly wonderful."

THIRTY-TWO

ELSA WAS OUTLINING HER eyes with kohl, naked from the shower. In the bathroom mirror I saw how her eyes flicked to the crystal glass as I set it beside her, then flicked back to me. There was an openness to her, an expectancy that I hadn't seen in months. She had left the doors open between the bedroom and the bathroom, remembering, perhaps—reminding me of a time, perhaps—when I would watch her as she prepared to go out.

I walked past her and into the bedroom, lay on the neatly made bed, glass in hand. I looked up to find her watching me, her own glass half-raised. She loosed her hair with her left hand. It hung heavy around her shoulders, glinting dully, the ends curling inward, trailing against her breasts.

She turned the glass in her hand. "Alchemy, Cal." Sunbeams cut the heavy viscous liquid. Tiny golden shards of ice, disappearing fast.

We held each other's gaze in the Norwegian way.

"*Skål*."

"*Skål*."

My phone rang.

I put down my drink untouched. Elsa watched me, her glass still by her lips, intrigued.

"Do you need to get that, Cal?"

I looked at her: at the keen intelligence in her wolf eyes; at the implied question in her gently parted lips. I looked down at the water droplets on her breasts, at the exhilarating angle of her thigh. I switched off my phone.

FOR THE FIRST TIME IN A YEAR we fucked. It was slow and intense, far too full of expectation and longing to be satisfying. Neither of us came, but there was an intimacy to it that I thought we had lost. Something simple and overwhelming and beautiful.

WE TOOK THE TRAIN INTO TOWN, SAYING nothing, each lost in our own thoughts. We stood for a while in front of the town hall, watched the cranes as they hoisted girders into place on the facade. Still we said nothing.

We headed into the East End of Oslo. People thronged the street, speaking languages we did not understand. There was dirt here, and color, and life, and noise. Kids on snakeboards glided through gaps in the crowds, bumped fists with friends as they passed. White boys with face tattoos and plaited Nordic beards sank beer from cans. Laughing women passed by in niqabs. Lesbian couples held hands or made out in the doorways of bars. There was an edge on these streets, something intoxicating and new.

Elsa put her arm around me. She rested her head on my shoulder and we stood stock-still, let the people flow around us, watched them as they surged and ebbed.

"Why did we never choose this, Cal?"

"We're choosing it now."

"We chose the part of town that's the very opposite of this," she said. "And we wondered why our daughters weren't happy."

"It was for six months."

"That's what we told ourselves. But we never chose this life anywhere we lived. We're not even forty. How did we become this old white married couple?"

"Tonight we chose this."

"No," she said. "No, tonight we chose a cocktail bar that has a barbershop on the second floor. They take thirty bucks for a peach Bellini. I don't know what that is, but it's not *this*."

I looked around me, at the ebb and surge of the crowd. "All right," I said. I led her to a bench table outside a dirty bar that opened onto the street. "Turn your phone back on. Tell your friends they're meeting us here."

"Hedda won't like it."

"No," I said. "She won't."

She put her handbag on the table. She rummaged.

"That bag," I said. "Not really you."

"And what do you know? No cigarettes."

"I'm trying to start a fight, Elsa."

"Okay." She leaned her head to the left, then to the right. "Okay, fuck you. I like the bag. And I like Hedda. Even if she doesn't like you."

"I knew it," I said. "I fucking knew it."

"Sorry," she said. "I'm sorry, Cal." But if this was the beginning of something more honest, I could take these little shards of pain.

We sat watching the people as they passed, our fingers entwined, saying very little. I kissed Elsa's neck; it was good to feel her skin beneath my lips: so familiar, so ordinary, so alive.

"Do you and Bror ever talk about me?" she said.

"I kind of assumed you wouldn't want me to," I said. "Though I think he'd like it if I did."

"What if I were to tell you a truly monstrous secret?" she said, her gaze level and easy.

"What if I already know your monstrous secret?" I said.

"You can't," she said. "You don't know the first thing." Her wolf eyes, all flecked with gold.

"What if I knew more than you think?"

"Not possible."

"Elsa," I said, "what have you done?"

She looked me in the left eye, then the right. She looked away. She said, "Do you ever scare yourself?"

"No."

"You're never frightened of what you might do?"

"Never."

She smiled. "Must be nice."

"Elsa," I said. "What have you done?"

"Nothing."

"Then what?"

The color disappeared from her eyes. Time slowed. She bit down on to her lower lip. She inhaled once, then paused, then inhaled again.

"Okay," she said. "So here's the thing . . ."

"Cal. Over here. Happy fucking anniversary, mate."

And so the moment passed, and we were on our feet and embracing our friends. And still I didn't know if Elsa was joking, or if she was about to tell me about the Glock.

"Great piece," said Jo, his arm across my shoulders.

"Yeah," said Edvard.

I stepped forward to hug Jo, felt his stubble raking mine.

"How are things?" I whispered.

"About the same."

But from his smile you would have thought nothing was wrong. "You really shook them up, Cal," he said, turning to Edvard. "Didn't he?"

"Yeah." Edvard stepped forward, hugged me with surprising warmth. "Yeah, management's freaking out."

"I'm sorry," I said.

"No," said Edvard. "They should freak out. Happy wedding anniversary, by the way."

Elsa embraced him warmly and said something that made him laugh, and she turned toward me and smiled.

Only Hedda was hanging back. Elsa's oldest friend, clutching defensively at the hem of her dress. She was made up for the cocktail bar, not for the street, in her too-short black dress and her too-high red shoes. She looked exposed, shrinking in the summer light.

"Hedda," I said. "Sorry about the change. You look beautiful."

And when Hedda leaned in and hugged me there was no hostility between us, no sense of putting on a show.

"Beer," said Jo. "The boyfriend's buying."

"Really?" said Edvard. "Am I really?"

"Handsome does as handsome gets told," said Jo.

Edvard looked from face to face, gave a what-can-you-do smile, and went inside.

"Seriously," said Jo as we sat down opposite each other, "seriously, Ed can't tell you this, but he's fucking delighted that someone said what you said about Tvist."

"I was worried," I said.

"Oh please." Jo laughed. "The police here are way too reasonable to harass you. And look . . ."

He passed me his phone. A newspaper front page. They had used a studio picture we had taken last spring: Elsa, Vee, Franklin on my shoulders, and at the front, looking straight down the barrel of the lens, Licia. In stark red text were the words:

Korrupsjon eller inkompetanse?

Elsa was laughing. "They put us on the front page of *Posten*?"

I said, "Does that mean what I think . . . ?"

"*Corruption or incompetence*," Jo translated. "*Three major police errors that cost us our daughter*. You really are taking the fight to the police, Cal. You didn't know they were doing this?"

The crazy euphoria of the moment. I handed the phone to Elsa. She stared at it, eyes shining.

Then Edvard was there in front of us.

"I thought I sent you to get beer," said Jo. "Go get these people some beer."

But Edvard simply stood there.

"What is it, *kjære*?" said Jo. "Ed?"

"I've been suspended."

And as we were staring at Edvard in disbelief, and as Jo was reaching out to comfort him, the phone in Elsa's hand began to ring.

"It's Tvist," she said. She passed me the phone.

I pressed answer. I raised the phone to my ear. I heard Tvist's voice say, "You and your wife will meet me at headquarters."

THIRTY-THREE

A MODEST CORPORATE SPACE at the end of the main office. Two blue plastic chairs waiting in front of the large white desk. We sat down, holding hands.

"Keep the faith," whispered Elsa.

"Yes," I said. "Keep the faith."

Tvist approaching from the far end of the office.

"No interrogation room?" I said as he reached us.

"The prosecutors have asked for the helicopter footage to be admitted into evidence. The Andersens have offered no objection. Well done."

We had expected anger, but Tvist looked tired. The past year had aged him. His shoulders curved forward; patches of puckered flesh gathered beneath his lower eyelids.

He opened a drawer, placed a typed sheet on the desk. A transcript of my broadcast. Then he reached across and switched on the recorder.

"Perhaps you wish to formalize your very serious accusations."

That strange solemnity as he looked from me to Elsa; that sense that he expected us to fill the silence.

"Edvard is not my source," I said.

"Edvard . . . is not the reason you are here."

We said nothing. Tvist sat drumming his fingers. Eventually he said, "I'm compelled to ask you how you came by your footage."

I looked at Elsa. She gave a tiny shake of the head.

I turned to Tvist. "No."

He gave a sharp, fleeting smile. "There are some dangerous people in our safe little country. It is my job to protect your family from those people. Agreed?"

That smile again.

Elsa glanced at me. Was he threatening us? It sounded nothing like a threat. I wondered how protective he would feel when he saw the front page of *Posten*.

"All respect, but this is not a difference of opinion." Elsa's voice, her fury barely contained.

"No?"

"Your tactical unit's boat sank; your armed officers hid in their car. These are hard truths, not opinions."

"Well, we could argue for hours about the difference between a fact and a truth and an opinion. But by making his 'truths' public, your husband has done the very thing that he is accusing my officers of." He turned to me. "When you put your needs before the needs of the nation you make my job difficult. There can be reasons why we do not wish *your* facts to emerge."

"And then," said Elsa, "you will smile and tell him that he's welcome here, and that in time he will learn how things work, and that for the sake of the country he should keep his foreign mouth shut, because his story could have consequences that he does not fully understand."

Tvist laughed. "Your husband is clearly not the only satirist in the family."

Elsa scowled.

Tvist turned to me. "There is one unsettling consequence to your posting the material. The video has traveled widely. Been widely seen. A viral hit."

Another pause.

Tvist pressed his fingertips against his forehead. "Cal, Elsa . . ." He turned to us each in turn. He seemed genuinely to be struggling to find the words. "We have for a long time assumed that your daughter was on the island. That Licia was the girl in the blue dress."

It struck me that perhaps for once he was not manipulating us; that there was a reason for his solemnity.

"As a result of the video you posted, another father has contacted us, claiming that it is his daughter in the film."

"It's Licia," I said. "Elsa spoke to her."

"Before she arrived at the island," said Tvist.

"We had texts," said Elsa.

"From a phone that was not on the island. It isn't Licia in the footage."

The impact of those words: so gentle at first, yet so firm, like an arm clamping around my neck. We had spent a year believing . . .

"This man is a Chechen. He lives in London. He had no idea that his older daughter was in Norway, let alone that she was on the island. You will see she looked a little like Licia." He opened a drawer, slid a picture across the surface of the desk. Elsa and I looked at each other. I picked it up.

"This girl was not known to us," said Tvist. "No records. Perhaps she came looking for a better life."

The picture had been taken in winter. Blond hair, plaited, worn under a fur hat that covered her ears. Red cheeks, a warm smile. A beautiful child, but not our child.

"From a distance one might indeed think this girl was your daughter. She was also fifteen."

Elsa took the picture from my hand. "Is this the girl whose body we were shown?"

"We have no record of that."

She laughed, a bitter, angry sound in that neutral white room.

"Mistakes were made on that day. However . . ." Tvist pinched the bridge of his nose. "This girl's name is Maria Krikk. My best guess is that Maria traveled unaccompanied, without papers. Disappeared from the radar. There are many such children seeking sanctuary here. Her father and sister have not seen her for eighteen months."

"She has a sister?"

"A year younger than your Viktoria."

"If she was living here illegally," I said, "why go to Garden Island?"

"Maybe she was an idealist? A feminist? Who knows?"

"Makes no sense."

"To this day we have no concrete evidence that your daughter was ever on the island."

"There's her dress," said Elsa. "Which you failed to find."

"You are right to point out our mistake." He looked up, addressed himself to me. "We have searched the island extensively since then. The dress does not make your case. No further evidence has emerged."

"Just like you found no evidence of an organization," said Elsa.

"Listen, please, to what I'm saying to you. Maria Krikk is a better fit than Licia Curtis."

Desperation in Elsa's eyes. "Search again. Please."

That same patient smile. "There is nothing more."

I said, "You have the print from Licia's shoe on the police boat."

"A similar shoe. Yes. But we have no such prints on the grass, or on the path, or in any of the other places you might expect."

"It was dry," I said.

"Precisely. Doesn't mean she wasn't there, but we can't say that she was. Look . . ." He leaned across his desk. "What I am about to say violates another family's right to privacy. I need an assurance that you will not publish what I am about to tell you, nor indeed will you discuss it outside this room. Either of you. Do you understand me?"

Elsa nodded. I nodded.

"All right. You have a right to know this, I think. Maria is unusual among the victims in that she was struck by three bullets. Her body was found in the water near the boat dock on the island. The first of those bullet holes matches the hole in the shoulder of her dress. From the first bullet fired, before she escaped from the main house and ran. We believe she removed the dress before she entered the water. As you know, we could find no trace of anything that could be said with certainty to be Licia's DNA."

I looked across at Elsa. A thought began to grow in me. The most exciting, dangerous thought, only Elsa had not seen it yet.

I said, "You found this other girl's DNA?"

"I cannot speak to you about procedure that does not relate to your case. But I may tell you that Maria is our best fit and you may read what you will between the lines . . ." He let his voice trail off, watching us to make sure we understood.

"This is wrong," Elsa was saying. "You're giving up on Licia."

"Love, I don't think that's what he's saying." Hope was coursing through me. "Elsa, if Licia wasn't on the island—"

"We can't, Cal," she said. "We can't let ourselves believe that she's alive. Because every time, that hope turns to nothing."

"But if she really wasn't there . . ."

We locked eyes. I could see that the thought terrified her.

I said, "Breathe, love."

"We had an independent witness confirm Maria's identity," Tvist was saying.

Elsa's eyes were locked onto mine. "Who?"

Tvist exhaled heavily. "Understand that I'm obliged to protect that witness's identity."

Elsa turned. She was staring very intently at Tvist.

"Why?" she said. "Why are you obliged?"

"Please understand what I'm saying to you."

"Oh. You mean it's a child," said Elsa quietly. She gave a little half laugh. She turned from Tvist to me. "He means Arno. That Arno confirmed her identity."

"Did he?" I turned to Tvist.

That warm, sympathetic smile. "You must respect my procedures, but again you may read between the lines."

Elsa couldn't quite let it go. "How would a person who doesn't speak confirm or deny anything?"

"By pointing and by nodding," said Tvist very simply. "Cal, Elsa, I know this doesn't bring your daughter back," he said. "But it's something to hold on to, no?"

ELSA, THOUGH, WAS IN SHOCK.

We sat on a bench on the dirty path that led down from the police station. The air was thick with barbecue smoke.

"Jesus fuck, Cal."

"But this could be good, love. This could be really good."

"We've spent a year believing she was a hero. When all the time it was Maria who saved Arno."

"I know. But if she's alive, Elsa . . ." I was struggling to contain my elation. "If she's alive, then we don't need Licia to be a hero. We just need to find her and bring her home. And we need to tell Vee."

"Please don't."

"She has a right to know."

"Know what? That her sister is not a hero? That we have no idea where she is?"

"Elsa," I said, "can't we please find the good in what Tvist just told us? Because what he's telling us is that she could be alive."

"Cal," she said, "the police have had a year to find her. And they're nowhere. We're nowhere. We're all starting from scratch."

VEE WAS AWAKE WHEN WE GOT HOME. She accepted the news about Licia, asked us very few questions. I made martinis. Vee sat with us on the dirty gray planter at the back of the apartment as Elsa scrolled through Twitter and I looked out over the hills in silence.

"Are we ever going to go home, Dad?" Vee said at last. I turned. The set of her jaw was heartbreakingly adult. "Or did this place just kind of become our home?"

"I don't know, Vee."

"Rhetorical question." She got to her feet, stood looking at me.

"What, love?"

"I was so sure it was her in the helicopter footage."

"Everyone was."

"People need to see it, though, right?"

"They do."

"Okay. Night, Dad. Mum." She leaned across and kissed me, nodded a good night to Elsa. "Don't stay up late, Mum," she said as she headed for bed.

Elsa watched Vee go. When we heard the tap running in the bathroom, Elsa said, "I keep trying to find reasons not to go back to the courtroom tomorrow. For Vee's sake, I know we have to. But the truth is we've spent a year fighting the wrong battles. Making enemies of the wrong people. Did you see what you get when you drop Tvist's name into Google these days?"

She reached for her phone, unlocked it with her thumb, handed it to me.

That image of Licia with the gun. Someone had Photoshopped Tvist's head on the left side of the card, as if Licia had him in her sights. Underneath were the words:

THIS IS WHAT THE #ARYAN #RESISTANCE LOOKS LIKE

I said, "So weird, the way this thing mutates and mutates."

She nodded. "It's the opposite of what it was when it started. The opposite of who Licia is. But it's an exact encapsulation of what those men believe. Pretty white girl taking out the country's first black police chief. Fuck, Cal. Our daughter became a white supremacist meme."

She picked up her glass, drained it.

"My love," I said.

"I can't stand the way all this hatred seems to seep into my soul. I don't have the stomach for it. I want us to go home, and we can't. So I guess we stay here and we pick ourselves up off the floor and we set about finding Licia. All over again."

"My poor tired horse," I said.

She leaned in to me. "Promise me you won't have me euthanized."

I knew I should ask her about the gun, but I could not. Because when we laughed our laughter felt very close to tears. And so we sat for the longest time, arms around each other, watching as the sky turned from gold to the deepest red.

THIRTY-FOUR

THE PROSECUTOR WAS PLAYING the video in short segments, taking the court through the timeline, reading from her notes: the names of the dead; the manner of each death. Elsa looked weary. Vee was alert, desperate to know what other people thought of the footage.

We could see whose children the prosecutor was talking about simply from looking at their backs. A small group would stiffen in anticipation. The Andersens would stare at the mothers and the fathers, the brothers and the sisters, of the children they had cut down. The family would clasp each other tightly, sit stock-still while the prosecutor read out her text. No one cried; no one was willing to hand the Andersens that victory.

The brothers showed neither pleasure nor shame; their eyes were unblinking and clear. In the face of such cruelty, the families' quiet courage was almost too much to bear.

When the helicopter crossed the fjord, when the screen showed the tactical unit foundering in their red rubber boat, people murmured. The chief judge sat with her hand across her mouth. Here and there people laughed in outrage, an eerie sound in this solemn place. When the boat turned around the laughter increased.

The Andersen brothers looked out across the rows of seats, at the survivors and the families of the victims, taking in the shock and the laughter. Then John Andersen turned to Paul Andersen, and the brothers laughed too, as if joining in a shared joke.

The laughter among the families stopped. Only the brothers were laughing now, hard and cold and cruel.

Vee leaned in. "Dad, is this making people feel worse?"

I pulled her to me. "People have a right to know the truth. You did a good thing."

The courtroom was silent but for the rustling of clothes and the catching of breath. The camera was above the shower block, silently looking down, while inside nineteen children were murdered.

When I looked up it was into the face of Paul Andersen. He made sure he had my attention, then gave the smallest of nods. He turned and said something to his brother, who laughed.

It was our turn.

They were staring hard at Vee, trying to lock onto her gaze.

"Eyes on the screen, Vee."

Elsa took Vee's right hand; I took her left.

There was the girl who matched Licia's description, down at the cliff's edge on Garden Island.

Vee leaned in to me. "Strange, once you know it's not her."

"Very."

It wasn't Licia, and didn't feel like Licia now. Hard to believe we could have thought it was.

I looked across at Elsa. She nodded. She was thinking the same thing. And so we emptied our faces of expression and kept our eyes on the screen. All the while I felt the eyes of the Andersen brothers boring into ours, trying to take pleasure in a pain that we no longer felt, because the girl on-screen was another family's missing daughter. You could feel the hope in this girl, in the way she stood, could feel through the screen the certainty that she was being rescued, that she was saved.

A terrifying cosmic joke. There would be no rescue.

You saw it as the camera drew away. You felt the melting away of certainty, as if the breath were gone from the girl's body. You saw beside her the other children who were to die with her, and the boy Arno who would survive but would never speak of it, and you saw in those children that same lack of hope as you saw in the girl. You saw the grown man in a torn T-shirt pushing through the children, deciding they were lost, but that he might yet be saved.

I felt Vee gripping my hand.

"Vee, are you okay?" I said as quietly as I could.

"The picture is wrong."

The blue of the dress was off. Too bright, too saturated. The rock beside the girl was too red. The grass beyond too green. Everything felt miscalibrated, over-intense.

"It's the colors, Vee."

"No. It's something else."

She looked about her. "Vee, eyes on the screen." But the brothers were no longer trying to lock eyes with her. They were staring at the screen, that same hungry look on their faces. The man in the T-shirt dropped out of shot as the camera outpaced him, racing along the path that led toward the cabins. They were curious, I guessed, to see the moment of their victim's death.

The helicopter stopped, abruptly, staring down. An empty frame. Nothing but yellowed grass, cut diagonally by the path. Then Paul

Andersen stepped into the shot at the right of the frame, moving toward the steps in the rock. He looked up at the helicopter. This time he did not raise his weapon. Instead he stopped; he looked left across the frame, down the path toward the steps.

A moment of nothing; of waiting. Then the man in the torn T-shirt stumbled into the shot, left of frame. He stood, as if dazed, facing Paul Andersen. I looked about the courtroom, trying to locate the man's family. If they were here, I could not see them.

On the screen Paul Andersen raised his pistol. He fired. The man in the torn T-shirt stopped. Paul Andersen fired again.

Two silent shots.

Around us people gasped.

The man in the torn T-shirt, crumpling, his body folding in on itself.

The camera held steady. The short man looked up toward the helicopter. He did not raise his weapon. He walked toward the dead man. He paused at the man's side, then continued out of frame toward the steps that led down to the fjord.

The helicopter veered off toward the mainland, leaving the children to their fate.

WE MARKED THE END OF THE FIRST trial week with pizza. Elsa and I sat up drinking beer on the sofa, watching bad films on Netflix.

At one Elsa fell asleep. I covered her in a blanket, went to check on the children. I found Vee at her computer, fingers hovering above the keyboard, the shower block on her screen. She looked up. I frowned. Vee mock-frowned back. "Why aren't you drinking beer, Dad?"

"Why aren't you asleep, Vee?"

"Because . . . So, I took this picture of the footage in the court-room. It's a little hazy. But look."

She squinted at the picture on her laptop, then adjusted it, tilting it so the top and bottom of the courtroom TV screen were roughly horizontal. She cropped it so all you could see was the image on the screen. The roof of the shower block, too red, against too-yellow dried grass above and below.

She double-clicked on a file. Pavel's helicopter footage opened, crisp and clean. Vee pulled the computer window down so that you could see the image of the roof, began scrolling till she found what she was looking for. The shower block.

She scanned backward, found the men as they were about to enter, clicked the image backward and forward until she was satisfied. "There."

I looked from the blurred image to the crisp image and back.

"Dad, it's the exact same frame."

"Okay. What am I looking for?"

"They resized it for the court, Dad."

I squinted. "I mean, maybe."

"No, Dad, they really did."

She adjusted both windows so they were exactly the same height, placed them side by side. Then she turned to look at me.

"Look at the grass."

"I'm looking at the grass."

"At the sides."

She was right. The courtroom version cut off the side of the image. Everything was larger. The grass and the steps were missing.

"Why do you think they enlarged the picture for the trial?" she said.

"I'm guessing there's some simple technical reason."

"And what if they were disguising something? This matters, Dad. It should matter to you."

"Vee," I said, "we're all exhausted. Please go to bed."

I WAS UP AT SIX, SHOWERING, WHEN I heard the scream. So very loud it was. So piercing, and so very close. I heard Elsa spring from our bedroom past Franklin and into the kitchen.

I pulled a towel around me, was there seconds behind her.

Elsa frozen by the sink, her eyes searching for the source.

Another scream.

She nodded toward Vee's room, and we were off, Elsa in front of me.

Vee's voice: "Get the FUCK away from me and out of my room!"

Elsa threw open the door. There was Vee, sitting upright in bed. And there, tall and angular in her simple gray dress, was our lost daughter Licia.

THIRTY-FIVE

"HELLO," SAID LICIA AS she turned toward me.

I heard myself speak her name.

"FUCK!" shouted Vee. "LICIA? REALLY?"

Only Elsa was silent. She stood there, her mouth open, gulping air.

I could feel the adrenaline coursing through me. "Licia," I said. "Oh, my Licia."

"Licia," said Vee, calmer now. "Licia, Licia, Licia."

"Alicia May Curtis," said Elsa. "My God. How?"

"Yeah," said Vee. "Actually, what the fuck?"

"My window was unlocked," said Licia simply, as if that were an explanation.

She had grown her blond hair. It hung in a simple plait halfway down her back. She was taller too. More like her mother than ever, though her clothes were formal. A plain gray smock. A gray skirt, unpleated. White socks. Around her waist a small gray cloth bag hung on a simple belt.

I laughed. "I knew it. Elsa, didn't I say she was alive?"

Licia smiled the most beautiful smile.

Elation spread through me. "Didn't I tell you?" I looked at Elsa. "Didn't I promise you she would come back?"

"I don't think you ever did." Elsa was dabbing at her eyes with the base of her palms. "But that's okay. Oh, Licia, honey . . ."

"Fuck," said Vee again, quieter now. "Licia."

"You can stop cursing. I'm here." An odd little formal smile.

I could feel the smile on my own face, a true smile, a smile over which I had no control. It was an alien feeling after all this time. Almost an ache.

"Oh, fuck, Licia," said Vee. "We all thought you were . . ."

"I'm home," said Licia. "There really is no need to swear."

"Where have you been?" said Vee.

Licia sat on the bed. "I'm home."

Vee threw her arms around her sister, crying and laughing.

I could see the weight beginning to lift from Elsa's shoulders. I felt that same weight begin to lift from mine as Licia sat there, all angular and long.

"Licia?" I said.

"Dad," said Licia. She was on her feet again, stepping toward me, and I was crying and laughing too, and brushing a stray hair from her eyes. She smiled—the most heartbreaking of smiles— and I threw my arms around her, lifted her from the floor.

"Jesus," I said. "You must have grown four inches."

"I guess. Again, no need to blaspheme."

I set Licia carefully down on the floor. "You're taller than your mother." I turned to look at Elsa. "I think."

Elsa was not laughing. She sent me a look that I could not read.

"What happened?" I said. "Licia, what happened to you?"

Licia turned to face Elsa. "Hello, Mum."

"Dad asked you a question." Vee was looking at her sister. Her eyes narrowed. "What did happen to you?"

"Hello, Mum," said Licia again. "I've come home." She stepped toward Elsa.

Elsa reached out, took Licia's hands in hers. Halfway to embracing they stopped, the air between them electric. Elsa's eyes sparked and flashed. I saw the tears that welled there, after all those months of strangulated fear, the long, hard battle against despair.

"Oh, Licia," said Elsa. "Licia, my sweetest child, where have you been?"

"Safe with friends."

Elsa drew away slightly, searching Licia's eyes.

"What friends? What happened, Licia?"

"Yeah, what kind of friends stop you from coming home?" said Vee. "Do you have any idea what it's been like here?"

"And I do want to talk about that," said Licia, still looking at her mother. "And why I really couldn't contact you. Only please don't ask me. Not yet."

"Why not?" said Vee.

Licia turned to her. "I've been safe," she said.

"What, like safe as in chained-to-a-pipe safe, or safe as in I-fell-in-love-with-my-captor safe?"

"Very, very safe." But she stammered as she spoke the words.

"Don't worry," said Vee. "Not an actual real question."

Licia laughed, relieved.

Vee smiled. "You hungry?" she said.

"So hungry!"

Vee disappeared from the room.

"So," said Elsa, "where have you been, Licia?"

I said, "Who were you with?"

"What did they do to you?" said Elsa.

"It's the same questions again," said Licia. "Why are you asking me all the same questions?"

"Because we all thought you were dead." Vee was back, standing in the doorframe, eyes blazing.

"Vee," I said, "go get your sister some food."

"Sure," said Vee. She began to turn. "Although . . ." She stopped. "I mean, at the start Dad and I both thought you were coming back. Mum never did, though . . ."

Licia looked stricken.

"Vee," I said.

"All right," said Vee, and headed for the kitchen.

Licia turned to Elsa. "There's so much I want to tell you, Mum, and I really promise I will. But this is . . . it's a lot . . ."

I could hear Vee in the kitchen, rummaging in drawers and cupboards, opening the fridge.

Elsa was clasping Licia's hand, trying hard not to cry. "The holes in your ears closed up," she said very quietly. "Did you stop wearing earrings?"

Licia seemed to hesitate. Her smile seemed to break; it faded from her face. There was something constrained about her gaze, something apprehensive and lost. Her right hand broke free from her mother's. Her thumb brushed her right ear, then her nose, then her left ear. An involuntary gesture, strangely nervy. She seemed to catch herself doing it; her smile returned; she took both her mother's hands in hers.

"Were you safe, at least?" said Elsa.

"I said that, Mum. Always. They took good care of me."

Vee returned, carrying a glass of orange juice and a plate stacked with cold pizza.

"Man," said Vee, "the police are going to freak when they see you. Those guys are completely convinced you are dead."

Licia stared at her sister. She gave a half smile. "I didn't eat pizza for a year. Can you believe that?"

"I can fetch you some toast instead. Or anything. What do you want?"

"No," said Licia. "Cold pizza is perfect. This is all perfect." And her smile could have lit up a room.

And so Vee sat, watching Licia eat her cold pizza, and Licia smiled at Vee, and Vee smiled back, and I began to wonder if perhaps we could be a happy family once more. And Elsa led me into our bedroom and I very quietly shut the door, and we argued in hushed whispers about when to take our daughter to the police. I was certain that now was the time. But Elsa could see, she said, that our daughter was in the most fragile state, and she convinced me to wait a few hours. "If she left us again, Cal, how would we ever find her?"

THIRTY-SIX

AT SEVEN LICIA FELL asleep on the living room sofa, her arms folded across her chest. Elsa tucked her in with a light quilt, though the day was already hot.

At seven-thirty Franklin padded out of his crib and into the living room. He took one look at his sister and screamed.

"Hey, buddy," I said. "It's your sister Licia. She's home, Franklin."

"Banda," said Franklin, pointing at a small scrape on Licia's hand, eyes wide. "Banda."

Vee fetched a Band-Aid, which she opened and handed to Franklin. Franklin reached out and half stuck the Band-Aid to Licia's hand. He smiled. "Banda banda." Licia did not stir.

I carried Franklin's high chair through from the kitchen. We threw open the windows and the door to the terrace so we could watch Licia as we ate. Elsa, Vee, and I drank coffee, seated on the edge of the planter, while in his high chair Franklin sucked a smoothie from a plastic pouch. From time to time we would catch each other's eye, and we would all grin.

"So, Dad," said Vee. "Aliens or Christians?"

I frowned, not sure what she meant.

Vee mock-frowned. "Which one abducted her?"

"Oh," I said.

"Christians, right, Mum?"

I looked at Elsa. "I'm not sure your mum's ready to joke about this yet, Vee."

Elsa smiled. "I'm going with militant atheists."

"Okay," said Vee. She walked back into the living room, sat down beside her sister, unhooked the cloth belt from her sister's waist.

"Vee," said Elsa, "no."

Vee looked at her mother. She opened the bag, tipped it onto the sofa. A few coins, and a simple gray cell phone like the ones Edvard had given us. She picked it up, turned it over in her hand, tapped a number into it, trying to unlock it.

"Vee," said Elsa, "put it down."

Vee scooped up the money and the cell phone and replaced them in the bag. "Also, clearly not abducted, or why would they just let her go like this? Seriously, where do the police think she's been?"

Elsa shot me an anxious look, which Vee intercepted.

"You didn't contact them?"

Elsa said, "We need to involve her. She needs to feel she's an agent in her own life."

"So, when she wakes up?" said Vee.

Elsa said, "Sure," and the tone of her voice was easy, but for a moment her expression was anything but.

Throughout it all Licia slept, hands folded across her chest. It was dark inside the living room, but Licia was lit by a single beam of sunlight that passed from her feet up her body as we sat, glancing at her and smiling. When the beam reached her hands, her fingers seemed to feel its warmth, began to clench and unclench, then stretch upward until her palms and her fingertips were pressed together.

"She looks like one of those stone saints." Vee laughed. "Like she's praying. Or giving thanks. Or something."

"Yes," said Elsa. "She really does."

The euphoria of it was a kind of madness.

Vee was looking at me, expectant. Elsa too. Vee raised an eyebrow.

I said, "What is it, Vee?"

"You really didn't hear that?"

I looked at Elsa.

Elsa smiled. "The doorbell."

"Oh."

On my way to the front door I paused at the bathroom. I checked my reflection in the mirror. How relaxed my face seemed; how at ease with the world. Such a strange, unfamiliar feeling. For the first time in a year I felt no trace of anger, or pain, or fear.

This time I heard the doorbell.

I stepped into the hall. I buzzed the entrance door open without checking. When I heard footsteps in the passageway I opened the front door.

Pavel.

The look in his eyes could have cut stone.

"You do not know," he said, "what you have unleashed."

Behind me, in the living room, I heard Vee and Elsa talking easily, their voices full of light and air. I stepped out into the passageway, pulled the door to behind me.

"You did not tell me you would use my footage for this," he said. "You are happy in your revenge against the police."

"No."

"It is not a question."

I stared at him. He was more disheveled than ever, though his black shirt was neatly ironed and his shoes freshly polished. He said, "I see through your window you are happy now. In your revenge."

"No."

"Yes."

I looked at him. Had he really been watching us from outside?

His phone chirruped. He took it from his pocket, checked the lock screen, and put it back. He waited until I was looking him in the eye. Then he said, "Since your broadcast I have received threats on my life. Because everybody googles Polish helicopter pilots who live in Norway and they find Pavel Lisowski. And eighty-seven of these people contact me to say they will kill me. This is a lot, no? Maybe eighty of these threats are not credible. These are from people who are angry that I did not share what I knew. People a bit like you, only without your good manners."

"Wait," I said. "Slow down. It was never—"

"Never your intention?" he said.

"No."

"Maybe you think I am being paranoid about these threats? Maybe you think I am a coward? And maybe you are right. Maybe even eighty-five death threats are not credible. But two of them are. I think actually more than two. These Andersen men have a lot of admirers."

"Why are you standing here? Why aren't you telling this to the police?"

He laughed. It sounded wild and hysterical, bouncing off the tiled walls of the stairwell. He stopped laughing. "You will say, Cal, that you are only telling the truth. But we know—we both *know*—that you are doing so much more than that."

He began to walk away from me.

"Pavel," I said. "You need to tell the police."

"You think I will trust the police?" he said without turning. "You think perhaps they are good enough for me, but not for you? No, I am going to run away and hide from these people. Like the coward you think I am."

"I don't think you are a coward. You did the right thing."

He laughed again: that same angry, hysterical laughter. Then he stopped laughing and turned, walked back to where I was standing. He brought his face very close to mine.

"To sacrifice me, this is not for you a big sacrifice, I think. But do not sacrifice your family in your quest for truth, Cal Curtis."

"HE MADE HIS CHOICE," SAID ELSA, WHEN I told her. "He knew that giving Vee the footage could have consequences."

"Do we need to worry?" I said.

She looked at me as if I were insane. "Cal," she said, "you cannot allow Pavel Lisowki's state of mind to become your state of mind."

"That's not what I'm saying."

"Licia is back. I will not let you just stand and watch happiness slip from your grasp."

"All right," I said.

"You have a duty now to be happy," she said. "A duty. To your daughters, to your son, and to your wife."

She locked her eyes on to mine, smiled the most beautiful smile, and her wolf eyes glowed blue-white and gold. I felt in my heart that she was right.

WE TIPPED LICIA'S POSSESSIONS INTO A BLACK plastic sack, which we placed in the hallway. Vee wrangled the mattress from the bed and stood on the narrow deck at the front of the apartment, beating out the dust for all she was worth. Elsa and I filled buckets with Pine-Sol and hot water and washed down the walls. When Vee had finished with the mattress she fetched a bucket, began to wash down the frame of her sister's bed.

We worked wordlessly, methodically, smiling all the while. And all the while Licia slept. Or so we thought. I was scrubbing at a mark on the skirting when I felt eyes on me. I stopped, looked up.

There she was, framed in the doorway.

"Hey," I said.

Licia frowned.

Elsa got to her feet, walked to the door.

Vee was smiling up at her sister. "We're cleaning up."

Again Licia frowned.

Vee's smile froze. I tried to catch her eye, to let her know that things were okay, but she swallowed hard and looked away.

Licia turned toward her mother, who was trying to embrace her.

"Please don't feel you have to, Mum."

Elsa laughed an uncertain laugh. "Have to what? Hug you, or tidy up your room?"

Licia gave Elsa a stiff little hug. "I tidy my own room, Mum. Please."

"You know what's weird?" said Vee pleasantly.

"What's weird?"

"We're all so happy to see you home. Like, really unbelievably happy. And you aren't. You aren't at all happy to see us."

"Vee," I said.

Licia was frowning at her sister.

"Well, she isn't, Dad." She turned toward Licia. "Are you?"

"Of course."

"Licia," said Elsa, "I don't think there's anything in your wardrobe that will fit you any longer."

"Are you really happy to see us?" said Vee.

Elsa put an arm on Licia's shoulder and began to turn her. "What say you come with me and pick out a couple of dresses from my wardrobe?"

Licia nodded. They walked from the room.

I looked at Vee. Vee looked at me. "What?" she said.

"It's early days, and your sister has experienced something unbelievably traumatic, Vee."

"Like, people dying? Or weird kidnap sex stuff?"

"I can't say for certain. But could you please lay off the direct questions?"

She looked at me, doubtful. "When are you going to take her to the police, Dad?"

"I'll go and talk to your mum."

NO ONE SPOKE MUCH AT LUNCH. ELSA and I smiled throughout, glad to have our family together, hoping that our happiness might spread to our daughters. But now that happiness felt strained, more a display than a spontaneous expression of emotion.

Only Franklin seemed truly happy. He waved his tiny fists, saying "Llll . . . Llll . . ." over and over. Impossible to believe he could remember his sister. Licia smiled warmly at him, but when I caught her eye there was an emptiness behind the smile that troubled me. She looked away, sat frowning at the food on her plate, then forced herself to smile and look up.

Vee stared at her sister. I could see she was on the verge of tears, though she would not let herself cry.

"May I go clean my room?" said Licia.

I looked at Elsa. Elsa nodded. "Of course, love," I said.

"Thank you." She got up, carried her plate to the dishwasher, knelt down, loaded it into the bottom drawer, the glass into the top, put her knife and fork into the cutlery basket. She closed the dishwasher and walked from the room. Still Vee was watching her sister, shaking her head as if trying to erase a thought.

I pulled my chair next to Vee's, put my arm around her. She leaned into me, sobbed silently for a time. "This will pass, Vee," I said.

"Llll," said Franklin.

"I promise you this will pass."

"It better."

"Your father's right, honey." Elsa was on her feet by Franklin, reaching down to pull him from his high chair.

Vee was staring sullenly up at her mother. "Did you even call the police?"

The smile froze on Elsa's face.

Vee looked from her mother to me. "Seriously? Neither of you called the police yet?"

Elsa sat down. "It's Saturday," she said.

"So? This is an active case."

"Vee," I said. "Vee, listen to me. Of course we are going to call the police. But in practical terms there's very little difference between us calling now, and us calling on Monday. We decided it would be good to have a bit more time. There's so much we don't yet know about what's happened."

"And, what? You're going to know that by Monday?"

"I mean—"

"Because you know what it looks like? It looks like you're trying to get a story straight." She was on her feet, heading toward the living room. "Thanks for the food."

"Vee," said Elsa.

"What?"

Elsa nodded toward Vee's plate.

Vee walked to the table, picked up her plate, loaded it noisily into the dishwasher.

I HEARD SHOUTING FROM THE GIRLS' ROOMS: Vee's voice raised, Licia's speaking calmly.

Elsa and I looked at each other. I got to my feet, was at the doorway to Vee's bedroom in four steps.

Licia moved quickly away from Vee's desk. She turned to me. "You shouldn't allow it," she said, her voice low and calm.

"It's rated fifteen," said Vee, "you cretinous freak."

"Vee," I said, "please."

"She ripped the controller out of my hand, Dad."

I looked across at Licia.

"It's inappropriate," said Licia in the same calm, measured voice. "Surely you can see that?"

"I'm am trying so fucking hard with her, Dad," said Vee. "Really I am."

"We allow this game, Licia," I said. "I'd expect you to remember that."

"You shouldn't. She just shotgunned a girl in the face."

"Well, we do."

Vee turned her arm over, thrust it in front of my face. Red welts where Licia had gripped her wrist, the nail marks still visible.

How quickly that old pattern was reasserting itself: Licia judgmentally pulling rank and Vee—always so quick to anger— punching low, insulting her sister's intelligence. Even now, even as Licia floated beautifully from room to room like a traveler returned from a strange land, wearing strange new clothes and speaking in strange new words: changed in ways we could not hope to understand.

Here was Elsa now, watching from the doorway. She sent me a questioning glance.

"Licia," I said, watching Elsa all the while, "do I really have to explain to you the difference between real and imagined violence?"

Elsa gave an approving little nod. I turned back toward Licia.

"Damn right," said Vee.

Licia looked at me. "You don't have to explain that difference to me. I'm not stupid."

I heard a telephone. An unfamiliar ringtone, tinny and small.

Licia stiffened. She looked down at the little gray canvas bag that she wore at her waist. She looked at her mother, then looked at me.

"Do you need to get that?" I said.

She stood there, paralyzed, as if she didn't dare lift the phone from its bag. I looked at Elsa, who was staring at Licia, eyes flashing white.

"Why don't you take the call, honey?" she said.

Licia opened the bag, took from it the simple gray phone, holding it in two fingers as if it were a foreign object. She turned it over and checked the screen. She looked at Elsa, then at me. She walked across Vee's room and opened the door into her own.

I said, "Should we—"

I heard Vee say, "Yeah, just use my room as a corridor, Licia!"

I heard Licia's door slam shut.

"We should . . ." said Elsa. She stepped into Vee's room.

We stood, the three of us, looking toward Licia's bedroom.

"What is this, Mum?" said Vee quietly. But Elsa simply shook her head.

We could hear Licia's voice through her door, though we could not make out her words.

"You need to make her tell you," said Vee.

"Vee," said Elsa, "do you see how fragile your sister is?"

"This is what you call fragile?" Vee held up her arm. Dark bruises were beginning to appear.

"I'd call that evidence of a fragile mental state. Wouldn't you, Cal?"

"I would," I said.

Vee made a scoffing noise.

I turned to Vee. "She doesn't have your strength, love."

Footsteps moved toward Licia's door. The door opened. "Viktoria," said Licia, "I want to apologize to you with all my heart."

"Who was that?" said Vee.

"I'm so sorry, Vee, I should never have gripped your arm like that. I don't know what made me do it."

"Why won't you tell us what happened?"

But Licia just smiled blankly.

THIRTY-SEVEN

ELSA INSISTED WE TAKE the boat out. And when Licia said she would wait for us at home, Elsa continued quietly to insist. We were a family, she said, and we must behave like a family. Eventually Licia gave in. And so we walked to the marina, set off down the fjord in our little red speedboat. The day was hot, the water flat. No one spoke much, but Vee and Licia did not argue.

When we reached Håøya we moored in the same natural harbor as we had a year ago, took the same path across the island. Heavy clouds were rolling in across the fjord.

As we passed Quisling's cabin, Licia stiffened. A group of goth kids were sitting on the porch by the carved wooden door, smoking a large joint. Licia stared at them as we passed. They seemed to recognize her, then us.

"We really should burn this cabin to the ground," said Vee, loud enough to hear. "It's like a magnet for assholes." The goth kids spoke words among themselves that we did not hear, stared defiantly at us.

We walked on in silence till we came to the willow tree. Elsa gathered the branches, opening them as if they were a curtain, and we stepped inside. The tree had grown more than we could have imagined, though we had to stoop. Only Vee and Franklin could stand upright. Elsa knelt and undid the cane-and-wire enclosure that Henrik had made, and we hunkered down in a circle, smiling at each other.

Elsa spoke. "Licia, we wanted to fix in our minds the image of you sleeping on your grassy bank at Garden Island."

Licia swallowed hard, looked at the ground.

Elsa said, "We imagined you lying there in your kingfisher dress, and we imagined that you were happy, before the knowledge of those men and the terrible things they did. We didn't know then, and we still don't know, what that must have been like for you. All we knew was that it must have been truly awful. And we chose this island because we wanted a happier place to come if we wanted to feel close to you."

How pale Licia looked here in the shade of the tree, as if she rarely saw daylight.

I looked at Elsa. I could see the cleverness in her bringing us here. Perhaps it would spur Licia to speak.

"So, here comes the weird part," said Vee. "We communicated with you through this tree, Licia."

Licia laughed. "You did not."

Vee was laughing too. "You didn't hear us?"

"No."

"We said some pretty great things," said Vee, eyes shining. "Mum was going to listen to you more. I was going to stop being a shitty sister, which I still kind of intend to do—I'm sorry too, by the way—and Dad talked about how much he missed your breakfast times together. It was super-spiritual. Pretty amazing, when you think the rest of us really don't do God."

"You could 'do God,' you know, Vee. It's not like you need any special skills."

"Yeah, don't get your hopes up," said Vee. "I'm kind of an empiricist."

"I don't know what that means." But Licia was smiling happily at Vee.

"You don't have to know, Licia," said Vee. She slid an arm around her sister.

I could hear Franklin cooing to himself just beyond the canopy. He must have slipped out. "I'll go get him," I said.

"Stay," said Elsa." She parted the canopy and stepped out. Vee and Licia stood, arms around each other, eyes shining, saying nothing.

I crouched down. The trunk of the willow had grown around the little band. Only the word *home* was visible now. "I planned to take this with us," I said, "only I don't think we can. And look . . ."

Someone had hung a handwoven woolen band around the trunk, a few centimeters lower down. On one side, black on white, the word *CHERISH*. On the other side, *PROTECT*.

Licia smiled. "Someone watching over our tree."

"Okay, that's it," said Vee. "I'm getting out before I cry."

Then Licia was kneeling beside me. She looked at the band, ran her thumb along its edges.

"I didn't know, Dad," she said, her voice like breath.

"What didn't you know, love?" I whispered.

"No one told me you would miss me so much."

"Licia," I said, "what did you expect?" I kept my voice as level as I could. "We've been out of our minds with worry and grief. I thought it was going to end us. I thought your mother was losing her mind."

"No," said Licia. "That wasn't supposed—"

"I was losing my mind too, Licia. It's been something very like Hell."

Licia began to cry, a terrifying deluge of tears, full of rage and fear and fury. I tried to take her in my arms, but she shook me roughly away. "I didn't know," she kept saying. "How was I supposed to know?"

She wrapped her arms around herself, began rocking backward and forward on the dark earth, her body racked by sobs that felt like the end of the world.

After a while I tried again. She didn't shake me off. I held her very tightly until she was all cried out.

I could see Vee's form on the outside of the canopy, could see her peering in through gaps in the branches.

"You go on, Vee," I called. "We'll follow."

"Did you ask her who was on the phone yet?"

"Please, Vee."

"Okay, fine, but you should ask her."

I looked at Licia.

"I promise I will tell you," she whispered. "I just need more time."

"Promise?"

"Promise."

We set off down the path to the harbor. The air tasted electric. Smoke wisped from the chimney of Quisling's cabin. It began to rain in huge drops, heavy, rhythmic, and slow. I thought the storm must be close, but the raindrops continued to fall in their strange even rhythm and the storm did not come.

Elsa captained the boat, while Franklin slept in my arms. And when I looked back at our daughters, they were reclining in the seats by the motor, arms around each other, talking easily, smiling and laughing.

AT ELEVEN THAT EVENING I OPENED THE door from Vee's room into Licia's. The slatted metal blind was closed, the light blazing. Licia had dragged the bare mattress into the middle of her room, had lain down on her side, fully clothed, was sleeping silently.

I pulled the door closed behind me. I crouched down beside Licia. How like her mother she looked in sleep.

"Licia," I said gently. "Licia."

She stirred, but would not wake. I took the phone from its cloth bag, but could find no way to unlock it, so I put it back into the bag.

When I came out, Vee was brushing her teeth. Elsa was lying on the living room sofa watching television. I lay down beside my wife, was asleep in seconds.

"DAD. DAD, WAKE UP."

I looked around, confused.

I sat up. There was Vee, cross-legged on the floor, my laptop between her thighs.

"Where's your mum?"

"Out, I guess. Once you know what you're looking for, it's obvious."

The footage from Garden Island. There was Paul Andersen

waiting on the yellowed grass for the man in the T-shirt. He looked like an avatar, like a graphic drawn on a map.

"How did you get into my laptop?"

"You were asleep," she said, as if that explained it.

I rolled on to the floor, put my arm around Vee, who leaned toward me, tilting the laptop screen upward.

"Watch."

A flickering around the bottom left of the frame. Vee stopped the footage, spooled back, ran it again. And there—I couldn't believe we had missed it—something passed through the frame. A gray sworl. Now there; now gone.

Vee rewound and ran it again. There was Paul Andersen, waiting on the grass, the camera looking calmly down at him. And there was the man in the torn T-shirt, running toward Paul Andersen. Andersen raised his weapon. The man stopped. You saw the pistol kick in Andersen's hand. You saw the man sway. Then came that horrible moment when you knew Paul Andersen would fire a second time, when you knew the man would fall. All silent. All filmed from directly above, so it looked almost like nothing.

That dark disturbance on the bottom left. That gray sworl. Vee looked at me, checking that I had seen it. She ran the cursor back along the timeline, found the first frame of it.

The image was softer in the corners; the contrasts were less clear. But once you saw that shape there was no doubting it. A man dressed in gray, crossing quickly through the bottom edge of the picture.

There.

Gone.

"Jesus Christ," I said.

"Yeah," she said. "Jesus Christ."

She parked the footage on the first frame of him. Gray clothes. Wild hair. She pressed the right arrow key. The smallest of movements, down and to the right. She advanced the frame once more. And once more. Something seemed to billow around the man's feet, to soften his outline. As if he were wearing a robe. She pressed the right arrow key three more times. Just the edge of his robe on the bottom edge of the frame now. She pressed the arrow key again, and the man in gray was gone.

"It really looks like him," said Vee.

"Seems so unlikely," I said.

"Not impossible, though . . ."

"No," I said. "Not impossible."

"We need to ask them, Dad. Because why did someone in the police enlarge past him? It's like they don't want someone to know."

I dialed Tvist. Vee leaned her head close to mine, the better to hear.

The line rang twice. "Cal Curtis."

"Are your people investigating Bror?"

"This is not a question I can answer. You know that."

Vee whispered, "I mean, he's only there in the middle of the frickin' film."

I made a *Shh* sign with my finger. Vee rolled her eyes.

I said, "There is a figure in gray in the Garden Island footage. When Paul Andersen shoots the man in the T-shirt."

"I wish you had a little more faith. These days my people are very thorough."

"Your people enlarged past it. You don't see it in the version shown to the courtroom. So either your people are investigating him and don't want him to know—in which case why don't you know that?—or someone is protecting him."

"Why the urgency? Can this wait until morning?"

"I realize it's inhumanly late," I said. "And maybe you'll tell me it isn't him. But it's got to be worth checking out, no? Just to eliminate him?"

"It is him, Dad," said Vee. "Any money you like."

"Is that Viktoria's voice I hear?"

"Vee found it," I said. "Seven frames. Maybe eight. A third of a second. You don't see it if you're not looking for it."

"Then why don't you send me the frames in question? With timings from the start of the shot?" We were trying his patience. I could hear it.

"Thanks," I said. "Has to be worth checking out."

"What are you doing?" Licia's voice, clear and bright.

I turned.

She was standing in the library, looking in. "Who's Bror?"

"Go to bed, Licia," said Vee loudly.

"I have to go," I said to Tvist.

"Then we shall speak in the morning, when we've both had a chance to reflect."

"Talk then." I hung up.

I looked at my daughters. If Tvist had heard Vee call Licia by her name, he had given no sign of it.

"Who is Bror?" said Licia again.

"This doesn't really concern you," said Vee. "Although, also, how can you not know?"

I could see Licia's face beginning to crumple.

"Oh, Vee," I said. "Please . . ."

"But Dad, I'm really not saying she's stupid."

"Vee . . ."

This time she heard the warning note in my voice.

"I'm very sorry, Licia. I wasn't implying anything. I won't do it again."

"Okay," said Licia as brightly as she could. "Good night, then."

Vee watched her go. "You know what's weird, Dad? I mean, even if she was locked away for a year, wouldn't you think Licia of all people would know exactly who Bror is?"

THIRTY-EIGHT

I COULDN'T SLEEP FOR thoughts of him. How easily he had attached himself to our lives, with his talk of heroism and the life well lived. How carefully he shielded his inner core. We knew nothing of what he actually believed. A compliment here, a deflection there, as his agile mind gently kept us at bay, all the while telling us we were close.

Had Bror been there on the island? And what did he want with my family?

AT THREE I FOUND MYSELF STANDING ON the threshold between my daughters' rooms. The in-in-and-out of Vee's breathing, so familiar, so like her mother's. Always that suggestion that it might stop on the in-breath. And Licia's breathing, no longer the same, a gentle in-and-out now, peaceful and assured. For that at least I was grateful, no matter what else she had experienced in the past year. Since coming home Licia had not used her inhaler once.

I WAS AWAKE BEFORE SIX. I STOPPED by Franklin's crib, watched his fingers flex and turn as he dreamed, watched his lips shape the words that he would soon begin to speak: the *D*'s and the *M*'s and the *L*'s and the *V*'s. Dada, Mama, Licia, and Vee.

I opened the door into Vee's room. I walked across, opened the connecting door into Licia's.

Licia had drawn the mattress to one side of the room, was reading, cross-legged, in the light from the open window. She was wearing a white summer dress that belonged to her mother.

She looked up. "It's Sunday." A glorious smile, full of peace.

"What are you reading, love?"

She held up the book so I could read the spine. *The Gnostic Gospels.*

"Is that a Sunday thing?"

She considered this. She smiled. "Maybe."

"Borrow it when you're finished?"

"Sure. Just . . . I don't think a person ever finishes reading the Gospels."

"That good?"

"Word of God. They say." She smiled again, put down the book. She stretched her arms in front of her, began to unfold her legs, stood up in a single fluid movement. "I would like to finish cleaning my room today."

"Your mum and I will help."

"No need."

I turned to look into Vee's room. Vee was sitting up in bed, squinting. "It's like nothing o'clock, Dad."

"I know."

Licia called through the door, "Maybe you'd like to help me clean, Vee?"

"Tell her to go back to bed," said Vee.

"I'll go make breakfast, Vee," I said. "You can get up when you want."

"Gee, Dad, thanks."

I WAS AT THE FARMHOUSE SHORTLY AFTER eight.

Bror was standing in the middle of the courtyard, waiting, but not for me. "Cal Curtis," he said as he embraced me. I had caught him off guard but he smiled his easy beatific smile. "You are always welcome here."

I said, "You told me to prepare for something utterly wonderful?"

"I did." He was looking over my shoulder. "Please, enter the house."

I heard car tires compressing the gravel. I turned. A little red cabriolet approaching, a woman at the wheel. Arno's mother, elegant in a headscarf and sunglasses. I waved. Mari waved back.

"Make your way to the kitchen," said Bror.

I walked across the courtyard, hovered on the threshold.

Silence in the hall. Around me the great wooden beams seemed to flex and settle. Again that strange sense of a living house, breathing. At the far end the door to the kitchen was open. And a sound from closer by. A soft object lifted from a hard surface.

"You may keep your shoes on," I heard Bror call after me.

"Thank you!" I shouted. I took them off all the same.

The second door on the left was ajar. A shadow crossed the doorframe. There was Arno, shoes in one hand, a small overnight bag in the other. His face betrayed him: something hasty and furtive, though he tried to smile it away.

"Hi, Arno," I said. "Good to see you."

"*Hei*." He stood facing me, pulling the door handle toward him.

"Did you just . . . ?" I said, unsure if I'd imagined it, but he stepped past me and down the hall, was on the porch now stepping into his shoes, waving to his mother.

I turned toward the door to the second room. *Imperceptibly ajar.*

In the courtyard Arno was climbing into the car, was embracing his mother. Bror was smiling down on them, benevolent and kind, his arms held wide.

What did Arno not want me to see? The door had not clicked shut. Tempting to lean against it, just to see. But if it gave, what then? Because when Bror turned I would be in his line of sight.

I heard Bror slam Arno's car door shut. I turned to watch him. He said a few words to Arno's mother and waved her away. Now he was striding toward the house as the red cabriolet arced out of the courtyard and along the track toward the main road.

I stood in the hallway, waiting, arms folded across my chest.

"What did you mean by 'something wonderful'?" I said as he crossed the threshold. "Was it Licia?"

He gave the broadest of smiles. "How is her breathing?"

"Cured," I said. "Almost."

"Then why do I see trouble in your eyes?"

"Was she living here with you?"

He laughed gently. "There would be a cruelty in that, would there not?" He put a steadying hand on my arm. "For Alicia Curtis to have been here, and for you to have been here, and for me not to have told you? Surely you do not think me cruel?"

The idea was absurd. And yet . . .

"Who was she with?"

"Good people." He must have caught the look in my eye.

"Why did she leave us?"

He smiled, but his eyes flicked to the side as he gathered his thoughts. "Wouldn't you rather hear the whole thing from her?"

"She hasn't spoken."

"You must have faith, Cal. I guarantee that Licia will speak. And soon." He placed his hand on my arm. For a moment I felt truly understood. He was so good at this, and yet . . .

I said, "Has she spoken to you?"

"Troubled young people are my stock-in-trade, and Alicia was indeed very troubled, and very lost, and I like to think I have been instrumental in bringing her safely back to you. She loves you very much, you know."

The quiet power of the man. That overwhelming sense of his goodness: so plausible, so gentle, so hard to counter, even for a cynic like me.

"Thank you," I said. "For everything." Did my words sound cynical? I didn't know. Bror seemed to accept that I was sincere.

"And finally I may accept your thanks. You are truly welcome, Cal Curtis. Now, follow."

At the sink he tipped coffee from a mortar into the filter, used his index finger to loosen the last of the grounds, examined the mortar closely.

He turned to me, and his eyes seemed to see my very soul. "You are not at peace, my friend," he said.

I thought of the gray sworl in the footage from Garden Island. I thought of the door ajar in the hall. I thought of Vee and Licia bickering and quarreling and fighting as they had always fought, when Licia was so clearly changed. So tempting to confront him, to accuse him outright. *I know.*

"Ask me anything you like."

Seven frames. The bottom left of the picture. Eight frames, perhaps. Blink and you miss it.

He narrowed his eyes. "What is troubling you?"

I said, "Were you ever on Garden Island?"

The slightest shake of the head.

His gaze was even. His smile was sincere. "Why do you ask?" His arm on mine, warmth flowing from him.

"Just my looping paranoia," I said.

He laughed. "Ah, the curse of the agile mind. Here's a crazy idea. Will you not have dinner with us tonight?"

And from the hall the sound of bare feet scuffing across flagstones. Milla, dressed all in gray, her hair again drawn into a tight bun. She saw me, looked meekly down at her feet. As if we had never met.

I said, "Good to see you again, Milla."

She glanced up at me, glanced at Bror, then looked away.

"Six rabbits from the refrigerator," said Bror. "Please skin them and joint them and have them ready for eight-thirty."

"Of course." She walked to the workbench by the sink. From a drawer underneath she took a long-bladed knife.

Bror turned to me. "Will you join us?"

"That's kind."

I must have frowned.

"You're concerned about logistics." He smiled.

I took a deep breath. "I am."

"You will drive home, collect your family, and return. I shall have Milla make up beds. You may then choose whether or not to overnight with us. Milla is an excellent cook. We will talk then, I hope, about things which we have alluded to but never quite spoken of. At the worst, you get a wonderful meal. At best, perhaps I can bring you all some peace. Go and call your extraordinary wife."

I stood for a moment looking down the hall, at its line of uniform doorways. I walked past the room from which Arno had emerged, stood by the front door, dialed Elsa.

"Cal."

"How's Licia?"

"Grimly pious. It's freaking Vee out. How's Bror?"

"He invited us to dinner tonight," I said, loud enough for him to hear.

She laughed.

"I think we should accept."

Shouting on the line. Vee's voice.

"One moment," said Elsa. I heard the phone hit a solid surface. I heard Vee shout. I heard Franklin cry. I heard Elsa remonstrating with Vee, and Franklin's rising wail.

I walked toward the door from which Arno had emerged, turned to face the kitchen. Bror was speaking Norwegian, all rising and falling tones. Milla was replying in monosyllables.

I leaned gently backward, felt the door slide open behind me. I turned.

Inside was a wooden table, and on that wooden table was a leather sports bag, brand-new. On the floor beyond were seven identical bags.

I knelt beside the table, put my phone on the floor, slipped the catch on the bag. A short-sleeved shirt, light blue in color. I removed it from the bag, found the police badge on the sleeve. I put the shirt down on the table, reached into the bag, pulled out the regulation black trousers with the checkerboard reflectors.

Blood pulsing in my ears, I stepped toward the open door. I looked toward the kitchen. Milla was speaking in long sentences, her voice flat and monotonous.

I took a photo of the uniform. I put the phone on the floor. I refolded the shirt, returned it to the bag, clicked the catch shut.

"Cal?" Elsa's voice, tinny and distant. "What's going on?"

I picked up my phone, spoke very quietly. "Elsa, whatever happens, I need you to stay on the line."

I heard her begin to reply.

"Please, love," I said. "I'll explain. Stay on the line."

I knelt on the floor, popped the catch on another bag. Another light blue shirt. Another pair of checkerboard trousers. The standard summer uniform of the police. I closed the bag, listened.

Milla was speaking in the kitchen.

The next bag I checked also contained a uniform. And the next.

Each bag had a single side pocket, zipped, flush to the surface. I slid my hand into a pocket. Nothing. I ran my finger along the inside seam, found something small and hard-edged.

I drew out the object. A microSD card, unlabeled. The same in the next pocket I checked. And the next. I took a card, pushed it into the slot on my phone.

There was a briskness to Bror's voice now; he was ending the conversation.

I could feel my pulse in my throat.

I checked the alignment of the bags on the floor. I zipped the side pockets shut. Everything as I had found it, except for a single missing microSD card, now in my phone.

I stepped out into the hall. From the kitchen I heard Bror's footsteps scuffing toward me across the flagstones. I pulled the door toward me, felt the lock begin to engage, stepped cleanly away. I turned, checked that it was as it had been, then took two long steps toward the front door, quiet as I could. I turned. I saw a shadow cross the kitchen doorframe. I leaned my left side against the wall, brought the phone to my ear.

"That's a shame, love," I said. "A great shame."

Bror appeared in the doorway to the kitchen. He sent me a quizzical look.

Elsa's voice in my ear. "Cal, are you all right?"

"I will give him your best. I love you so much."

I ended the call.

Bror simply standing there, watching me from the other end of the hall. Did his eyes glance at the door I had opened?

"I'm really sorry," I said. "Licia isn't up to seeing anyone right now. Even you."

"You're right. That is a great shame." The warmest smile. The most unwavering gaze. "Perhaps you will join us. On your own? There is much to tell."

"I . . ." I turned apologetically toward the front door. I blinked hard, gathering my thoughts. I knew now. I knew. I turned toward him, returned his gaze with the sincerest smile I could manage. "I'm sorry."

"You feel the need to be with your family. I understand."

"We are so grateful." I stepped on to the porch.

"Go in peace, Cal Curtis," he called after me.

"Go in peace, Bror," I called back.

I could hear the dogs in their low wooden building, their growls dark and melancholy, though the day was still bright. I stepped into my shoes, walked as casually as I could across the gravel of the courtyard, certain with every step that I was giving myself away.

When I reached the car I drove slowly away. If Bror or Milla were to follow me, I wanted to know.

I stopped at the first gas station I came to.

I bought a coffee to calm my nerves.

I sat in my car, shaking.

On the microSD card was a single video file. I put my headphones on and pressed play.

THIRTY-NINE

IT BEGAN WITH A simple caption:

TRUE HEROISM

Then a girl's right eye, filling the frame. Licia. My Licia, all concentration. So close you felt you could touch her.

Another caption:

MIDSUMMER'S EVE, A YEAR AGO

Licia was checking something on the camera. A glimpse of a lip, half-bitten. In the half dark I caught sight of a gas cooker on gimbals and a small porthole. I heard Licia's fingers depressing buttons, changing settings. Then she turned the camera toward herself, placed it with care on a surface in front of her. A wooden chart table, with raised edges to prevent objects from falling.

A boat cabin. Licia in a plain gray shift dress.

She took a step away from the camera. From a shelf she took a cloth belt. She looped the belt around her waist and tied it easily at one side.

She reached across for a black-strapped harness that lay on the map table, fit it over her shoulders. She reached for the camera. For a moment her fingers obscured the lens. The camera thunked softly into place on the harness. When her hand cleared the frame it showed Licia's point of view.

A queasy feeling in the back of my throat.

Licia turned, opened the hatch, climbed the three steps out onto the deck, barefoot. The water by the floating dock was mirror-flat, the sunlight harsh and unforgiving. There were her shoes, neatly placed in the bow beside two pairs of men's shoes. Near the stern stood two cracked leather travel bags and a rusted blue box.

I recognized that box. Maria Krikk had hidden it from the Andersen brothers on Garden Island that day. Surely Licia could not know its significance?

Licia's attention was caught by something else. On the next floating dock, a little boy was running barefoot and half-naked toward a large dog that was pacing up and down, tongue out, staring into the water. The dog wore an orange life jacket. The boy wore only shorts. On other boats people were adjusting fender ropes, setting chart plotters, lowering motors into the dark water of the fjord. They did not see the boy as he ran toward the dog.

No one but Licia was watching the boy. The camera panned left and right, as if Licia were scanning for his parents. And there they were, tiny in the frame, at the wire-mesh gate near the road, arguing in the summer heat. They had not seen their son as he ran down the concrete pontoon toward the water.

For a moment I could hope that everything was all right. That this was the Licia Curtis I knew, that this was a video of a girl who would save a child from drowning. True heroism. My Licia.

Somewhere out of sight a hydraulic winch rattled and whined.

An ignition chirped.

An engine turned twice, then died.

The camera swung toward the boy and the dog. The dog dropped clumsily into the water, began to swim out into the fjord, buoyed by the orange life jacket. Still the small boy ran toward him.

I could hear Licia's breath catch.

Licia, you know what you have to do, I thought. *You know, because we taught you right from wrong.*

But the camera turned toward the center of town.

Standing in front of Oslo town hall was a large white van. With a vertiginous lurch I realized this mooring had been chosen with care. From here the town hall almost filled the frame. Two tiny black-clad figures were walking briskly away toward a small white car.

I thought of the men who must have chosen to place my daughter here, in this boat, so close to the epicenter of the coming explosion, and I was filled with rage.

The white car was driving away. In that car, I guessed, were John and Paul Andersen. And on the shoreline there were people.

Licia looked down at her watch. A counter. Seventeen seconds.

She looked up. At all those people whose lives they were about to change. Who did not yet know.

She was at the port side of the boat, loosening the mooring line. Compensating, I guessed, for the coming surge. The movement was practiced; natural; rehearsed. She raised her wrist, looked down at her watch. Nine seconds. Now eight.

The camera panned around. The boy had stopped; he stood unsteadily at the water's edge, then hunkered down, watching his dog as it swam, facing away from the town hall. He did not see the white van; he did not see his mother, running full-tilt toward him along the pontoon.

The camera swung toward the town.

Licia raised her watch.

Five seconds.

The only sound the mother's frenzied footfalls.

Everything else was still.

The van disappeared.

Was there a flash? Hard to be sure. The van was there. Then it was not.

For a moment nothing else changed. The town hall looked peaceful, solid. Then the entire facade seemed to sway forward. It crumpled. It folded in on itself, silent in the summer sun. Bricks fell like rain. Smoke billowed from the empty space inside, curled across the piers in huge enveloping waves.

At the end of the next dock the mother scooped her child into her arms. She had not seen the explosion. She did not yet know.

The air tightened. The surface of the water grew opaque. The boat lifted, as Licia must have known it would when she loosened her mooring rope.

And now the gathering roar, like a world ending. The pontoons lifted from the water. Ropes strained upward; boats pulled hard against their fenders, groaned against the metal of the mooring spars.

Licia turned again. I saw the boy and his mother, frozen, as the blast from the bomb reverberated across the fjord. Such stress in that child's sinews. Did my daughter feel a stab of regret at the terror she had visited upon this woman and her tiny son?

The pontoon dropped gently back into place. The water became still.

You could hear the sobs of the boy very clearly: it was the only sound beyond Licia Curtis's easy breathing.

The shock wave from the bomb had passed.

THOSE MEN HAVE MADE THIS GIRL A terrorist. And that change happened in our home, while we were looking elsewhere.

New country.

New son.

New life.

And here is Licia on the screen of my telephone, and here is the boat she will give to the men. And soon the men will be heading toward Garden Island on this boat, while the police head toward the town hall. And Licia is calm because the thought of all those people—of all those possible lives soon to be ended—because the thought of this does not trouble her. Because something fundamental in my daughter has changed. And every fiber of me grinds against every other fiber, and it is all that I can do not to scream.

What have you done?

And yet.

And yet.

This girl is my daughter.

This day marked the end of her youth. She was fifteen.

Was a girl.

Is a terrorist.

And so Alicia Curtis travels to meet the men who will murder ninety-one people, the majority of them children, two bullets at a time. She brings to them ammunition and uniforms and shoes, and on their boat she will leave her footprint.

These men will rob my Licia of everything: all that life ahead of her; all those people not yet met; all those choices not yet made. All of that will be gone.

Please, God, tell me there is a way back from this.

LICIA STARTED THE ENGINE. SHE REACHED DOWN for the mooring line at her side, unhooked it from its cleat, drew it free from the rings on the dock, coiling it neatly onboard. She dropped the boat into gear and set out down the fjord.

My daughter did not once look back. The engine was so quiet and the water so flat that you could still hear the boy sobbing uncontrollably. There were sirens too, mingling with the sobs, though all you could see on the screen was perfection: the majestic tranquility of the fjord, the calm beauty of the islands with their pristine rows of waterfront cabins.

FORTY

IN THE KITCHEN ELSA was sitting, nervy and out of sorts.

I said, "I need to take Licia to the police, Elsa. It needs to be low-key and without fuss, and it needs to be now."

"Fi'e tlu'!" shouted Franklin.

I looked across at my son, who was sitting, his back to the wall, an iPad propped against his legs.

Elsa said, "Yeah, honey, fire truck. Good job." She turned to me. "This is all too weird."

"There's a connection," I said. "Between Bror and Licia."

"There can't be."

"He told me he cured her breathing. He told me he's the reason she's with us now."

Elsa's eyes narrowed.

I handed her my phone. "Watch this. In the bedroom. Away from the girls."

LICIA'S ROOM WAS IMMACULATE. SHE HAD REMOVED from it everything that she did not want. There was one chair, one table, one reading light on the table, another reading light by the bed. On the wall above the bed was a small devotional picture that showed a knight's tomb, lit by a shaft of sunlight. Beside the picture was the plain card with the verse on it, ripped after the last word:

> *Be simple*
> *Be pure*
> *Be true to the faith*
> *Be mindful*
> *Be kind*
> *Be true*

She was sitting in the chair in her gray shift dress, a long bolt of plain gray cloth spread out before her, sewing.

I said, "I thought your mother lent you some dresses."

She looked down at her gray shift. She smiled. "I like this one."

"Sure." I watched her work for a while, her fingers nimble and quick. And even now—now that I knew—a part of me tried to explain away the film. Though I had seen it with my own eyes. There could be no doubt that she was the girl in the video.

I crouched down beside her. "The police are at work today. We need to get things started."

"It's Sunday."

"Your mother and I realize coming home is very hard," I said, softening my voice. "We realize you've experienced things that you aren't ready to talk about. But I need you to come with me so we can at least let the police know you're home."

"It's Sunday."

"You're officially missing, presumed dead. We need to do this, honey."

Then Elsa was standing in the doorway. "There's so much we don't know about what you've experienced, Licia." She said it calmly, but her face was colorless, the worry lines etched deep. She had seen the video. She knew.

"Because you can't, Mum. Because you don't understand the praxis."

Elsa's eyes met mine. That word. Bror's word.

I said, "We all need you to help us understand."

"The police are not on our side," said Licia. "You know this."

"Love, these guys are human beings. I know we said we'd give you time, but there's a process." I looked at Elsa. Elsa nodded. "Your mother and I agree we need to get things started."

LICIA CHANGED BACK INTO ELSA'S WHITE SUNDRESS. Around her waist she wore her small cloth bag on its cloth belt.

On the train into town she sat staring about her, nervy and ill at ease. Her eyes kept falling on a group of young Somali men in the seats across the aisle. One caught her eye and smiled. Licia looked away. The men laughed and joked, said something about her in Norwegian. I don't think there was any ill intent, but the exchange seemed to terrify her. She spent the rest of the train journey staring straight ahead, ignoring my attempts to start a conversation.

In the park below the police station men with dark skin were grilling meat on charcoal barbecues, playing football with their sons, shirts off, laughing and shouting. Licia walked stiffly past them, eyes set on the building in front of her.

"Hey," I said. "What is it, Licia?"

"How can this be happening? Right by the police station?"

I looked around. The park was abuzz with voices: children's voices; women's voices, a clamor of activity.

"But Licia, there's nothing illegal going on here."

She gave me an uneasy smile.

I wondered what change Bror could have wrought in my daughter, that she should be so afraid of the city in summertime.

Tvist had been right: Bror was a dangerous man. How cleverly he had guided our suspicions, how easily he had nudged me toward the belief that it was Tvist who was my true enemy. He had seen my anger at a flawed system and guided it toward something darker and more confrontational, quietly and skillfully urging me to act. If he could do that to me, what could he do to the mind of my sweet child?

A WAITING AREA ON THE SECOND FLOOR. Blue sofas on three sides of a glass table. Beyond us, men and women sat at uniform desks, in front of uniform computers, drank coffee from uniform cups.

"They shouldn't be here," said Licia. "Not on a Sunday."

"Things changed after the attacks, love."

A reaction I could not read.

I filled two paper cups with water from the cooler, handed one to her.

Footsteps on carpet. "Cal?" I felt a hand on my shoulder. It was Edvard, tired-looking but still darkly handsome in his shirt-sleeves. We hugged. Stubble on stubble.

"I thought you were at home."

"My union rep got me reinstated." He leaned close. "I'm really not your source."

"I know." I turned. Licia was staring at us, unsmiling.

"This has to be Licia." he said, as if noticing her for the first time.

"This is Licia."

"So like her mother . . ." He squeezed my shoulder, smiled the most infectious smile. "I am so fucking pleased for you all."

"Licia," I said, "do you know Edvard?"

"Why?"

The hostility of that simple word. I looked at my daughter, shocked.

"Hello, Licia," said Edvard, all smiles. "Amazing that you're back." He offered his hand. Licia held it limply, then released it and sat down again.

"Early days," I whispered.

"You don't have to explain," he replied.

I took the seat beside Licia. She watched Edvard go, then turned to me. "Why did you let him touch you like that?"

"Edvard's a friend," I said.

She considered this. "Edvard looks like a homosexual. So emotional."

"Are you asking if Edvard is gay?"

"Is he?"

"He is your godfather Jo's partner. You didn't realize? And he's emotional because he's glad, Licia. For us. For you. Because you're back from the dead."

"You didn't think I was dead."

"We did," I said. I took her hand in mine. Made sure she met my gaze. "By the end we all did."

She frowned, looked away. "You're wrong," she said, as if correcting a simple mistake. "They sent you proof that I was alive. Time-stamped before and after. So that you would know."

"Before and after what?"

She shook her head as if shaking away a thought.

"My God. Alicia Curtis!"

Mikkel Hansen was standing before us in his stained suit. Strange to see him smiling; I had grown used to his hangdog look. I reached forward to shake his hand, but he bear-hugged me. "Your daughter! She's here." I patted him on the back and ended the embrace. He stood, dirty, in clothes that were days old, smiling the most radiant smile. I tried hard to return the smile. His pleasure was genuine. I had been wrong about this man, I thought. I had judged him very harshly.

Licia was sitting stiffly on the blue sofa, staring studiedly ahead of her. I crouched down beside her. "Licia," I said, "this is Mikkel Hansen. He has been working on your case for a year."

"Didn't make a lot of difference," she said.

Hansen pretended he hadn't heard. He held out his hand. "I'm so pleased finally to meet you, Alicia. Perhaps we could speak somewhere quieter?" He turned to me. "Tvist will be more happy than you can imagine. Everyone will."

Licia looked at his hand. "Why?" But she got to her feet and followed him as he led us through the office and into the interrogation room at the end.

"Be right with you," said Hansen. "Going to get the boss." He disappeared. Licia and I sat in facing chairs. I leaned forward, took her hands in mine. "Licia, you know no one sent me any proof you were alive."

"Two videos."

Of course. The near-black screen. The faint profile. The in-in-and-out of the breathing as she slept.

I laughed. "I'm an idiot."

Licia looked at me, not understanding.

"We thought someone was trying to cast suspicion on your mum."

"Why are you laughing?" Licia looked as if she were about to cry.

"Because it's like some horrible joke, Licia. It never once occurred to us that it could be you. Who did you say sent the videos?"

"I didn't."

A tinny chiming sound. She reached into the cloth bag that hung from her belt, produced her gray plastic phone. She looked at the screen. She frowned, typed a short reply, returned the phone to the bag.

"Does Bror know you're here?" I said as gently as I could.

Her eyes flicked away. "Bror's really just a name for something bigger."

"Bigger?"

"It's a network of helpers. Other people aren't good at implementation because they think too much and believe too much. Bror is about the praxis."

"So people come to him . . ."

". . . to Bror . . ."

". . . and Bror helps them plan . . ."

She exhaled heavily, gave a slight shake of the head. "They told me you learned nothing from the action."

"The action?" I felt the blood pulsing cold in my hands, felt my chest tighten.

She took a deep breath. "I didn't believe them."

"By action, you mean the murders?"

Her phone chimed again. She ignored it.

"How can you not see the message, Dad?"

In her eyes burned a dangerous fire. I took her hand, chose my words with care.

"But Licia, love, the message of the 'action' *is* murder. You can't separate it from what those men did."

Her expression softened. She gave a sad little smile. "Why are you criticizing something you can't understand?"

"Make this right," I said. "Tell the police what you just told me."

The phone chimed. Licia took it out, read something from the screen. She looked at me.

I seized the phone from her hand.

Time you accepted your parents' limitations.

"Licia," I said. "We have to tell the police."

"Why are you trying to hurt us?"

"To hurt you?" For a moment I thought I'd misheard. Then I understood.

"You don't regret any of it," I said. "Do you?"

Licia laughed. She actually laughed.

"I used to think of all the lives you saved, Licia. All based on a footprint that you left on that fake police boat. We thought it had to be you who took the ammunition case. We thought you shortened the massacre. 'Our Licia,' we would say, 'hero of Garden Island.' Without that thought I think we would have gone under. Except that the Hero of Garden Island was a girl called Maria. You were never on the island."

She looked at me, and I saw that it was true.

I tried to marshal my anger, spoke as quietly as I could. "Those men in court aren't smart enough to execute a plan of this complexity. Not without help. But Bror's smart. And Milla's smart."

She took a breath. Held it. Released it. Took another breath.

"Is that a breathing technique?" I said as gently as I could.

She nodded.

"Did he teach you that?"

She exhaled, nodded again.

Bror, with his breathing and his meditation and his warm reassuring manner. How easily he would have bypassed Licia's defenses.

"What else did he teach you?" I said.

My daughter looked at me, and she saw that I understood. And in her eyes was something cold and complex and entirely without love.

She took a deep breath in through her nose. She paused, holding the breath in her lungs. She exhaled through her mouth.

"Bror planned the attacks," I said. "Didn't he?"

She was on her feet. "I'd like to leave now."

I could feel my desire to tell her that all was forgiven—my absurd father's desire to tell her we could still be a family—though I understood now what she had done and knew that it could never be forgiven.

FORTY-ONE

IMAGINE A GIRL.

Imagine that this girl has turned her back on her parents, on everything they have taught her, on everything they hold dear. This girl has found happiness elsewhere; with a man who has offered a clear path to salvation. This is a girl with purpose now; with a sense of duty to a "race" and to a "faith."

Imagine this girl, if you can, her head full of timings, expectant and excited, counting off the seconds until the bomb.

Imagine that this girl is your daughter.

THE THOUGHT WAS UNBEARABLE. AND SO I carried on speaking. "That friend you met at the station: that was Maria Krikk, wasn't it?"

"Friend." She made a little scoffing sound.

"Did you meet her at the house church?"

"Not a believer."

"I guess she didn't have to be. You gave her your dress and your bangle because she looked like you. You let her think you were friends."

She sniffed hard. "I met her at an outreach group. For illegals." She lengthened the word *illegals* for emphasis, as if it explained everything.

"Did you give her your ticket to Garden Island?"

"I gave her lots of stuff."

I could see that poor girl lying alone on her steel gurney under the white canvas of the tent, could see the two bullet wounds that had shattered her left clavicle; surprisingly neat; washed clean of blood by the water of the fjord.

I said, "She didn't know you were recruiting her, but that's what you did, isn't it? Licia?"

"She was an illegal, Dad. A thief. She thought she was smarter than me."

How could she speak so casually about what she had done to this girl?

I swallowed down my anger, spoke as calmly as I could: "You gave your phone to Bror so he could plant it on the island. You wanted us to believe you were there; you wanted us to believe that you had been killed. You let us carry on believing that."

Licia's eyes clouded. Her posture became less certain. "You were meant to know I was safe," she said. "They sent you proof."

"What they sent wasn't proof."

"You were meant to know."

"At best it was a riddle. It was cruel, Licia. We never knew you were okay."

This threw her off balance. She stood, swaying slightly, weighing her thoughts.

I held out my hand, which she took. For a moment I thought she might cry.

"Sit with me," I said.

She began to sit.

"Licia, love, you need to tell the police what you know."

At the mention of the police her resolve returned. It was instant. She was on her feet again, moving swiftly toward the stairs.

I sprang after her.

Striding toward us along the corridor was Tvist, his dark head glistening, his eyes alive, laughing as he spoke.

"What a momentous day. I am so pleased for you, Cal, my friend. So very, very pleased. Lovely to meet you, Alicia."

"Licia," I said, "this is Mr. Tvist. He's the chief of police."

Licia stepped past him. The smile froze on his face.

"I'll explain," I said. "We're coming back. Licia!"

She was at the stairs. I followed her down until we were out of sight of Tvist.

I took her wrist, spun her around. "Tell me I'm wrong about the attacks. Licia, please."

"Why do you think you can make this okay? Dad, I have blood on my hands. I'm non-recuperable."

"Listen to yourself. *Non-recuperable*. That's not your word. You're following someone else's script."

"You never believed I could be something better." That look in her eye. Utter contempt. She pulled her hand free. She stood, eyes locked onto mine, as if amazed by her own strength. "You've always thought I was stupid."

"No, love. No."

She set off down the stairs, two at a time. I followed, but she was nimbler than me, her movements efficient and smooth, her left hand skimming the banister on each turn, releasing on the straight.

We were in the main hall, abruptly, where on the weekdays people stood in line for passports. Licia's leather soles skidded on the polished floor.

Behind glass screens near the exit two uniformed officers smiled pleasantly.

"Stop her!" I shouted. "Please."

The officers turned uselessly, but we were past them and out in the evening heat.

I was gaining on her. In the park outside, the day was bright. People sunned themselves on benches. Children played in the monumental fountain.

I caught up with her, took her by the wrist, spun her around.

"Did you prepare the attacks?"

"Get off!" she shouted.

People began to turn.

"Get him off me!"

"You were in touch with them for months. The police presented us with evidence and we just didn't think it could be you. You were too good. Too obedient. You weren't a rebel. Do you know, at one point we actually started to wonder about Vee being radicalized—"

"Let go."

"What happened, Licia?"

She was struggling hard. The strength of her was terrifying.

"I'm not your possession. You don't control the truth."

"These people are destroying your mind. They've made a murderer of you."

Her scream echoed out across the square. "Let go of me!"

A small crowd gathering around us, faces filled with concern.

"Licia," I said, keeping my voice as low as I could. "Licia, I need you to come back."

"What's going on?" someone said. "*Hva skjer?*"

She leaned very close to me. "There's more . . ."

A half smile.

Then she was pulling violently away. "Attempted kidnap. Call the police!"

I reached for her but she was gone. The crowd closed between us. Arms restrained me. I could not follow. And I realized with a shuddering lurch that my daughter had rehearsed precisely this moment, that her lines had been chosen with care.

"Please," she was saying, "protect me from that man. I'm scared of what he might do." Then the same words in Norwegian. And all the time she was slipping farther away, and all the time people were closing around me.

"That's my daughter," I kept saying. "I'm Cal Curtis. She's Licia Curtis. The hero of Garden Island. Don't you recognize her? Don't you know who we are?"

But people simply stared at me as I stared after her.

She had been here. I had held her. She was gone, lost in the Sunday crowds.

Then Tvist was standing in front of me, dark eyes blazing. His voice rang out across the park. "*Hva er nå dette?*" What's all this?

From the crowd someone said, "*Trakasseringssak.*" Harassment.

He turned to me. "Explain."

In my pocket my phone rang. I began to reach for it. Strong arms locked around my torso.

"I need to answer my phone," I said. "Please."

Tvist glared about him. "This crowd is to disperse. At once."

He turned slowly, locking eyes with each of the men at the front. Such authority he had. Such total command.

The arms released me. I raised the phone to my ear.

"I have not been entirely honest with you," said the voice.

"Bror," I said, "what did you have her do?"

"What did I have her do?" he repeated.

I pressed loudspeaker on the phone. Laughter in Bror's voice. "Alicia Curtis really is the most uniquely dutiful girl. She wanted so badly to be exceptional. She packed explosives and set fuses without regard to her own life. When the day came, she made the call that began the countdown that detonated the bomb that drew the police into town." Even through the phone speaker his voice was full of honeyed warmth. I knew he was telling me the truth. "In time, perhaps you would have understood our position, but given recent developments . . . Tell your wife that your daughter Alicia is lost to you. We are severing ties."

And he was gone.

I looked up into Tvist's dark, dark eyes. "Will you arrest him?"

"If only life were that simple." Tvist put an arm on my shoulder. "We're building a case. One step at a time. This brings us very close."

Voices murmured. Eyes watched us from all around.

Tvist took his arm from my shoulder. He looked about him at the faces in the crowd. "Do I really have to point out to these people that they are"—he brought his head very close to the face of a young man with a plaited beard—"one hundred meters from police headquarters? This crowd *will* disperse." The young man shrank back.

I reached into my pocket. I found on my phone the picture I had taken.

Tvist was turning a slow circle, making sure the crowd had understood.

I passed the phone to Tvist. "I took this at Bror's farmhouse three hours ago."

Tvist stared at the screen.

"Eight uniforms," I said. "In eight bags. And in each of those bags was one of these . . . It's like a motivational film. With my daughter Licia in a starring role." I handed him the memory card. "He's supplying strategic and logistical support to these people. And he's grooming Arno to step into his shoes."

"Three hours," said Tvist quietly. "When this is actionable intelligence—"

"I thought if I laid everything out in front of Licia, with you there, I stood a chance of not losing her a second time."

He looked at me appraisingly. "And now she's gone," he said quietly.

"And now she's gone."

I heard myself laugh. It was bitter and hollow.

I said, "I underestimated her intelligence."

The Hunter

FORTY-TWO

AT HOME ELSA'S EYES were cold and white, her fury measureless. She listened silently to what I told her, then got to her feet and walked toward the front door. "Don't follow me," were her only words.

I stood on the lawn outside, watching her go. And when she was gone I stayed where I was, staring out into the evening. Despair ate at the edges of my thoughts. Licia had been here; we had held her; she was gone.

Then Vee was at my side.

"Where's Licia?"

I raised my hands. A gesture of surrender. "I don't know," I said.

"Dad," said Vee. "Is everything fucked?"

I could think of nothing to say.

I STOOD WITH MY HEAD PRESSED HARD against the slick tile, showered till long after the water ran cold, trying desperately to find clarity.

Why had Licia come back? Had she thought she could pick up her life where she had left off? Was mass murder something she believed she could put behind her? Or had she hoped to draw us gently toward a new way of thinking?

Two heroines, Bror had said once. Had they been setting their sights on Vee?

"WHY ISN'T MUM BACK?"

I sat up. A shaft of gray-white light across the bed. Vee's shape in the doorway. Elsa not beside me.

"Dad? Where is she?" Fear in her voice this time.

"Not home yet, I guess."

Through the window the trees were black. There was color in the sky above the hills.

I turned on the bedside light.

"Vee," I said. "Why are you up?"

"Forget it," she said.

"No, it's three in the morning. What's bothering you?"

"I heard something outside. Like maybe footsteps."

"It's a footpath, Vee. People walk there."

But my brave little daughter stood there shivering in her night-gown, eyes filling with tears, so I got up, pulled on a T-shirt and underpants, fetched a heavy flashlight from the kitchen drawer, and headed outside.

Someone had spray-painted the outer wall by Licia's bedroom window. White paint on black brick:

CHERISH

I looked out across the parkland. Lights shone bright above the black tarmacked paths. Whoever had done this was gone.

Vee stood staring at the word. "Is this a threat?"

"I don't know," I said.

She must have seen something in my eyes. She began backing toward the door of the building.

"Vee," I said, "we're calling the police now."

She nodded, turned, walked into the apartment. I found her in the kitchen, checking the door latches. She pulled at the blind cord. On the other side of the window the metal slats dropped into place.

"How can they threaten Licia? She's not even here."

"We don't know for certain it's a threat, Vee."

But she wasn't listening. Not to my words. Her head was tilted to one side.

"The bedrooms," she said very quietly.

"Vee," I said, "listen to me . . ."

"No, I heard something . . ."

"I don't hear anything."

Again she tilted her head. "You really don't hear that?"

I listened. Nothing.

"Oh my God," she said. "Franklin."

She threw open the passageway door. At the end the door into Franklin's room was open, and the door beyond that from Franklin's room into ours. You could see our bedroom window at the back of the building, and the stepped hills beyond.

"Your window," she said. "Was it open?"

"Vee," I said, "please . . ."

"GET OUT!" She shouted the words at the top of her voice.

"Vee, we are both very tense."

"*GET OUT!*" A scream this time.

A movement in the shadows. Franklin's room. Then a figure, black-clad, framed in the doorway, darting away.

I ran at the figure.

Franklin's voice; a loud wail.

I stopped level with his crib. Franklin was on his feet, hands locked around the bars, terror etched into his face.

On the white wall above the crib a word painted in black paint, still wet:

PROTECT

"Vee," I shouted. "Pick him up."

The figure was at the bedroom window, pushing the lower edge of the frame outward.

I launched myself into the room and across our bed, saw the right leg lift from the floor and disappear through the frame.

The figure half turned. A moment of hesitancy.

It was all I needed. I threw myself at the torso as the left leg landed on the terrace outside, held the figure by the neck, tried to drag him in through the window.

Her.

The figure turned. A woman.

I stopped.

She swung at me with her right hand.

From behind me I heard Vee say, "No!"

Something cold and hard connected with my cheek. A tooth bit through my lower lip. I tasted blood. I grabbed at her, saw a flash of silver-blond hair.

The woman struck me a second time, from high up. The blow landed on the crown of my head. A metal surface, hard, textured.

I stood stupefied. The woman tore herself free. She ran across the terrace, turned and lowered herself to the grass below, ran out of sight toward the parking lot.

I turned to see Vee in the doorway, Franklin in her arms, a look of horror on her face.

"It's okay," I said. "It's all right."

"It's not," said Vee. "Get away from the window."

I closed the window, lowered the blinds, turned the slats till they blocked out the light.

"You see?" I said. "It's okay." But I was breathing hard, and she could hear it.

I walked to the living room, checked the lock of the door to the terrace.

I heard Vee's feet padding behind me. "Dad, please."

I checked the window lock. I turned.

Vee, standing there, furious. Because anger was easier than fear.

"He has a gun," she said.

Of course. The texture of the metal. A pistol grip.

"She," I said dully. "It was a woman."

Vee, staring at me in horror.

"Dad, you need to get back."

I reached toward the window, released the metal blind.

"She's gone, Vee. It's okay."

Franklin was screaming. I reached out to take him and he shrank away. Vee put a protective arm around him.

"Am I bleeding?" I said.

"From your cheek. And your lip. And from the top of your head."

TWICE I PUT FRANKLIN TO BED. TWICE he lay silent, staring upward. As I left the room he began to cry despairingly: long rasping sobs, disturbingly adult.

"You can't blame him," said Vee.

"No," I said. "You can't."

I was afraid of what the police would say: that I should have kept us out of the public eye, that I had drawn attention to my wife and my children. But when Mikkel Hansen arrived he was nothing but kind and helpful. He interviewed Vee and me together. Franklin sat on my knee, anxiously gripping my thumbs, determined not to be left alone.

Hansen asked only one question that I could not answer. "Mr. Curtis, where is your wife?"

But as I tried to find something that worked, Vee answered. "She's out a lot these days. Drinking and such. With friends. Only she turns her phone off so my dad can't track her."

Hansen looked at me. I nodded. I could think of nothing to add that was not a lie.

"Perhaps we should write that your wife could not be reached, Mr. Curtis?"

I could see what he was thinking, though he tried to disguise it: the cuckold and the wife-errant.

"Okay," I said. "Thank you."

"I'll put a uniformed officer at the entrance to your apartment," he said.

"We need two," said Vee.

"Vee," I said. "Please."

"Dad, she came in through the back." She turned to him. "The officer at the front should sit in the kitchen. That way they cover both entrances."

"All right," said Mikkel Hansen. He looked at his watch. "I'll make a few calls."

It was half past four. I gave him a key. I closed the blinds on the front of the house, double-locked the front door.

Franklin, Vee, and I lay on the double bed in my bedroom, arms entangled. Vee kept getting up to peer through the window blind; it was only when the uniformed officer appeared on the grass below that she wrapped herself tightly around Franklin and seemed to fall into the deepest sleep.

ELSA RETURNED AN HOUR LATER. SHE WAS red-eyed and sour-breathed, her fists clenching and unclenching, her breathing ragged. She had spent the night pacing the shore, she told me later, had come home ready to lay her cards on the table. But she could taste, she said, the tension in the apartment. She knew at once that something very serious was wrong. *What cards?* I should have said. *What do you want to confess, Elsa?*

I was so strung out I didn't ask.

We stood in silence in Franklin's room, where some admirer of the Andersens had stood above our baby's crib, spraying PROTECT in red letters a meter high.

Whether or not there was a connection between Bror and the Andersens—and surely there could be no doubt now—we had come to the attention of their admirers. People for whom children were simply a strategic tool in the planning of the coming war. They wanted us to know they could reach any of us.

There was a worse thought, which I kept from Elsa, though surely she must have thought it too: What if the plan had been to take our baby son?

EDVARD CALLED, OFFERING A PLACE TO STAY. A cabin farther down the fjord; a place where no one would find us; two hours' drive. We packed, Vee, Elsa, and I, nodding to each other as we passed in the hallway or the living room, touching each other's hands, standing cheek to cheek for a moment, then moving on. We needed time to fit dead bolts and cameras in the apartment. I needed time to speak to Elsa. Vee and Franklin needed peace.

Tvist offered to send a uniformed officer with us to the cabin. We said no, but we did ask him to place officers at the top and bottom of the road as we left, to make sure that we were not seen. I drove, while Elsa sat facing backward, watching out of the rear window. No one followed us. We were certain of it.

We arrived when the sun was still high above the fjord, bought shellfish from a trawler down by the harbor wall, rowed out in a tired wooden boat to an island halfway across the sound. And later, while our children slept, Elsa and I drank cold martinis and ate grilled flounder and crab from a fire that we made on the stone beach in front of the cabin.

When I asked Elsa what she had meant about putting her cards on the table she smiled and said she didn't want to speak about herself, not tonight, that it was all too raw, that she was frightened she would cry and never stop. And there was such sadness in my wife's smile that I smiled too, and held her in my arms, and we sat for an age, watching the embers of the fire, listening to each other breathe.

Then we talked long into the night about our daughter Licia Curtis, who was not on Garden Island that day, and about Bror, who was.

WHEN SHE FELL ASLEEP I WENT TO her handbag, and in its reinforced side pocket I found her pistol.

I get it, Elsa, I thought. *I understand that you would want this.*

I stood for the longest time, looking out across the fjord toward the mainland. The Glock felt comfortable in my hand. Lighter than I expected. Balanced. I returned to the cabin. I wondered whether I should wipe my prints from the gun, but I had done nothing wrong, so I simply put it back in Elsa's bag.

FORTY-THREE

I PUT MY SON in a harness on my back and walked the coastal path. Set out with my daughter in a tiny boat to catch fish from the fjord. Watched my wife across the flames as we grilled mackerel on a fire of driftwood gathered on the shore. I needed to feel the weight of the sky and the sea as they darkened, and reddened, and lightened again.

But more than that, I needed closure.

At five the next morning I took the gun from my wife's gray handbag. I rowed across the sound, pulled the rowboat up onto the rocky beach beside the harbor. I walked into the center of the village, all white clapboard houses standing on piles driven into the rock.

I was no longer a journalist. No longer a satirist. What, then? I stared at the screen of my phone, wondering what I was planning.

I DROVE, WINDOWS DOWN, TASTING THE COMING storm.

The heat haze simmered above the cornfields. Birds perched on power lines. Clouds rolled in. The evening roads were empty and straight, the air electric. My thoughts were full of murder. That man, who had taken my daughter and done with her— what? What had Bror done to Licia, that she had betrayed so many children? How had he turned her mind?

Make him confess.

On the passenger seat my phone rang. I looked across. Tvist. I picked it up in my right hand, swiped my thumb across the screen, brought it up to my ear. "Yeah?"

"Cal, the Andersens wish to return to Garden Island. They say they have extra information they wish to impart. Some of that information concerns Licia. They wish to have the families present."

"Oh please. That has to be against pretty much every law going."

"Exceptional circumstances," he said. "I have a free hand."

"You didn't say no?"

"It's been formalized by the court."

I laughed. "This country . . ."

"Maybe it won't yield any useful operation intelligence—"

"You think?"

"But it could."

I laughed again. "Those men want to extract every last fucking ounce of outraged emotion from us. And you're giving them that platform. So my reaction to what you've just said is fuck them. And fuck the court. I'm sorry. This is a parody of justice. I can't take part, Tvist."

"Your wife has already said yes; also on Viktoria's behalf."

"Then my wife and I will talk."

"She tells me you are not at the cabin. Perhaps you would like to come in to see me?"

"Have you arrested Bror?"

"Soon."

"Then no," I said. "But let's talk when you do."

AT THE FIRST WOODEN SIGN I REVERSED up the track a few meters, parked the car at the side.

I looked at the farmhouse. I could hear the barking of the dogs. I could see no movement beyond gray clothes drying on a line. A woodpecker swooped between the ash trees that lined the path. I drove an arc across the dried grass of the field, turning so the car faced away from the farm—in case I needed to run. I took the gun from the glove box, held it in my hand for a time, enjoying its comforting weight. Then I carefully replaced it and got out of the car.

I was no killer.

The gravel was loud beneath my shoes. Crickets jumped before me as I walked the path toward the farmhouse. It was windless here, the sun beating down, though on the cornfields you could see the shadows of clouds rolling in from the fjord.

How perfectly Scandinavian it all looked. The split beechwood, stacked neatly in rows; the wild strawberry plants in the meadow, studded with tiny red fruits; the dizzy drone of insects on the wing. Swallows dipped and dived through the orchards. Past the house, near the horizon, a single fighter jet, then another, skirting the shoreline far beyond. A phalanx of white doves took flight, circled the yard, began to settle again in the pear trees.

The front door stood open. If there was anyone in the house, they could hear me. But all was still. No faces in the upstairs window.

I stopped five meters from the house. "Bror," I said, and again, louder, *"Bror!"*

Nothing. I approached. That sign:

YOU ARE ENTERING A PLACE OF CONTEMPLATION

No, I thought. Whatever this place was, it was not that.

My footsteps echoed off the polished stone floors. Every door was open. Here, just beyond the staircase, was a living room, decked out as a classroom. The paneled walls were painted white. Four benches, placed in a row, and a lectern at the front. Above the lectern an image: an eagle carrying off a lamb. No desks on which to write, and in the bookcases no books. No evidence of what anyone here believed. Not a place of learning. A place of indoctrination.

The kitchen had been emptied. The refrigerator stood open, light off. Above the sink a tap dripped. I crossed the floor, turned off the tap.

I made my way toward the staircase.

"Hello?"

The house breathed. Wood shifted against wood, beam against beam.

I began to climb the stairs, quietly, aware of my own breath. Six steps, then a landing, then seven steps up to the next floor. Hung by the landing window was a needlepoint square. A nun dressed all in white holding a small tapestry on which were the words:

Be simple
Be pure
Be true to the faith

Be mindful
Be kind
Be true to the race

A child's rhyme, designed to bypass rational thought. Licia had cut the last three words from the print on her wall, hiding from us their murderous intent.

ON THE FLOOR ABOVE WERE THREE BEDROOMS of roughly equal size, and a large windowless bathroom. There were toothpaste spatters by the sink and on the gray-painted floor, but the room was clean and free of dust.

In the first bedroom were four single beds, stripped down, arranged at the corners of the room. Two spartan white cupboards gave the only storage space. The second bedroom was arranged identically. Four single beds, stripped down; two plain cupboards. On the gunmetal bedframe was a small green label with the letters RS inked on. I checked the next bed frame. JT. I found Licia's bed in the first of the rooms. LC, the ink of the letters fading slightly. So she had been living here. Bror had lied about that too.

I sat on the bed, tried to feel Licia's presence, but felt only a sadness: That this had in some way been better than life with us. That Bror had made her feel exceptional when we could not.

My little girl. Did we do you some quiet violence, and not know it? Did we make you feel that good enough wasn't good enough? When, Licia, you were everything to me . . .

I checked both cupboards. I ran my hands along the undersides of the shelves, pulled out the drawers, and stacked them by the door. I turned the cupboards on their sides, though I was sure that there was nothing on top of them. I checked the gaps around the skirting boards, began pushing at the floor planks in the hope that one of them would give.

She had erased herself from our lives. There was nothing left of Alicia Curtis.

OUT IN THE COURTYARD I FELT THE whipcrack and roar of thunder. The air smelled metallic; I could taste it on the side of my tongue.

I walked across the dried mud to the red-painted barn. Nothing here. No sign of life. I pushed open the great wooden doors, stood looking in. The archaeology of the farm: the broken machinery and the abandoned coal store, the carriages and the winter sleighs: all dead now, their time long past. Enamel flaked from a large white tub that had once fed cattle. Hay stood in neat bales, aged and yellowed. Gasoline stood in rusting red cans.

In a corner was a gun rack. Four shotguns and a small-bore rifle, recently cleaned. Not comforting, but nor was it evidence of intent. This had once been a working farm. In the drawer beneath I found rifle bullets, and in the drawer beside that, pellets, gunpowder, and shot. Nothing that spoke of the massacre on Garden Island.

Still the barking of the dogs. They could feel me on their territory.

I drew the barn door closed behind me, walked slowly toward the dogs. The dry mud was marked with rain now, the first spots from the coming downpour. The barking rose to a frenzy. They could see me. You could feel their movement through the slats, see the height of them, hear the chains that bound them as they dragged across the concrete floor.

I drew the door gently outward. Inside I could see three looming shapes, black in the gray-black gloom. I stood for a while, letting my eyes adjust.

To my left was a light switch. I reached out, ready to withdraw my hand at the slightest change in the dogs, but the panting continued. I flipped up the switch. Three pairs of keen yellow eyes; three powerful chests. Their coats were dry, the kennel dusty. A low, guttural, breathy sound. Tendons tight, bodies crouched in readiness. *Look down*, I remembered. *Look to the side.*

"Hey," I said softly. "Hey, dogs."

Bror had left them with water. They had long since knocked over the stainless steel dish, were growing desperate in the afternoon heat. I crouched down and they cowered away from me. As I reached for the dish the animal beside me licked its chops. A dry rasping sound.

I froze, but there was no malice in her.

"It's okay, girl," I said. "It's all right."

There was a sink in the far corner. They watched as I got to my feet.

I had put the dogs between the exit and me. Stupid, perhaps, but I had committed myself. I inched forward across the floor. The dogs turned to face me.

The water in the pipes was hot. I guessed that it ran through a surface pipe in the yard. I stood, facing the dogs, my finger under the tap, trying not to look them in the eye.

They were beautiful, though. Magnificent, really. Higher at the shoulder than at the hip, with heavy, muscular chests and long, slender legs. Doberman crosses, and fighting fit. Two dogs and a bitch, every nerve aquiver.

The water was cooling now. I filled the dish, holding it in two hands.

The dogs began to pace, their chains tangling each other.

"It's okay," I said. "Shh."

They had their eyes on my hands. I stepped into the middle of the floor, placed the dish down.

All three dogs stared at me, as if waiting for a signal. I took a step back. Still they did not move.

"Come on," I said. "Drink."

The bitch approached first. She sniffed at the bowl, then began to lap, paws splayed. The larger male looked at me, then at the bitch, then pushed in beside her. Then the smaller male bent down and began to drink too.

When I had filled the bowl three times the dogs began to relax. I looked around, found a packet of kibble on a high shelf, poured it out onto the floor. The bitch and the smaller male ate hungrily. The larger male simply stared at me. I knelt down, held out the back of my hand. He sniffed it, then sneezed a surprised sneeze. He turned around twice on the floor, then lay down. When the others had eaten their fill, they joined him.

Soon all three dogs were asleep.

I noticed now what I should have noticed before: in the far wall was another metal door. I opened the door. This room beyond was walled in concrete, not wood. Along one wall was a workbench, scrupulously clean.

Nothing in any of the drawers. Nothing in the cupboards. Everything was stripped clean, washed down. But there were taps here, and porcelain sinks, and gas burners. And in the far wall, yet another metal door, which I had to bend to enter. How confident Bror had been that I would not dare open it when he encouraged me to visit his dogs. How certain he had been of my limits.

It was warm in this little room. The air smelled of burnt feathers and lighter fluid. Something worse too. Some memory of the air in town after the bomb, as Vee and I tried to make our way home.

In the far corner was a pit dug into the mud floor, filled with sand. I stepped forward. The heat intensified.

I thought at first that Bror had been burning banknotes. There were scraps here, charred at the edges: thin papery sheets, baled together with wire. I reached out, then realized the edges of the bale were smoldering. The charcoal he had used glowed dully. I kicked the bail out of the pit and on to the floor. There was writing on the edge: printed lettering in red and blue.

I returned to the kennel room. The dogs were sleeping peacefully now, snoring quietly to themselves. I took their metal dish, filled it with water, returned to the fire pit. I doused the bale on the floor, then went to refill the dish.

The fire-damaged paper was fragile, especially now that it was wet, but I managed to free the outer sheet. It was dark in here. Too dark to read the tiny print. I walked past the sleeping dogs, stood blinking in the harsh summer light.

It was part of a thick paper sack, heavily charred. I squinted at the print. Phosphate-based fertilizer. Product of the People's Republic of China. The basic ingredient of so many terrorist bombs.

I called Tvist, asked him to come as soon as he could. Then I set about finding tools so I could split the chains and free the dogs.

HE CAME ALONE IN HIS GRAY GULL-WING Tesla. The dogs were milling about, walking large arcs around the farmhouse, patrolling the perimeter, staring out into the gathering twilight. They stopped as Tvist approached, turned to face him, silent statues, their sinews sprung with steel. Still the storm had not broken.

"Another couple of hours and the evidence would have been gone." I handed Tvist the fire-damaged paper. "Here's your fertilizer-bomb factory."

"It's rarely that simple, Cal." He took out a flashlight, held the paper up to the light.

"You had evidence Bror was on the island," I said. "But it wasn't enough. That's why you didn't want it in front of the court."

"Interesting theory." He stared at me, an unreadable look in his eye.

"How long has he been a suspect?"

He shook his head. He wasn't going to discuss procedure with me.

"Have you at least issued an arrest warrant?"

"We have," he said. "I can give you that assurance."

FORTY-FOUR

THE APARTMENT WAS SECURE. Electricians had installed a panic button and a camera in every room. Everything was professional, everything reassuringly neat. But really, if someone wants to harm you, they will find a way.

I drove south. By eleven-thirty I was at the beach by the harbor. I dragged the rowboat across the stones and into the water, rowed slowly across the sound. The water was ink-black, the sky red, streaked through with white.

I tied up the boat in front of the cabin. Elsa had placed Franklin's crib on the wooden veranda that gave onto the shore. She heard my footsteps on the shingle, came out to meet me, stood beside the crib as I approached, watching over our sleeping son. Franklin lay on his back on his giant sheepskin, covers thrown off, arms raised, the tips of his fingers gently exploring each other as he slept.

"We have to talk," I whispered as we kissed. Elsa nodded, looked meaningfully at Vee, who was watching us intently from the doorway.

Not yet.

They had dredged mussels from the bay with a snow shovel. Elsa laid the shovel straight onto the fire to cook the mussels, turning them with steel tongs, then scooped them onto plates filled with seagrass and new potatoes. We poured a small glass of wine for Vee, which she did not touch, and a larger glass of wine for each of us. Together we sat on a wooden bench that faced out across the fjord, Vee between us, watching as the last of the sun's rays played on the brow of a far hill and the sky above us faded purple-black. Water lapped at the shore. Oystercatchers gathered in small flocks, swooping and soaring, calling out across the sound.

The mussels were sweet, the wine dry, the seagrass salty and delicate.

"Vee," I said, "you're barely eating." But Vee did not reply.

Elsa looked across at me, smiled. Vee's eyes were closed. She was asleep where she sat, upright, breathing gently. That slow, familiar in-in-and-out. Her mother's daughter.

"Vee?" I said gently. "Vee, I'm going to lift you, and carry you into bed."

"Mm," said Vee.

"Want me to help?" said Elsa.

"I've got this."

I hoisted Vee as gently as I could, a hand on each side of her chest, below her arms, her head lolling on to my right shoulder. *Little Vee. This has been far too hard on you,* I thought. I carried her into the cabin and over to the divan by the kitchen window, laid her gently down on top of the sheets.

Elsa was standing in the doorway, watching.

"Elsa," I said. "Licia's with Bror."

"Yes," she said. "I know."

I frowned. How could she possibly know?

"Tvist called me himself this time," she said. "Fuck, Cal."

"Those videos," I said. "I was so caught up in my jealous thoughts that I was sure it was you."

"I guess I thought it was me, also. I fell asleep at Hedda's a bunch of times. I kind of assumed she was gaming us, seeing how far she had to push before it broke us apart."

"When in reality it was Licia. Before and after the attack."

She bent down, kissed Vee on the forehead. "Let's go outside."

I nodded. I took a bottle from the fridge, found an opener in the drawer, carried them out, and set them beside the fire.

We sat there, cross-legged, staring into the flames. Elsa took a long slug of wine. "Can I share with you a thought I'm not proud of, Cal?"

"You know you can."

"I used to look at those grieving women in their headscarves," she said. "With their daughters gone to marry foreign fighters. Because there's a definite urge—don't you have it?—to say you radicalized your daughter . . . you and your husband must have . . . something in your family cannot be right . . . You know, they chose the wrong mosque, or they put the wrong holy texts in front of her, or they beat her, or I don't know what they did . . . And that's what people are going to think about us."

"We didn't do anything wrong."

"Most likely, neither did those poor grieving women." She took a long slug of wine. "Ninety-one counts of accessory to murder, Cal. How is this possible? She was this . . . average girl."

"I guess maybe average wasn't good enough."

"Maybe," she said, quiet as breath. "Cal, did we do that to her? Did we make her feel not good enough?"

"We're never going to know."

"That's an unbearable thought."

We sat for a while, barely touching.

"Elsa," I said, "that girl who welcomed Licia to the house church that time . . . was she wearing gray clothes?"

"A gray shift dress. A belt tied at the waist."

"That day when I sent you back to the boat, did you get a look at the woman I met?"

She shook her head. "Why?"

"I'm beginning to wonder if they could be the same person. I think Milla recruited her."

We drank wine and watched the fire and did not speak. Neither of us would say it, but I could see she was thinking it too: that we had failed Licia; that these people had stepped in to provide something we could not. In Licia's own eyes she had become something exceptional.

After a time I took my wife in my arms. Elsa cried then, a long, keening wail that rang out across the fjord. And I cried too, silently, as men are taught. We cried for our family, and for Franklin and Vee, and for what the last year had done to them. Most of all we cried in mourning for our daughter Licia, who was lost to us now; who was never coming back.

FOR FIVE DAYS WE BARELY SPOKE. WE caught fish in the fjord, we collected wild strawberries, and we slept in the sun. None of us spoke about Licia—not once—though we were locked into place by her crimes. On Monday the Andersens would speak about her. Then the world would learn what she had done.

On Saturday Tvist rang to tell me he had arrested Bror personally. "We've got him this time," he said.

All we could do now was wait.

FORTY-FIVE

I WAS STANDING NAKED outside the cabin, spitting toothpaste and water onto the grass, when Tvist called again. I picked up my phone. It was five-fifteen on Monday morning.

"We're up," I said. "Thanks for checking."

"This is about Bror." I could hear the strain in his voice.

"Have you charged him?" I said.

"We don't yet have enough. The case we are building will be strong. I give you my word."

"Please tell me you haven't released him."

"We expect to rearrest him soon."

VEE HAD BREAKFAST ON THE TABLE. SHE looked burned out, pale, a little shaky.

"Nice outfit," she said as I passed. "Very Scandinavian."

"Sorry. I'll get dressed."

"You okay, Dad?"

"Are you?"

"Sure."

I dressed. We ate with the door to the cabin thrown open. We could see through the window the headlights of a police Volvo as it drew up by the harbor. And as we crossed the fjord in the rowboat I sat in the bow, vibrating with rage, watching the police driver as he smoked a cigarette down by the dock. Vee rowed carefully, turning regularly to check her position, dutiful and cautious, while Elsa sat in the stern with Franklin in his car seat, her stiff gray bag at her feet. The motion of the boat had lulled Franklin to sleep again. He was smiling as he slept, fingers exploring the contours of his cheeks.

Henrik had promised to meet us on shore and there he was, leaning on the hood of the police car, his own car doors open, speaking easily to the driver. As we approached, he got up. Vee put the car seat gently on the ground and stepped forward to kiss him. Elsa threw her arms very tightly around her father, whispered something to him, then stepped back awkwardly, as if embarrassed.

Henrik smiled. "How is my most excellent grandson?" he said, looking down at Franklin. "Ready for a day of soft play and as many smoothies as he can eat?"

"You know those things are basically just sugar?" said Vee.

"Thanks for doing this, Henrik," I said.

He stepped toward me and bear-hugged me. "Just . . . don't hand these men any sort of victory."

"We won't."

Elsa was leaning down, strapping Franklin's seat into her father's car.

I turned to the police officer. "I need our car for after Garden Island. I'll follow you."

Elsa sent me a questioning look. *Please*, I thought at her. *Don't ask me why.*

Elsa nodded.

Vee stared at me for a moment, but got dutifully into the rear seat of the police car.

"See you there, love," I said.

WHEN WE HIT THE TWO-LANE HIGHWAY I dropped my speed, let a pair of Teslas fall in between me and the police Volvo. After five minutes I let myself fall out of sight.

BY SEVEN I WAS PARKED ACROSS THE road that led to the farm-house. There were the doves, turning lazy circles in the air above. And there was the Land Cruiser. I had guessed Bror would be here, that he was weary after a weekend of question-ing, that the farmhouse would have seemed the easiest option. He would be no match for me now. But here he was, striding across the yard to his car.

I walked to the gate, opened it.

The Land Cruiser drifted forward. Bror glared out. I waved him past, closed the gate.

He came to a stop beside me. "Your car is impeding my car's progress," he said.

"It is."

"Perhaps you are more stupid than I realized." Any charm, any hold he ever had over me, was gone.

"Perhaps I am," I said. "Where is she?"

"Do I not make myself clear?"

"You made an implicit threat. Where's my daughter?"

He got out of the Land Cruiser, stood staring into my eyes. "Move your car."

"Was that Milla you sent? Standing over my son like that?"

"Move your car."

I folded my arms across my chest. "Was it Milla who recruited Licia?"

"Weak little believe-nothing centrist cuck scum."

"Nice."

"Sorry." He smiled. "That was Licia's verdict on you, Cal. Her actual words when we spoke on the phone. I had tried to warn her that she wouldn't like what she found, but she needed to see for herself."

I thought of Licia behind her bedroom door, mumbling words that we could not hear. I thought of Bror advising her to apologize to her sister. But then I thought of Licia's tears when we visited the tree we had planted in her memory: Surely those tears at least were genuine?

Bror smiled. "Licia was pregnant and broken when she came to me. Not unlike her mother at that age . . . Very receptive, desperate to be heard, delighted to find me a good listener . . ." That same easy, charming smile that had comforted me a year ago. The sledgehammer blow of his words. "Sorry to be the bearer of bad news."

"No," I said. "No, none of that's true."

"Tempting to think, though, surely? Would that bring you some closure, an explanation of how she ended up believing what she does? She's her mother's daughter, after all, and to be pregnant at fifteen . . . Oh, so she was *traumatized*. Oh, so she was *brutalized*. Oh, so she was *brainwashed*. Maybe that's how we did it?" He adjusted his stance, made himself tall. "Now move your car."

"No."

He looked me up and down. "Or perhaps she despised you,

Cal, and everything you stood for. What if she simply looked at us and liked what she saw?"

"No," I said.

We taught her right from wrong.

Still, the accusation caught me off guard.

Bror made a scoffing sound at the back of his mouth. "Oh, I can see that's an unbearable thought to the great Cal Curtis . . ."

"Fuck you, Bror."

Bror laughed. "Let's not forget *I* fucked your wife. What if Licia were my daughter all along? She found that argument very persuasive. *Father Bror.*"

I tried to slow the racing of my mind. I made a point of laughing, of looking him in the eye.

I said, "The dates don't work."

"If your wife is to be believed, they don't . . ."

"And you told Licia that?"

"You'll never be sure exactly what I told her. She isn't coming back, Cal. Sorry." He stepped away. "Now, why don't we take my implicit threat and make it explicit? There are no safe countries anymore. Wherever you think you will find sanctuary, there we will find you."

"Except that I'm not afraid of you."

"Your son will not see his second birthday." He spoke the words so quietly. For a moment I thought I had misheard.

"Say that again," I said.

"Victoria will not see adulthood. Your children are as good as dead. Your only legacy will be Licia Curtis and the Garden Island massacre, and even then people will argue over whose daughter she is."

My right arm swung toward his left temple.

I saw a moment of panic in his eye. He tried to lean away from the blow.

Too late.

His jaw moved toward me as his temple moved away. I struck him with all the anger and the frustration and the grief of the past year.

He remained on his feet, took half a step backward.

He ran his tongue experimentally around his mouth, spat blood onto the yellowed grass. He smiled. "That's assault."

"It is." I smiled back.

He looked down at the blood, then looked up at me, locking eyes. "Here, assault is a grave offense. The police take it very seriously."

I laughed.

Bror laughed too, holding my gaze, eyes full of revenge.

I said, "Are you going to murder my family before or after you report me to the police?"

"Very satirical."

I knew we were in danger; I knew the threat was real; I would not be cowed.

I laughed again.

Bror's laughter stopped. Mine did not. I could hear it echoing across the courtyard. Something in his gaze, though, as if he were trying to send a signal. His eyes flicked. I turned, and in the upstairs window I saw a thin male figure in a black suit.

Edvard, caught as if in a spotlight.

Time stopped.

Of course.

Oh, you traitorous man.

I thought of Edvard and of the help he had provided. Of the Post-it note that he must have passed to Milla, of the photograph of the boat that had fallen into our hands, of his own lost uniform, for which he had blamed Jo. All that evidence of a failing police culture. And all of it was true, and all of it was damning. That was the brilliance of the scheme. Brick by brick Edvard had helped build a narrative of police incompetence at the best, of a conspiracy at the worst. Bror had fed that narrative to me in tantalizing morsels, and each time I had reacted as he guessed I would.

Edvard returned my gaze, level and unblinking. How could he feel no shame? He had betrayed us; he had betrayed Jo; he had betrayed the memory of all those children on Garden Island. I thought of him down on the shore, collecting information about the missing. I thought of the anonymous gray telephones he had given us, and the anonymous gray telephone that Licia had carried. I thought of the eight police uniforms in the room off the corridor in the farmhouse. Was it Edvard who had enlarged past Bror in the video, hiding his presence on the island?

While I was watching him and wondering at his treachery, Edvard nodded and he smiled his introverted smile. The betrayals were not over. Edvard and Bror were enacting a plan.

Edvard stepped away from the window. Bror was walking stiffly to his car. Had Edvard known who he was aiding? Or had Bror convinced Edvard that he too was a teller of great truths?

I welcome the fallen. Bring them back to the fold.

Bror was sliding himself into the driver's seat, pulling his door shut behind him. He wound down the window. "You, Cal Curtis, are a dead man." Then he drove across the stones at the side of the path, past my car, and onto the single-track road.

My pulse beat heavy in my ears, and in my throat. Soon, perhaps, the fear would come. But for now my blood was up.

I got into my own car. I drove forward, turned in the courtyard, set off along the single-track road. A swirl of dust hung like a spirit in the morning air. Bror was gone.

I pushed the car as hard as I could along the dried mud and gravel, felt stones kicking up into the wheel wells as I turned.

At the main road I made a guess, joined the four-lane highway heading north. Trucks lined the inside lane, but the outside lane was empty of cars and I cruised easily past the trucks.

As I passed Sharif's tire warehouse I wondered if I had miscalculated. I slowed to the speed limit, began to consider my options.

I dialed Elsa, held the phone jammed between my neck and my shoulder as I drove.

The line rang twice.

"Hey. Where are you?"

"Elsa, tell your dad to get Franklin to a police station. Tell him not to stop en route."

"Cal, what's going on?"

"I have to go."

Because there was a silver Land Cruiser, standing alone in front of a gas station.

"Fuck," I said, and again, "fuck."

"Cal, what's going on?"

"Tell him that, Elsa."

I dropped the phone onto the seat beside me, began looking for a break in the inside lane. I accelerated till I saw a gap in the wall of trucks, pulled across the lane and on to the shoulder, braking hard. Angry horns sounded. I came to a stop. To my left, an endless flow of trucks; to my right, fields and sky. I looked behind me.

From here I could see only the gas station roof, red against the dark trees beyond.

Was I sure I had seen Bror's Land Cruiser? I sat watching the flow of traffic to my left: the endless parade of trucks driving north, and in the outside lane the occasional car.

There, in a gap between the trucks, a silver flash. So brief that I barely saw it. I kicked the car forward on the narrow hard shoulder, pushed it up to 110. To my left, a truck driver sounded his horn, warning me off. There was a gap in front of his cab, barely large enough for my car. I swerved in. The driver sounded his horn again, flashed his lights as he braked to avoid me. "Thanks, friend," I said under my breath, and pulled into the outside lane. Empty space, then Bror, disappearing over the brow of a hill. I pushed the car forward.

After a minute I was on him. I sat on his tail, matching his speed, a car length behind.

Twice he stood on his brakes, guessing perhaps that my nerves were dulled by worry and by lack of sleep. But my nerves were sharpened by the certainty of the righteous man. And so I braked when he braked, and accelerated when he accelerated, tracking him move for move.

Twenty minutes out I knew he was heading for Garden Island. He took an exit from the highway, timed very late. I swerved out behind him and onto a lazy back road that led across endless flat fields of maize. Bror slowed. Impossible to shake me on this narrow road. I eased off the accelerator, allowing the gap to increase. We drove at a steady sixty all the way, parked next to each other on the road that led to the slipway.

The ferry was heading toward us across the sound. On Garden Island people were disappearing up the rise. I sat watching Bror in his car. He made a telephone call. I wondered, almost casually, whether he was ordering our deaths. We were at the end of something. I knew that. Still the fear that Bror wanted me to feel was obliterated by a seething rage.

Why was this man not in jail?

I got out of my car, walked down to the water's edge, waiting as the ferry moored. I turned to find Bror walking down the slipway toward me.

Security on the mainland was light. Informal, almost. I watched Bror as the police officer patted him down. He stood patiently, watched as I was patted down in my turn. He smiled. I was not expecting the smile. It was warm and inclusive, as it had been the first time we had met. That same quality of understanding and— even now—a part of me wanted to interpret it as kindness. But I was no longer seduced by his charm. He did not wish me well. To Bror I was merely a means to an end.

"Have they euthanized your dogs yet?" I said as we walked onto the ferry.

He considered this. Again he smiled. "Perhaps."

Anyone watching us might have thought we were friends as we stood together at the bow of the ferry, facing Garden Island. Just the two of us, and the ferryman in his cab above the deck, as the man on shore cast off the rope.

The ferry edged out into the sound.

I turned to Bror. "You're clever. You see the problems with what the Andersens believe."

"I do."

"You made me believe that you despised their beliefs."

"Any sane person does."

"I think the reality is worse. I think what they believe is irrelevant to you. You care about what they do. It's the praxis of terrorism that excites you. You're in love with the chaos and the pain."

"Interesting theory." The most charming of smiles. "Impossible to prove."

"You can't explain away the fertilizer on your farm," I said.

"And yet, that's exactly what I had my lawyer do. We are a farm. We use fertilizer."

At the boat dock on Garden Island I could see Tvist. At his side was an escort of firearms officers.

Bror had a look in his eye, like a dog on the hunt, expectant and keen. And as I looked toward the officers a terrible wrenching thought began to form. Because I saw now that Bror was planning the murder of Police Chief Ephraim Tvist.

FORTY-SIX

BROR STEPPED BRISKLY ASHORE, nodded to the firearms officers, ignored Tvist, continued up the rise toward the buildings.

"Tvist," I said. "You have to end this."

Tvist watched Bror for a moment. He turned to me.

"No," he said. "Not yet."

"You don't realize the danger you're in."

"I really do."

"He spent the night at his farmhouse."

"Yes."

I narrowed my eyes. How did he know?

I saw him think for a moment. The tiniest of frowns. "Perhaps I can tell you this, Cal. We've picked up six of his followers so far," he said. "All armed, all wearing police summer uniforms."

"Here?"

"Here. Bror does not know, because we have disabled all telephone signals."

"That leaves two."

"Possibly. And if I arrest Bror before I arrest them, these men will go to ground. But on this island I have a hundred armed men and women. A hundred and eleven, in fact. And this time they are properly trained and they are primed. Bror will be arrested as soon as he attempts to leave. In the meantime we will be watching him like a hawk and noting who he speaks with. You and your family are perfectly safe."

"The target is you."

Tvist laughed. "Then I must hope my people are as effective as I believe."

"I'm serious," I said. "Edvard was there at the farmhouse. He's been feeding information to Bror."

Ephraim Tvist simply smiled his level smile.

"You knew?" I said.

"I can't discuss procedure. But Edvard is no traitor."

"You suspended him."

"He fell under the spell of a man who promised him salvation. And when Edvard saw the harm he had done, he wanted to put that right. I reinstated him. Now . . ."

We began to walk up the hill. There were fewer of us on Garden Island today. The survivors and the families of the deceased were outnumbered by Tvist's men and women. There was a readiness in the air, a strange sense of anticipation.

"So, Edvard . . ." I said.

"A good man may do evil if the devil crosses his path. Are we not all fallible? But Edvard passed on information about today, so I'd say he has redeemed himself."

Those dark, dark eyes. That patient smile.

"All right," I said. "I accept that you're better at this than I realized."

Tvist shook his head, amused. "It's my job, Cal. Have some faith."

I SAW THEM AT ONCE. VEE WELCOMED me with smiles and with hugs. Elsa embraced me warmly, then took a half step back, let her hands rest easily on my shoulders. I looked about me. Tvist did have the island locked down. His men and women were everywhere. And there was Bror on the far edge of the group, smiling at me across the clearing. I looked away. I would not play his games.

"We can leave at any time, Vee," I said.

"I know," said Vee. "All good."

Our brave little daughter, growing up fast. My best beloved Vee. Sleek and streamlined. A world away from the stick-thin child she was a few short months ago, with her knotted fists and her dark suspicious eyes.

Tvist placed himself close to Bror. These two men, each using me to get to the other. Though I understood Tvist's reasons now. He smiled. I nodded, glad of his presence. For as long as we were on the island we were safe.

"So we're ready?" said Elsa.

There was a warmth in my wife's voice I had not expected. I searched her face, looking for anger, or bitterness, but there was no edge to her words. Instead there was a glow in her ice-blue eyes that I had thought was gone, an intimacy in her gaze that I thought had been lost to me. So gentle she looked, so kind and so strong.

"Viktoria Curtis," said John Andersen.

"What?" said Vee.

The world grew quiet. John Andersen was staring very intently at Vee. The judges and the police were watching; the victims' families; the survivors; Bror too. Only Paul Andersen was facing away.

"About your sister," said John Andersen.

Paul Andersen turned toward us too, so close that I could smell the chewing tobacco on his breath. Like candy, with a dark, cancerous edge. I felt the fear in my Vee, felt her struggle as the men tried to hold her with their gaze. I reached out to her with my free arm, tried to turn her toward me. But Vee would not be turned.

"Look down, love," I said.

"I won't," said Vee.

From across the clearing I felt the smile curling across Bror's lips. I saw the cruelty in him now, though he was a cleverer man than the brothers, better at disguising his true self.

"Your sister sends warm wishes," said Paul Andersen, enjoying the moment.

"We hope one day you will join us," said John.

"My sister is dead to me," said Vee.

Elsa stepped in front of our daughter, eyes blazing, facing the men. Any trace of gentleness was gone from her. She would strike them down if she could, I thought to myself.

The birdlike judge stepped forward. "John Andersen; Paul Andersen: you will address all remarks to me; most particularly you are not to address minors. Is this understood?"

The Andersen brothers said nothing.

"Is this understood?"

The men nodded. Bror turned away, unable to disguise his smile. I saw now the pleasure he took in our pain, and something in me wanted him dead.

"Let's go home," I said. "They have nothing for us."

"No, Dad," said Vee.

"Come on."

"Dad, it was always going to be like this."

I caught Elsa's eye. She nodded.

"Okay," I said. "All right."

The men had prepared a statement. It was long and dissociative, full of diversions and paranoia: all *Arabs*, and *Jews*, and *Marxist Cabals*. It contained no new information, except that they wished to be known by new Nordic names. Mjölnir and Torshammer. They demanded that the court recognize these names, which seemed unlikely. Hard to believe that two such childish men could inflict so much damage on a country. Unlikely that they could have done it without Bror's help. Or Licia's.

We broke for lunch at eleven. The men were led away.

"I used to think this was the last place where Licia was happy," said Elsa. "I would imagine her waking up on the grass by the boat dock, and looking out across the water. It gave me some sort of peace, you know, thinking that for a time on this island Licia was at peace. But she was already lost."

THROUGH THE GAP IN THE TREES I saw a table and two chairs. John and Paul Andersen were looking out across the lake.

"Sitting there, eating and drinking like normal people," said Vee. "Unbelievable."

To the left the armed guard: three policewomen on stools, keeping watch. Paul Andersen wiped his mouth on a napkin. He took out a small tin, opened it, formed a lump of tobacco into a rough cube, and inserted it between his upper lip and his gum.

"Yes," I said. "It is unbelievable."

There was something obscene about the men at their picnic table, looking out across the fjord, wiping their mouths on their napkins, joking with their guards. As if nothing, to them, had consequence. As if this were just another day and theirs were just another family.

"Vee," said Elsa. "I want to speak with your father."

Vee hesitated, but she could see Elsa meant it, and she sloped off toward the lunch line. Bror was watching our daughter too, though he was careful to keep his distance.

"When this is done," said Elsa, "please help her to forgive me."

"She does forgive you."

This surprised Elsa. She laughed. "For what?"

"For bringing us to this country. You couldn't know what that would mean. None of us could."

"You're a good man, Cal, but you really haven't understood. Not yet."

Vee was smiling at us from the lunch line.

Elsa turned to me. "I need you to understand that I will forgive you, Cal," she said. "Though it will cost me."

"Forgive me for what?"

"For the women. In the bars."

"What women in bars?"

"Did you think I didn't know?"

She was smiling as if nothing were wrong. Still, the accusation stung.

"Elsa, nothing has ever happened."

"It will. For you, there will be a new life with one of these women. But I will forgive you, in time, because the man I married is a good man."

"Elsa," I said. "Please."

Her eyes were clouded with tears. "Perhaps in time you will forgive me too."

I took a step toward her. "Elsa, what have you done?"

For a moment I thought she would step toward me too, that she would let me take her in my arms. But she stood where she was.

She swallowed hard. She wiped her eyes with the pad of her right hand. "You're a good man, Cal Curtis. I love you with all my heart. But you still haven't understood."

"Then help me understand."

"We are going to spend some time apart."

"Love, whatever this is, we can talk it out."

Before she turned, she gave the slightest shake of her head. Then she left me standing, alone and forlorn.

And all the while Bror stood watching us, his arms folded, smiling.

FORTY-SEVEN

WHEN I REJOINED THE group I could not see Elsa.

"Cal Curtis," said Paul Andersen. "Ask me a question."

I looked at him.

"Anything you like," he said.

The judges were standing in a huddle farther down the path. I could not see Tvist. Without him, his officers seemed unsure as to how to act.

I looked Paul Andersen in the eye. I could feel his cruelty, could feel the sheer terrifying energy of the man. But I would not be cowed.

"I have no questions," I said.

"Ask my brother."

"No questions," I said. "Not one."

This surprised him. He looked about him, then drew himself up to his full height. "We are knights. One day we shall return to battle. This is no metaphor."

He was studying my reaction. He had prepared these words. He wanted the journalists around us to quote him, in English.

"Good for you," I said, as if to a child. I looked away.

That's when I saw Elsa. She was on one knee by the rocks that led down to the fjord, her body facing away. She stood slowly, turning as she did, leaving her gray bag at the side of the path. Now she was walking swiftly, knees slightly bent, eyes fixed ahead.

At first no one reacted. A few stragglers sat on white chairs at white tables, finishing their waffles and their coffee. As Elsa reached the Andersens she said something I did not hear. The brothers turned to face her. Paul Andersen began to stand. John Andersen too. Still the scene was calm. Elsa's stride was purposeful, measured.

I called her name.

Her eyes met mine but would not settle on me. She replied in whispered words that I did not hear. Beside me a policeman got to his feet. At the food tent people turned to watch.

The brothers stood, arms folded across their chests. Elsa raised her right hand. I saw something dark and metallic.

Elsa's left hand braced across her right.

"STOP."

A policewoman shouldered her weapon. Two more officers began to stand. The policeman beside me reached for his pistol.

Elsa assumed a stance.

I saw Tvist pulling Vee toward him, trying to turn her, to shield her from whatever was coming, but Vee struggled in his arms.

The first gunshot. Paralyzingly loud. The shock of it rooted me to the ground.

In Tvist's arms Vee froze, eyes wide. My own eyes flicked toward Elsa, her hands locked around the pistol, then to the rifle in the policewoman's arms.

Not a blade of grass moved.

I seemed to hear Vee inhale, then pause, then inhale. Tvist's hands clasped her shoulders. Around us everyone was upright. Everything was rigid; every muscle aquiver. My jaw was locked tight, braced for the second shot.

That same paralyzing intensity.

Elsa's body barely reacted.

The gunshot whipcracked across the fjord, reflected off the hills beyond.

Vee screamed.

"Mum!"

I was running across the clearing toward my wife.

Elsa stood, hands raised high, fingers clenched around the pistol.

The Andersen brothers stared back at her, blank-faced.

Vee broke free from Tvist and stood, frozen, watching her mother.

Then the sinews in Elsa's body seem to loosen. Paul Andersen took a step toward her.

"Throw down your gun." The policewoman, her rifle inches from Elsa's chest.

"Dad," said Vee. "Dad, help her."

I was almost at Elsa's side.

A policeman stepped in front of me. "You will stay where you are."

"Dad, we have to—"

"Viktoria." Tvist stepped forward, tried to guide Vee away. Again she broke free.

"All of you," shouted a uniformed policeman. "Stay where you are."

Paul Andersen took another step toward Elsa.

"Drop your gun." The policewoman again.

Only now did I see the blood pooling red on Paul Andersen's white shirt. Only now did I see the tremoring of his hand as he reached to stanch the flow. Only now did I see the smoke that wisped from the barrel of Elsa's Glock 17.

The pistol slid from her fingers. It glanced off her leg, landed on the path nearby.

Paul Andersen fell forward, crumpled to the ground.

I saw fear now in his brother John, saw in his eye the moment of realization. I felt a horrifying thrill of pleasure. *Good*, I thought. *Now you know.*

Then Elsa was on the ground. The policewoman had a knee in the small of Elsa's back. Her rifle was pointed directly at Elsa's head. A second policewoman was reaching to cuff her hands.

"Dad," said Vee. "Dad, we have to help her."

"Stay where you are, Vee."

"Are you just going to let them—"

Elsa had her head raised. "Cal."

I looked at the rifle; I looked at the pistol on the ground; I looked at my wife.

The policewoman with the rifle saw me. "No closer," she said.

I stayed where I was.

"I want you to know that I do love you," said Elsa, her voice loud and clear. "I want you to promise me that you know that."

"Cal Curtis," said Bror's voice. I ignored it.

"Sir," said the policewoman. "Sir, step away."

I stood staring at my wife.

"Cal Curtis."

I turned, saw Bror at the side of the path, his face twisted, full of wrath.

"Cal Curtis!" he shouted. "Øvre Øvrebøhaugen four, Oslo, Norway."

Vee at my side, grasping my hand. "What's he doing, Dad?"

Two officers stepped forward, stood one on each side of Bror. I looked around, saw the look on Tvist's face. He understood full well the danger of this man.

Vee turned to me. "He's threatening us, isn't he?" She turned to face Bror. "You're fucking threatening our family."

Bror heard her speak. He turned, looked her full in the face.

"Viktoria Steen Curtis," he shouted. "At the same address."

Issuing an instruction, I realized.

"Franklin Steen Curtis. Same address."

He was summoning the murder of my children. Calling on his admirers to make good on his threat.

I looked toward the food tent. Every face was turned toward Bror. It only took a sympathizer among the staff . . .

"The cameras," said Vee. "The fucking cameras, Dad." I heard the panic in her voice. I turned.

The TV crews. Two cameras, one pointed at Elsa where she lay on the ground, the other at Bror. I began to walk toward them.

"This way." A policewoman at my side, trying to lead me away.

"Daniel Curtis." Bror was screaming at the top of his lungs now. "Spring Bank Drive fifty-two, Washington D.C., United States of America. Daisy Curtis and Lyndon Curtis, also of Spring Bank Drive fifty-two."

"This way," repeated the policewoman.

"Wait," I said. "You need to seize the cameras."

"No, Mr. Curtis, you need to come."

"Douglas and May Curtis. Inverleithen Terrace forty-three, Edinburgh, Scotland."

Bror was a powerful man. The police were struggling to drag him down the path.

"Henrik Steen, Lundeveien eight, Drøbak, Norway."

Tvist's voice. "Come away, Cal. Now."

The cameramen filming, saying nothing.

I stepped toward Tvist. "You need to seize this material. If it goes out, it's going to imperil my family."

Tvist turned to the camera team. "Stop filming."

The cameraman near me put down his camera.

"*Begge to*," said Tvist. *Both of you.*

Tvist looked at the second cameraman. You could feel the man's reluctance; the instinct for a story trilling in his blood. Tvist nodded toward a policewoman, who stepped forward. The second cameraman put down his camera.

"Cal," said Tvist, "we are going to take you to a place of safety."

People were turning. I looked down at the Glock, lying a meter or so from me. I crouched beside it.

"Whatever the provocation," said Tvist, very quietly, "don't."

I sensed fingers tightening on triggers. I looked up, into the faces of armed police, their rifles shouldered, ready. I ignored the rifles. Something had broken in me, I thought. This last year had been too much. I looked down at the pistol on the grass.

Vee was at my side.

"Dad," she said softly.

That look on my daughter's face: so adult. She crouched down beside me, brought her face very close to mine.

"Dad, stand up."

"All right." I stood up.

I looked about me. All around me rifles were shouldered. I raised my hands.

"Step away. It's okay." Tvist's voice. I turned, met his gaze, nodded.

Vee was fast. She reached down, picked up the pistol. She stood.

Those rifles, trained on my daughter now.

"Vee," I said. "No."

"What are they going to do, Dad?" She turned toward the police. "Are you guys even allowed to shoot me?"

She began to walk, the pistol in her right hand, her intention clear.

"Stop this girl," shouted John Andersen. "You must stop her."

The police were looking to Tvist for guidance.

"Viktoria," said Tvist. "Viktoria, you must stay where you are."

Vee walked briskly past Tvist, past John Andersen.

Everything else was still. Every eye was on my daughter. She stopped a pace in front of Bror, a little to the side. She began to raise the pistol.

I looked about me in terror, waiting for the rifle shot that would end this.

Vee paused, the gun at Bror's chest, as if she too were surprised by her action. The gun swayed in her hands, and for a moment I thought this was no more than a child's game.

Bror smiled a lacerating smile.

"No," he said, "I didn't think so." He turned to the nearest police officer, held his hands together at the wrists. "*Skal vi?*"

Fingers hovered on triggers. All eyes on Bror.

"Shall we?" said Bror, this time in English.

"No," said Vee, her voice clear and level. Her stance became confident. Her gun was steady now, level with the man's heart. Other hands reached for Vee, ready to pull her clear. But she tightened her grip on the gun. "Back off," she said, and they did.

"Vee," I said, "you aren't going to do this."

"Look what he's done to us," she said.

"Viktoria," said Bror, trying to force calm into his words. "Viktoria, this can be undone."

"No, it can't," she said simply.

"I hereby cancel the order."

Vee looked him in the eye. "You can't."

Still I waited for the rifle shot, but no one here was willing to shoot a child.

The past year had changed my daughter. There was a hardness to her that was not there before.

"Vee," I said, "this is not who we are."

"It is now." She stiffened her stance.

"Please, Viktoria," said Bror, and I heard his rising panic. "Listen to your father."

IMAGINE A GIRL.

Imagine a girl pushed to the breaking point, in a world where kindness and forgiveness no longer make sense. This girl stands in front of a man, now, who has promised her a better life. He has approached her many times, and each time she has resisted a little less.

Her father was seduced easily into this man's world, with coffee and with clever talk. But it began long ago with her sister Licia.

Now Licia is gone.

Now they know who this man is.

This man has ordered her death, and the death of her parents, and the death of her tiny baby brother. That is the reality of Bror. And she sees in Bror's eyes his fear, and she understands now that he is mortal, and that he has no greater truth to offer. He has nothing beyond breathing exercises and a belief in praxis, whatever *praxis* really means.

In her hands the Glock feels balanced and cool and she wishes the moment did not have to end, wishes Bror could feel this fear for all eternity, though she knows that he will not, because the moment must end. She must put down the gun, or she must fire it. If she puts down the gun this man will go to jail, and from his cell he will continue to amplify his signal and glorify the attacks. And if she fires it, what then? She will not be jailed, but it will break her family apart.

She breathes deeply. She is her mother's daughter. She believes very strongly in revenge. And on Garden Island all is still, and every face is watching this girl now.

Killer or victim, she thinks. *Which is it to be?*

ABOVE THE CLEARING, MAYFLIES danced in the heavy summer air.

"Vee," I said. "Time to go home now."

I reached to take the gun from my daughter's hand, but she sidestepped me and raised it to Bror's temple.

"No," she said quietly.

Bror inclined his head as if he were asking a question.

On Garden Island in that instant nothing breathed.

Vee pulled the trigger, twice. And when Bror fell to the ground, my daughter stood over the dying man, and before she could be stopped she pulled the trigger twice more.

ACKNOWLEDGMENTS

Cecilie Lilaas-Skari of the Oslo Police has advised me on Norwegian police practice and procedures; any exaggerations are mine alone. Peder Anker and Tor Øverbø helped form the idea of the novel. Stein and Signe Lundgren showed what it means to live by the Scandinavian ideals of fairness, openness, and freedom; so too did Line Michelsen and Pia Lundgren. Thorgeir Kolshus, Leslie Gray-O'Neil, and Eleanor Moran read and advised me on drafts. James Bradley and Tim Lott encouraged me when the writing got tough. And I couldn't have written this book without Charlotte Lundgren, who has done so many of these things, and more. She can't possibly know how grateful I am.

ALSO BY BEN McPHERSON

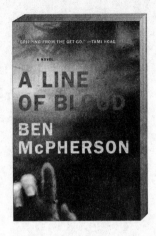

Whose secrets cut deeper?
Your family's.

Whose secrets do you fear?
Your neighbor's.

Whose secrets can kill?
Your own.

For Alex Mercer, his wife, Millicent, and their precocious eleven-year-old son, Max, ar
everything—his little tribe that makes him feel all's right with the world. But when he an
Max find their enigmatic next-door neighbor dead in his apartment, their lives are suddenl
and irrevocably changed. The police begin an extremely methodical investigation, an
Alex becomes increasingly impatient for them to finish. After all, it was so clearly a suicide

As new information is uncovered, troubling questions arise—questions that begin t
throw suspicion on Alex, Millicent, and even Max. Each of them has secrets it seems. An
each has something to hide.

With the walls of their perfect little world closing in on them day after day, husband
wife, and son must decide how far they'll go to protect themselves—and their family—
from investigators carefully watching their every move . . . waiting for one of them t
make a mistake.

A Line of Blood explores what it means to be a family—the ties that bind us, an
the lies that can destroy us if we're not careful. Highly provocative, intensely twisty an
suspenseful, this novel will have you wondering if one of them is guilty—or if all of the
are—and will keep you on edge until its shocking final pages.

You will never look at your loved ones the same way again. . . .